SHIGERU MIZUKI'S

KITA!

THE BIRTH OF KITARO

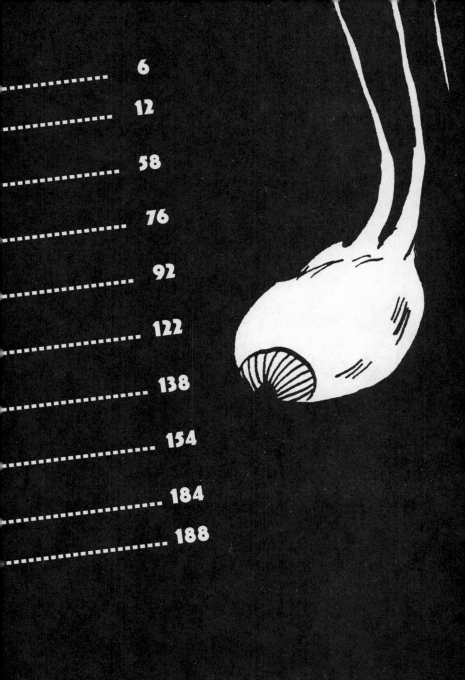

HISTORY OF KITARO PART 1 ZACK DAVISSON

Once upon a time, in a graveyard far, far away, a little yokai boy dug his way up from under the dirt and into a world that didn't understand him. He was the last living member of the Yurei Zoku—the Ghost Tribe: a race of monster people that once freely roamed the earth until they were chased underground by humans. The Ghost Tribe slowly died off until only two remained, a husband and wife who hid themselves in an abandoned temple. Desperate to save their baby, they reached out to a human who they hoped would help them. And that's how the story of Kitaro began.

But it isn't the whole story. Even though Kitaro is one of Japan's most famous and beloved characters, few know his actual origin and history. Most would say that he is a creation of manga artist (and eccentric genius) Shigeru Mizuki. After all, Mizuki drew the adventures of Kitaro and his yokai companions for over fifty years. If you go to Sakaiminato city in Tottori prefecture to visit the Kitaro wonderland and eat the delightful yokai food, you are visiting Shigeru Mizuki Road. But like many yokai, the true story behind Kitaro's origin is older and more mysterious. We must go back in time almost four hundred years.

Japan during the Edo period (1603–1868) was a time of monsters. Every dark corner, every deep forest, every dank graveyard, was filled with yokai— an unimaginable variety of strange creatures, weird phenomenon, and mysterious beings. The entire country was consumed with belief in the supernatural. Some of these monsters were ancient legends from prehistory, but most of them were

born right in the Edo period, in a game called *Hyakumonogatari Kaidankai*—A Gathering of 100 Weird Tales.

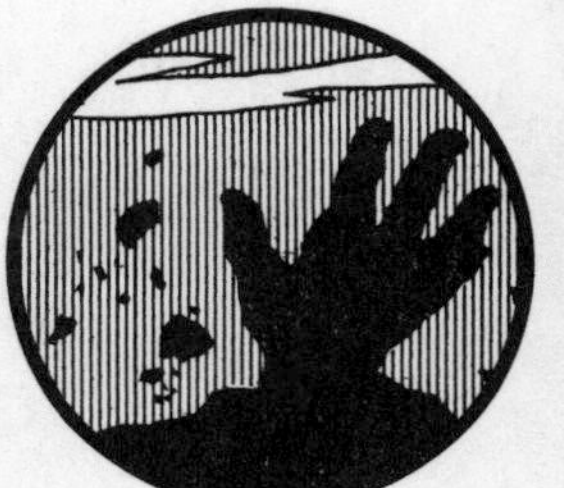

The way to play was simple. Players would light a hundred candles in a room, then take turns telling stories. With every story, they would douse a candle, so the room got slowly darker. People swapped stories about something they had heard. Or they told of their own mysterious encounters with strange lights at night. It didn't matter if these stories were complete, it only mattered that they were true. And that these spooky encounters sent a shiver down the spine on a hot summer night.

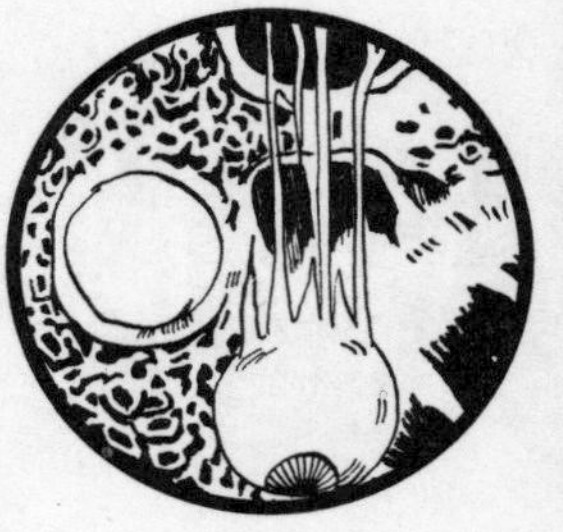

Edo period artists and writers saw an opportunity in Japan's mania for yokai. They began to produce art prints and little books of stories called *kaidanshu*. Some of these recounted spooky true life encounters with ghosts and bizarre monsters. Some were tales of supernatural beasts from countries like China and India. Some were just made up. But regardless of origin, almost all of the yokai stories we know today come from these Edo period collections. There were so many monsters that in 1776 artist Toriyama Sekien decided to catalog them, and created his yokai encyclopedia series called *Gazu Hakki Yagyo—The Illustrated Night Parade of 100 Demons*. Although there were a lot more than a hundred!

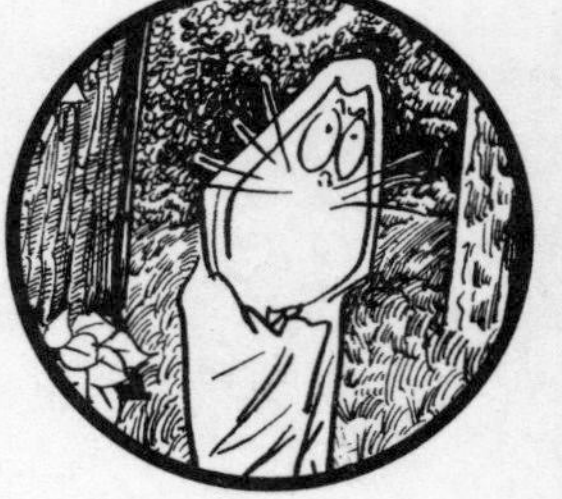

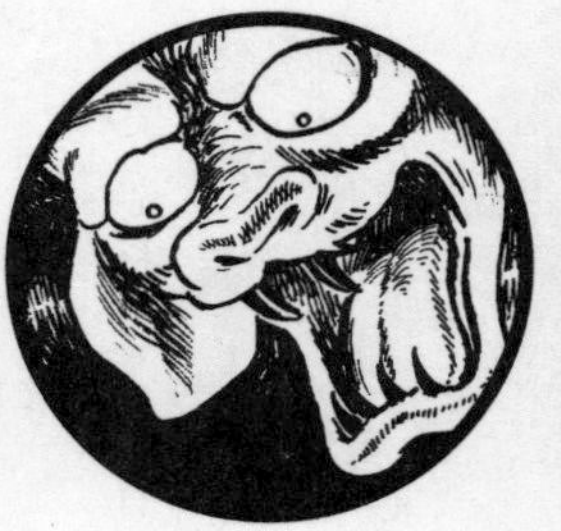

One of the yokai in Toriyama's encyclopedia was a lonely ghost mother called an *ubume*, or sometimes called a *kosodate yurei*—a child-raising ghost. This told the story of a woman who died

while pregnant. She was buried with her living baby still inside of her. Because she was a good mother, every night her ghost would rise from the grave to buy candy and treats for her little child. When some people noticed this, they dug up the grave and found the ghost mother's son had been born alive inside the grave. There were many tales of ubume in Japan, and the children of ubume were said to possess unique abilities.

Eventually the Edo period ended and Japan's belief in the supernatural faded. The Meiji period (1868–1912) brought contact with the West, as well as science and invention. Yokai faded before the electric lights of the modern world. By the time of the Showa period (1926–1989), most people had forgotten about yokai, except as funny children's stories.

But during the early Showa period, there was a popular form of entertainment called *kamishibai*—meaning paper theater. This was a time before TV or radio or even comic books. Artists would create characters and stories in the form of paintings, then storytellers would wander the countryside to bring the stories to life. Storytellers had a small wooden theater they used to show the pictures, pulling them out one at a time while the story unfolded. Just like today, there were many popular characters who appeared over and over again. Children eagerly anticipated the next chapter in the story of some of their favorites, like the skull-faced Orgon Bat who flew with a big red cape and lived in a secret base in the Alps.

In 1933, two popular kamishibai artists dug up old Edo period yokai stories for a series of kamishibai adventures starring a peculiar young boy. Writer Masami Ito and artist Kei Tatsumi took the legend of the ubume to create their character Hakaba Kitaro—Graveyard Kitaro.

Very little is known about this original version of Kitaro. Most of the illustrations and storynotes were destroyed during WWII. Of the few bits and pieces that survive, we know that Hakaba Kitaro was a boy born in a graveyard. His parents had met with some unjust fate, and Kitaro was cursed by their legacy. He was a monster, terrible to behold. His teeth jutted out of his mouth like planks of wood. One of his eyes was huge and seemed like it was trying to escape his head. His hair was wild and crazy. He looked like some version of Quasimodo—the famed Hunchback of Notre Dame.

This original version of Hakaba Kitaro ran for about two to three years, and was said to be as popular as Orgon Bat. The storytellers tromped all over the major cities of Japan, telling the story of the bizarre yokai boy, Graveyard Kitaro. However, by all accounts they never made it to the small fishing town of Sakaiminato, Tottori prefecture, where a small boy named Shigeru Mura had arrived eleven years earlier in 1922.

It was this boy who would continue the story of Kitaro, and spread his wonderous tales to the whole world.

To be continued...

THE BIRTH OF KITARO

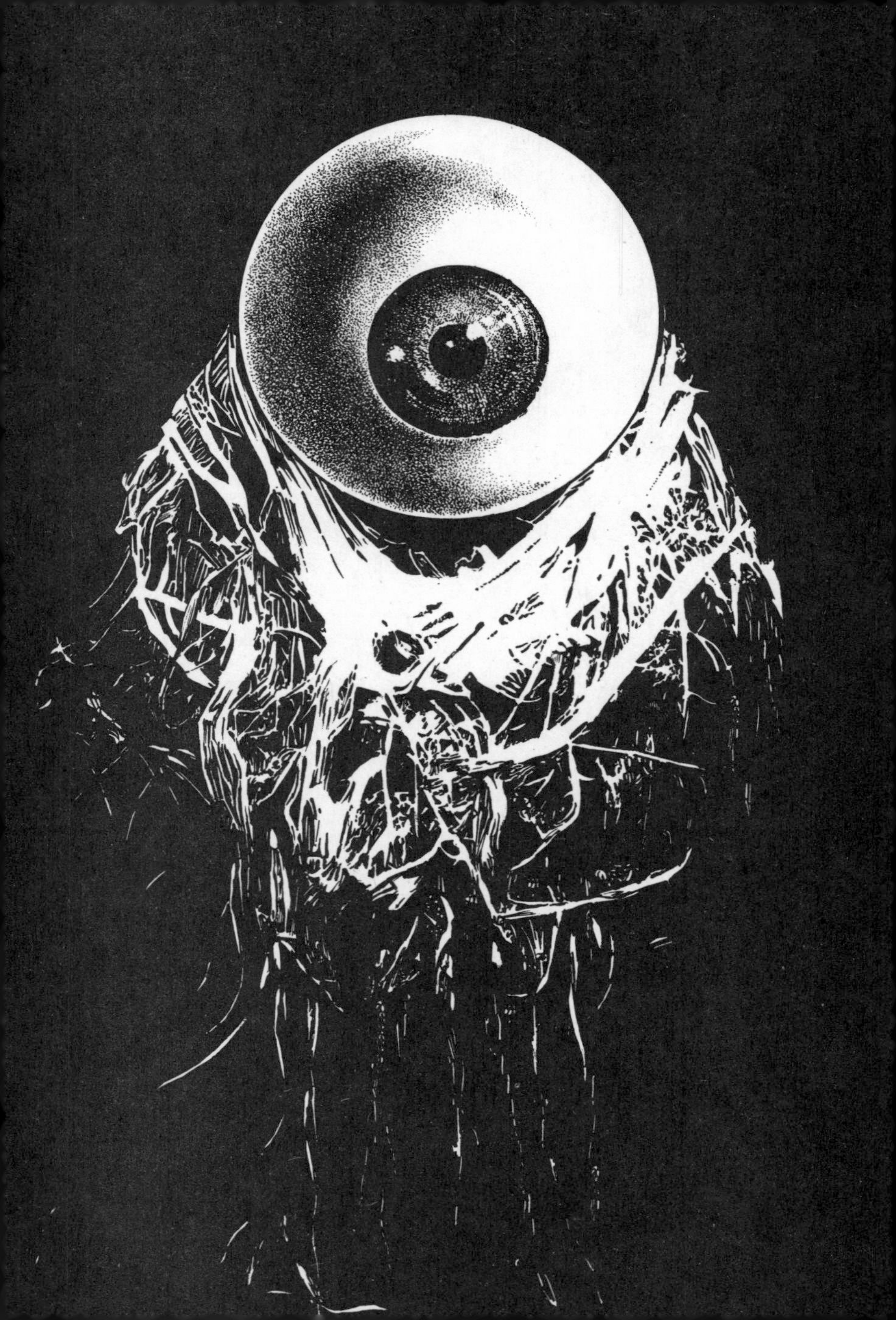

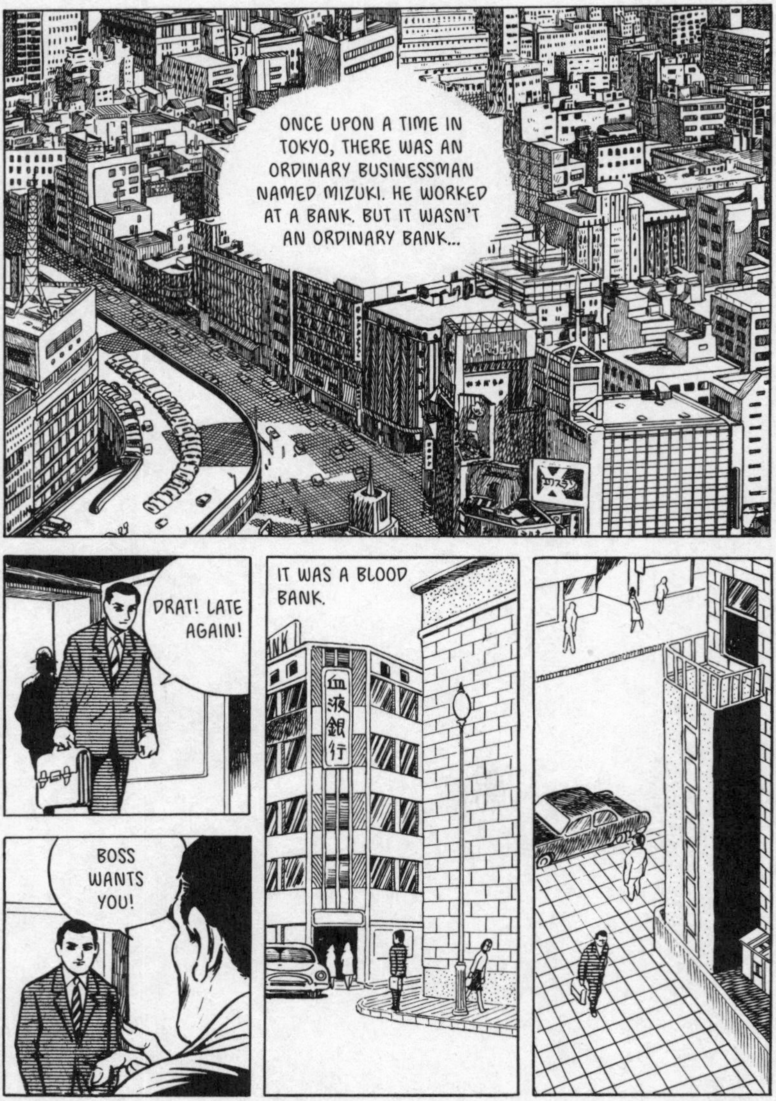
ONCE UPON A TIME IN TOKYO, THERE WAS AN ORDINARY BUSINESSMAN NAMED MIZUKI. HE WORKED AT A BANK. BUT IT WASN'T AN ORDINARY BANK...
MARUZEN
IT WAS A BLOOD BANK.
血液銀行
DRAT! LATE AGAIN!
BOSS WANTS YOU!

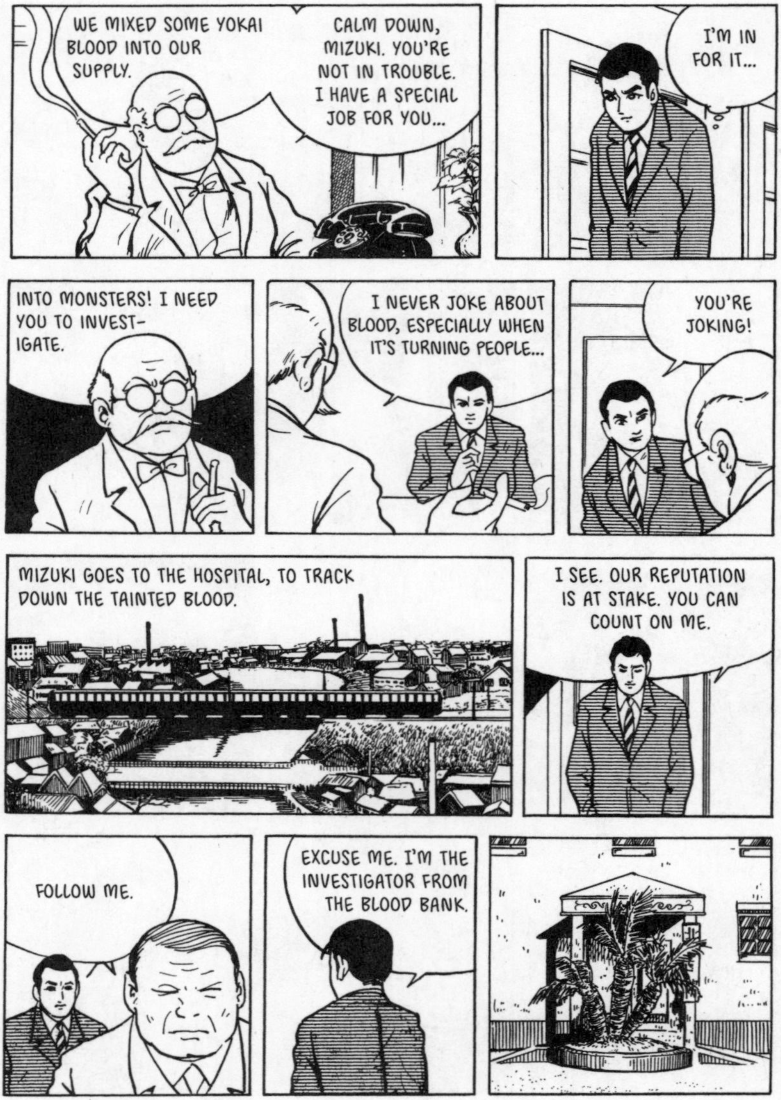
I'M IN FOR IT...
CALM DOWN, MIZUKI. YOU'RE NOT IN TROUBLE. I HAVE A SPECIAL JOB FOR YOU...
WE MIXED SOME YOKAI BLOOD INTO OUR SUPPLY.
YOU'RE JOKING!
I NEVER JOKE ABOUT BLOOD, ESPECIALLY WHEN IT'S TURNING PEOPLE...
INTO MONSTERS! I NEED YOU TO INVEST-IGATE.
I SEE. OUR REPUTATION IS AT STAKE. YOU CAN COUNT ON ME.
MIZUKI GOES TO THE HOSPITAL, TO TRACK DOWN THE TAINTED BLOOD.
EXCUSE ME. I'M THE INVESTIGATOR FROM THE BLOOD BANK.
FOLLOW ME.

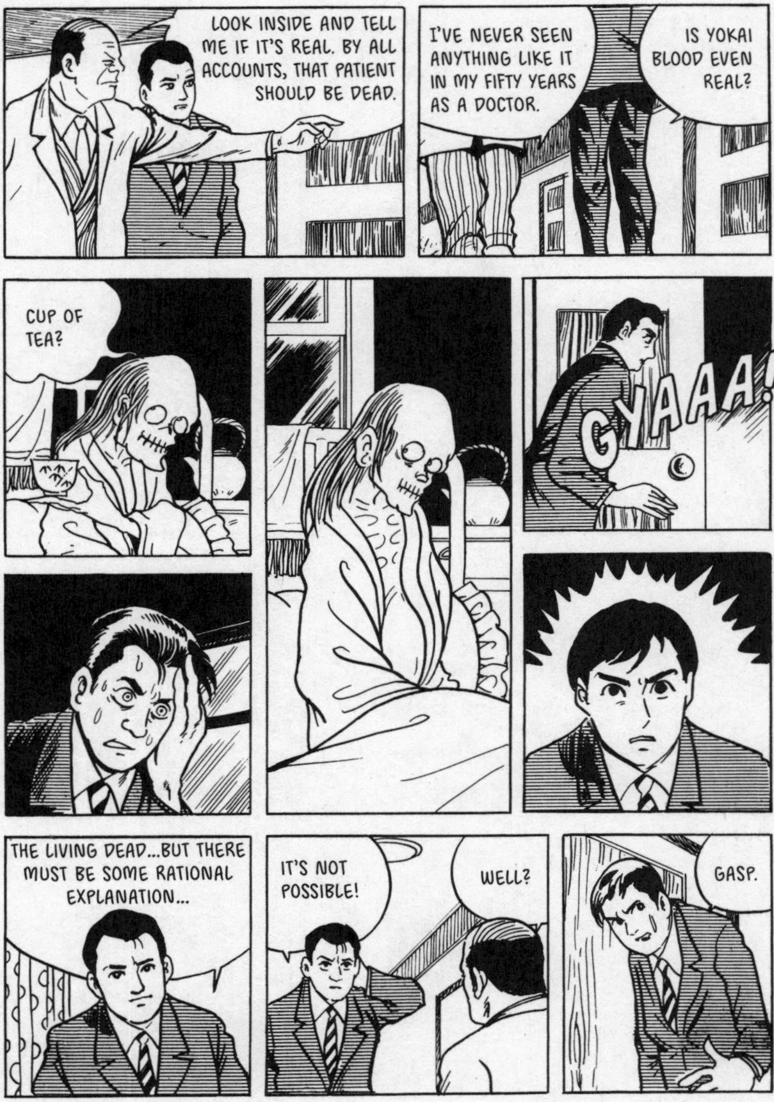
IS YOKAI BLOOD EVEN REAL?
I'VE NEVER SEEN ANYTHING LIKE IT IN MY FIFTY YEARS AS A DOCTOR.
LOOK INSIDE AND TELL ME IF IT'S REAL. BY ALL ACCOUNTS, THAT PATIENT SHOULD BE DEAD.
GYAAA!
CUP OF TEA?
GASP.
WELL?
IT'S NOT POSSIBLE!
THE LIVING DEAD...BUT THERE MUST BE SOME RATIONAL EXPLANATION...

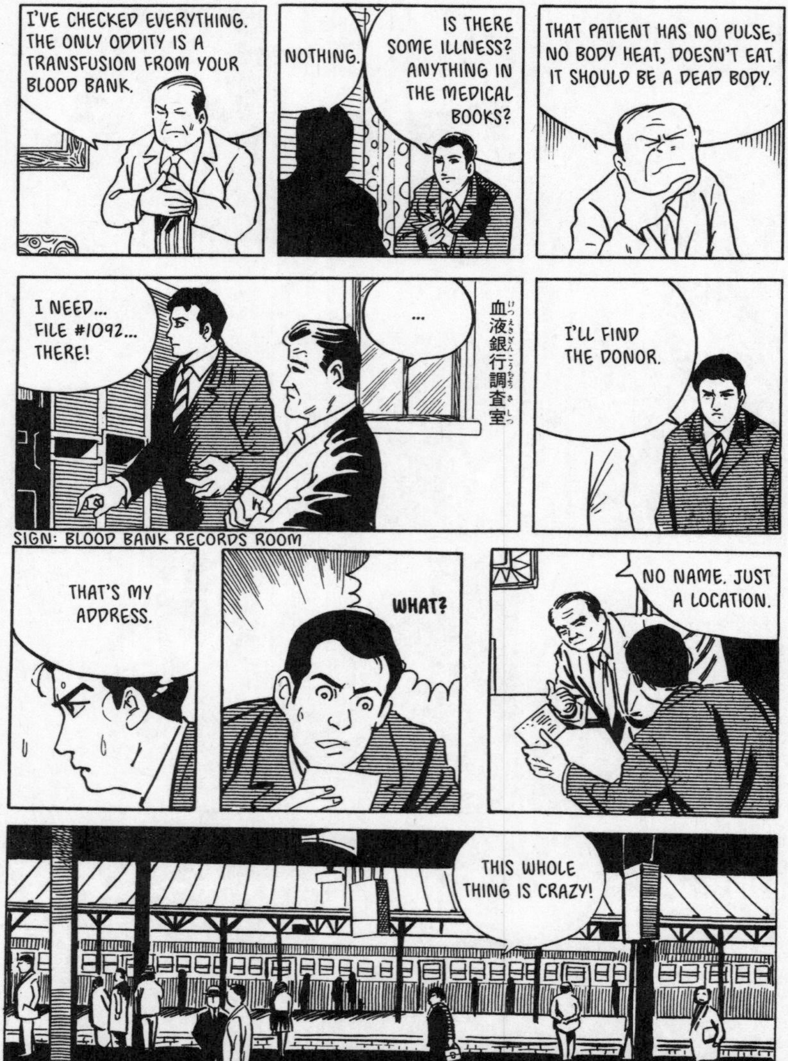
THAT PATIENT HAS NO PULSE, NO BODY HEAT, DOESN'T EAT. IT SHOULD BE A DEAD BODY.
IS THERE SOME ILLNESS? ANYTHING IN THE MEDICAL BOOKS?
NOTHING.
I'VE CHECKED EVERYTHING. THE ONLY ODDITY IS A TRANSFUSION FROM YOUR BLOOD BANK.
I'LL FIND THE DONOR.
...
血液銀行調査室
I NEED... FILE #1092... THERE!
SIGN: BLOOD BANK RECORDS ROOM
NO NAME. JUST A LOCATION.
WHAT?
THAT'S MY ADDRESS.
THIS WHOLE THING IS CRAZY!

DOES ANY-
WHERE ELSE
SHARE THIS
ADDRESS?

DON'T BE
RIDICULOUS.

HAS
ANYONE
MOVED IN
RECENTLY?

I'M HOME.

THAT JUNK
PILE...?

MAYBE THAT ABAN-
DONED TEMPLE
OUT BACK.

THAT TEMPLE SCARES
ME. I'VE SEEN LIGHTS
ON AT NIGHT...

I DON'T
KNOW
YET.

IS SOMETHING
WRONG?

I'LL HAVE TO
GET A CLOSER
LOOK.

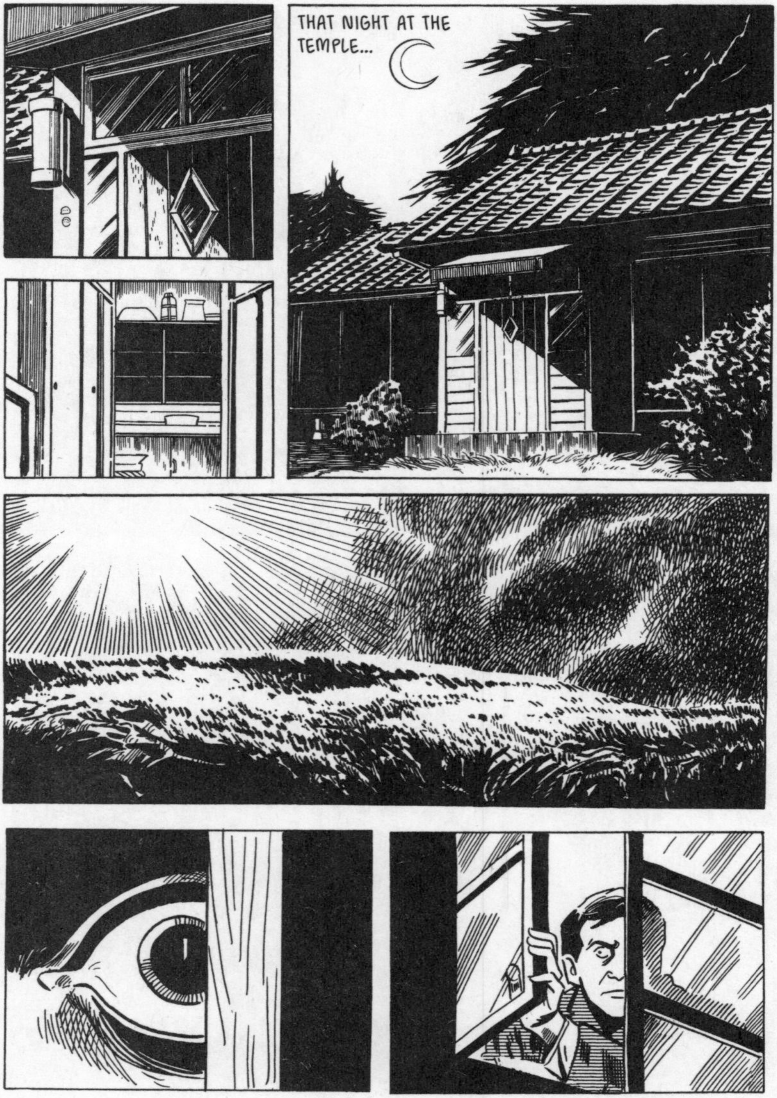
THAT NIGHT AT THE TEMPLE...

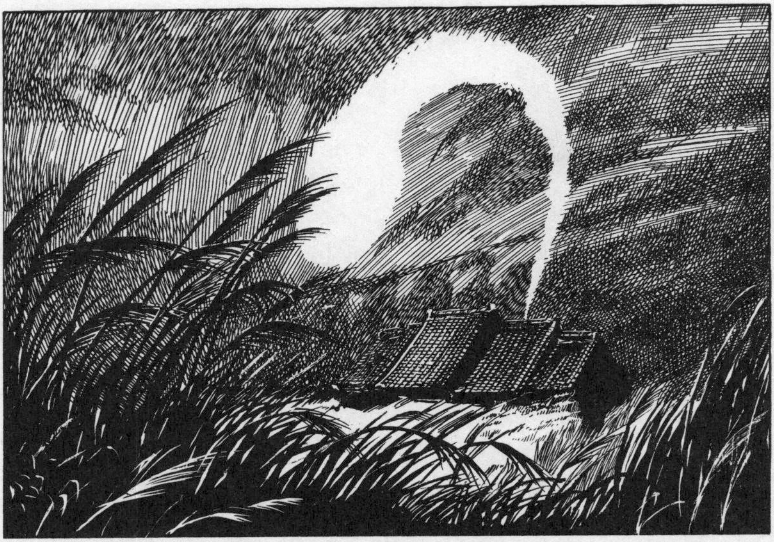

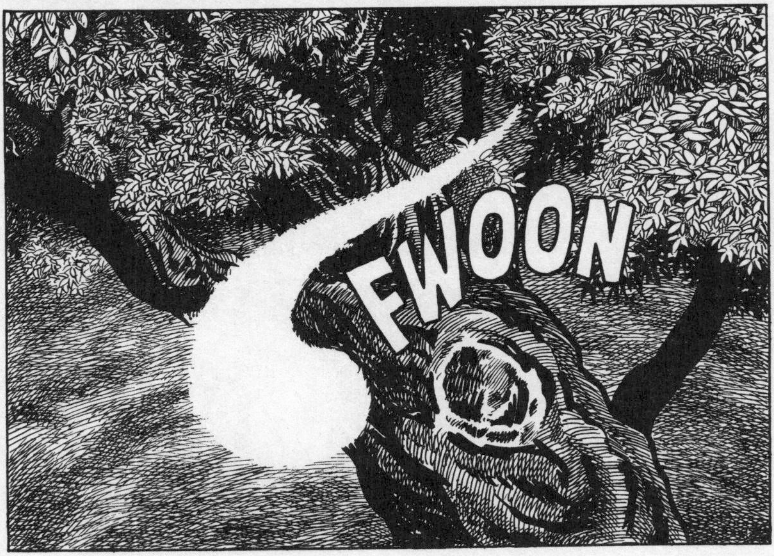
FWOON

IT'S LEADING ME SOMEWHERE.

A HITODAMA!

FWOON

FWOON

FWOON

SWISH

FWOON

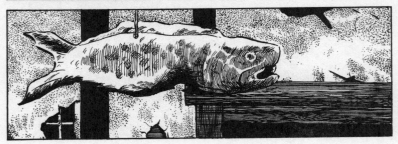

22

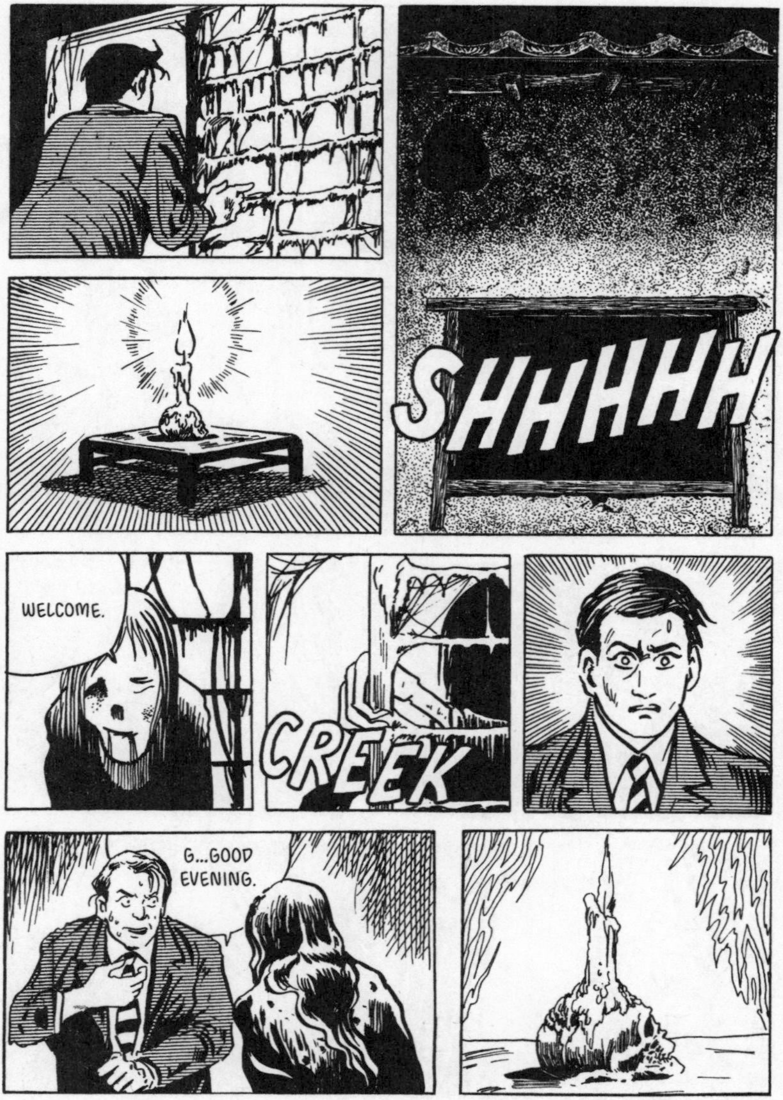
SHHHHH
CREEK
WELCOME.
G...GOOD EVENING.

COME IN. MAKE YOURSELF AT HOME.
I JUST HAVE SOME QUICK QUESTIONS...
WE'D LOVE TO HAVE YOU FOR DINNER. HE HEE HEE.
IT'S POOR FAIR, BUT FRESH.
SQUISH
SQUISH
SQUISH
I PLUCKED THEM MYSELF.
FROG'S EYEBALLS.
YUM.
POP POP POP

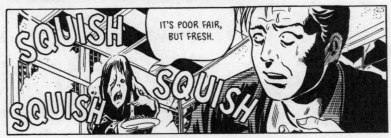

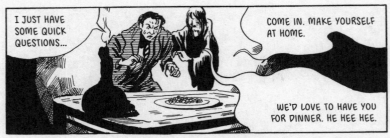

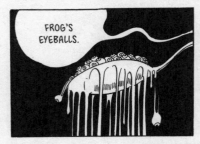

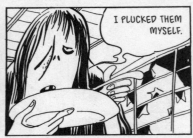

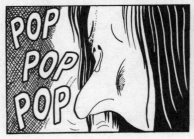

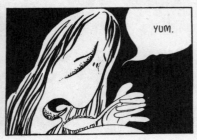

AND NOW FOR YOU, I THINK IT'S TIME YOU MET...

MY HUSBAND...

WHOMP

GWRAAR

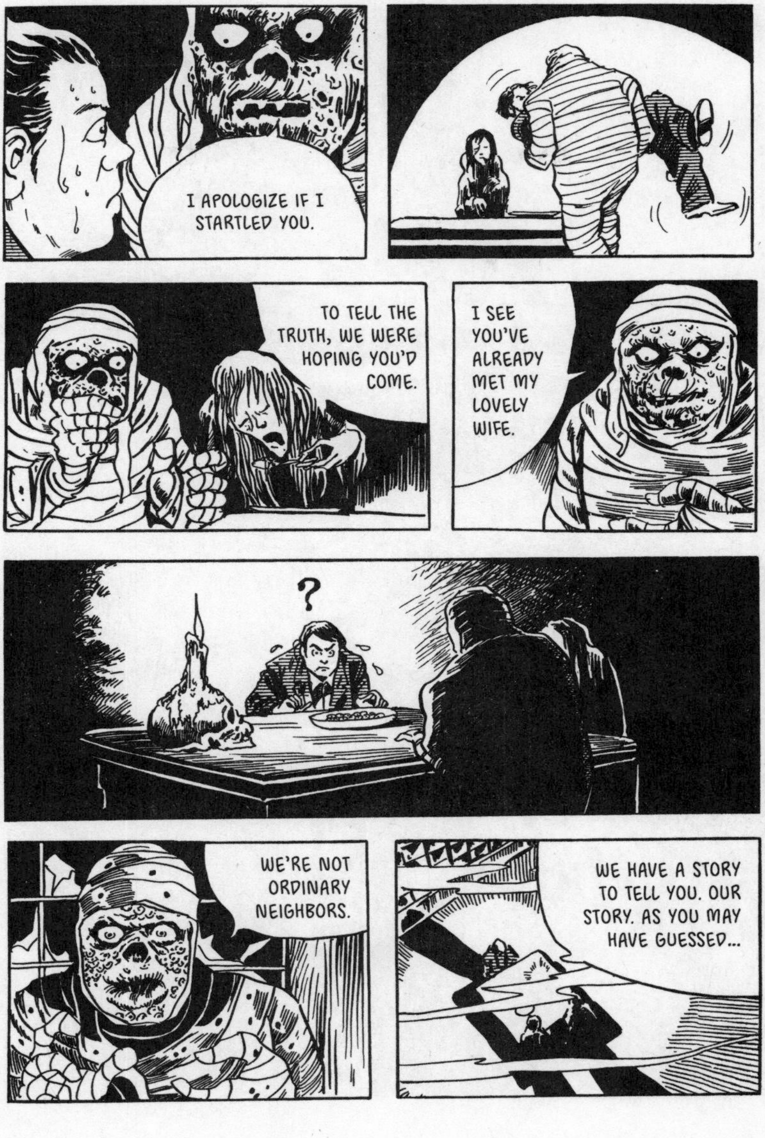
I APOLOGIZE IF I STARTLED YOU.
I SEE YOU'VE ALREADY MET MY LOVELY WIFE.
TO TELL THE TRUTH, WE WERE HOPING YOU'D COME.
?
WE HAVE A STORY TO TELL YOU. OUR STORY. AS YOU MAY HAVE GUESSED...
WE'RE NOT ORDINARY NEIGHBORS.

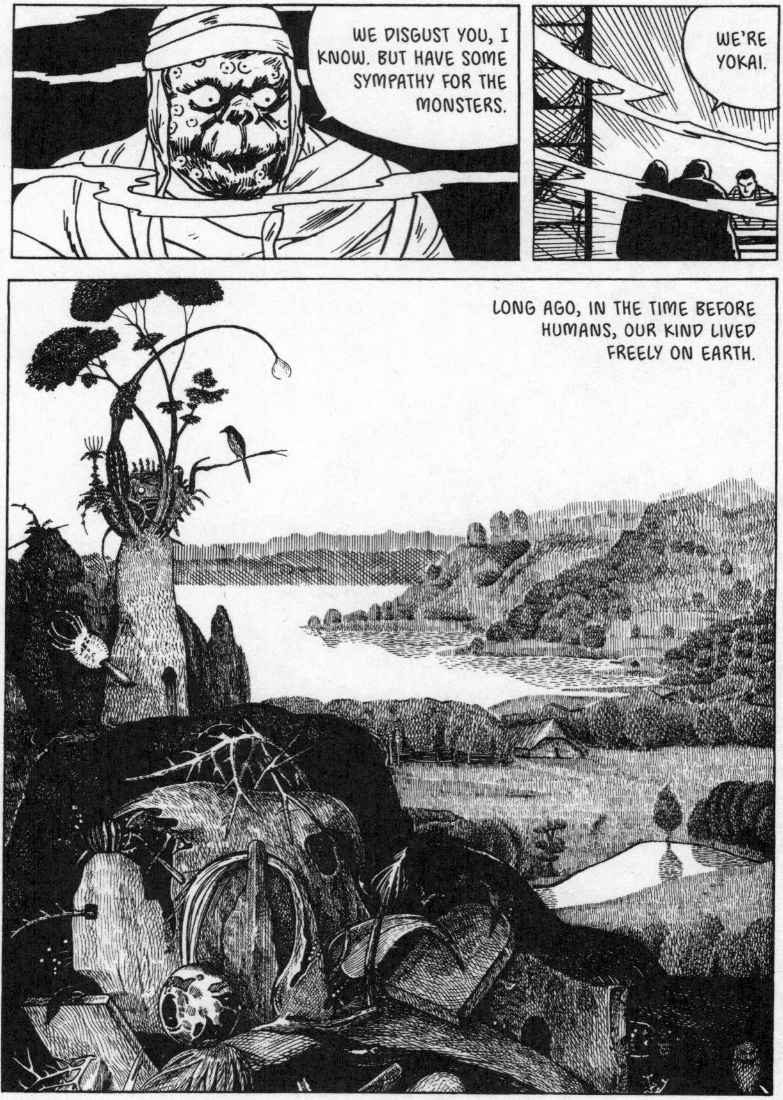
WE'RE YOKAI.
WE DISGUST YOU, I KNOW. BUT HAVE SOME SYMPATHY FOR THE MONSTERS.
LONG AGO, IN THE TIME BEFORE HUMANS, OUR KIND LIVED FREELY ON EARTH.

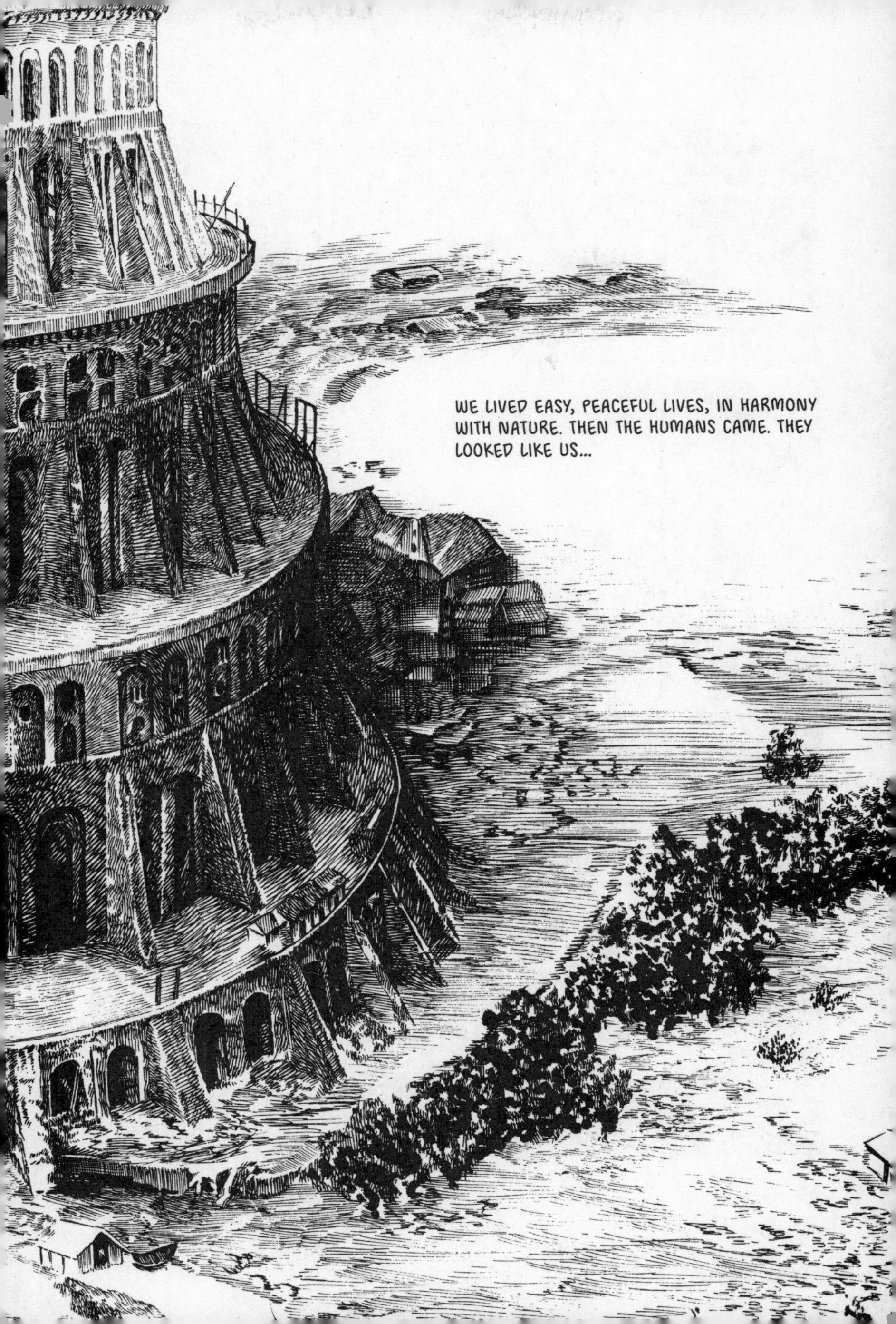
WE LIVED EASY, PEACEFUL LIVES, IN HARMONY WITH NATURE. THEN THE HUMANS CAME. THEY LOOKED LIKE US...

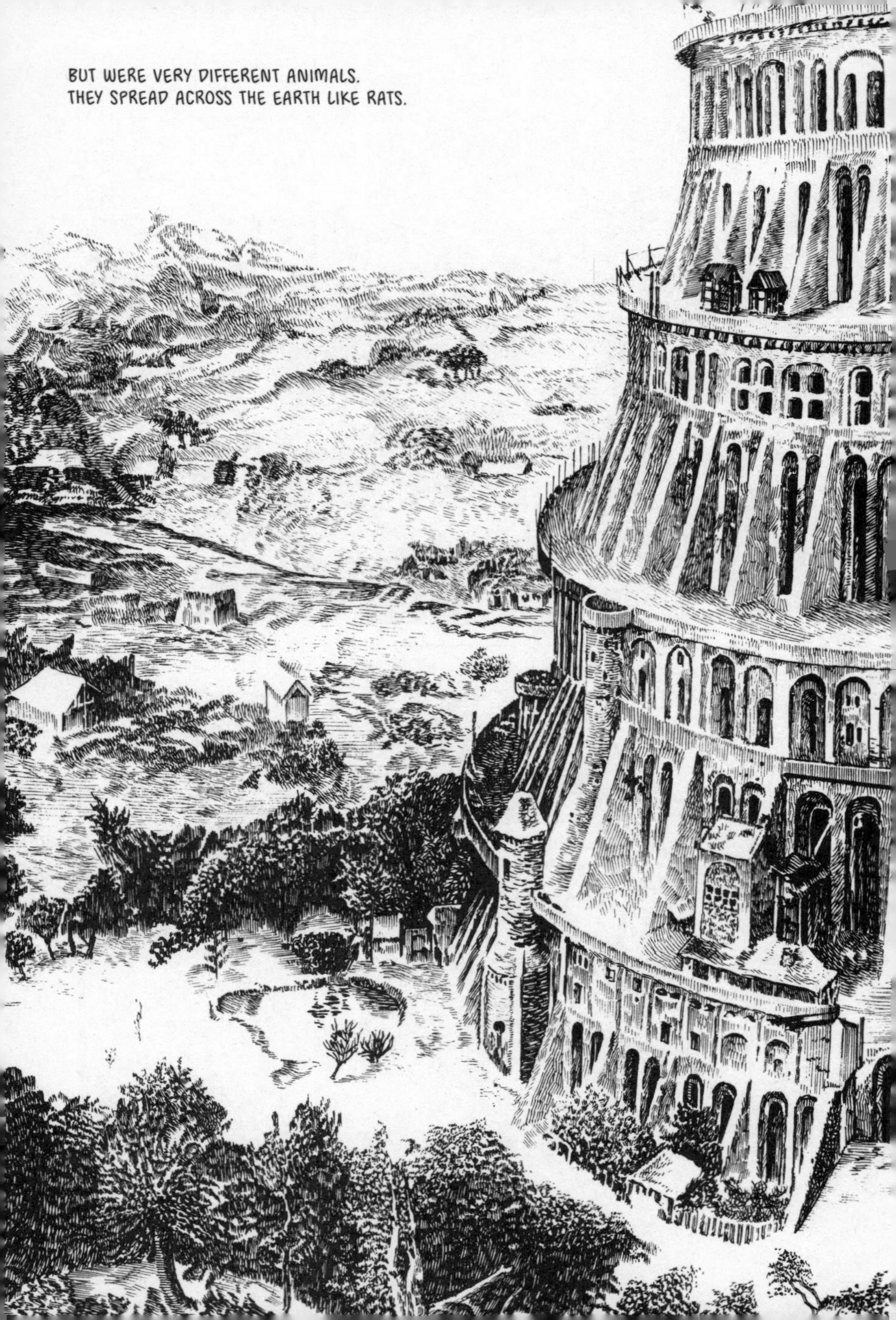
BUT WERE VERY DIFFERENT ANIMALS.
THEY SPREAD ACROSS THE EARTH LIKE RATS.

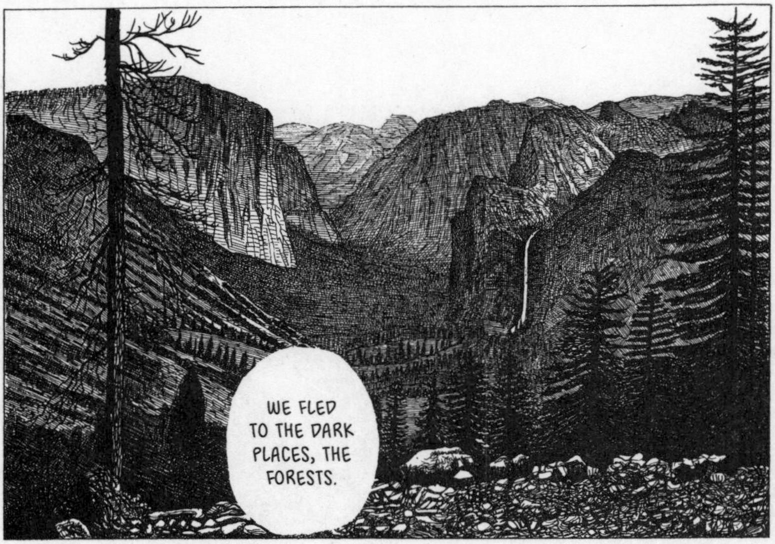
WE FLED TO THE DARK PLACES, THE FORESTS.

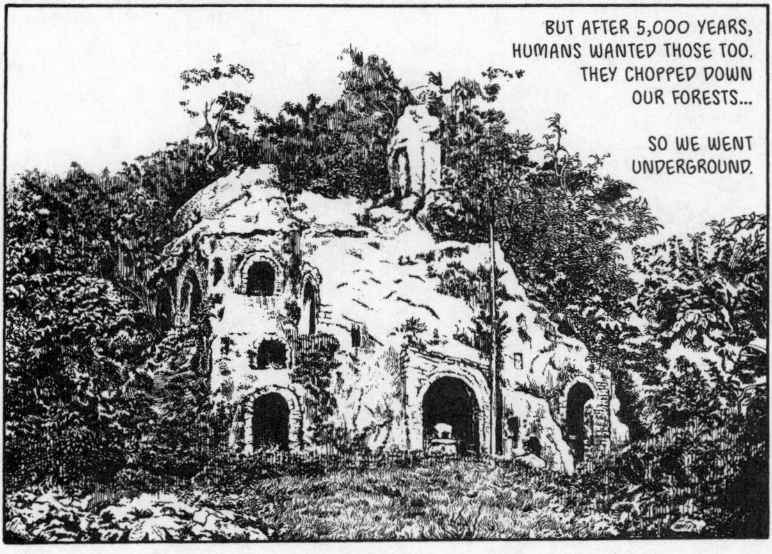
BUT AFTER 5,000 YEARS, HUMANS WANTED THOSE TOO. THEY CHOPPED DOWN OUR FORESTS...
SO WE WENT UNDERGROUND.

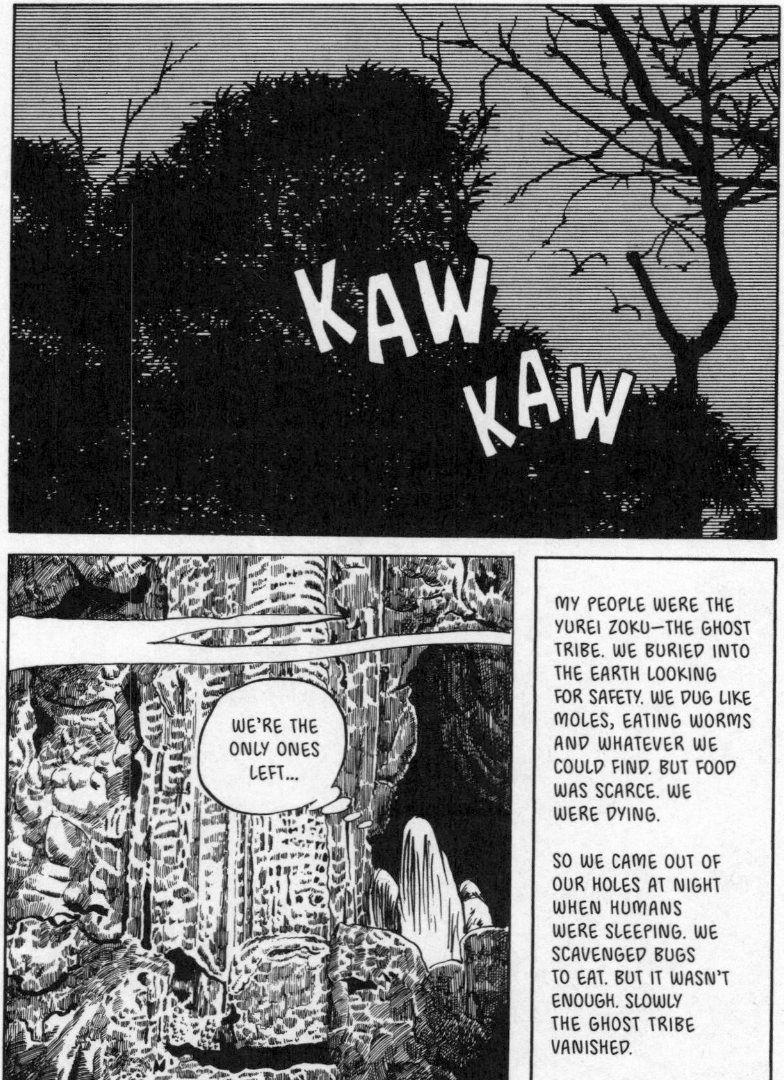
KAW
KAW
MY PEOPLE WERE THE YUREI ZOKU—THE GHOST TRIBE. WE BURIED INTO THE EARTH LOOKING FOR SAFETY. WE DUG LIKE MOLES, EATING WORMS AND WHATEVER WE COULD FIND. BUT FOOD WAS SCARCE. WE WERE DYING.
SO WE CAME OUT OF OUR HOLES AT NIGHT WHEN HUMANS WERE SLEEPING. WE SCAVENGED BUGS TO EAT. BUT IT WASN'T ENOUGH. SLOWLY THE GHOST TRIBE VANISHED.
WE'RE THE ONLY ONES LEFT...

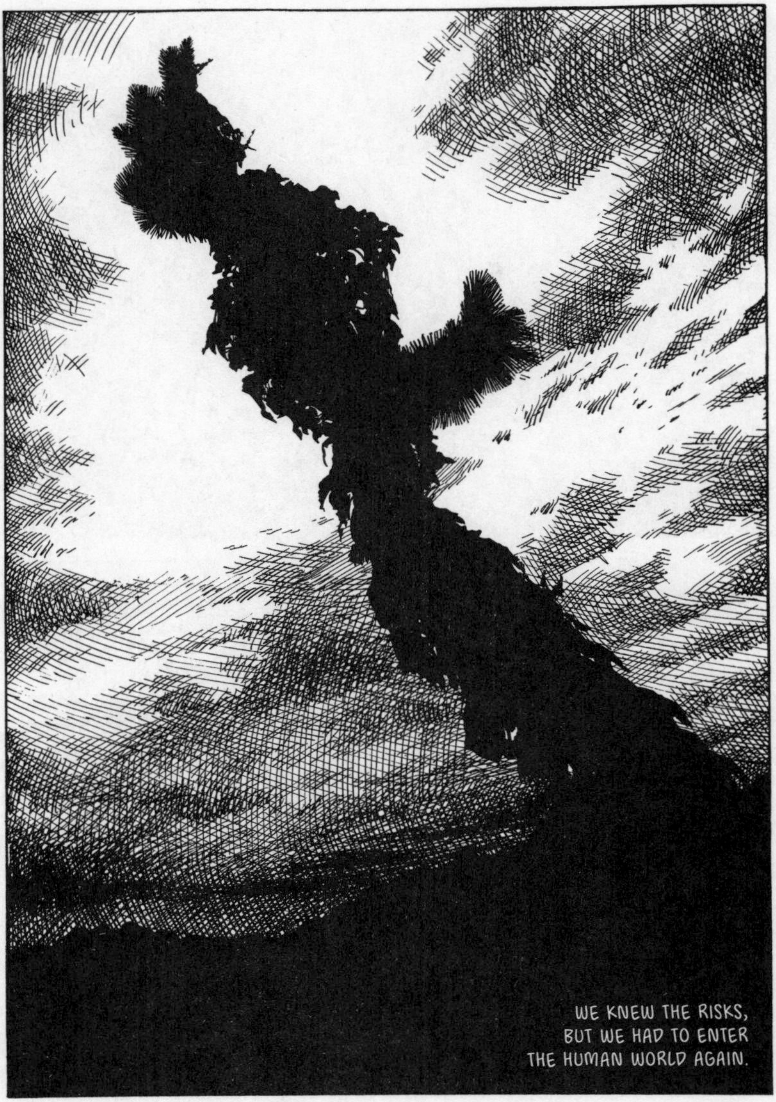
WE KNEW THE RISKS,
BUT WE HAD TO ENTER
THE HUMAN WORLD AGAIN.

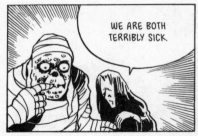

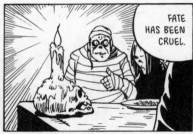

FATE HAS BEEN CRUEL.
WE ARE BOTH TERRIBLY SICK.
OUR LAST HOPE WAS HUMAN MEDICINE...
BUT YOU NEED MONEY FOR THAT...
THAT'S WHY YOU SOLD YOUR BLOOD!
YES. TO BUY MEDICINE.
I DISGUISED MYSELF IN HUMAN CLOTHES.
BUT...

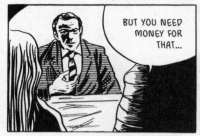

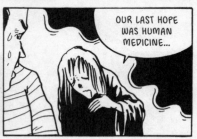

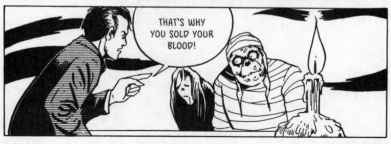

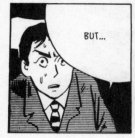

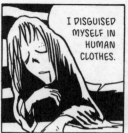

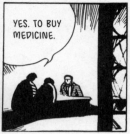

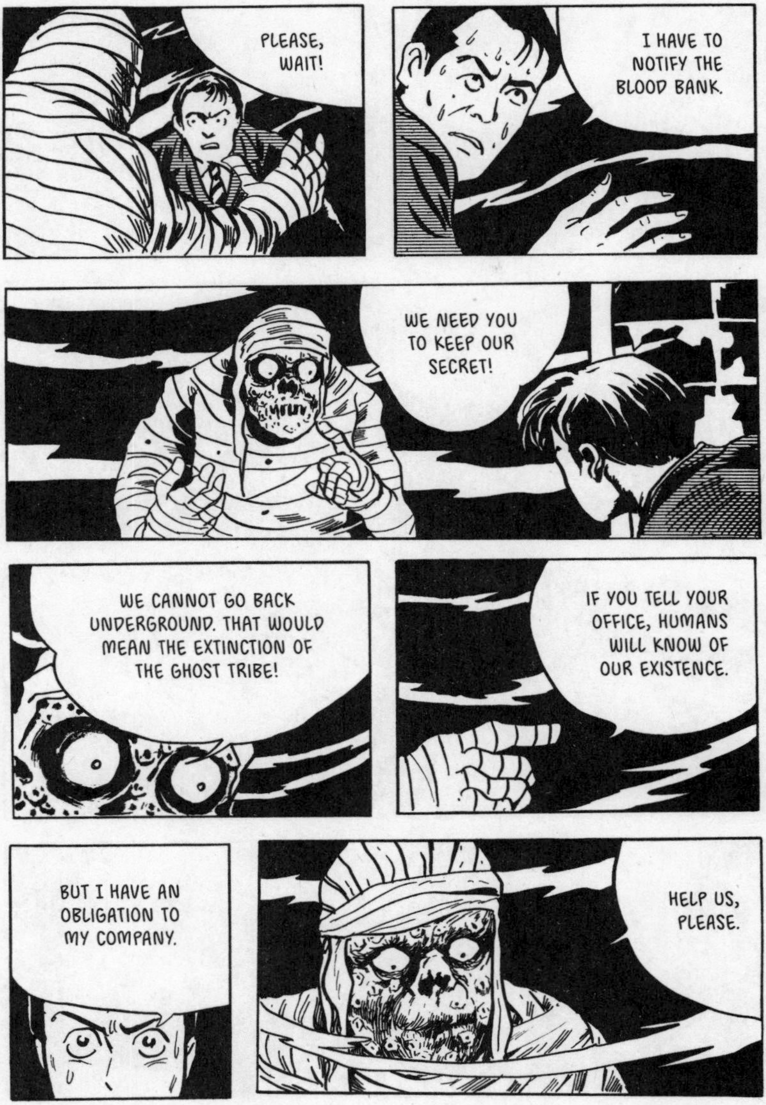
I HAVE TO NOTIFY THE BLOOD BANK.
PLEASE, WAIT!
WE NEED YOU TO KEEP OUR SECRET!
IF YOU TELL YOUR OFFICE, HUMANS WILL KNOW OF OUR EXISTENCE.
WE CANNOT GO BACK UNDERGROUND. THAT WOULD MEAN THE EXTINCTION OF THE GHOST TRIBE!
HELP US, PLEASE.
BUT I HAVE AN OBLIGATION TO MY COMPANY.

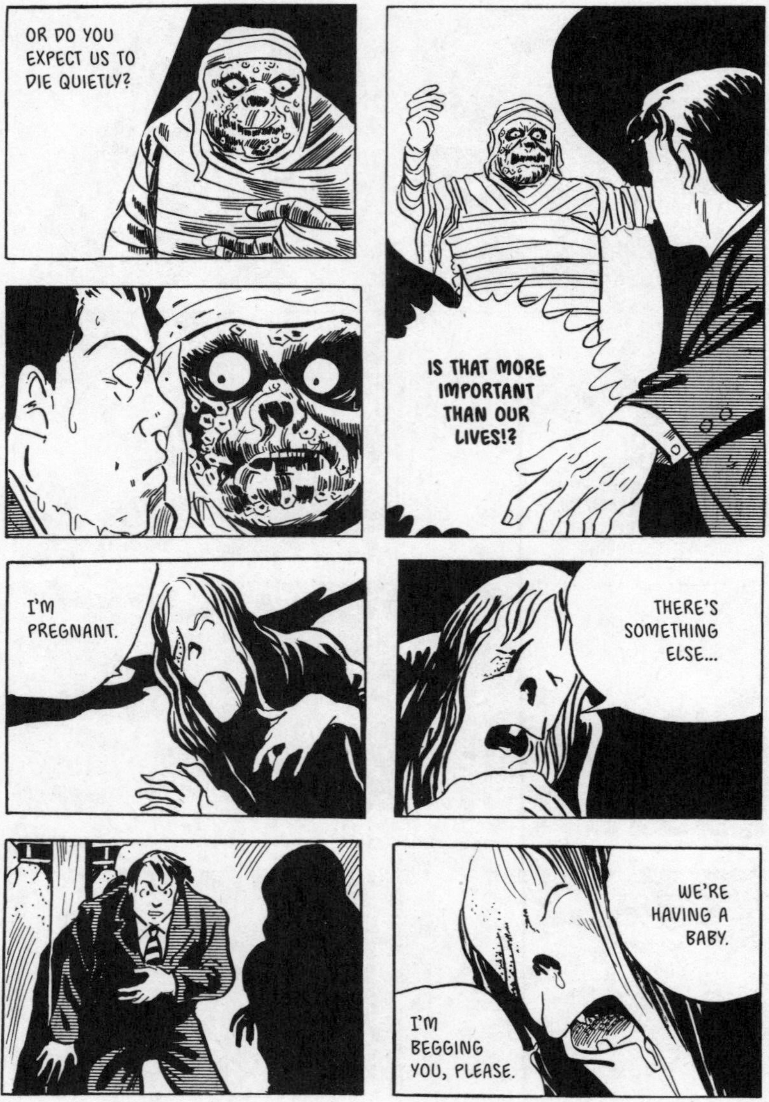
IS THAT MORE IMPORTANT THAN OUR LIVES!?
OR DO YOU EXPECT US TO DIE QUIETLY?
THERE'S SOMETHING ELSE...
I'M PREGNANT.
WE'RE HAVING A BABY.
I'M BEGGING YOU, PLEASE.

THIS IS TOO BIG OF A DECISION FOR ME TO MAKE!
I CAN GIVE YOU EIGHT OR NINE MONTHS...
HEE HE HEE HE HE
YOU HAVE OUR SINCERE GRATITUDE.

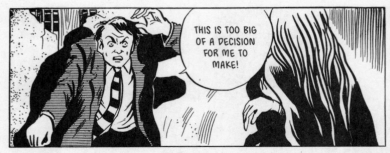

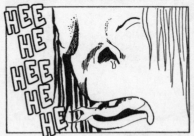

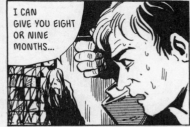

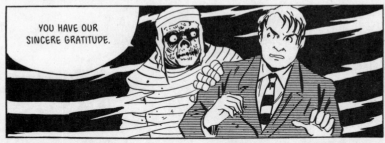

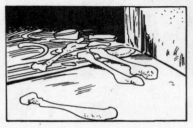

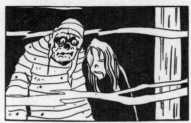

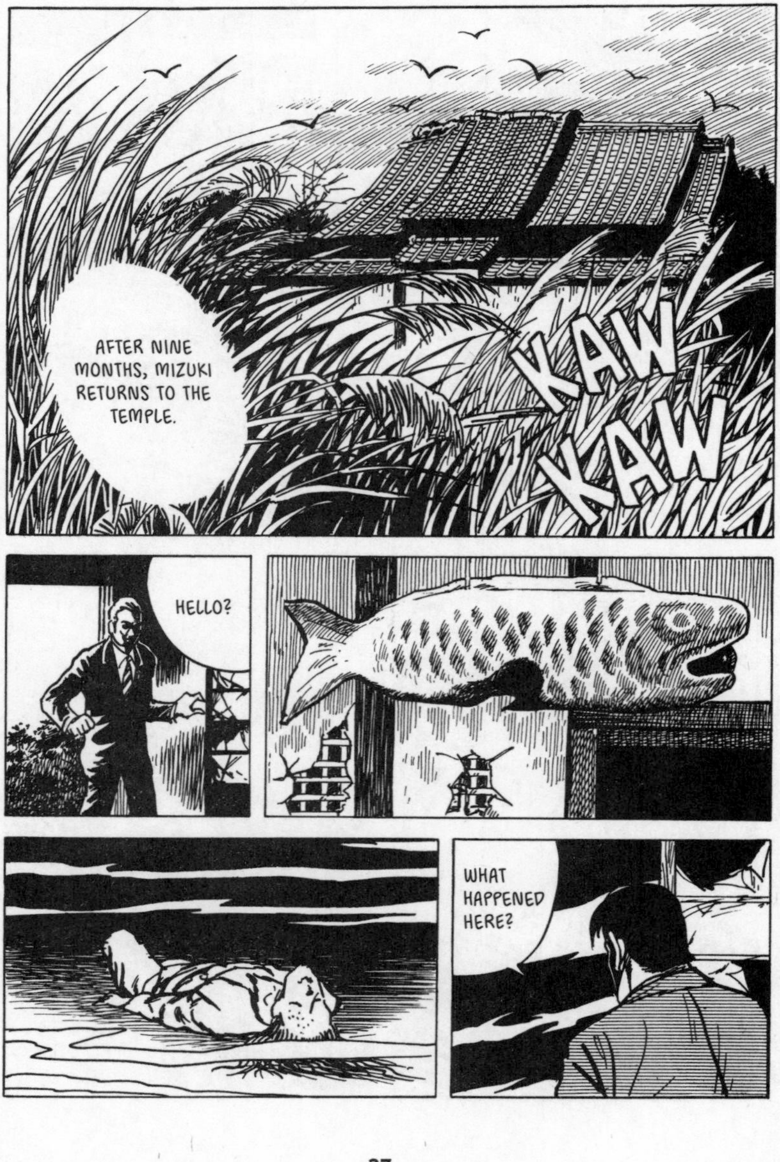
AFTER NINE MONTHS, MIZUKI RETURNS TO THE TEMPLE.
KAW KAW
HELLO?
WHAT HAPPENED HERE?

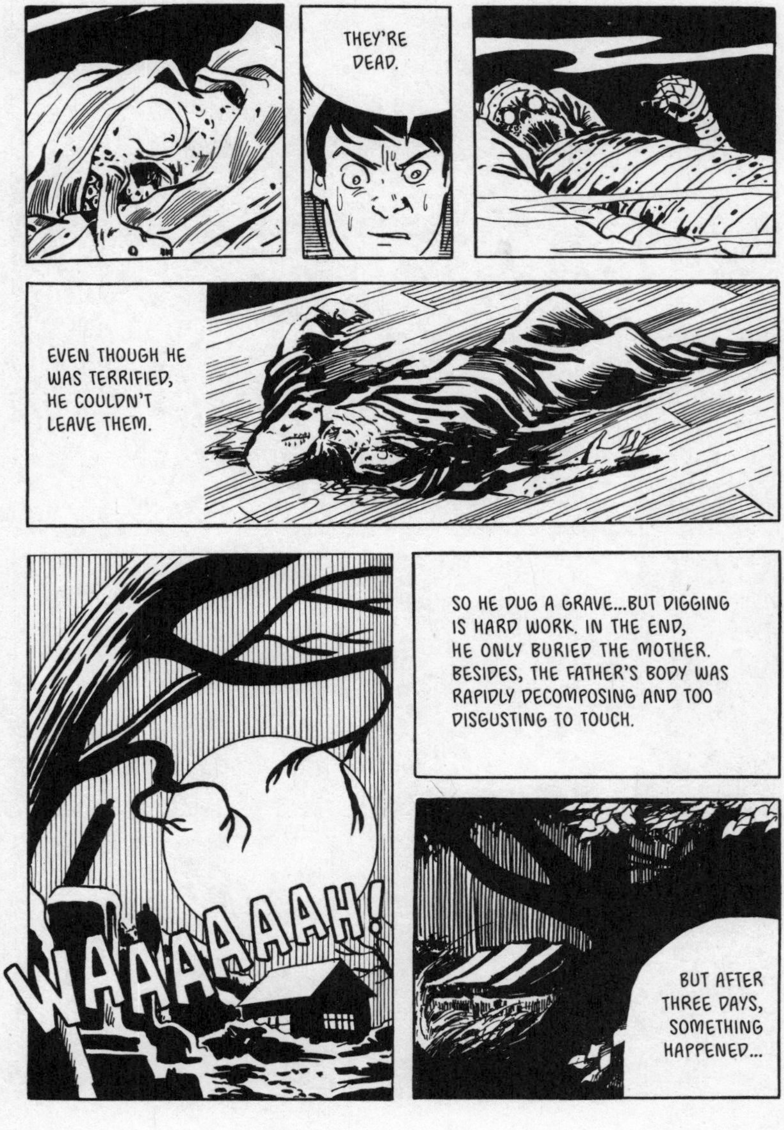
THEY'RE DEAD.
EVEN THOUGH HE WAS TERRIFIED, HE COULDN'T LEAVE THEM.
SO HE DUG A GRAVE...BUT DIGGING IS HARD WORK. IN THE END, HE ONLY BURIED THE MOTHER. BESIDES, THE FATHER'S BODY WAS RAPIDLY DECOMPOSING AND TOO DISGUSTING TO TOUCH.
BUT AFTER THREE DAYS, SOMETHING HAPPENED...
WAAAAAAH!

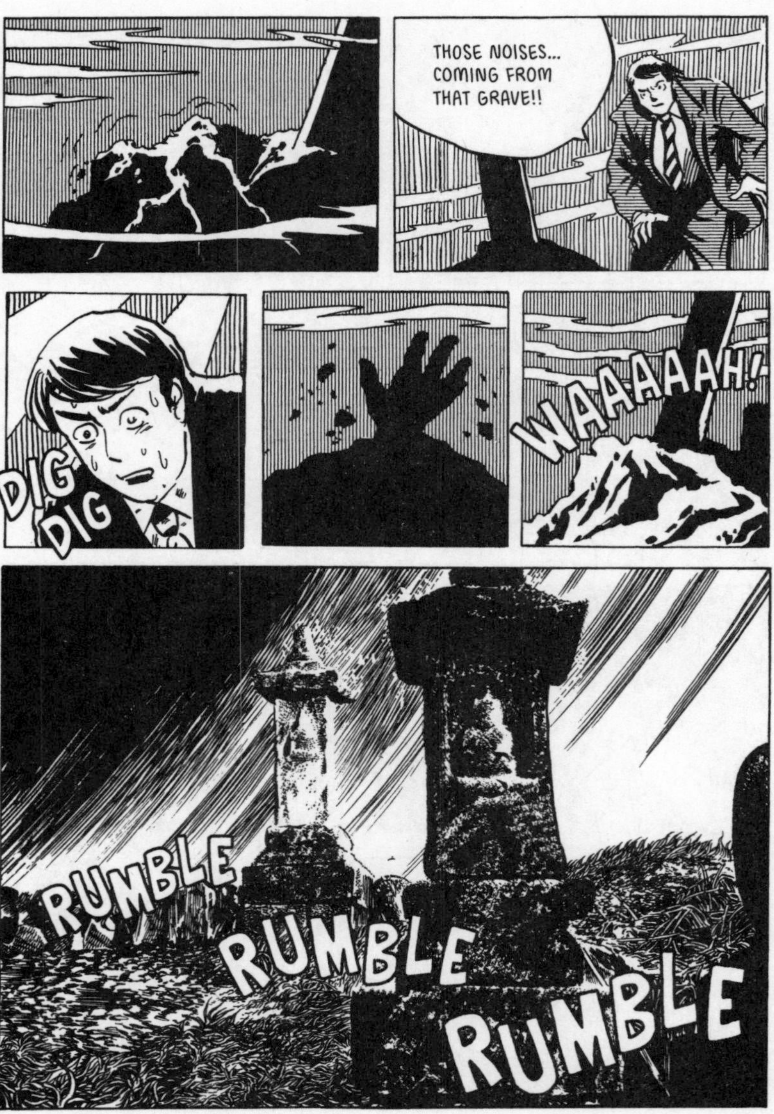
THOSE NOISES... COMING FROM THAT GRAVE!!
WAAAAAH!
DIG DIG
RUMBLE
RUMBLE
RUMBLE

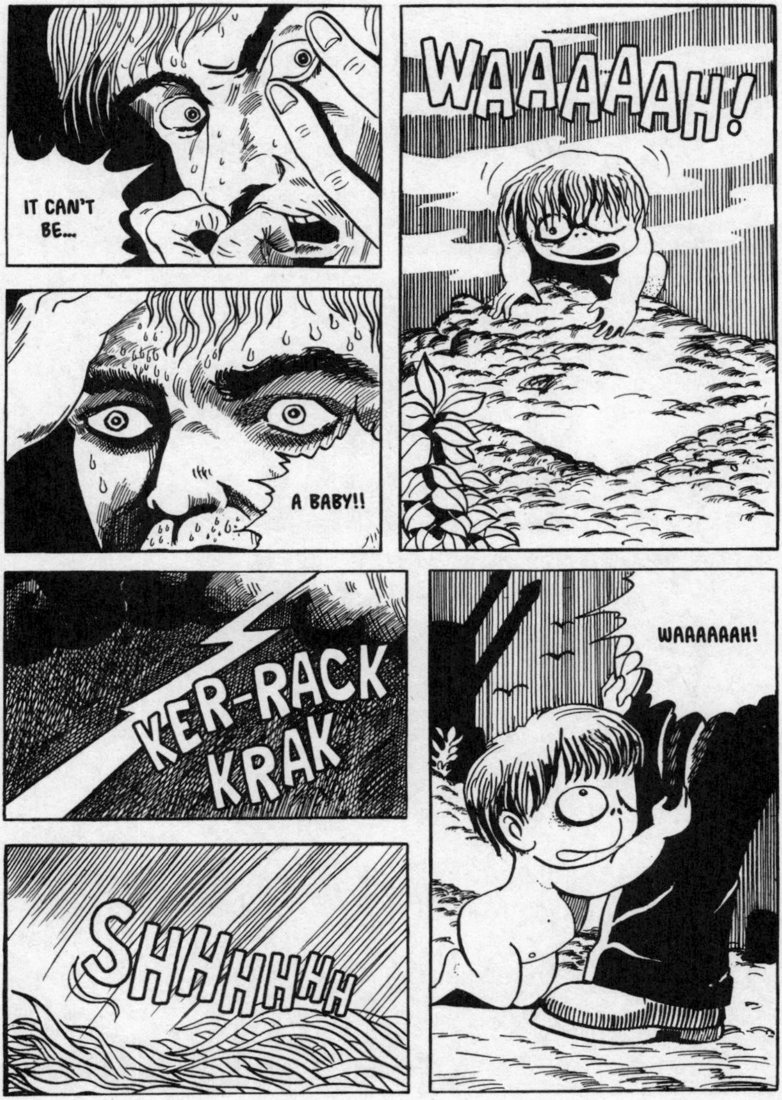
WAAAAAH!
IT CAN'T BE...
A BABY!!
WAAAAAAH!
KER-RACK
KRAK
SHHHHHH

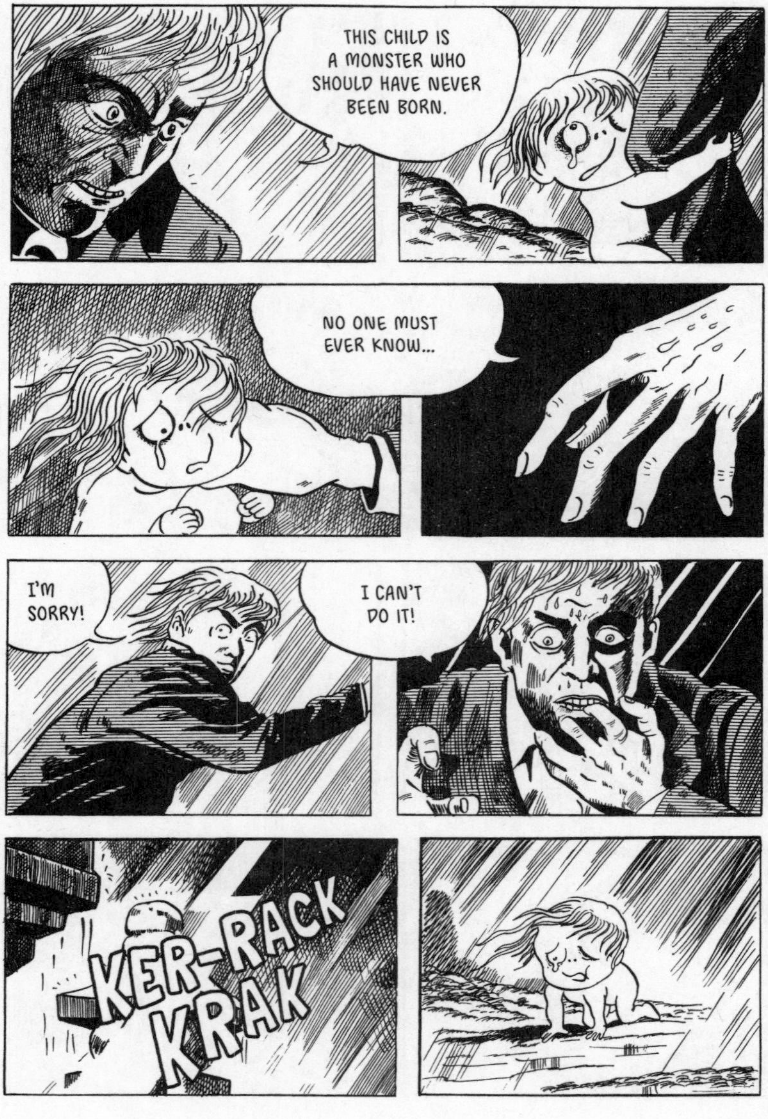
THIS CHILD IS A MONSTER WHO SHOULD HAVE NEVER BEEN BORN.
NO ONE MUST EVER KNOW...
I CAN'T DO IT!
I'M SORRY!
KER-RACK KRAK

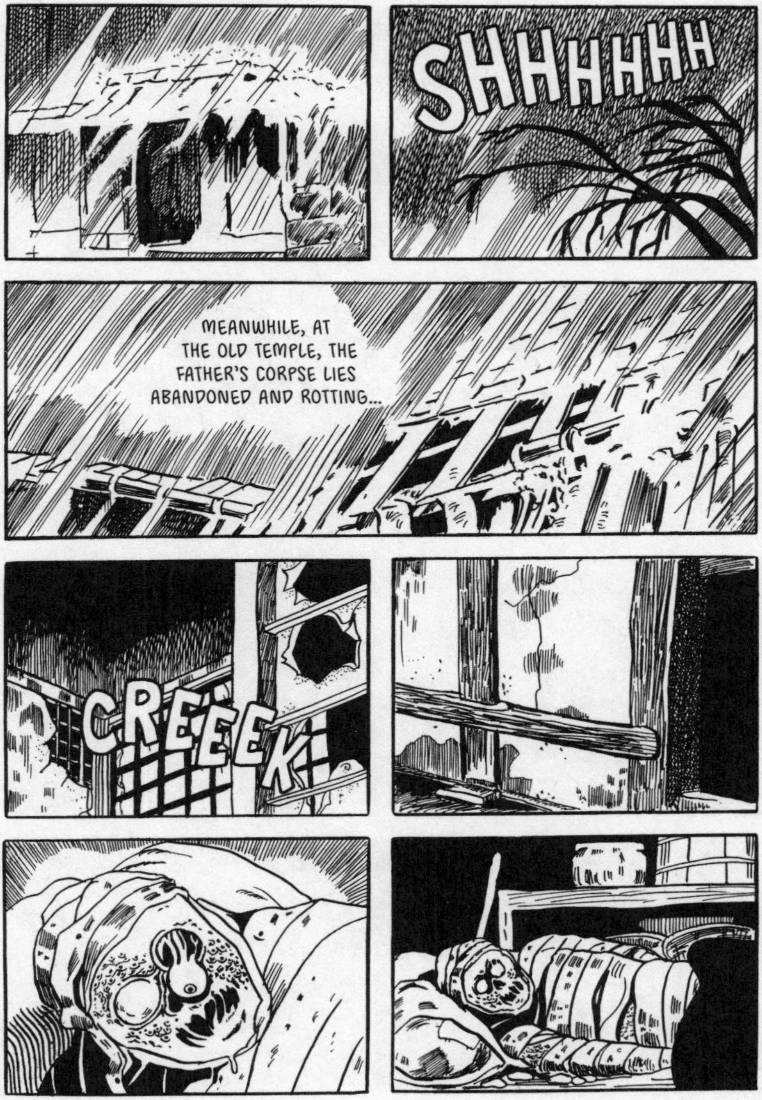
SHHHHHH
MEANWHILE, AT THE OLD TEMPLE, THE FATHER'S CORPSE LIES ABANDONED AND ROTTING...
CREEEK

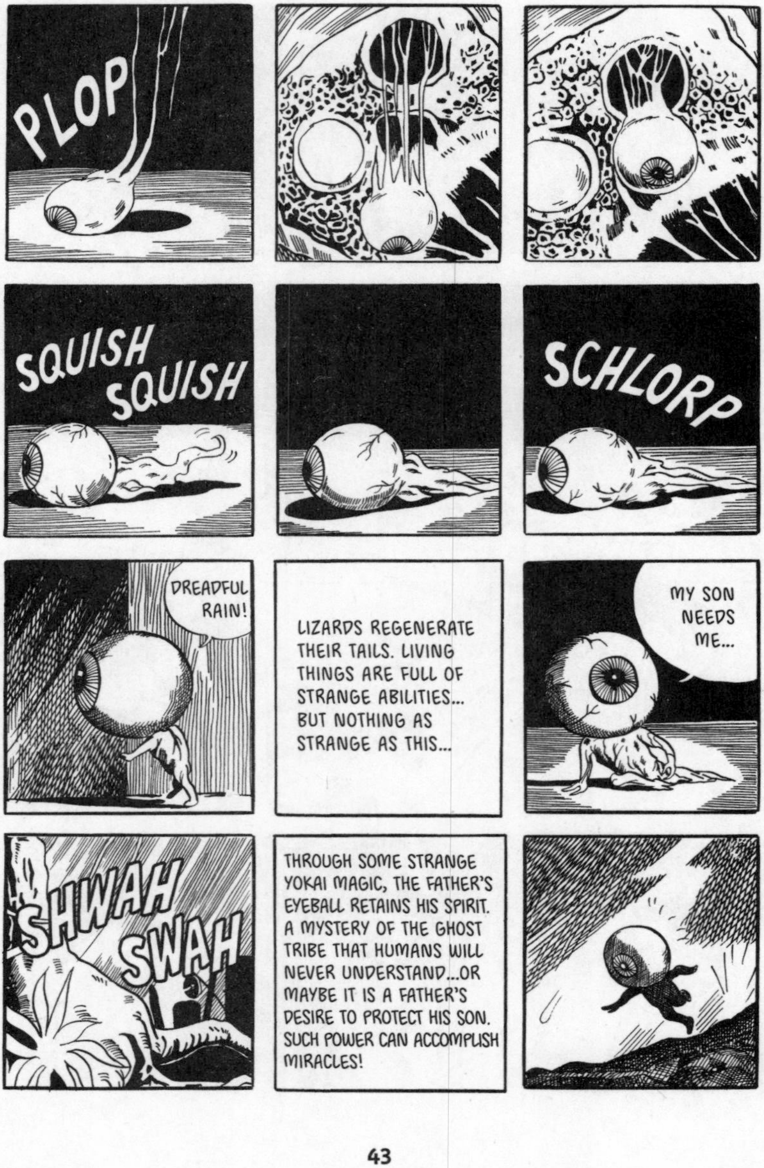
PLOP
SCHLORP
SQUISH SQUISH
MY SON NEEDS ME...
LIZARDS REGENERATE THEIR TAILS. LIVING THINGS ARE FULL OF STRANGE ABILITIES... BUT NOTHING AS STRANGE AS THIS...
DREADFUL RAIN!
THROUGH SOME STRANGE YOKAI MAGIC, THE FATHER'S EYEBALL RETAINS HIS SPIRIT. A MYSTERY OF THE GHOST TRIBE THAT HUMANS WILL NEVER UNDERSTAND...OR MAYBE IT IS A FATHER'S DESIRE TO PROTECT HIS SON. SUCH POWER CAN ACCOMPLISH MIRACLES!
SHWAH SWAH

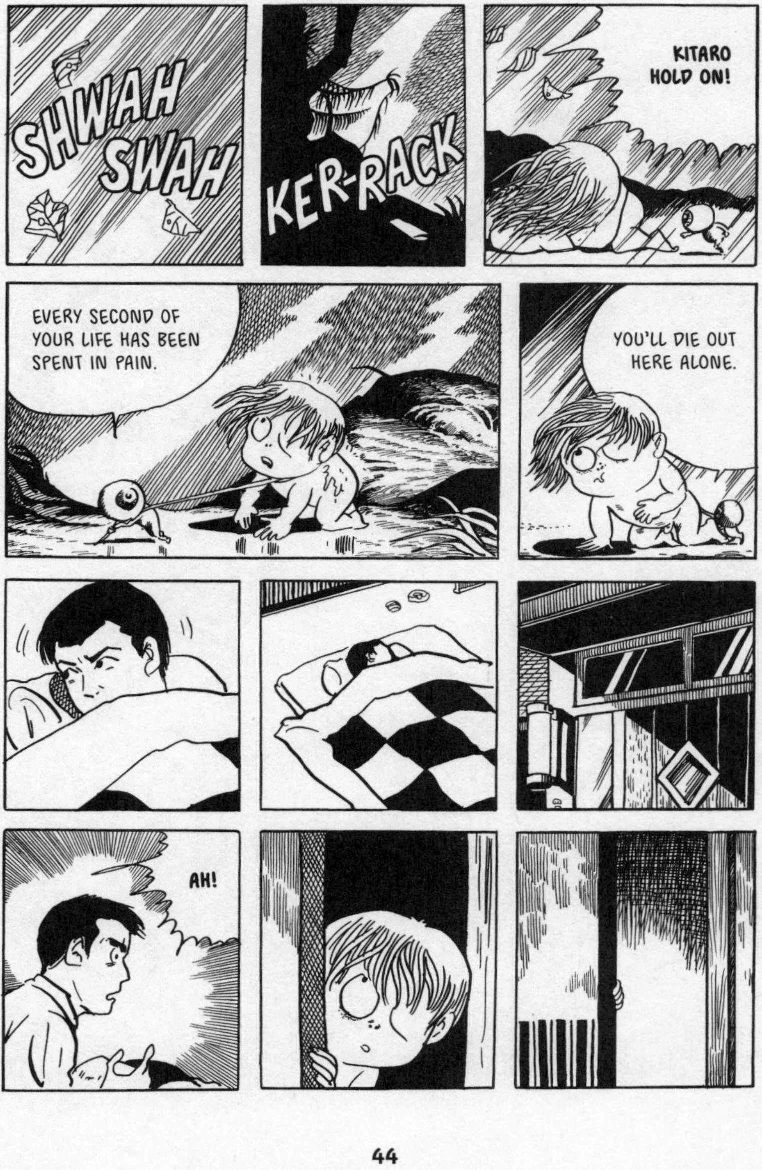
KITARO HOLD ON!
KER-RACK
SHWAH SWAH
YOU'LL DIE OUT HERE ALONE.
EVERY SECOND OF YOUR LIFE HAS BEEN SPENT IN PAIN.
AH!

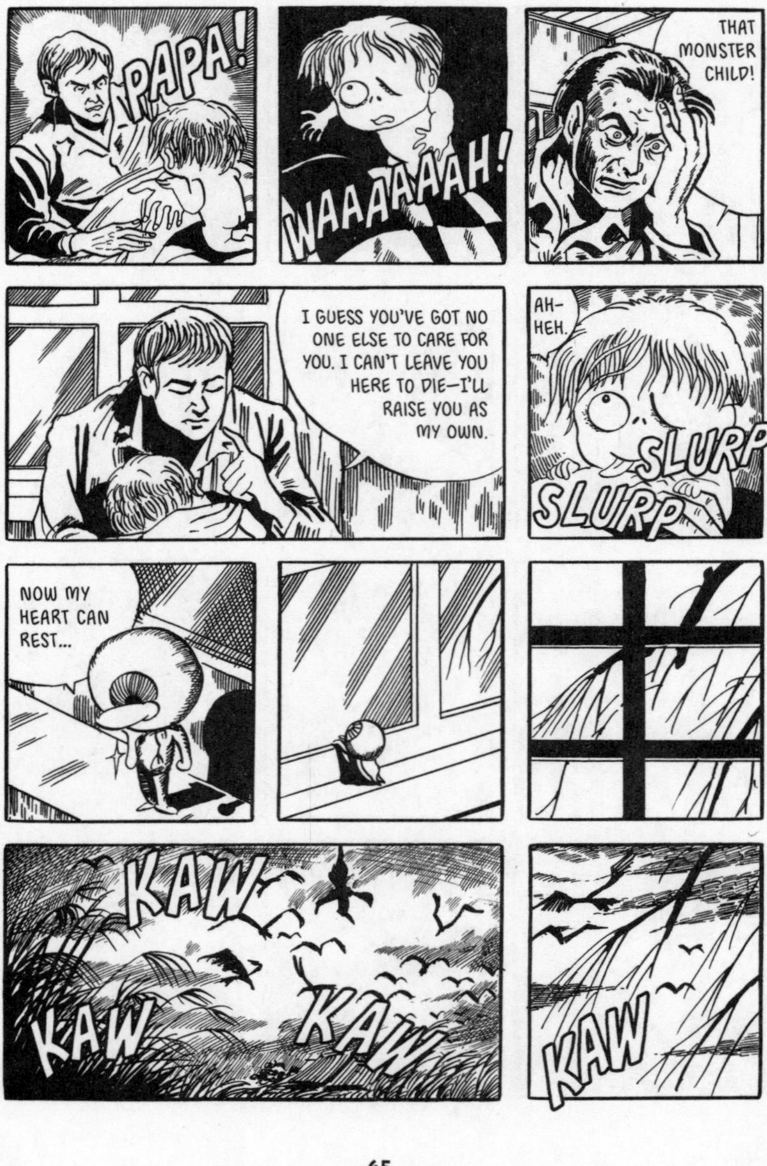
THAT MONSTER CHILD!
WAAAAAAH!
PAPA!
AH-HEH.
SLURP
SLURP
I GUESS YOU'VE GOT NO ONE ELSE TO CARE FOR YOU. I CAN'T LEAVE YOU HERE TO DIE—I'LL RAISE YOU AS MY OWN.
NOW MY HEART CAN REST...
KAW
KAW
KAW
KAW

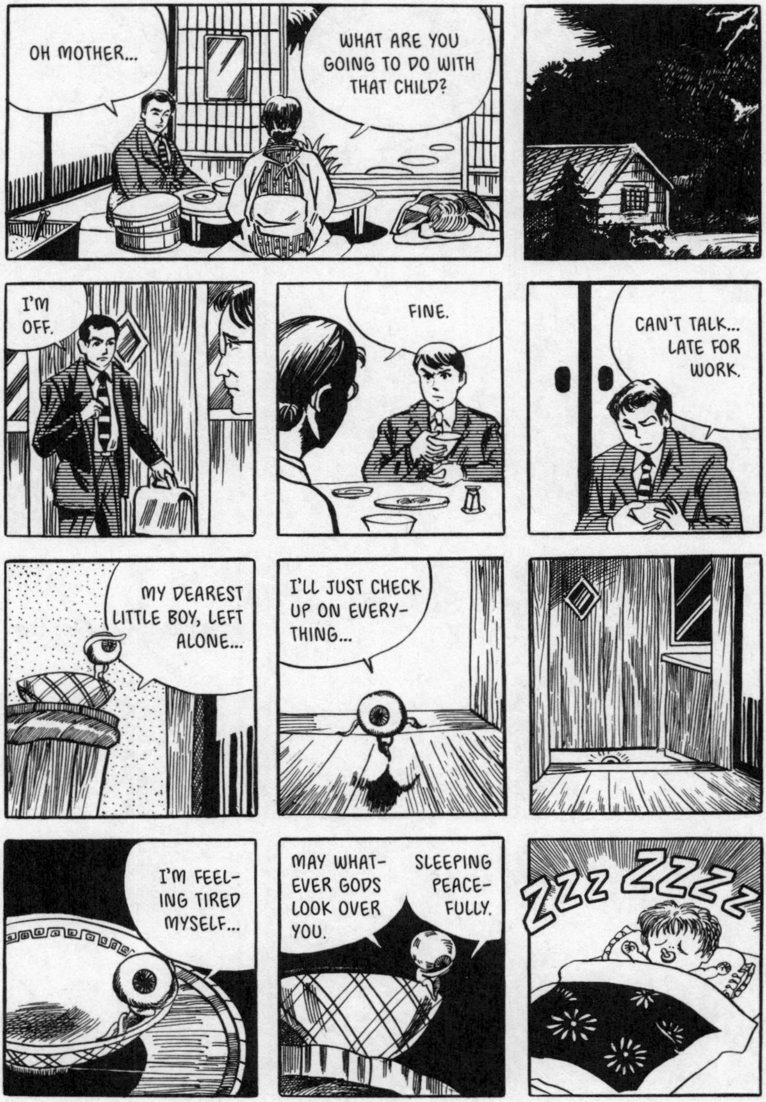
WHAT ARE YOU GOING TO DO WITH THAT CHILD?
OH MOTHER...
CAN'T TALK... LATE FOR WORK.
FINE.
I'M OFF.
I'LL JUST CHECK UP ON EVERY-THING...
MY DEAREST LITTLE BOY, LEFT ALONE...
ZZZ ZZZZ
SLEEPING PEACE-FULLY.
MAY WHAT-EVER GODS LOOK OVER YOU.
I'M FEEL-ING TIRED MYSELF...

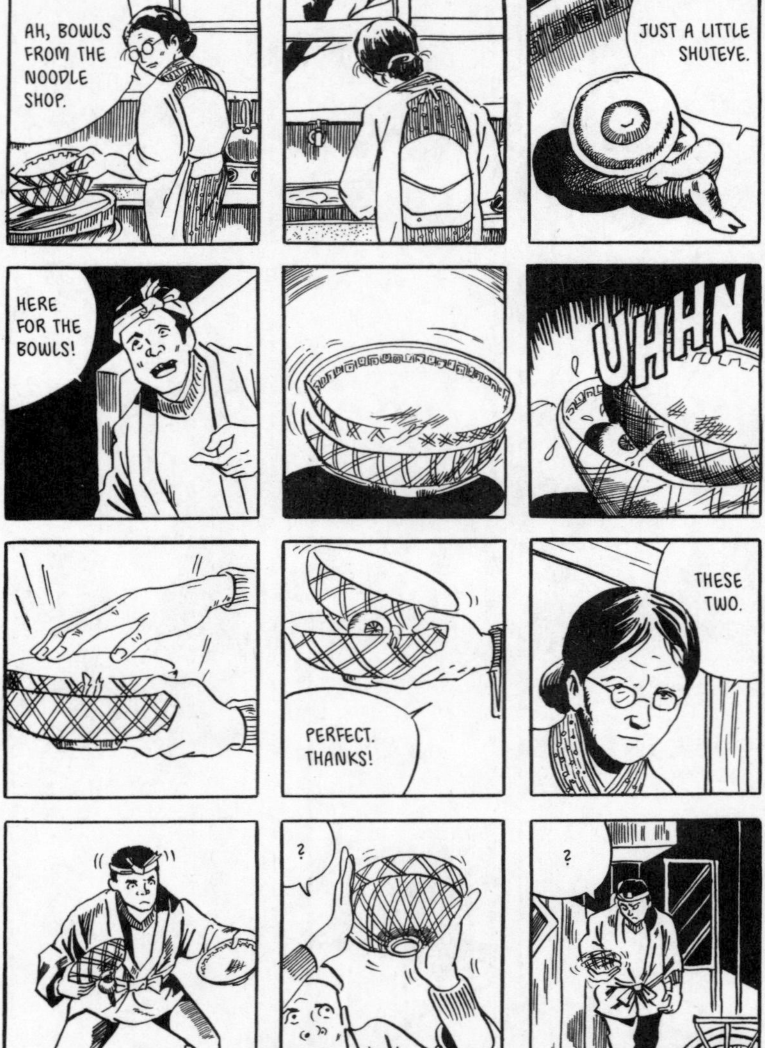
JUST A LITTLE SHUTEYE.
AH, BOWLS FROM THE NOODLE SHOP.
UHHN
HERE FOR THE BOWLS!
THESE TWO.
PERFECT. THANKS!
?
?

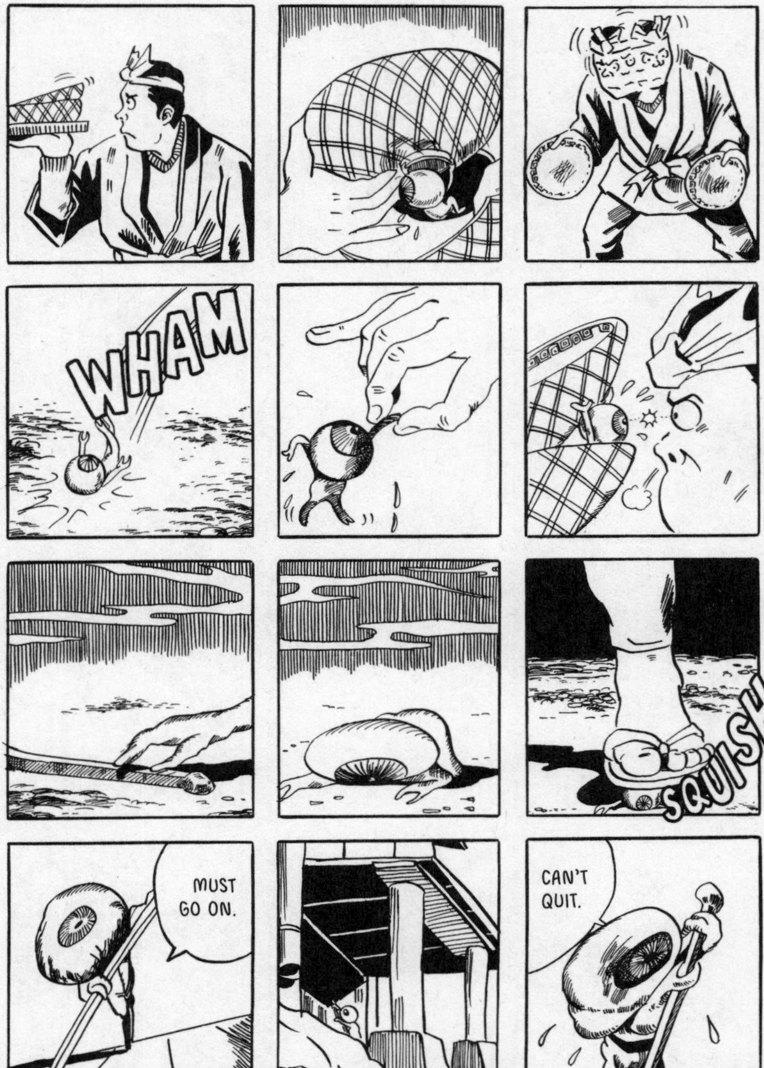
WHAM
SQUISH
CAN'T QUIT.
MUST GO ON.

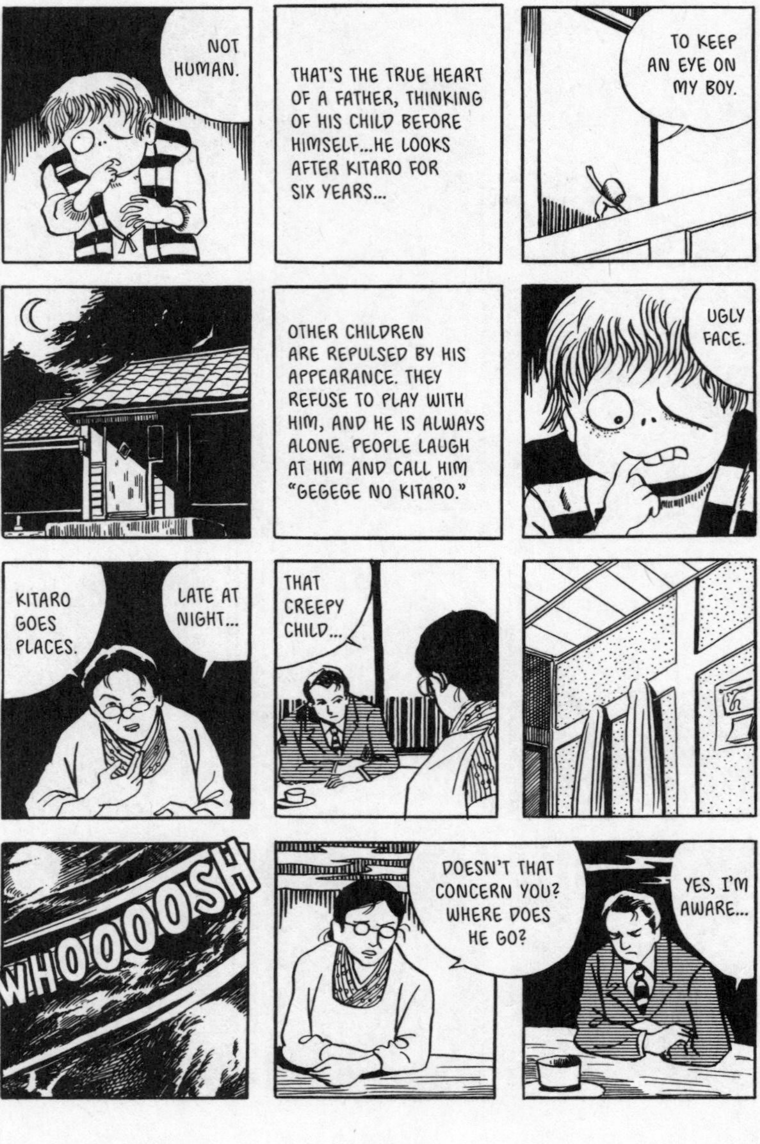
TO KEEP AN EYE ON MY BOY.
THAT'S THE TRUE HEART OF A FATHER, THINKING OF HIS CHILD BEFORE HIMSELF...HE LOOKS AFTER KITARO FOR SIX YEARS...
NOT HUMAN.
UGLY FACE.
OTHER CHILDREN ARE REPULSED BY HIS APPEARANCE. THEY REFUSE TO PLAY WITH HIM, AND HE IS ALWAYS ALONE. PEOPLE LAUGH AT HIM AND CALL HIM "GEGEGE NO KITARO."
THAT CREEPY CHILD...
LATE AT NIGHT...
KITARO GOES PLACES.
YES, I'M AWARE...
DOESN'T THAT CONCERN YOU? WHERE DOES HE GO?
WHOOOOOSH

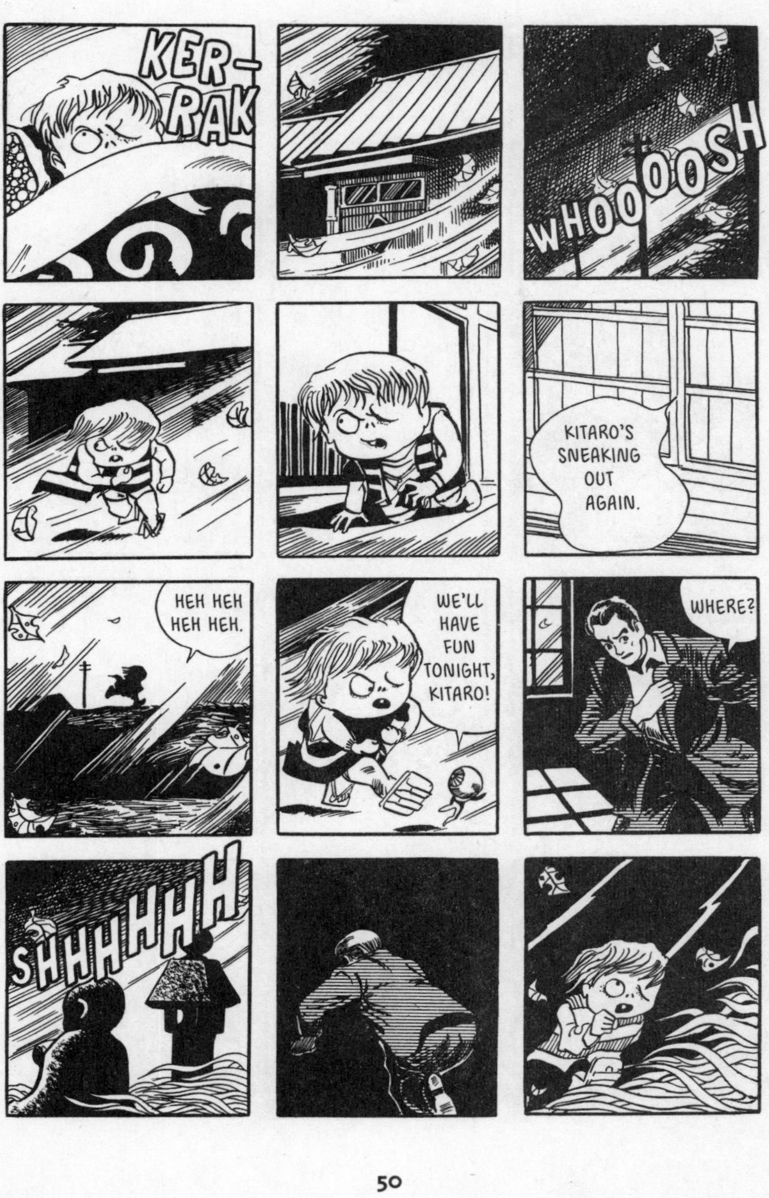
WHOOOOSH
KER-
RAK
KITARO'S SNEAKING OUT AGAIN.
WHERE?
WE'LL HAVE FUN TONIGHT, KITARO!
HEH HEH HEH HEH.
SHHHHHH

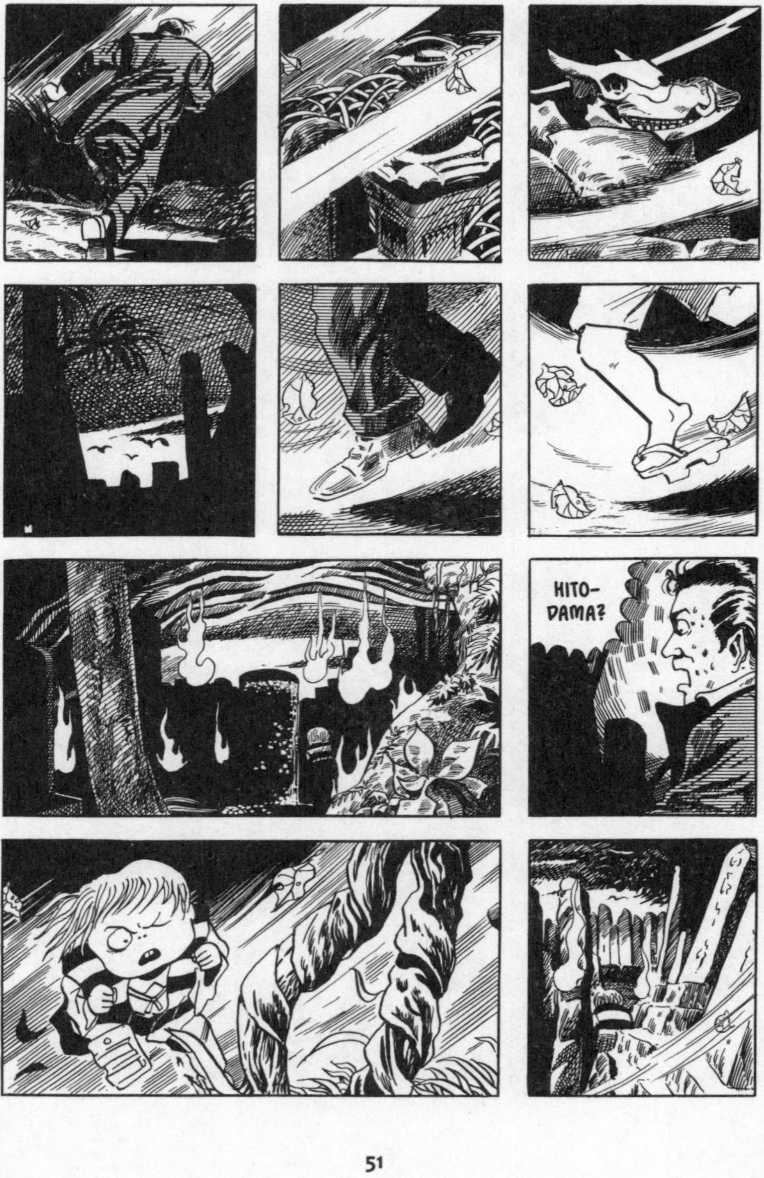
HITO-
DAMA?

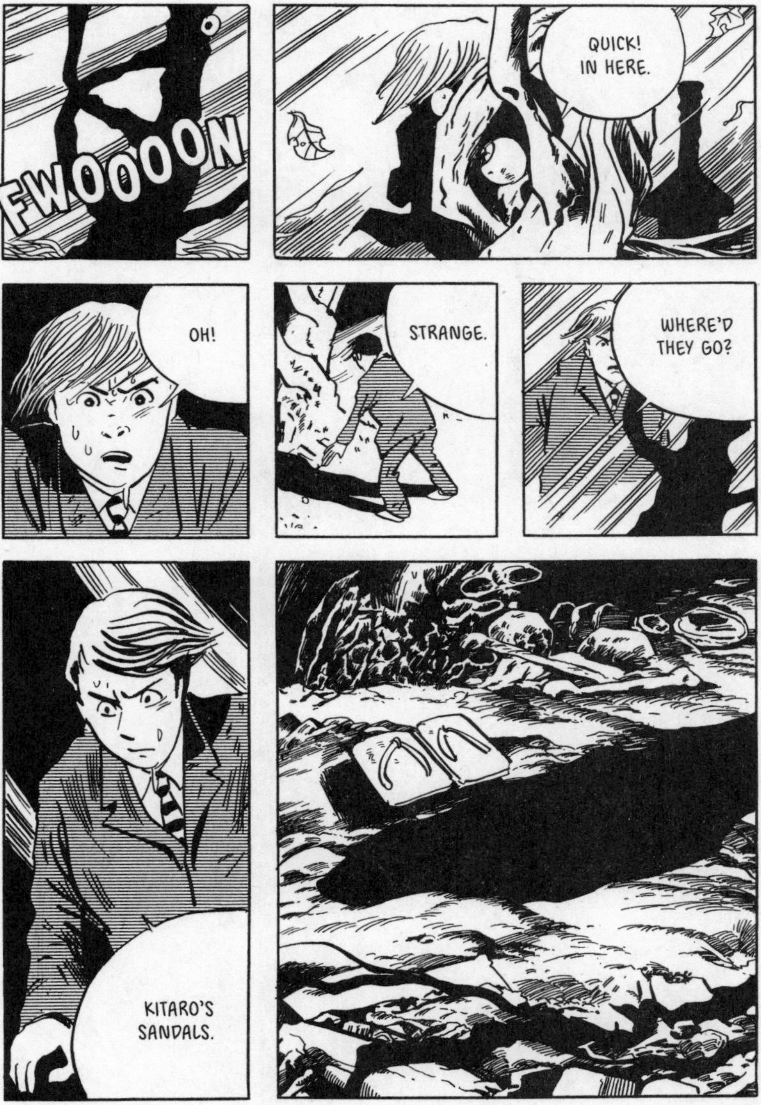
QUICK! IN HERE.
FWOOOON
WHERE'D THEY GO?
STRANGE.
OH!
KITARO'S SANDALS.

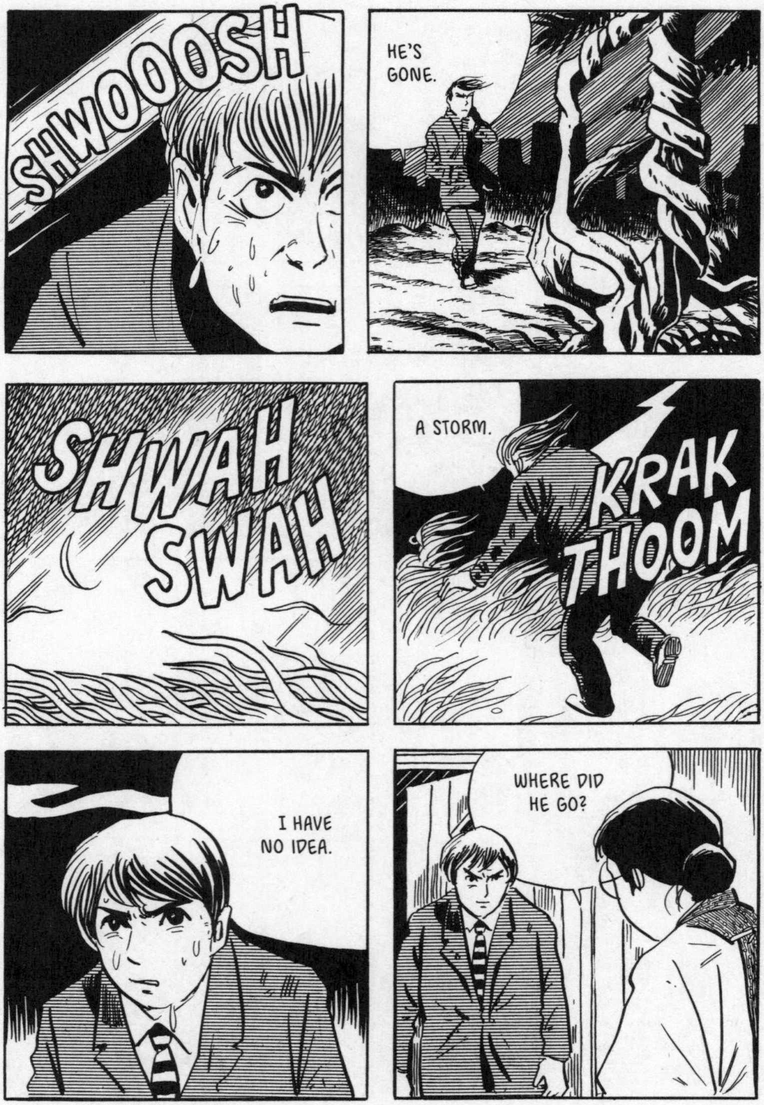
HE'S GONE.
SHWOOOSH
A STORM.
KRAK THOOM
SHWAH SWAH
WHERE DID HE GO?
I HAVE NO IDEA.

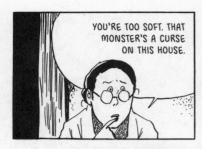

WHAT SHOULD WE DO?
ISN'T IT PRETTY CLEAR?
YOU'RE TOO SOFT. THAT MONSTER'S A CURSE ON THIS HOUSE.
KITARO!
GOOD MORNING.
CREEEEK
AH...NICE WEATHER TODAY.
KITARO, TELL US WHERE YOU GO AT NIGHT.
...WHAT DO YOU MEAN?

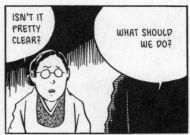

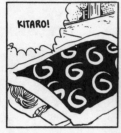

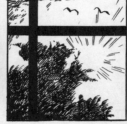

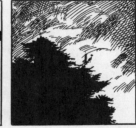

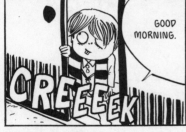

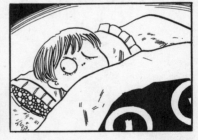

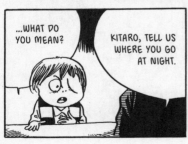

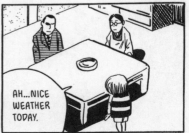

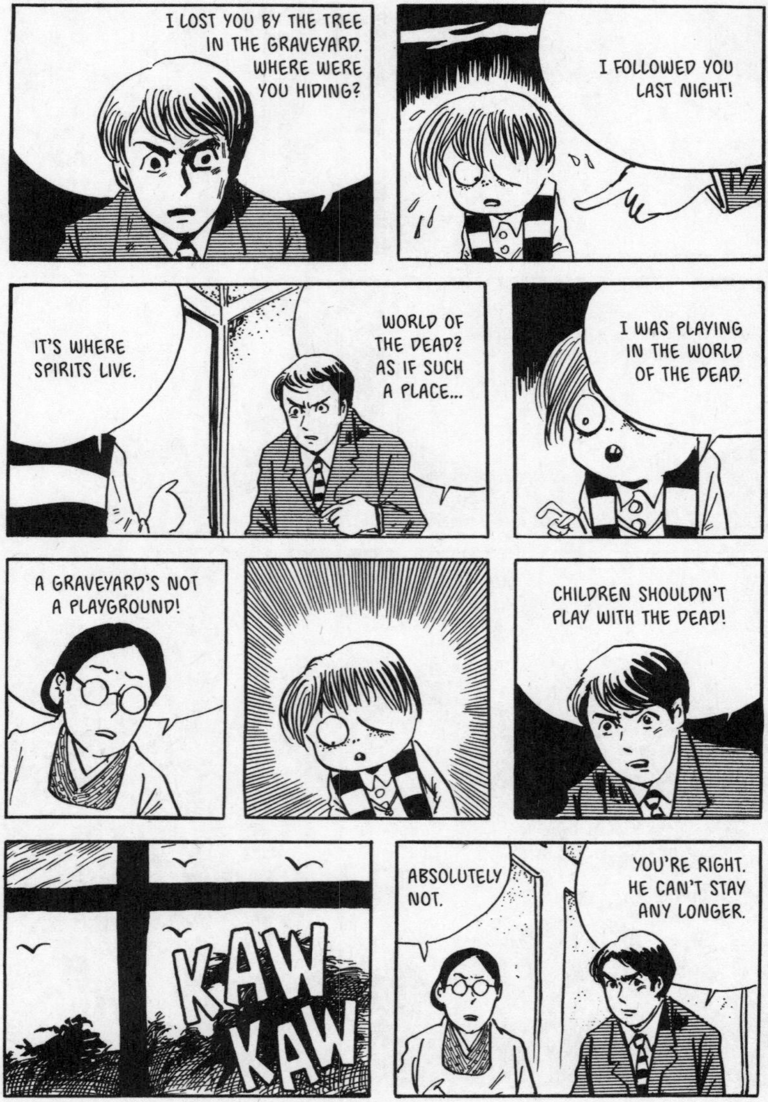
I FOLLOWED YOU LAST NIGHT!
I LOST YOU BY THE TREE IN THE GRAVEYARD. WHERE WERE YOU HIDING?
I WAS PLAYING IN THE WORLD OF THE DEAD.
WORLD OF THE DEAD? AS IF SUCH A PLACE...
IT'S WHERE SPIRITS LIVE.
CHILDREN SHOULDN'T PLAY WITH THE DEAD!
A GRAVEYARD'S NOT A PLAYGROUND!
YOU'RE RIGHT. HE CAN'T STAY ANY LONGER.
ABSOLUTELY NOT.
KAW KAW

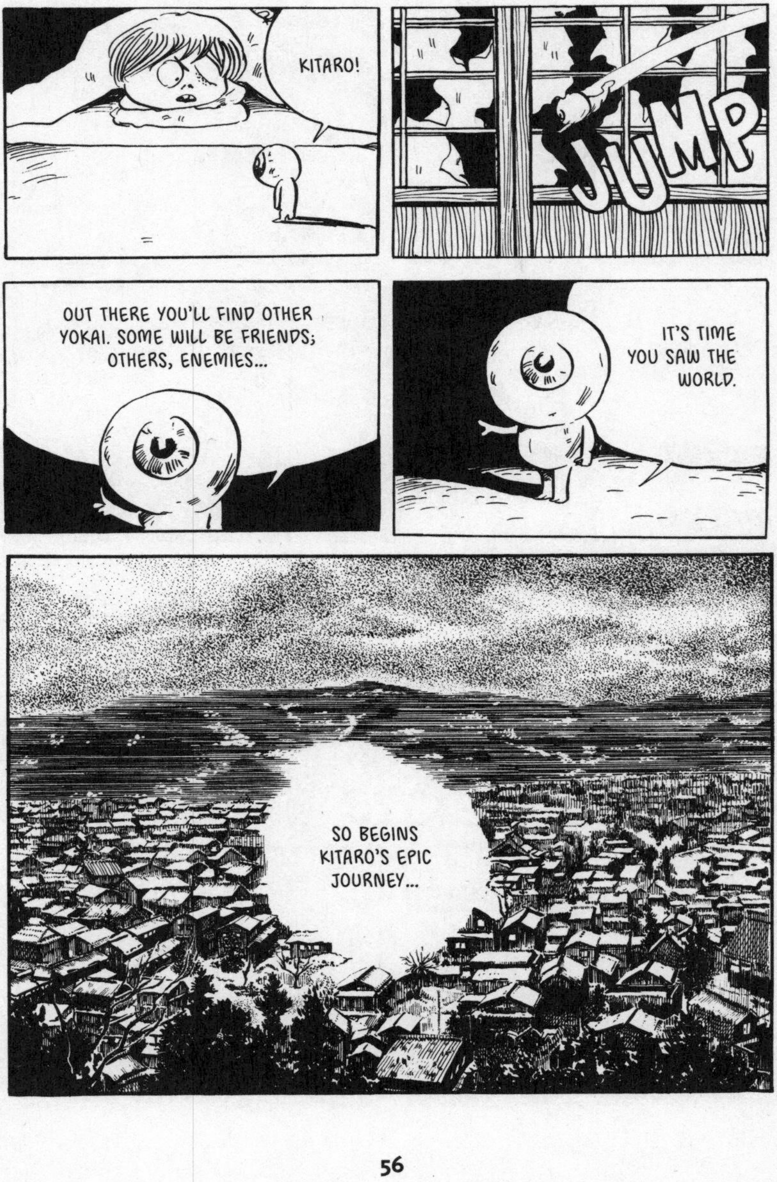
JUMP
KITARO!
IT'S TIME YOU SAW THE WORLD.
OUT THERE YOU'LL FIND OTHER YOKAI. SOME WILL BE FRIENDS; OTHERS, ENEMIES...
SO BEGINS KITARO'S EPIC JOURNEY...

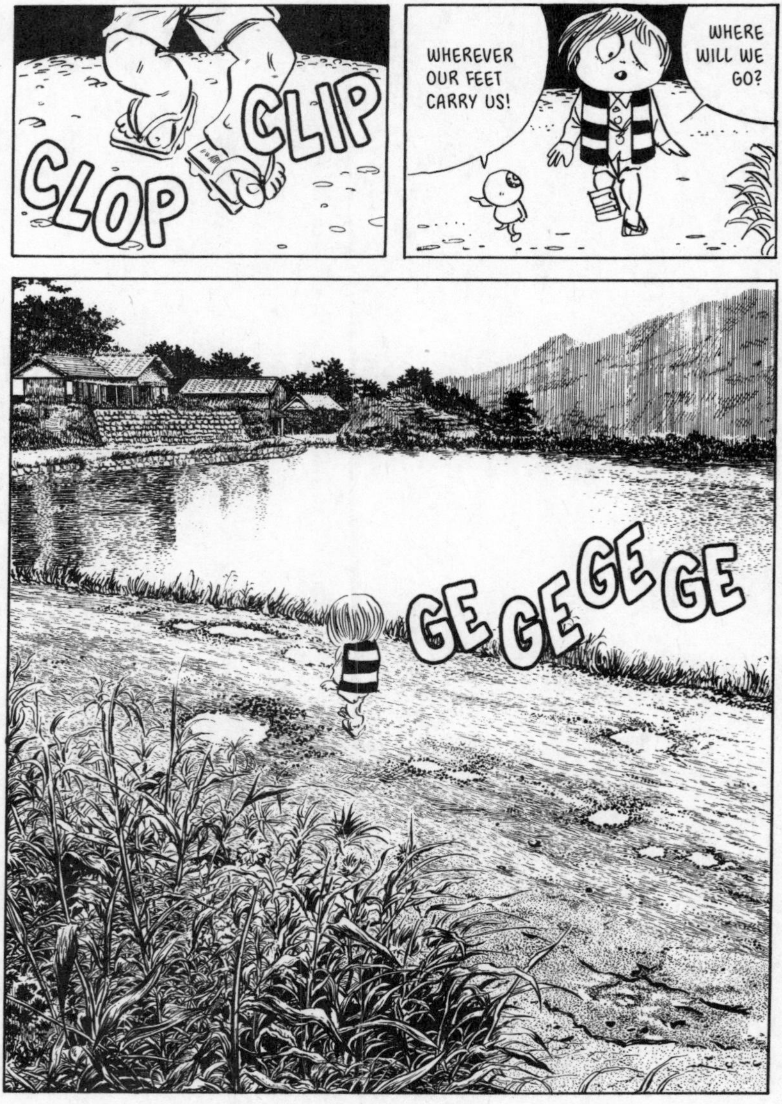
WHERE WILL WE GO?
WHEREVER OUR FEET CARRY US!
CLIP
CLOP
GE GE GE GE GE

NEZUMI OTOKO
VERSUS NEKO
MUSUME

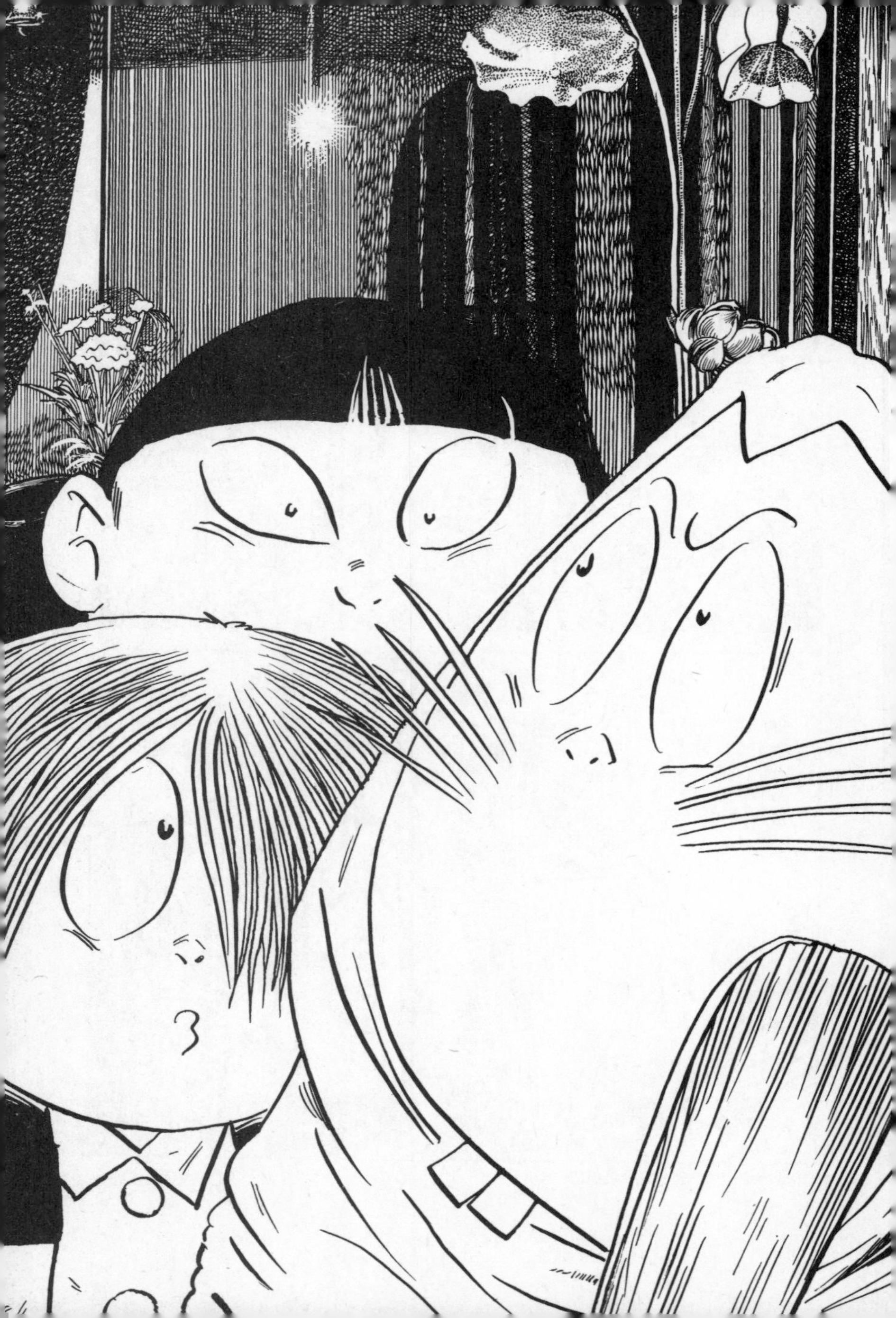

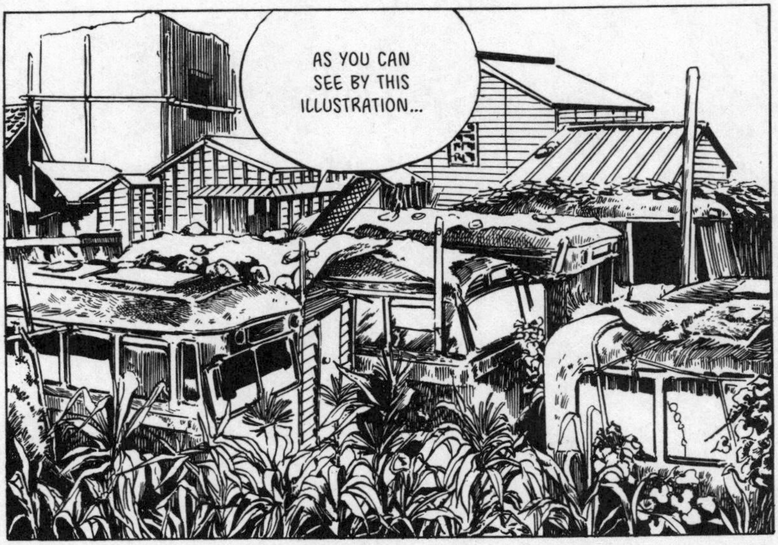
AS YOU CAN SEE BY THIS ILLUSTRATION...

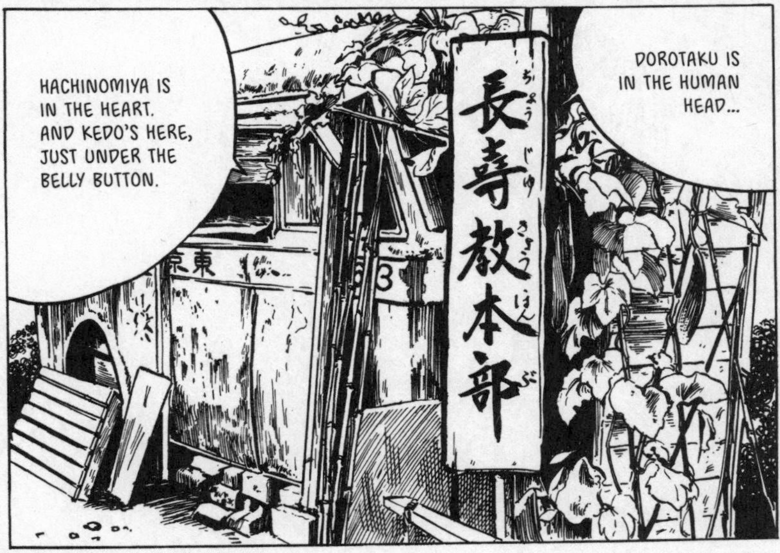
DOROTAKU IS IN THE HUMAN HEAD...
HACHINOMIYA IS IN THE HEART. AND KEDO'S HERE, JUST UNDER THE BELLY BUTTON.
長寿教本部

SIGN: INSTITUTE FOR LONGEVITY

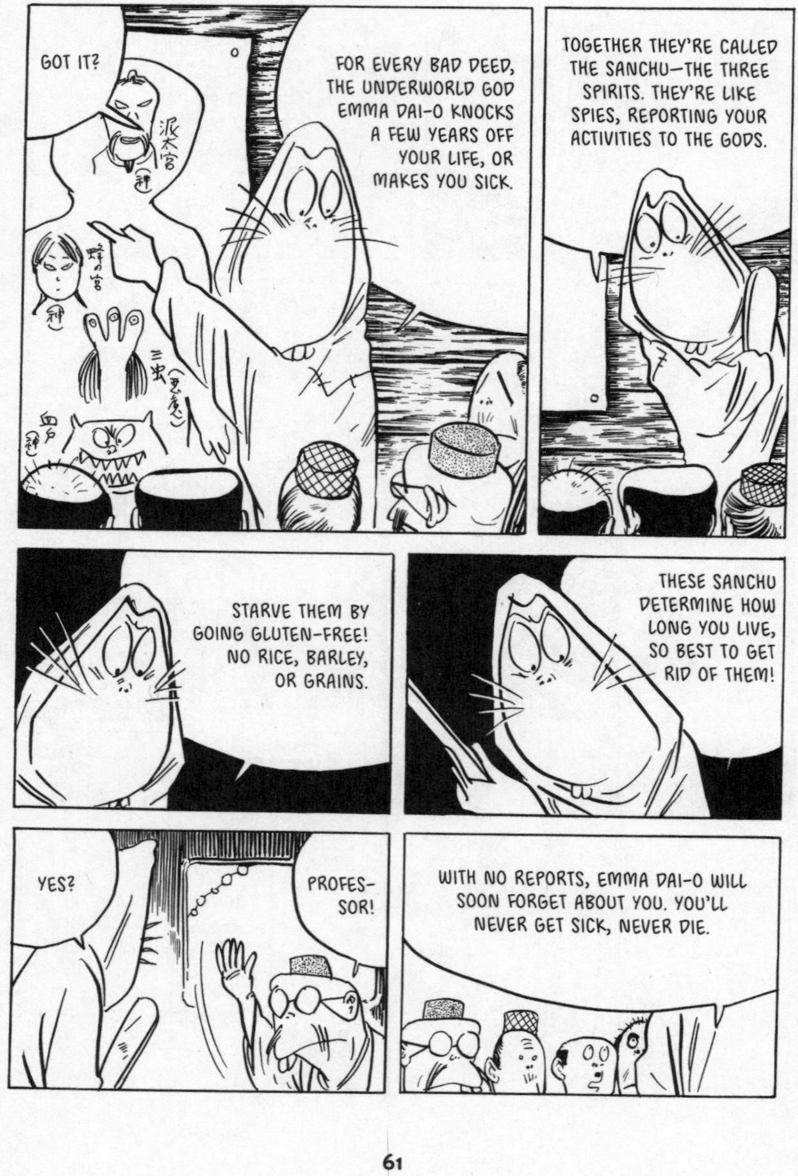
TOGETHER THEY'RE CALLED THE SANCHU—THE THREE SPIRITS. THEY'RE LIKE SPIES, REPORTING YOUR ACTIVITIES TO THE GODS.
FOR EVERY BAD DEED, THE UNDERWORLD GOD EMMA DAI-O KNOCKS A FEW YEARS OFF YOUR LIFE, OR MAKES YOU SICK.
GOT IT?
THESE SANCHU DETERMINE HOW LONG YOU LIVE, SO BEST TO GET RID OF THEM!
STARVE THEM BY GOING GLUTEN-FREE! NO RICE, BARLEY, OR GRAINS.
WITH NO REPORTS, EMMA DAI-O WILL SOON FORGET ABOUT YOU. YOU'LL NEVER GET SICK, NEVER DIE.
PROFES-SOR!
YES?

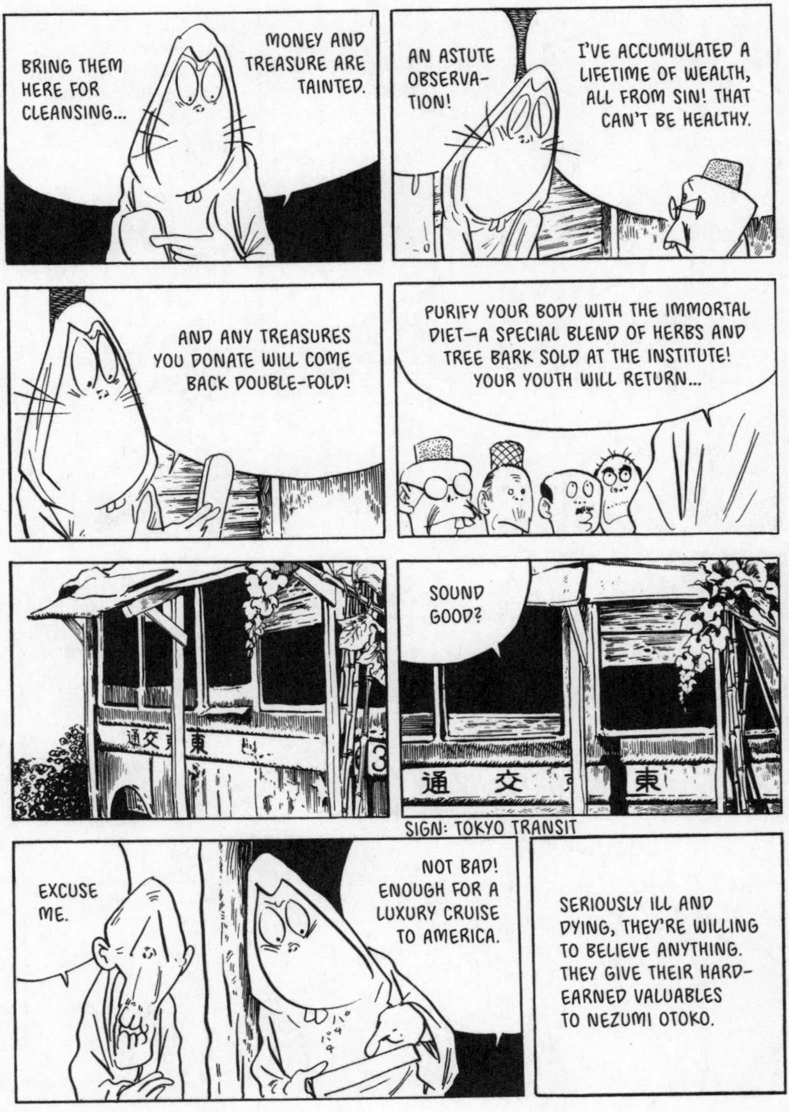
I'VE ACCUMULATED A LIFETIME OF WEALTH, ALL FROM SIN! THAT CAN'T BE HEALTHY.
AN ASTUTE OBSERVA-TION!
MONEY AND TREASURE ARE TAINTED.
BRING THEM HERE FOR CLEANSING...
PURIFY YOUR BODY WITH THE IMMORTAL DIET—A SPECIAL BLEND OF HERBS AND TREE BARK SOLD AT THE INSTITUTE! YOUR YOUTH WILL RETURN...
AND ANY TREASURES YOU DONATE WILL COME BACK DOUBLE-FOLD!
SOUND GOOD?
SIGN: TOKYO TRANSIT
SERIOUSLY ILL AND DYING, THEY'RE WILLING TO BELIEVE ANYTHING. THEY GIVE THEIR HARD-EARNED VALUABLES TO NEZUMI OTOKO.
NOT BAD! ENOUGH FOR A LUXURY CRUISE TO AMERICA.
EXCUSE ME.

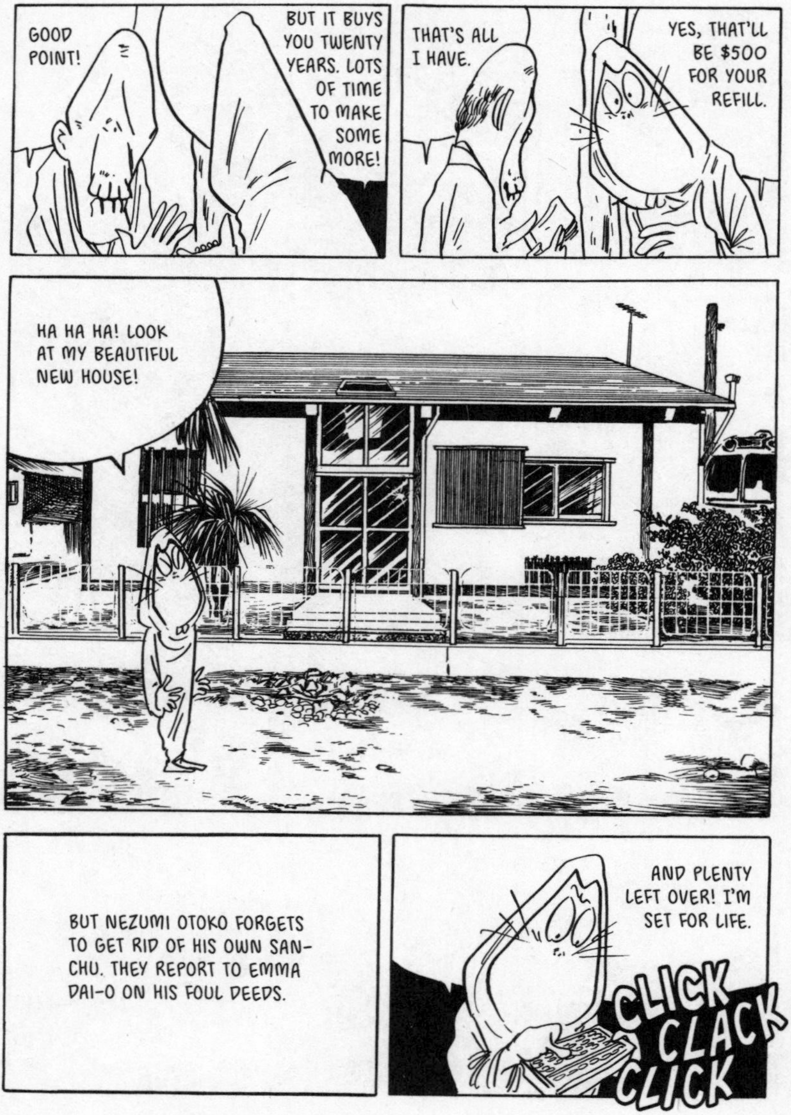
YES, THAT'LL BE $500 FOR YOUR REFILL.
THAT'S ALL I HAVE.
BUT IT BUYS YOU TWENTY YEARS. LOTS OF TIME TO MAKE SOME MORE!
GOOD POINT!
HA HA HA! LOOK AT MY BEAUTIFUL NEW HOUSE!
AND PLENTY LEFT OVER! I'M SET FOR LIFE.
CLICK CLACK CLICK
BUT NEZUMI OTOKO FORGETS TO GET RID OF HIS OWN SAN-CHU. THEY REPORT TO EMMA DAI-O ON HIS FOUL DEEDS.

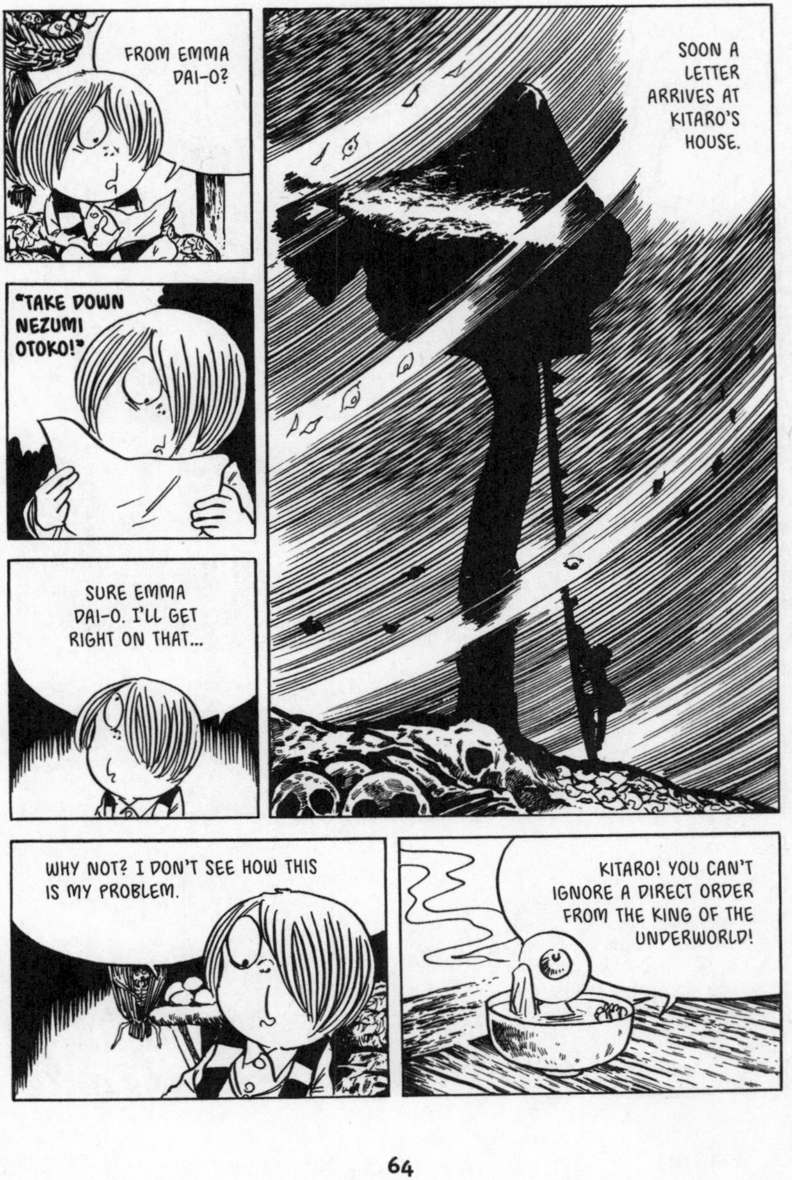
SOON A LETTER ARRIVES AT KITARO'S HOUSE.
FROM EMMA DAI-O?
"TAKE DOWN NEZUMI OTOKO!"
SURE EMMA DAI-O. I'LL GET RIGHT ON THAT...
KITARO! YOU CAN'T IGNORE A DIRECT ORDER FROM THE KING OF THE UNDERWORLD!
WHY NOT? I DON'T SEE HOW THIS IS MY PROBLEM.

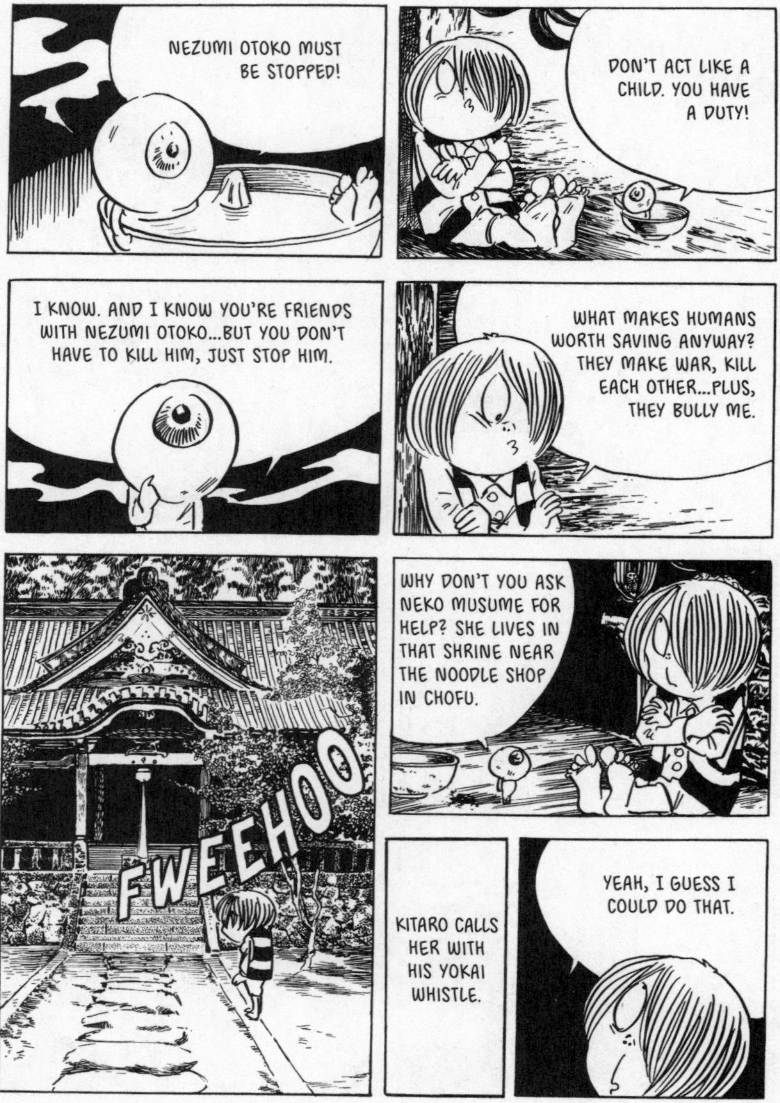
DON'T ACT LIKE A CHILD. YOU HAVE A DUTY!
NEZUMI OTOKO MUST BE STOPPED!
WHAT MAKES HUMANS WORTH SAVING ANYWAY? THEY MAKE WAR, KILL EACH OTHER...PLUS, THEY BULLY ME.
I KNOW. AND I KNOW YOU'RE FRIENDS WITH NEZUMI OTOKO...BUT YOU DON'T HAVE TO KILL HIM, JUST STOP HIM.
WHY DON'T YOU ASK NEKO MUSUME FOR HELP? SHE LIVES IN THAT SHRINE NEAR THE NOODLE SHOP IN CHOFU.
YEAH, I GUESS I COULD DO THAT.
KITARO CALLS HER WITH HIS YOKAI WHISTLE.
FWEEHOO

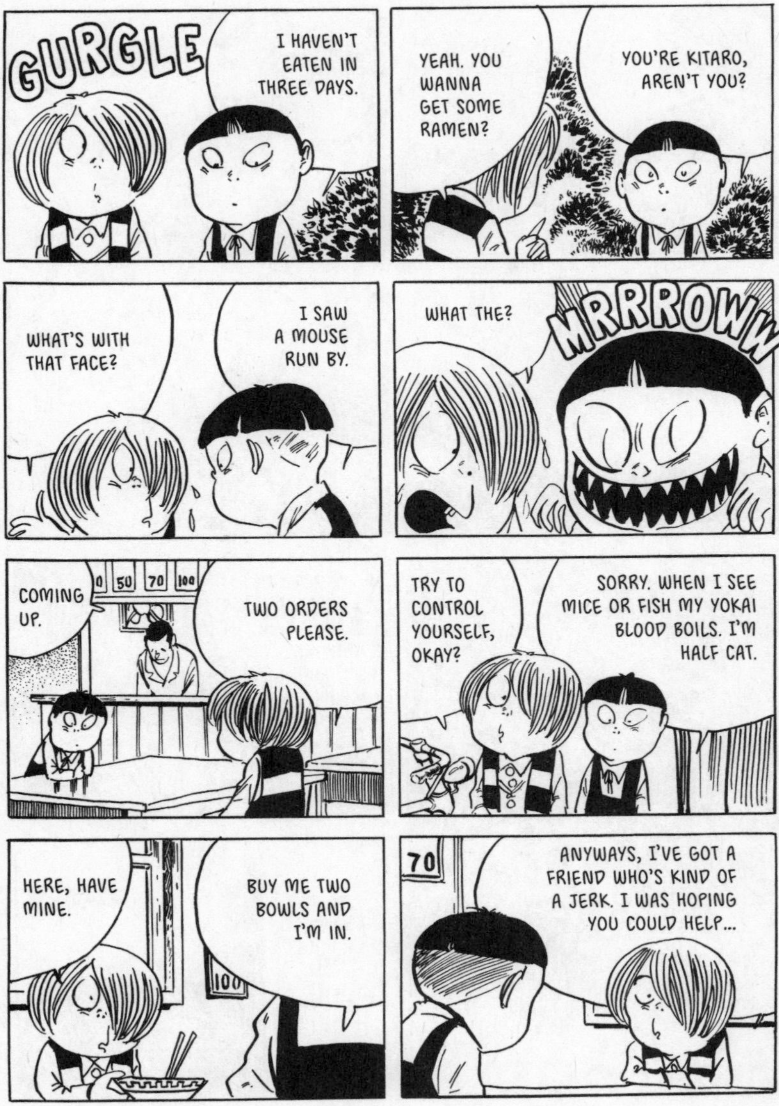
YOU'RE KITARO, AREN'T YOU?
YEAH. YOU WANNA GET SOME RAMEN?
I HAVEN'T EATEN IN THREE DAYS.
GURGLE
MRRROWW
WHAT THE?
I SAW A MOUSE RUN BY.
WHAT'S WITH THAT FACE?
SORRY. WHEN I SEE MICE OR FISH MY YOKAI BLOOD BOILS. I'M HALF CAT.
TRY TO CONTROL YOURSELF, OKAY?
TWO ORDERS PLEASE.
COMING UP.
ANYWAYS, I'VE GOT A FRIEND WHO'S KIND OF A JERK. I WAS HOPING YOU COULD HELP...
BUY ME TWO BOWLS AND I'M IN.
HERE, HAVE MINE.

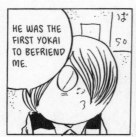

YOU SURE?
うどん 70
THAT'S ALL I CAN AFFORD.
WHY ARE YOU FRIENDS WITH THAT DIRTY YOKAI ANYWAY?
SLURP
SLURP
ぱ 50
HE WAS THE FIRST YOKAI TO BEFRIEND ME.
COME WHEN I CALL YOU.
SURE.
KITARO SEES THE DEVASTATION NEZUMI OTOKO HAS CAUSED.
THE STREETS ARE LITTERED WITH THE SICK AND DYING.
HE'S GONE TOO FAR THIS TIME.
LOOK AT THAT NEW HOUSE!
OH HEY, KITARO!
YOU BRING A HOUSEWARMING GIFT...?

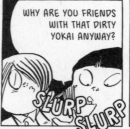

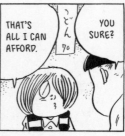

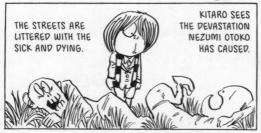

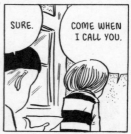

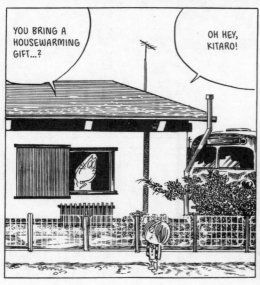

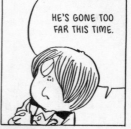

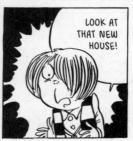

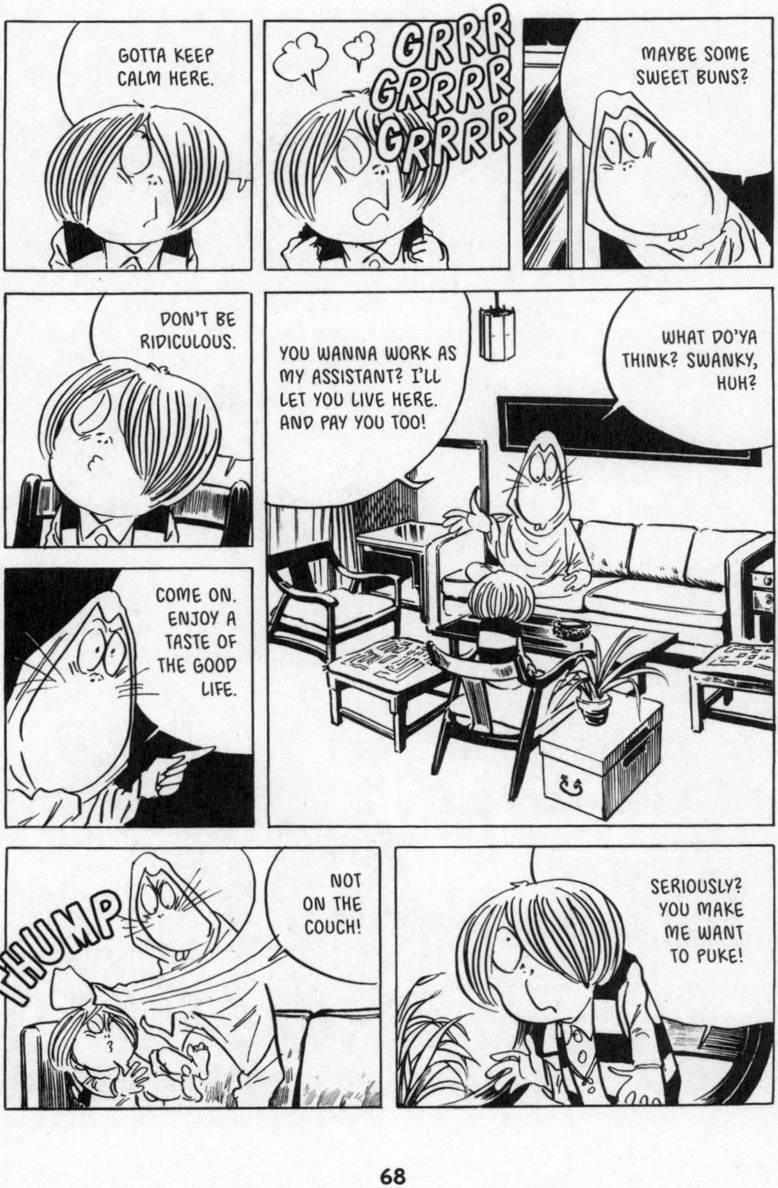
MAYBE SOME SWEET BUNS?
GRRR GRRRR GRRRR
GOTTA KEEP CALM HERE.
WHAT DO'YA THINK? SWANKY, HUH?
YOU WANNA WORK AS MY ASSISTANT? I'LL LET YOU LIVE HERE. AND PAY YOU TOO!
DON'T BE RIDICULOUS.
COME ON. ENJOY A TASTE OF THE GOOD LIFE.
SERIOUSLY? YOU MAKE ME WANT TO PUKE!
NOT ON THE COUCH!
THUMP

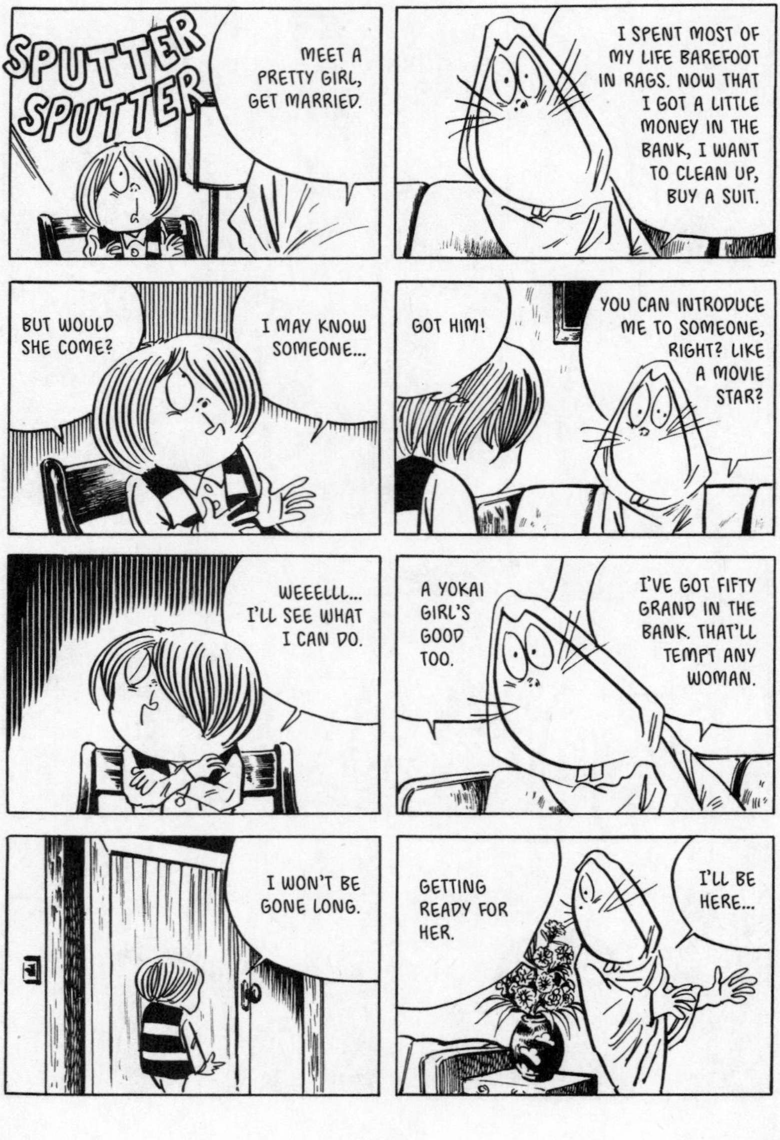
I SPENT MOST OF MY LIFE BAREFOOT IN RAGS. NOW THAT I GOT A LITTLE MONEY IN THE BANK, I WANT TO CLEAN UP, BUY A SUIT.
MEET A PRETTY GIRL, GET MARRIED.
SPUTTER SPUTTER
YOU CAN INTRODUCE ME TO SOMEONE, RIGHT? LIKE A MOVIE STAR?
GOT HIM!
I MAY KNOW SOMEONE...
BUT WOULD SHE COME?
I'VE GOT FIFTY GRAND IN THE BANK. THAT'LL TEMPT ANY WOMAN.
A YOKAI GIRL'S GOOD TOO.
WEEELLL... I'LL SEE WHAT I CAN DO.
I'LL BE HERE...
GETTING READY FOR HER.
I WON'T BE GONE LONG.

THINGS ARE LOOKING UP FOR ME!

HERE, MY DEAR.

PROFES-SOR?

OHHH...HE LOOKS GOOD ENOUGH TO EAT. KEE HE HEE!

THAT'S HIM.

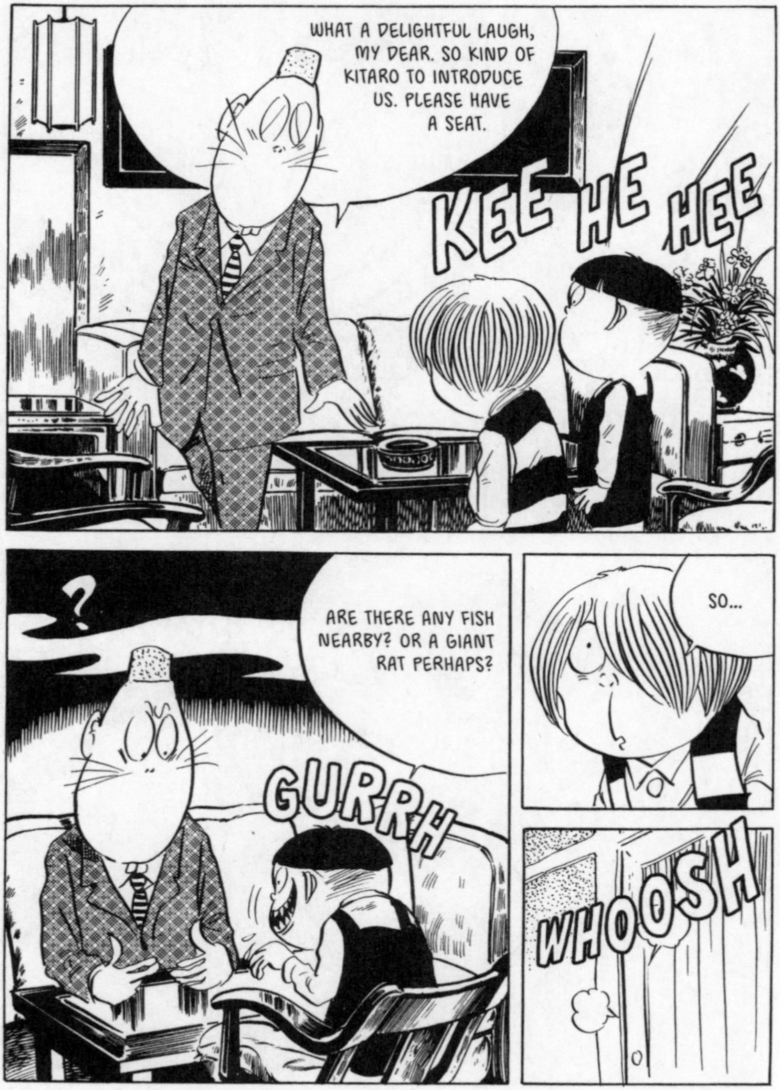
KEE HE HEE
WHAT A DELIGHTFUL LAUGH, MY DEAR. SO KIND OF KITARO TO INTRODUCE US. PLEASE HAVE A SEAT.
SO...
WHOOSH
ARE THERE ANY FISH NEARBY? OR A GIANT RAT PERHAPS?
?
GURRH

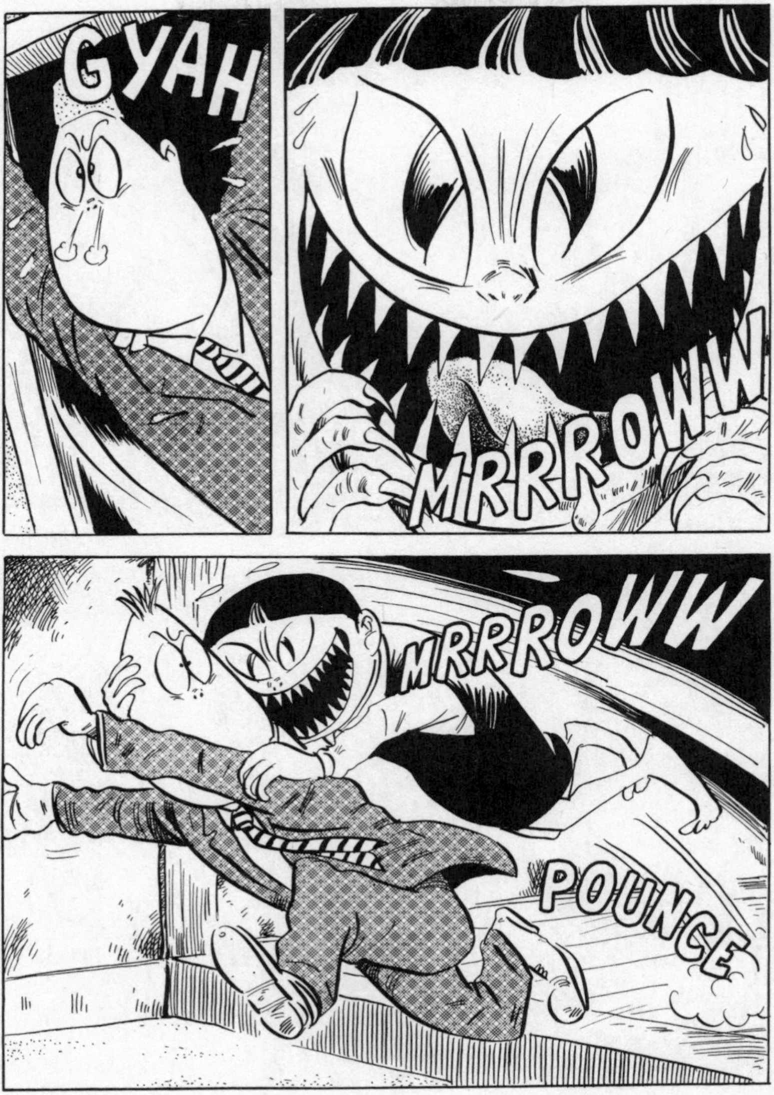
MRRROWW
GYAH
MRRROWW
POUNCE

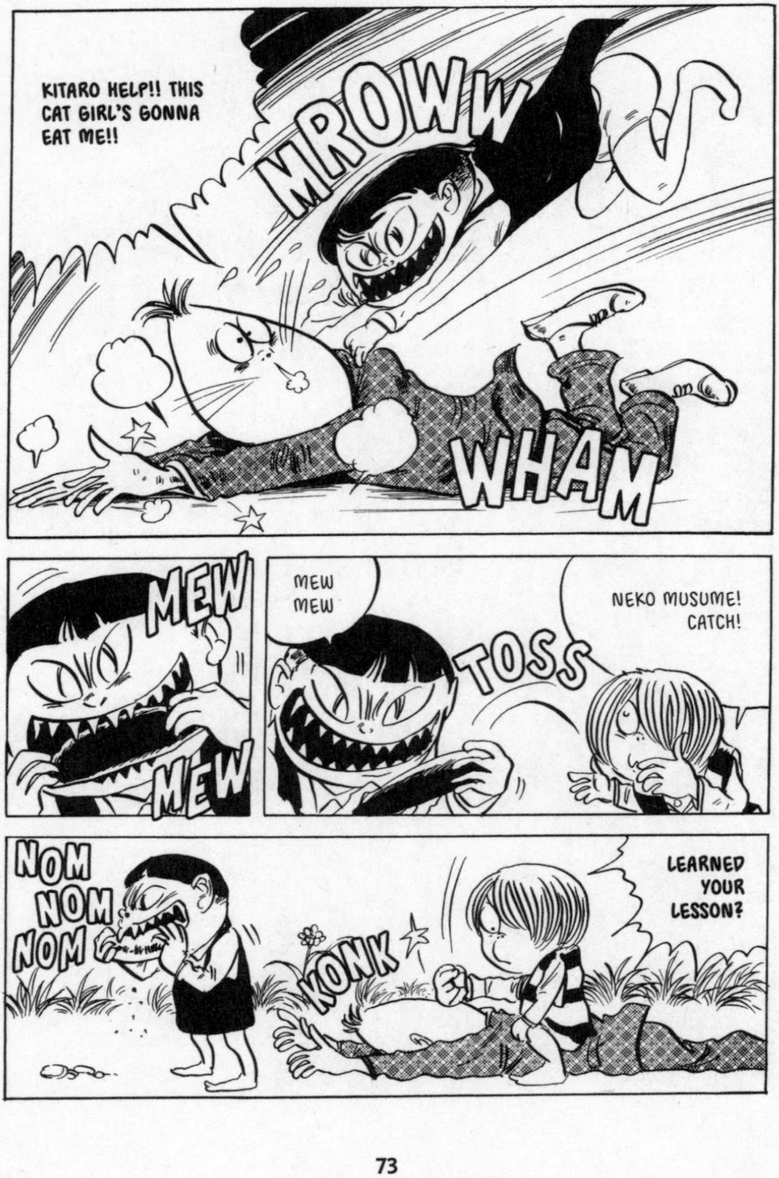
MROWW
KITARO HELP!! THIS CAT GIRL'S GONNA EAT ME!!
WHAM
NEKO MUSUME! CATCH!
MEW MEW
TOSS
MEW
MEW
LEARNED YOUR LESSON?
KONK
NOM NOM NOM

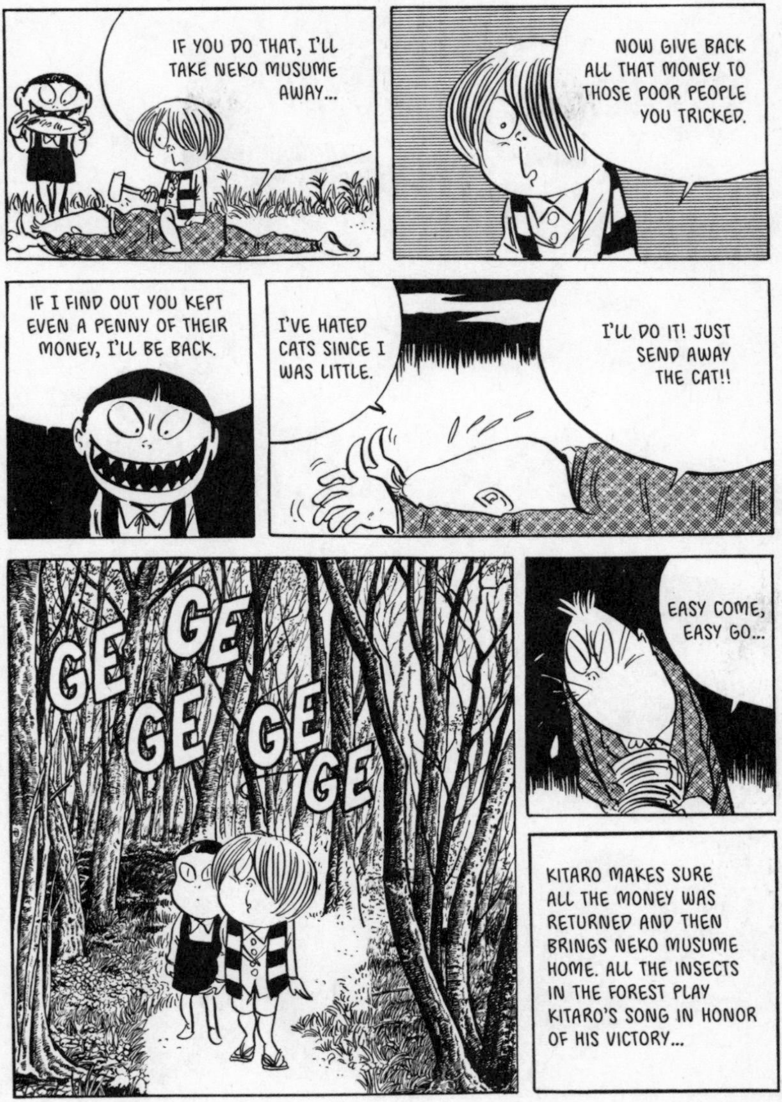
NOW GIVE BACK ALL THAT MONEY TO THOSE POOR PEOPLE YOU TRICKED.
IF YOU DO THAT, I'LL TAKE NEKO MUSUME AWAY...
I'LL DO IT! JUST SEND AWAY THE CAT!!
I'VE HATED CATS SINCE I WAS LITTLE.
IF I FIND OUT YOU KEPT EVEN A PENNY OF THEIR MONEY, I'LL BE BACK.
EASY COME, EASY GO...
KITARO MAKES SURE ALL THE MONEY WAS RETURNED AND THEN BRINGS NEKO MUSUME HOME. ALL THE INSECTS IN THE FOREST PLAY KITARO'S SONG IN HONOR OF HIS VICTORY...
GE GE
GE GE
GE

NOPPERABO

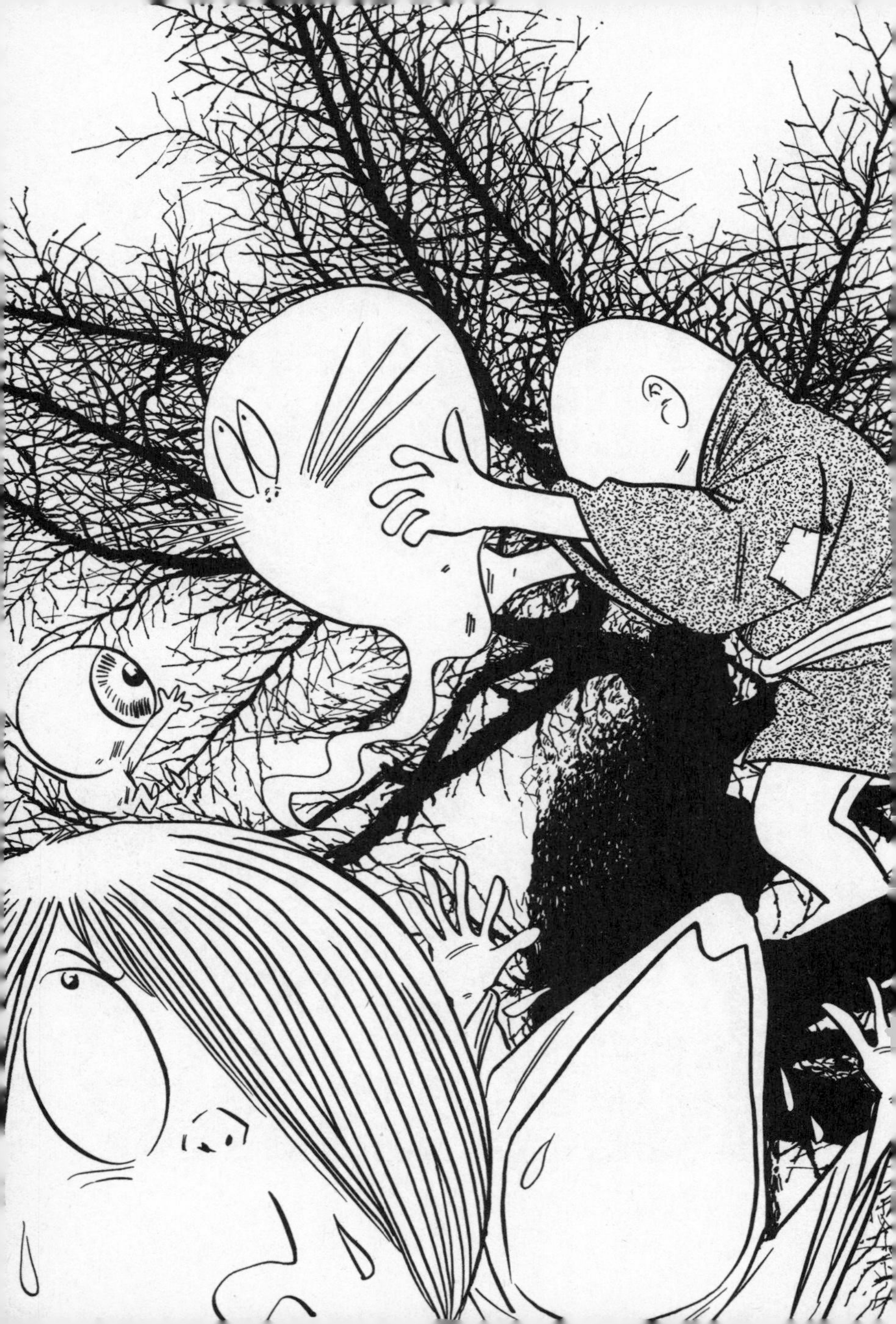

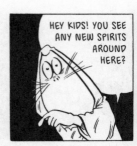

HEY KIDS! YOU SEE ANY NEW SPIRITS AROUND HERE?
NEW SPIRITS?
YEAH— ANYONE DIE?
UHH...YES. OVER AT MR. JINBE'S HOUSE.
CLEVER LADS. YOU GOT BIG THINGS AHEAD OF YOU! BWA HA HA!

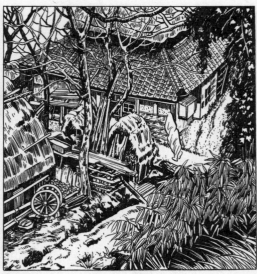

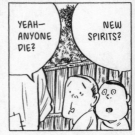

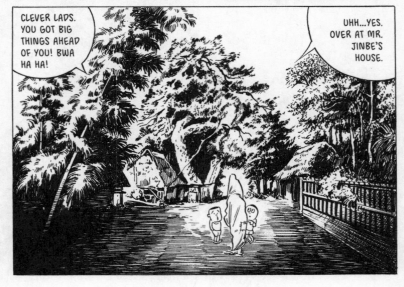

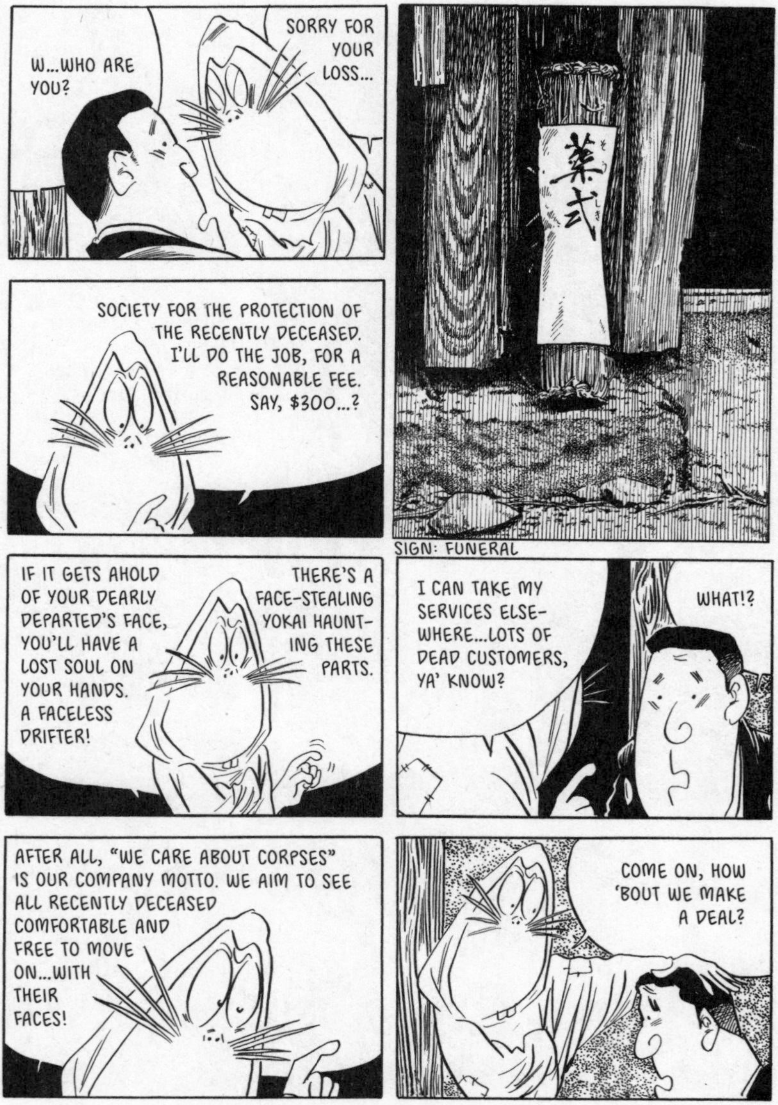
葬式
SIGN: FUNERAL
SORRY FOR YOUR LOSS...
W...WHO ARE YOU?
SOCIETY FOR THE PROTECTION OF THE RECENTLY DECEASED. I'LL DO THE JOB, FOR A REASONABLE FEE. SAY, $300...?
WHAT!?
I CAN TAKE MY SERVICES ELSE-WHERE...LOTS OF DEAD CUSTOMERS, YA' KNOW?
THERE'S A FACE-STEALING YOKAI HAUNT-ING THESE PARTS.
IF IT GETS AHOLD OF YOUR DEARLY DEPARTED'S FACE, YOU'LL HAVE A LOST SOUL ON YOUR HANDS. A FACELESS DRIFTER!
COME ON, HOW 'BOUT WE MAKE A DEAL?
AFTER ALL, "WE CARE ABOUT CORPSES" IS OUR COMPANY MOTTO. WE AIM TO SEE ALL RECENTLY DECEASED COMFORTABLE AND FREE TO MOVE ON...WITH THEIR FACES!

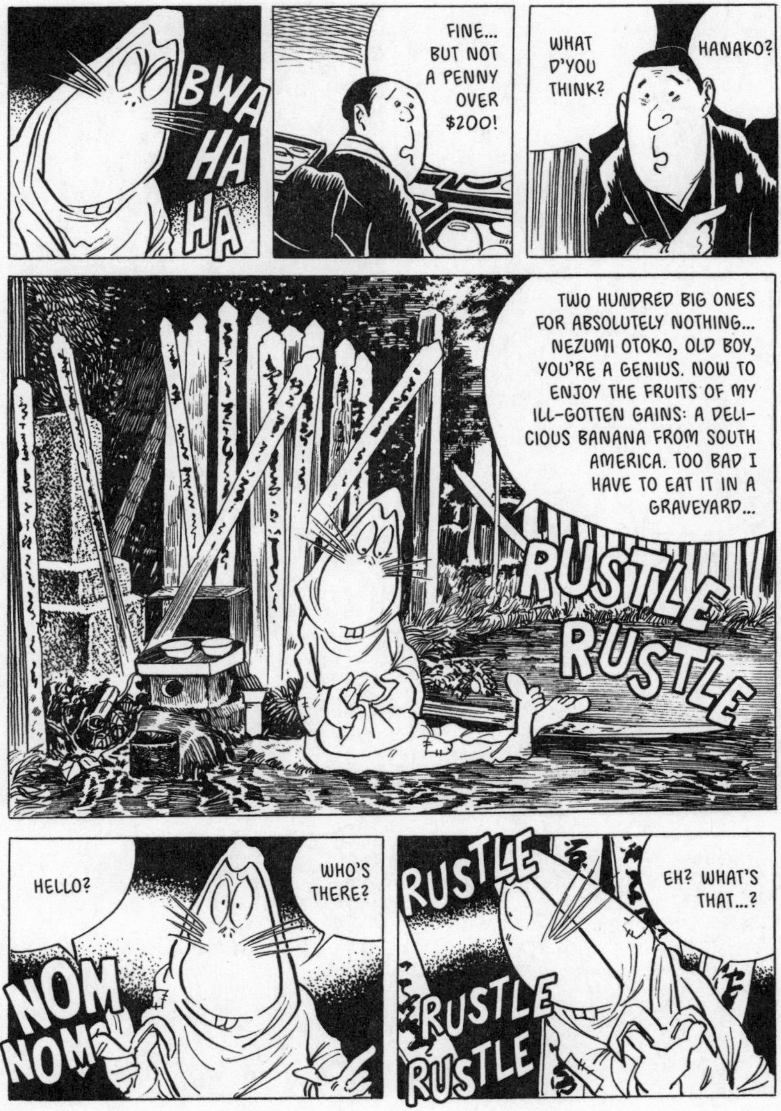
HANAKO?
WHAT D'YOU THINK?
FINE... BUT NOT A PENNY OVER $200!
BWA HA HA HA
TWO HUNDRED BIG ONES FOR ABSOLUTELY NOTHING... NEZUMI OTOKO, OLD BOY, YOU'RE A GENIUS. NOW TO ENJOY THE FRUITS OF MY ILL-GOTTEN GAINS: A DELICIOUS BANANA FROM SOUTH AMERICA. TOO BAD I HAVE TO EAT IT IN A GRAVEYARD...
RUSTLE RUSTLE
EH? WHAT'S THAT...?
RUSTLE
RUSTLE RUSTLE
WHO'S THERE?
HELLO?
NOM NOM

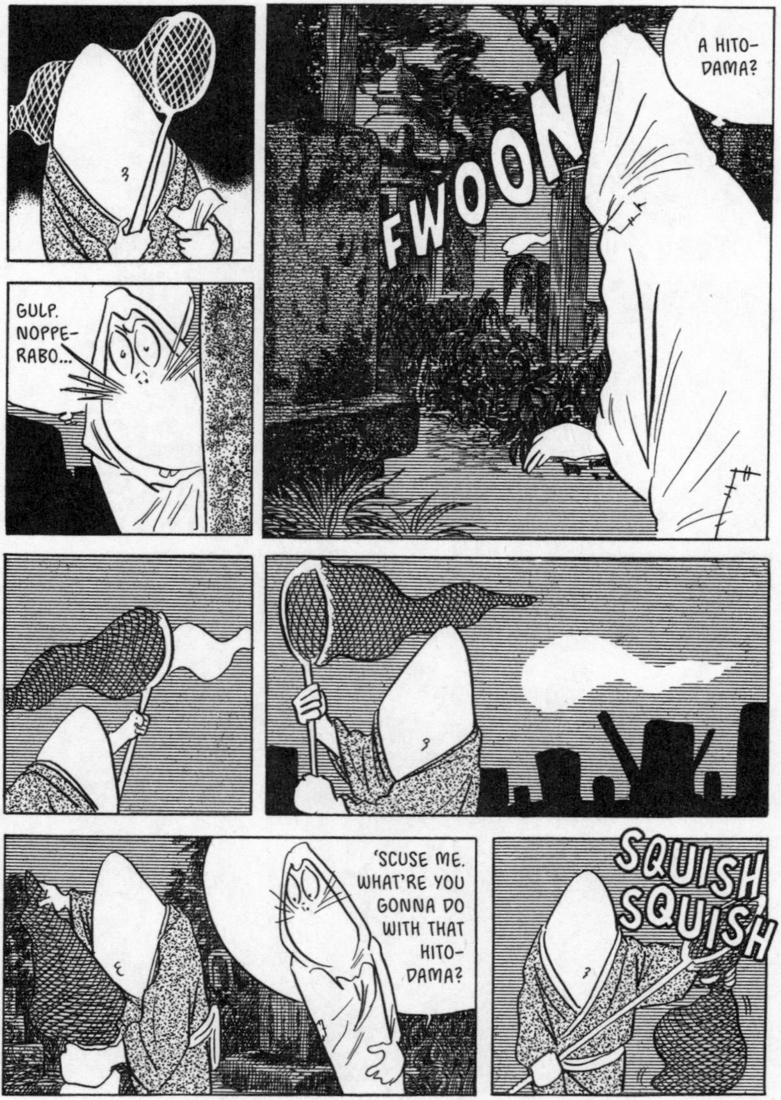
A HITO-DAMA?
FWOON
GULP. NOPPE-RABO...
SQUISH SQUISH
'SCUSE ME. WHAT'RE YOU GONNA DO WITH THAT HITO-DAMA?

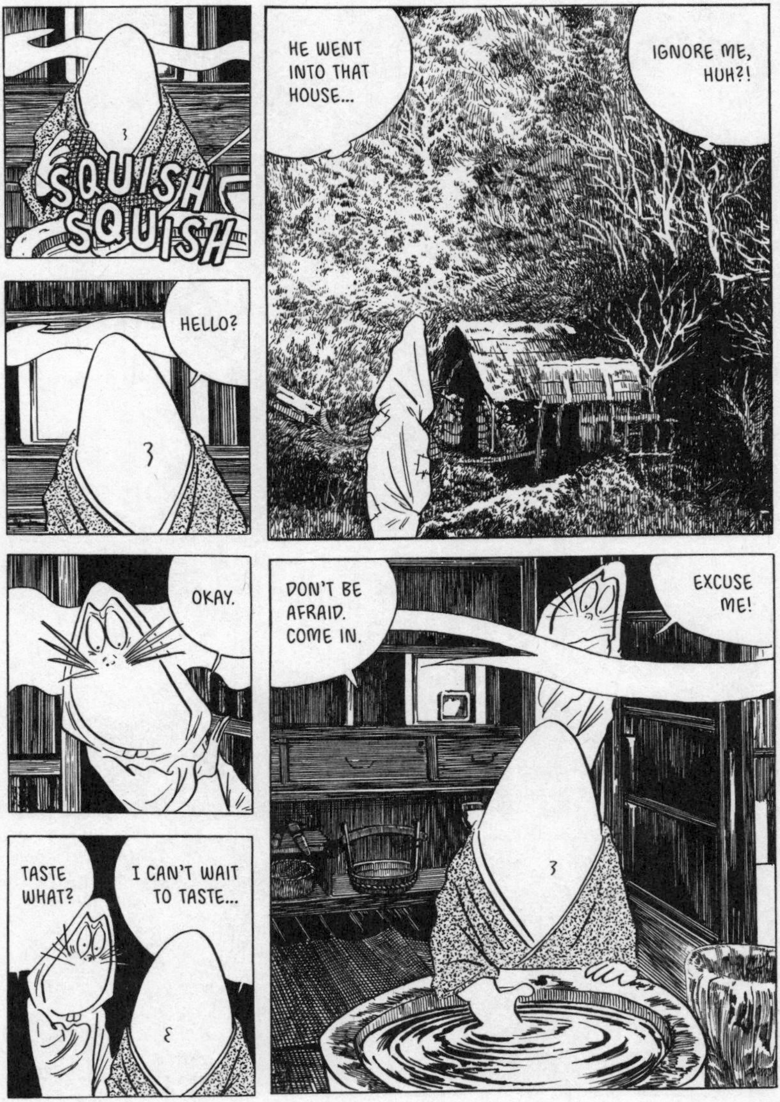
IGNORE ME, HUH?!
HE WENT INTO THAT HOUSE...
SQUISH SQUISH
HELLO?
EXCUSE ME!
DON'T BE AFRAID. COME IN.
OKAY.
I CAN'T WAIT TO TASTE...
TASTE WHAT?

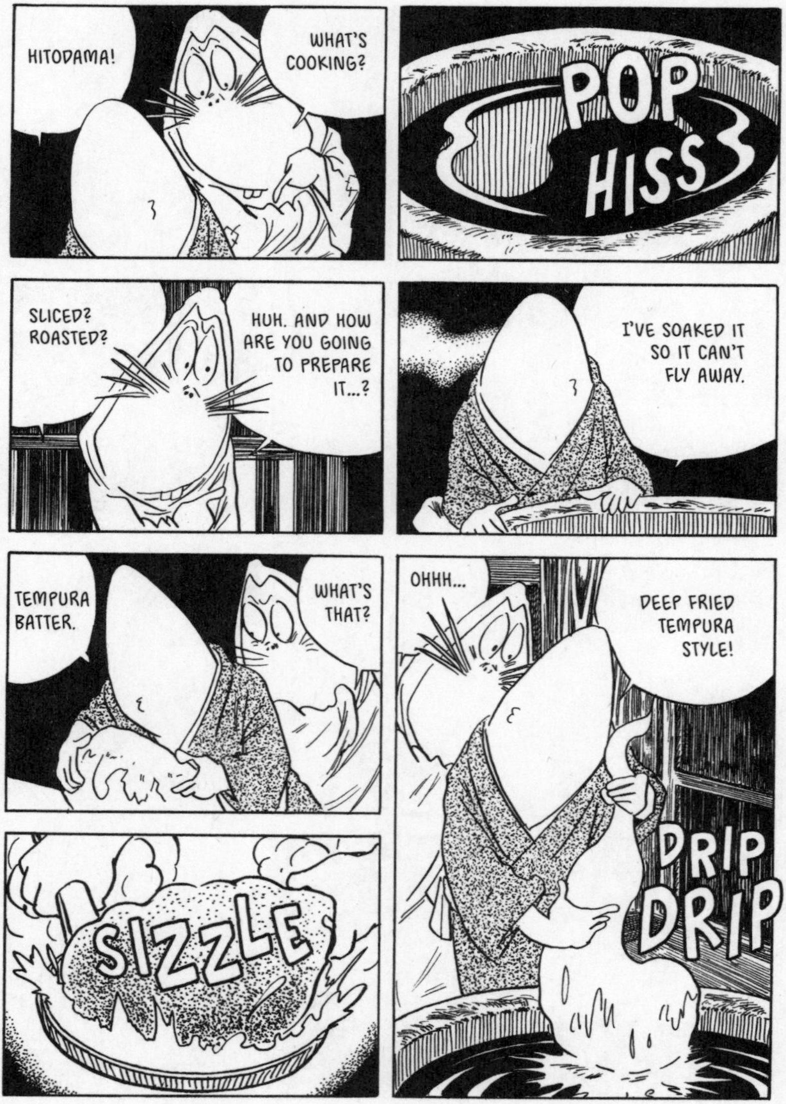
POP
HISS
WHAT'S COOKING?
HITODAMA!
I'VE SOAKED IT SO IT CAN'T FLY AWAY.
HUH. AND HOW ARE YOU GOING TO PREPARE IT...?
SLICED? ROASTED?
DEEP FRIED TEMPURA STYLE!
OHHH...
DRIP DRIP
WHAT'S THAT?
TEMPURA BATTER.
SIZZLE

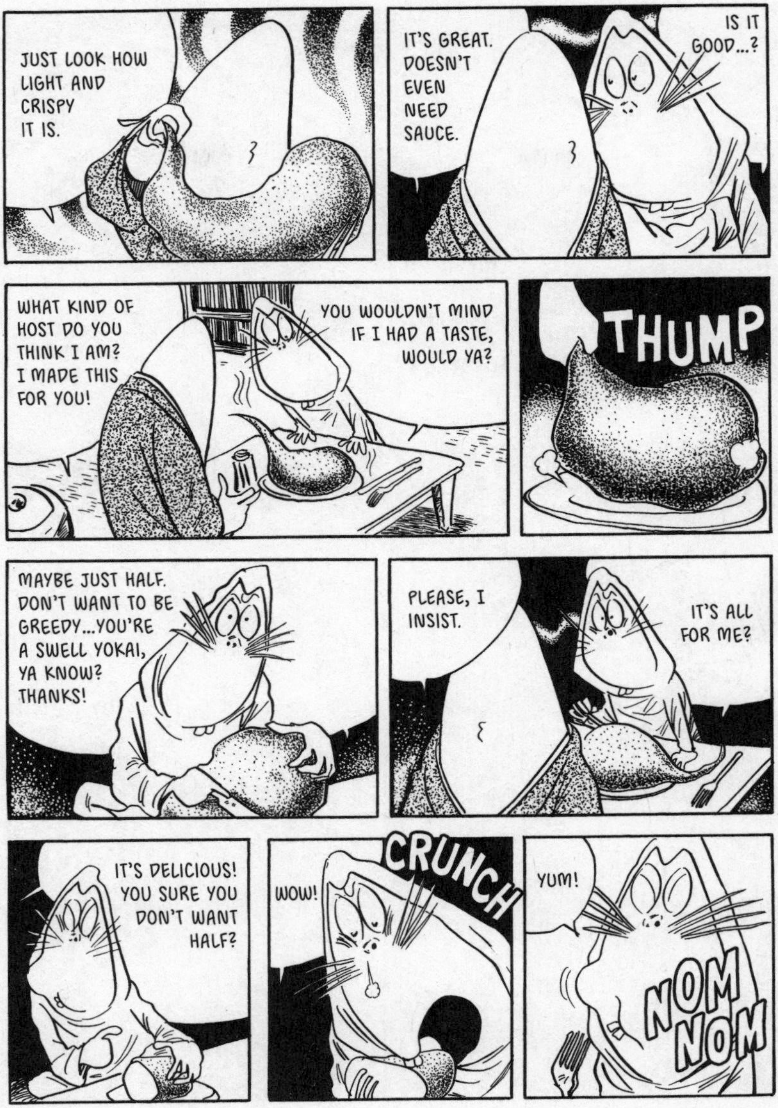
IS IT GOOD...?
IT'S GREAT. DOESN'T EVEN NEED SAUCE.
JUST LOOK HOW LIGHT AND CRISPY IT IS.
THUMP
YOU WOULDN'T MIND IF I HAD A TASTE, WOULD YA?
WHAT KIND OF HOST DO YOU THINK I AM? I MADE THIS FOR YOU!
IT'S ALL FOR ME?
PLEASE, I INSIST.
MAYBE JUST HALF. DON'T WANT TO BE GREEDY...YOU'RE A SWELL YOKAI, YA KNOW? THANKS!
YUM!
NOM NOM
CRUNCH
WOW!
IT'S DELICIOUS! YOU SURE YOU DON'T WANT HALF?

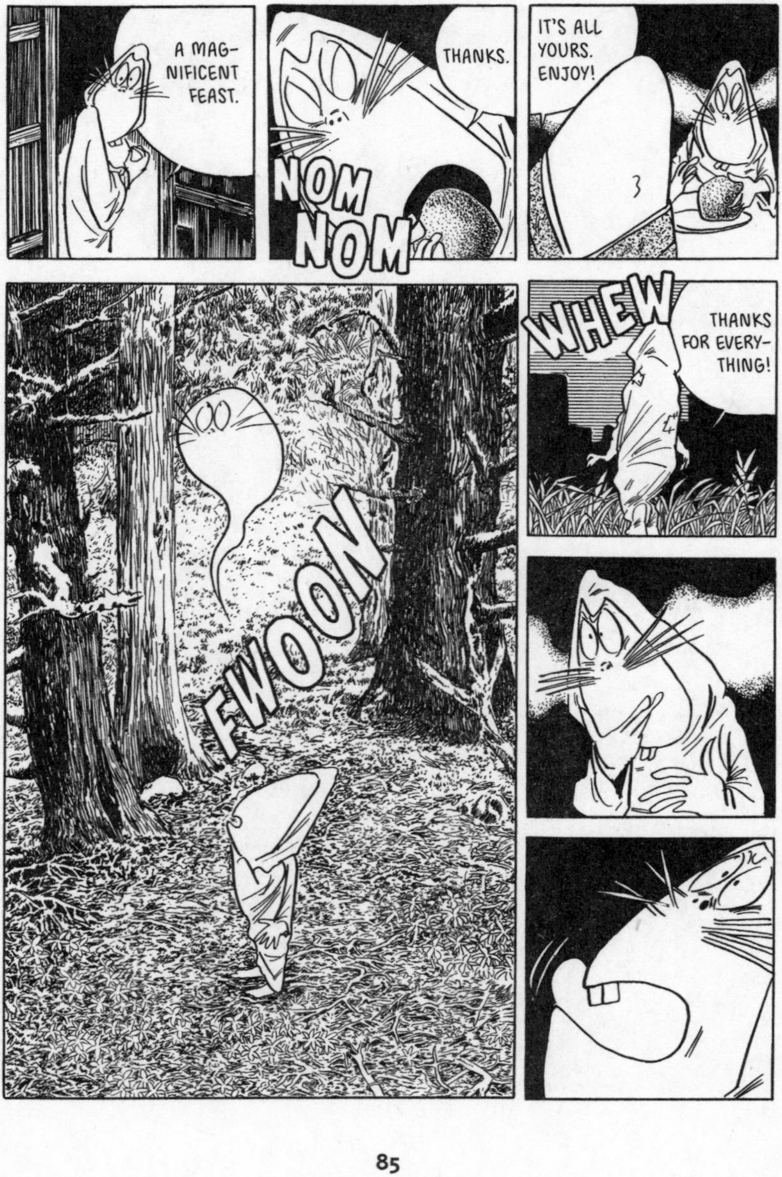
IT'S ALL YOURS. ENJOY!
THANKS.
NOM NOM
A MAG-NIFICENT FEAST.
WHEW
THANKS FOR EVERY-THING!
FWOON

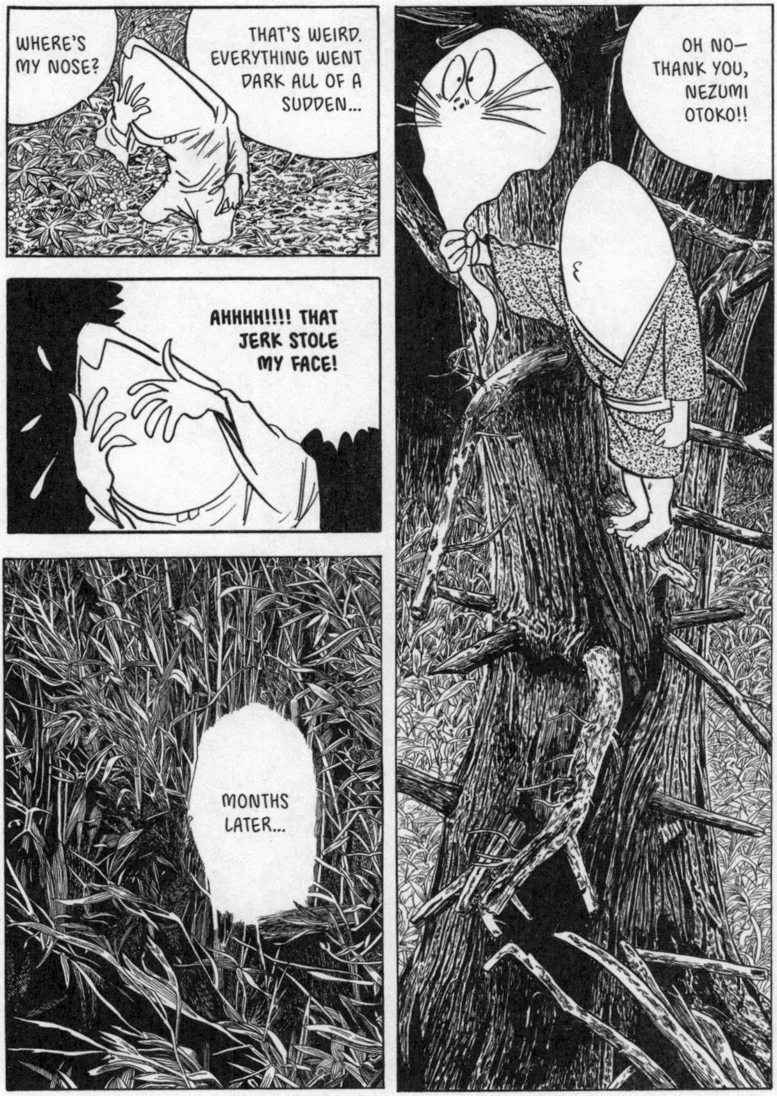
OH NO—
THANK YOU,
NEZUMI
OTOKO!!
THAT'S WEIRD. EVERYTHING WENT DARK ALL OF A SUDDEN...
WHERE'S MY NOSE?
AHHHH!!!! THAT JERK STOLE MY FACE!
MONTHS LATER...

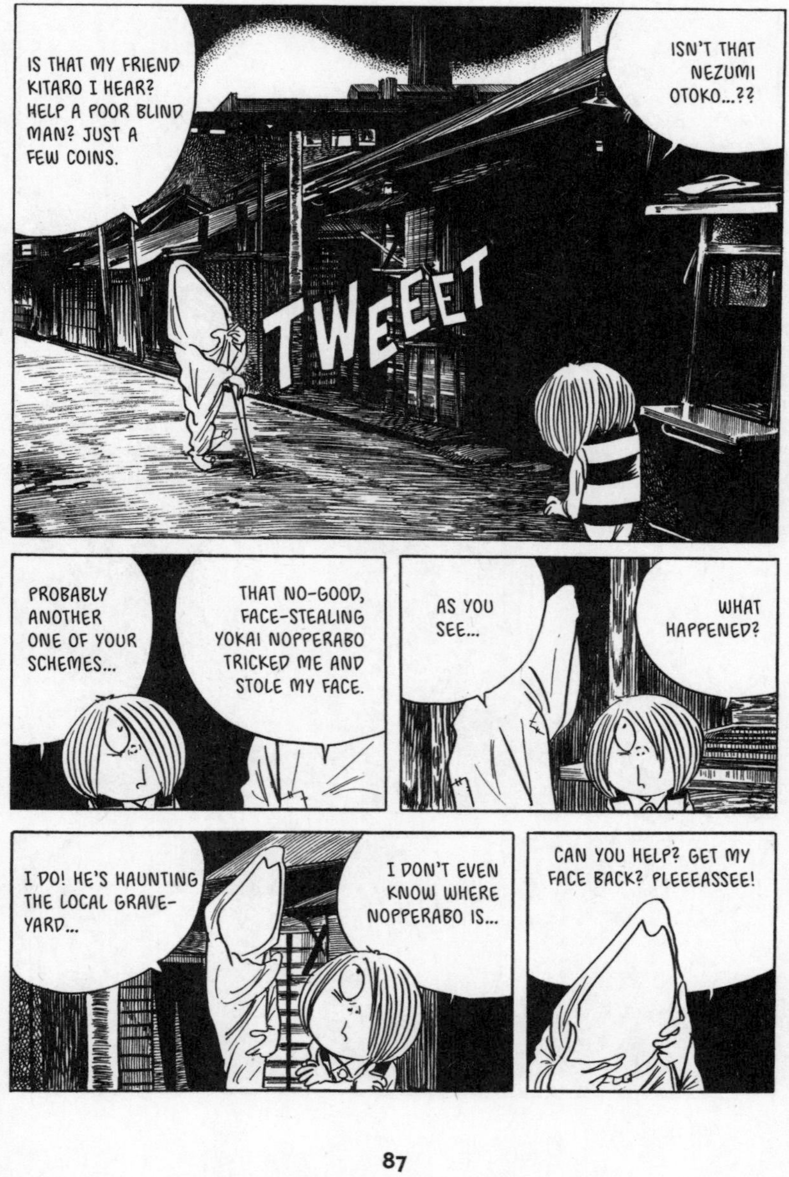
ISN'T THAT NEZUMI OTOKO...??
IS THAT MY FRIEND KITARO I HEAR? HELP A POOR BLIND MAN? JUST A FEW COINS.
TWEEET
WHAT HAPPENED?
AS YOU SEE...
THAT NO-GOOD, FACE-STEALING YOKAI NOPPERABO TRICKED ME AND STOLE MY FACE.
PROBABLY ANOTHER ONE OF YOUR SCHEMES...
CAN YOU HELP? GET MY FACE BACK? PLEEEASSEE!
I DON'T EVEN KNOW WHERE NOPPERABO IS...
I DO! HE'S HAUNTING THE LOCAL GRAVE-YARD...

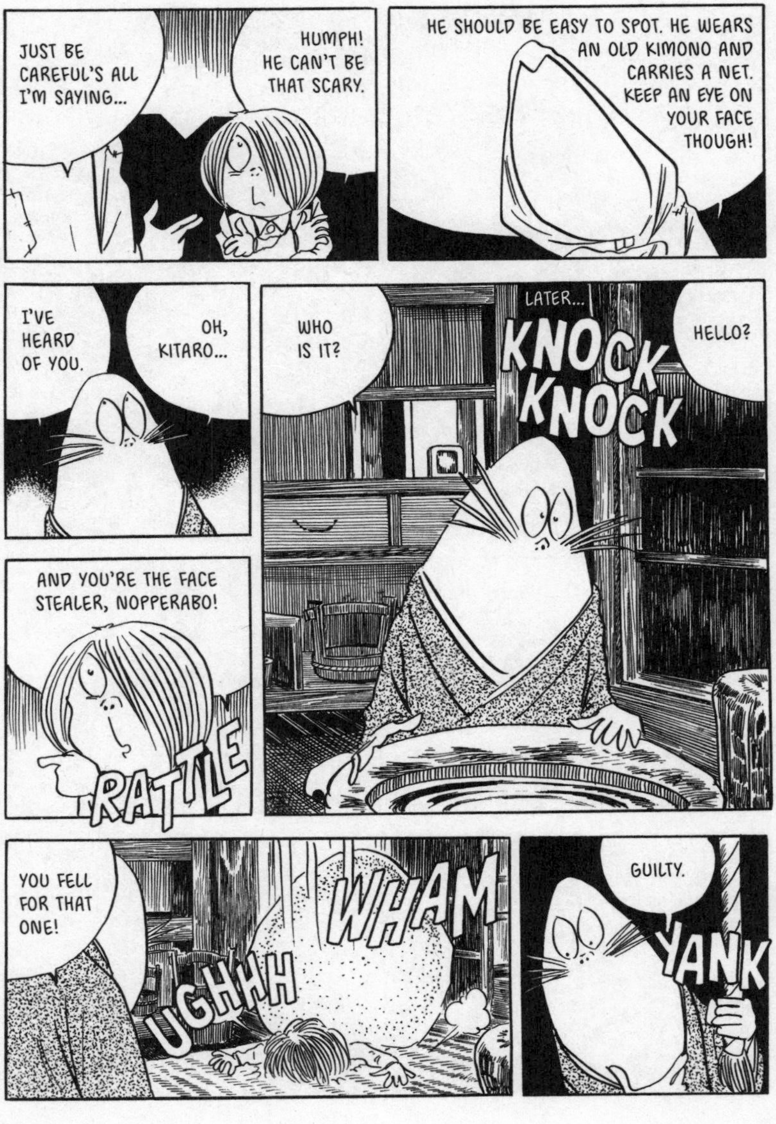
HE SHOULD BE EASY TO SPOT. HE WEARS AN OLD KIMONO AND CARRIES A NET. KEEP AN EYE ON YOUR FACE THOUGH!
HUMPH! HE CAN'T BE THAT SCARY.
JUST BE CAREFUL'S ALL I'M SAYING...
LATER...
KNOCK KNOCK
HELLO?
WHO IS IT?
OH, KITARO...
I'VE HEARD OF YOU.
AND YOU'RE THE FACE STEALER, NOPPERABO!
RATTLE
GUILTY.
YANK
WHAM
YOU FELL FOR THAT ONE!
UGHHH

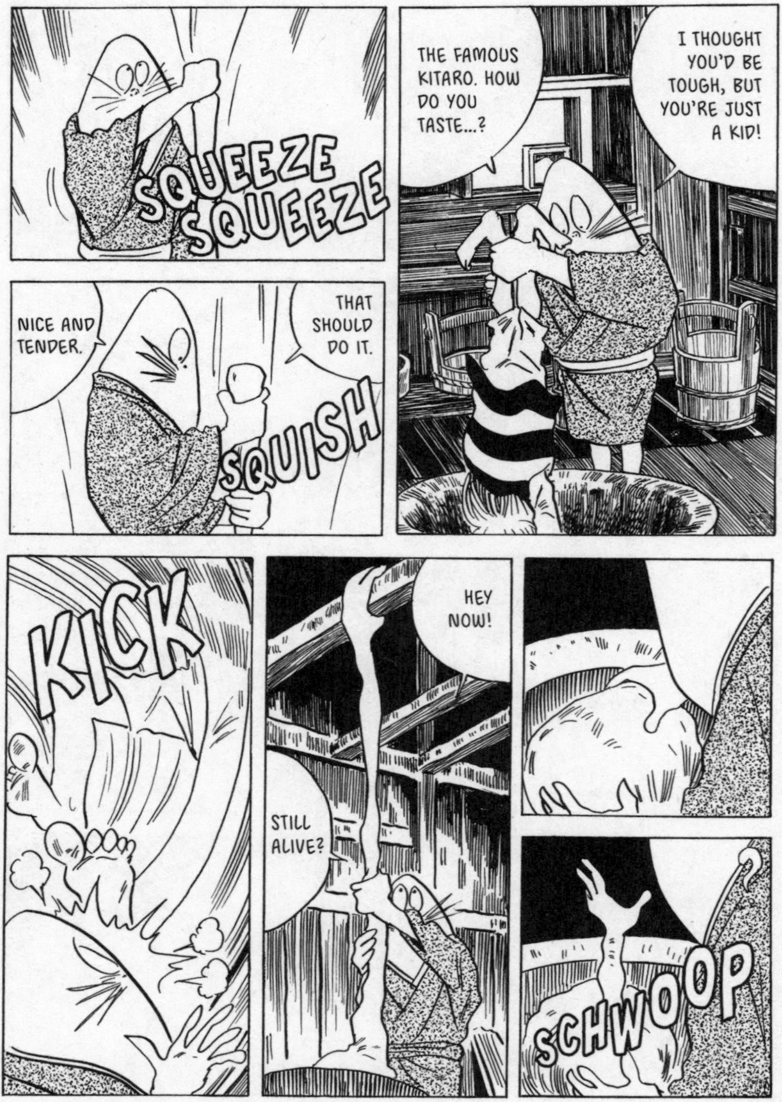
I THOUGHT YOU'D BE TOUGH, BUT YOU'RE JUST A KID!
THE FAMOUS KITARO. HOW DO YOU TASTE...?
SQUEEZE SQUEEZE
THAT SHOULD DO IT.
NICE AND TENDER.
SQUISH
SCHWOOP
HEY NOW!
STILL ALIVE?
KICK

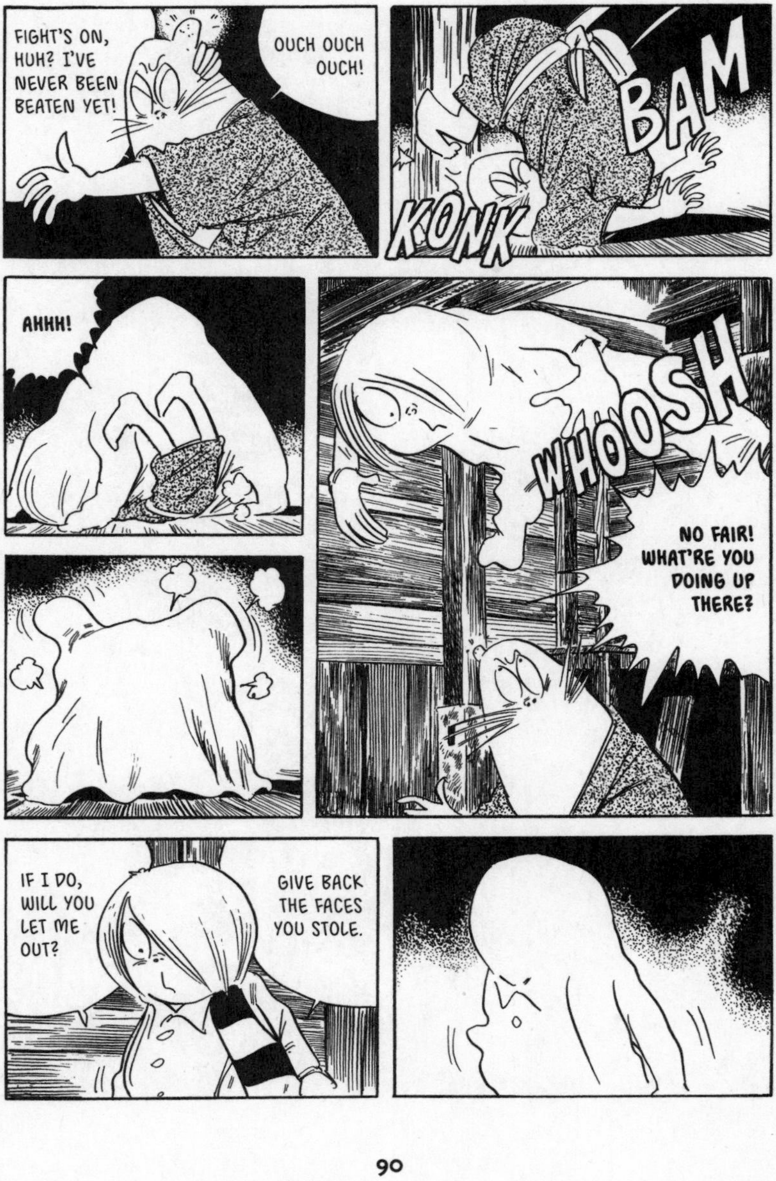
BAM
KONK
OUCH OUCH OUCH!
FIGHT'S ON, HUH? I'VE NEVER BEEN BEATEN YET!
WHOOSH
NO FAIR! WHAT'RE YOU DOING UP THERE?
AHHH!
GIVE BACK THE FACES YOU STOLE.
IF I DO, WILL YOU LET ME OUT?

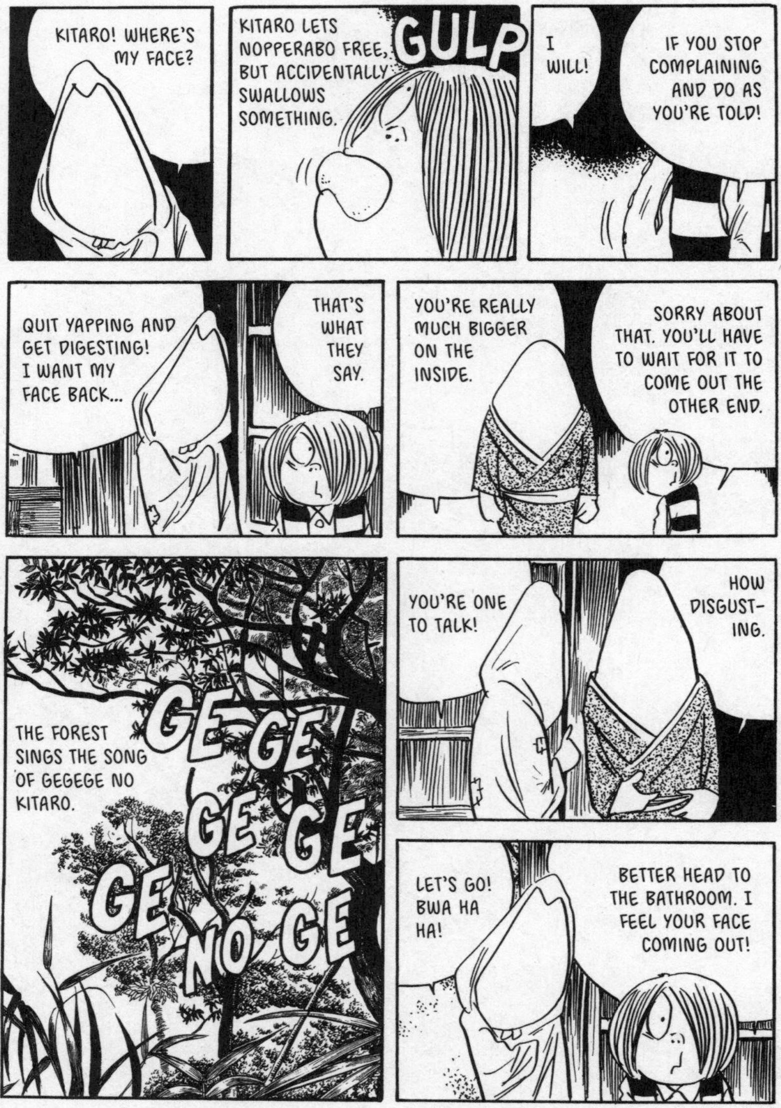
IF YOU STOP COMPLAINING AND DO AS YOU'RE TOLD!
I WILL!
KITARO LETS NOPPERABO FREE, BUT ACCIDENTALLY SWALLOWS SOMETHING.
GULP
KITARO! WHERE'S MY FACE?
SORRY ABOUT THAT. YOU'LL HAVE TO WAIT FOR IT TO COME OUT THE OTHER END.
YOU'RE REALLY MUCH BIGGER ON THE INSIDE.
THAT'S WHAT THEY SAY.
QUIT YAPPING AND GET DIGESTING! I WANT MY FACE BACK...
HOW DISGUST-ING.
YOU'RE ONE TO TALK!
BETTER HEAD TO THE BATHROOM. I FEEL YOUR FACE COMING OUT!
LET'S GO! BWA HA HA!
THE FOREST SINGS THE SONG OF GEGEGE NO KITARO.
GE GE GE GE GE GE NO GE

GYUKI

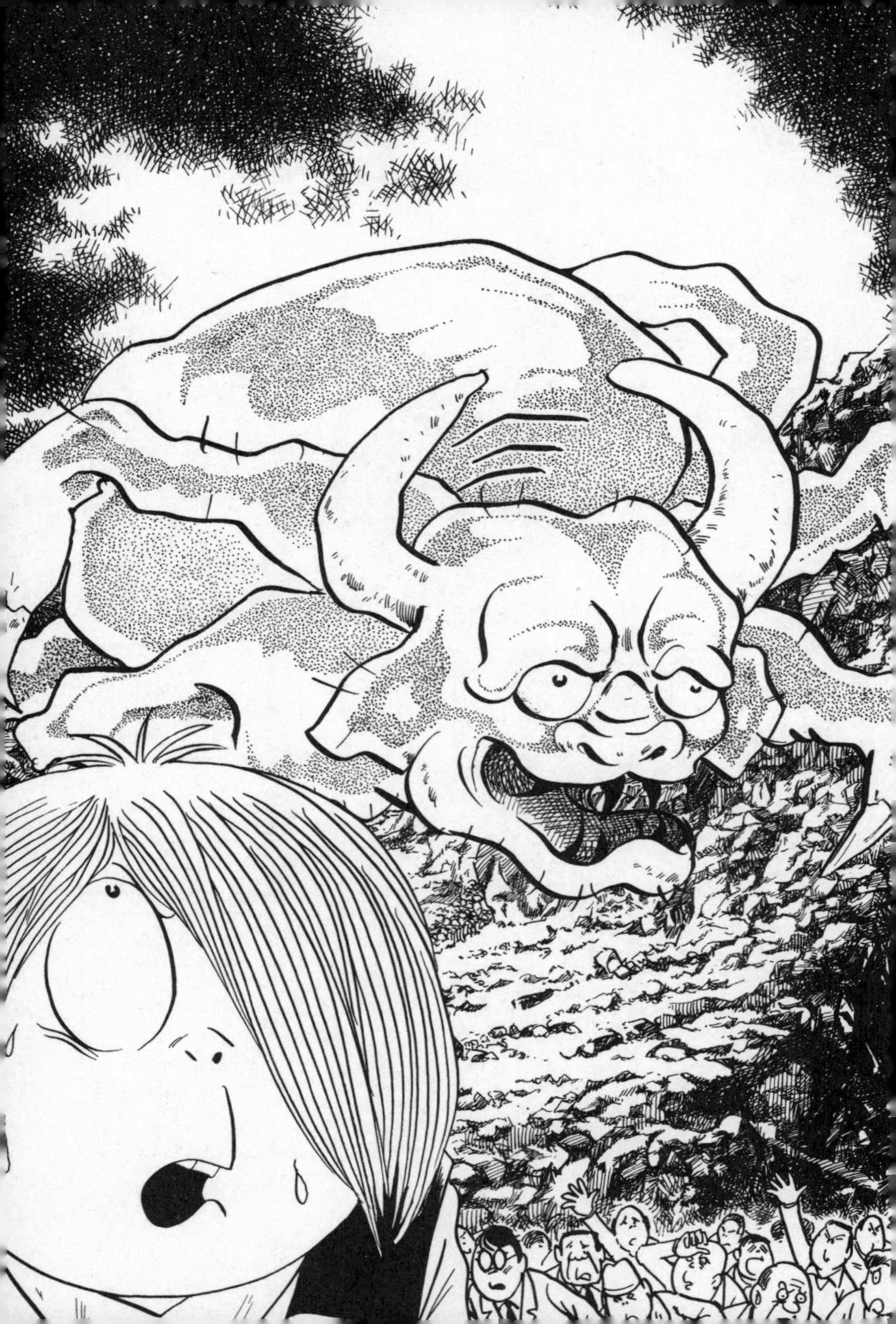

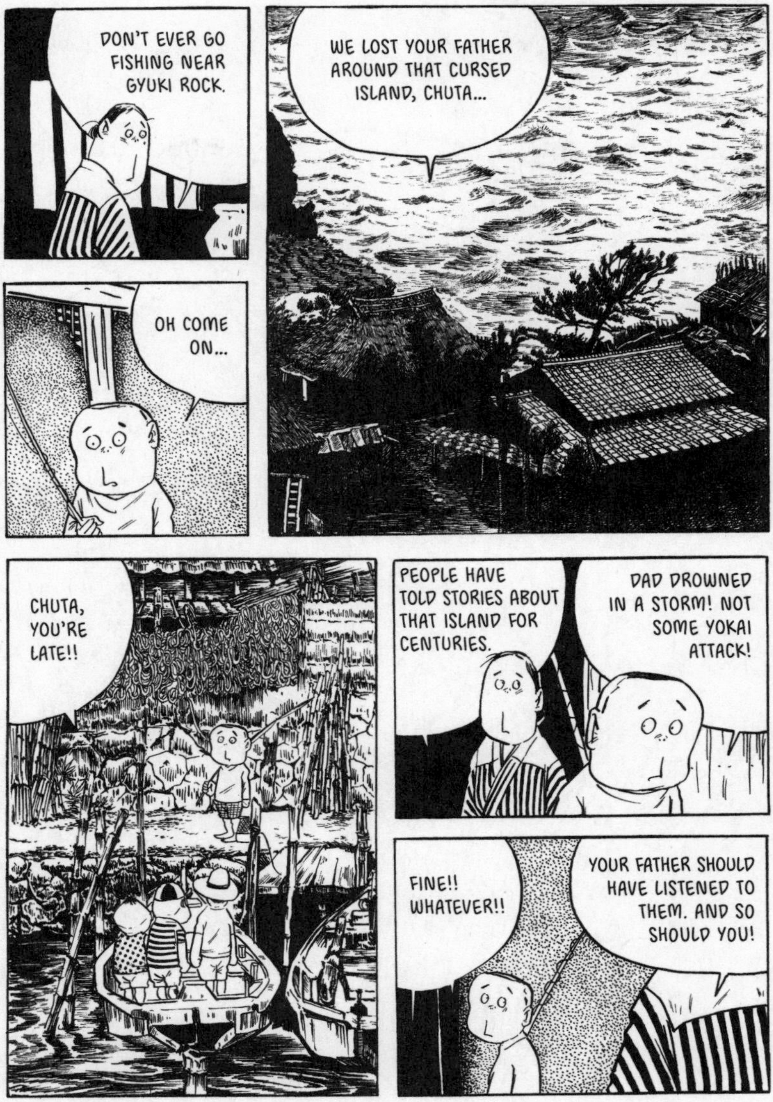
WE LOST YOUR FATHER AROUND THAT CURSED ISLAND, CHUTA...
DON'T EVER GO FISHING NEAR GYUKI ROCK.
OH COME ON...
DAD DROWNED IN A STORM! NOT SOME YOKAI ATTACK!
PEOPLE HAVE TOLD STORIES ABOUT THAT ISLAND FOR CENTURIES.
YOUR FATHER SHOULD HAVE LISTENED TO THEM. AND SO SHOULD YOU!
FINE!! WHATEVER!!
CHUTA, YOU'RE LATE!!

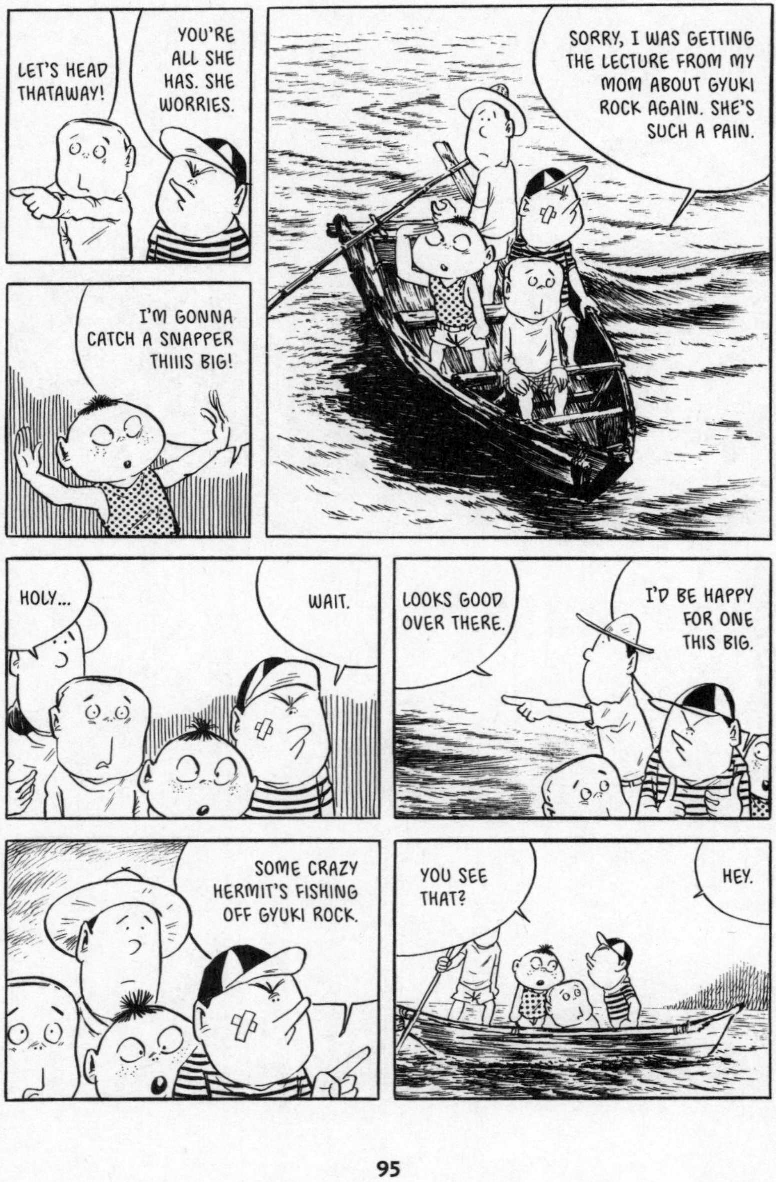
SORRY, I WAS GETTING THE LECTURE FROM MY MOM ABOUT GYUKI ROCK AGAIN. SHE'S SUCH A PAIN.
YOU'RE ALL SHE HAS. SHE WORRIES.
LET'S HEAD THATAWAY!
I'M GONNA CATCH A SNAPPER THIIIS BIG!
I'D BE HAPPY FOR ONE THIS BIG.
LOOKS GOOD OVER THERE.
WAIT.
HOLY...
HEY.
YOU SEE THAT?
SOME CRAZY HERMIT'S FISHING OFF GYUKI ROCK.

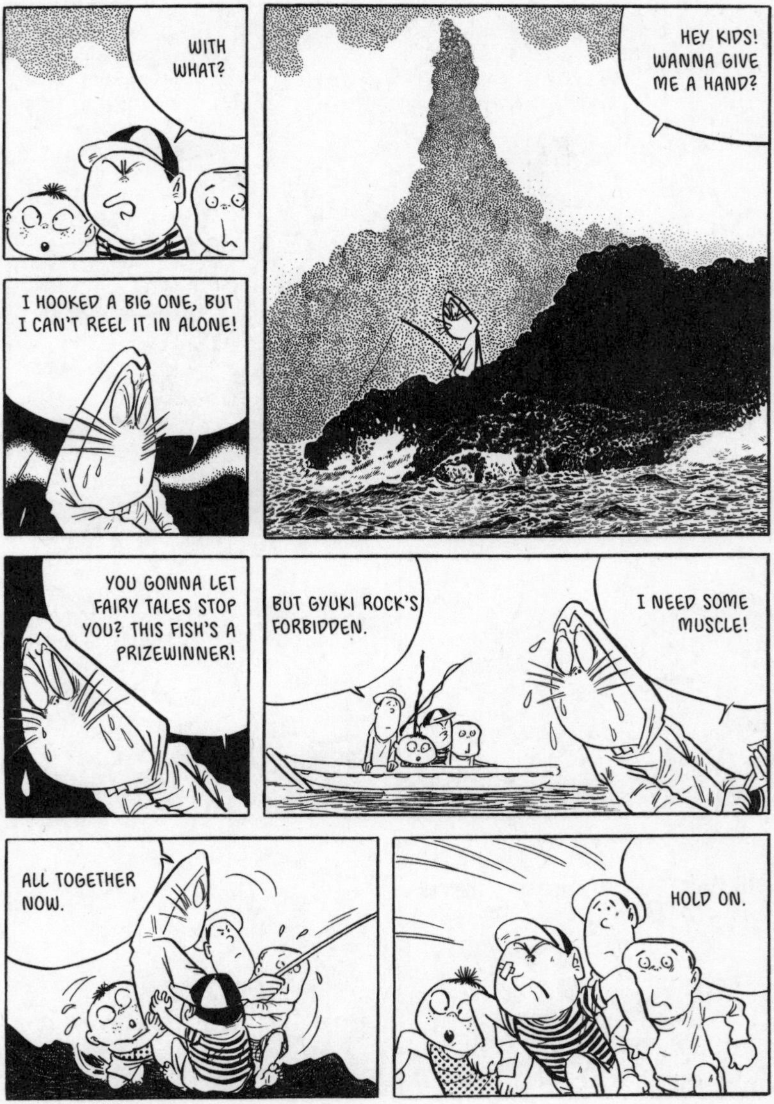
HEY KIDS! WANNA GIVE ME A HAND?
WITH WHAT?
I HOOKED A BIG ONE, BUT I CAN'T REEL IT IN ALONE!
I NEED SOME MUSCLE!
BUT GYUKI ROCK'S FORBIDDEN.
YOU GONNA LET FAIRY TALES STOP YOU? THIS FISH'S A PRIZEWINNER!
HOLD ON.
ALL TOGETHER NOW.

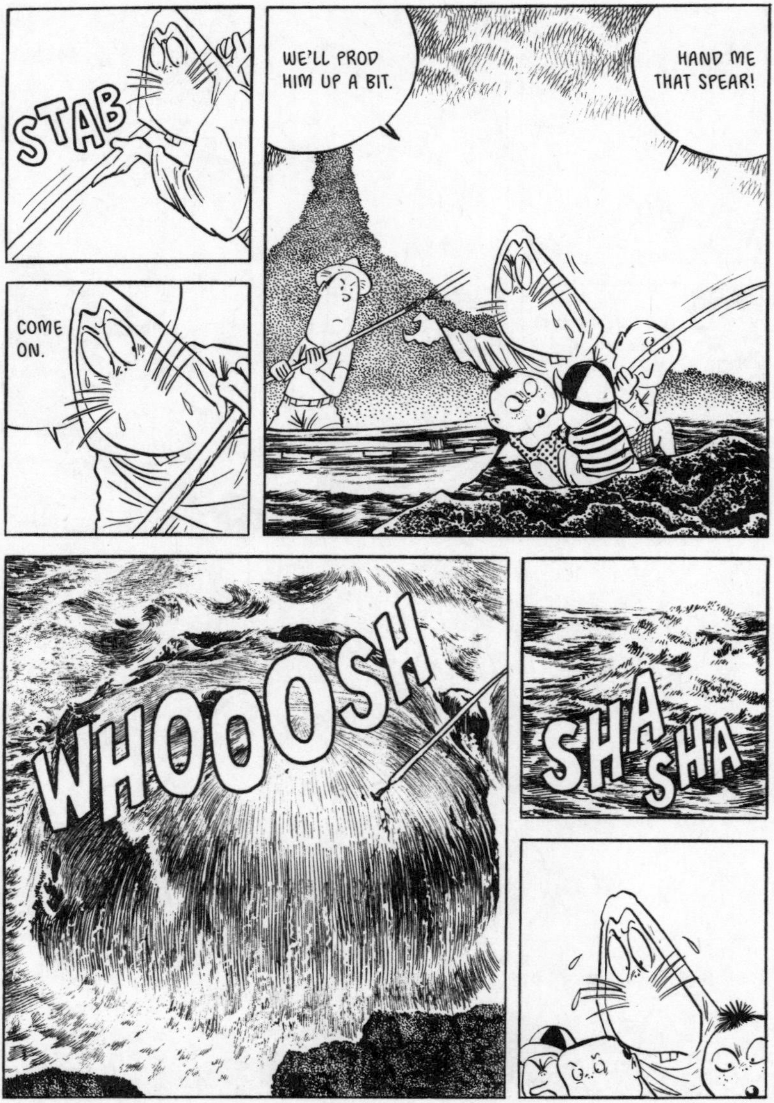
HAND ME THAT SPEAR!
WE'LL PROD HIM UP A BIT.
STAB
COME ON.
SHA SHA
WHOOOSH

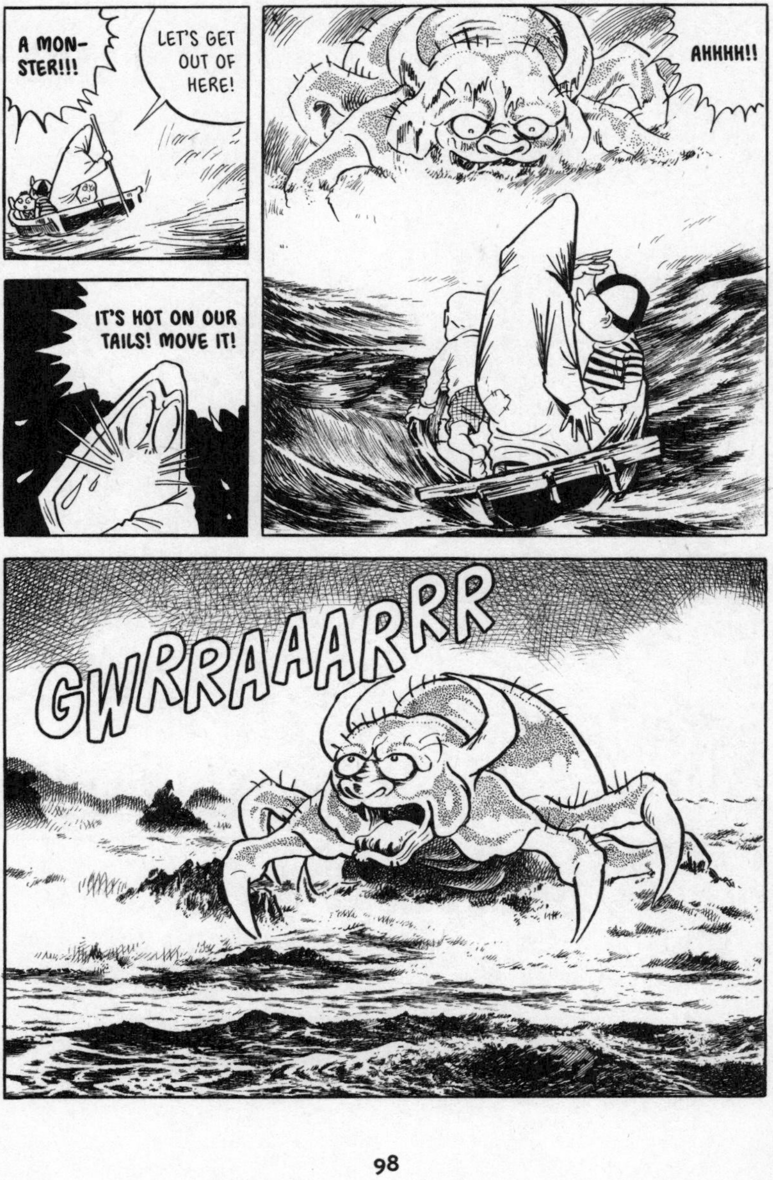
AHHHH!!
LET'S GET OUT OF HERE!
A MON-STER!!!
IT'S HOT ON OUR TAILS! MOVE IT!
GWRRAAARRR

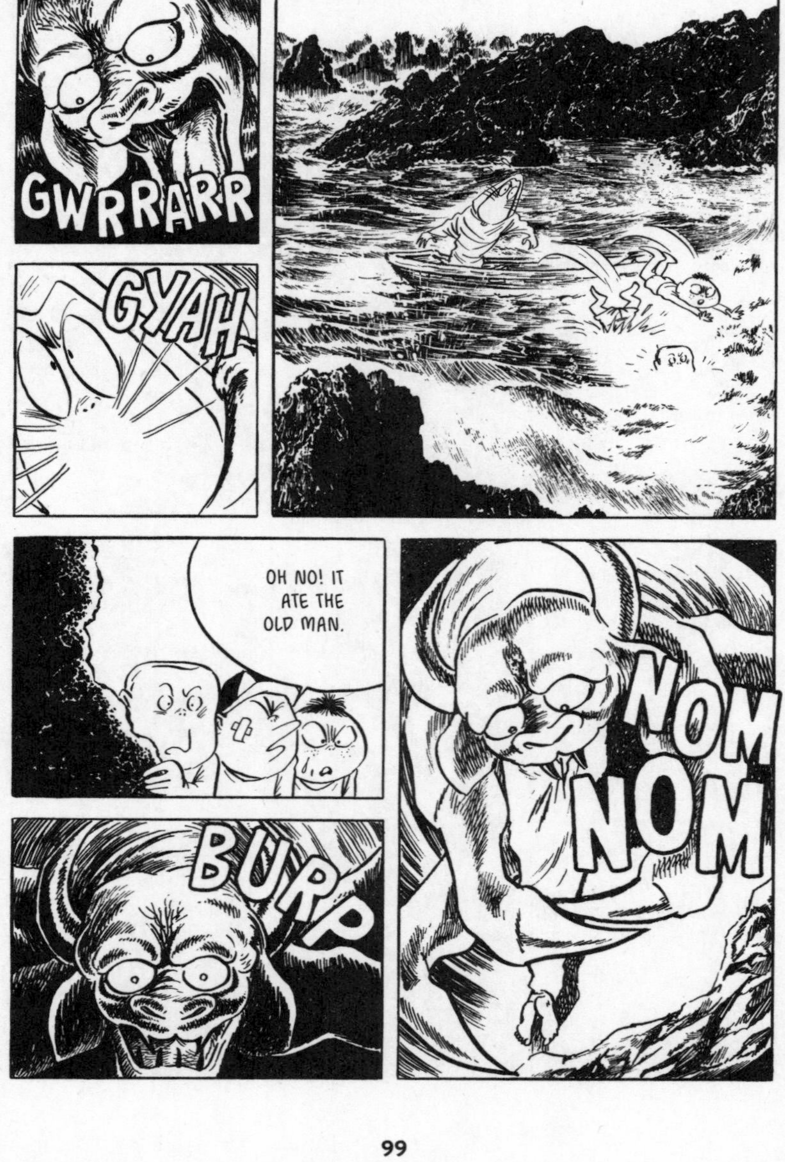
GWRRARR
GYAH
NOM NOM
OH NO! IT ATE THE OLD MAN.
BURP

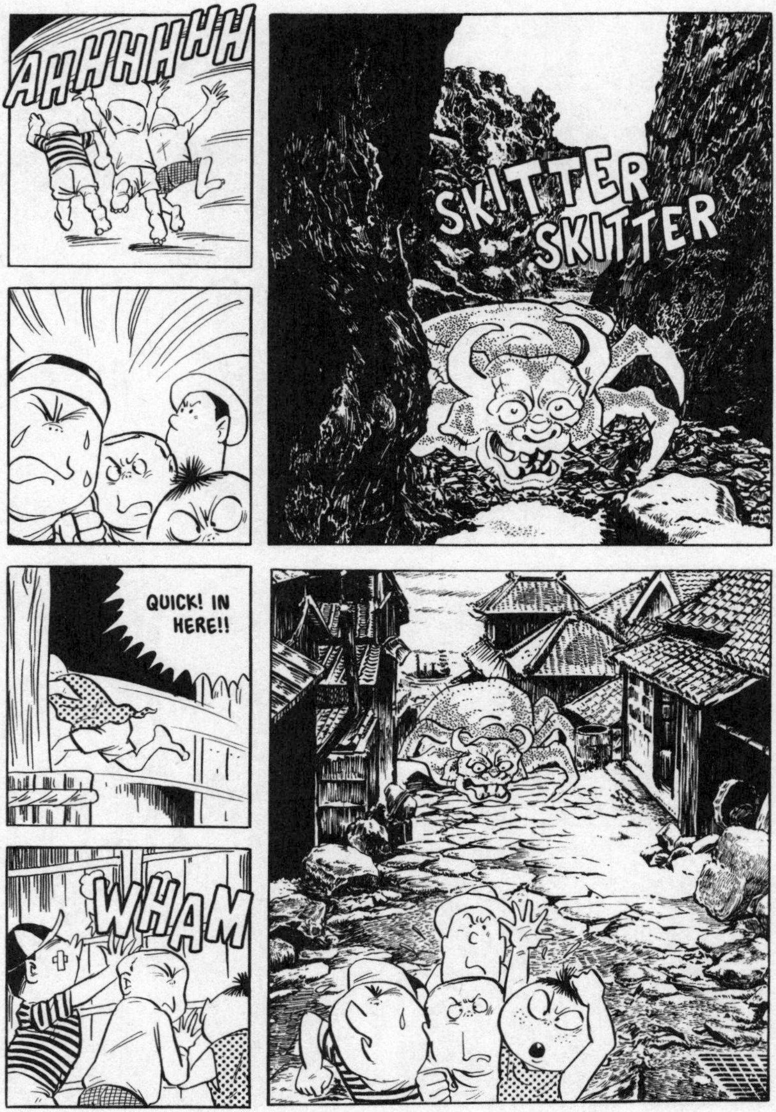
SKITTER
SKITTER
AHHHHHHH
QUICK! IN HERE!!
WHAM

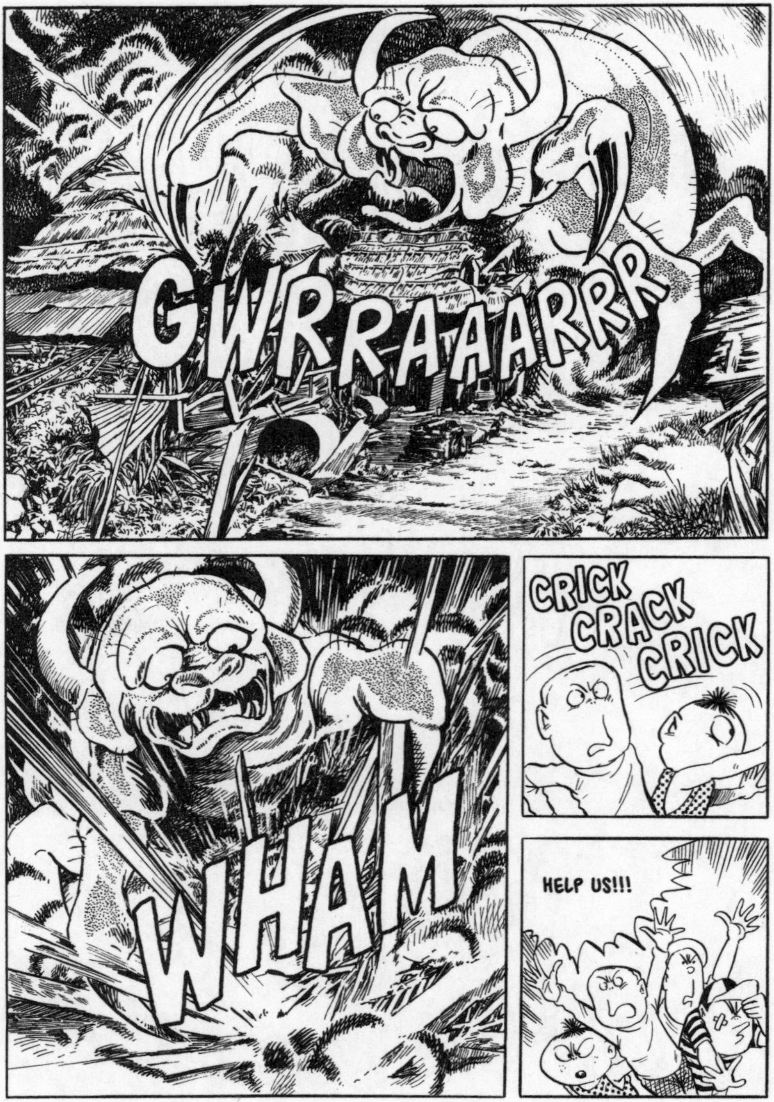
GWRRAAARRR
CRICK
CRACK
CRICK
HELP US!!!
WHAM

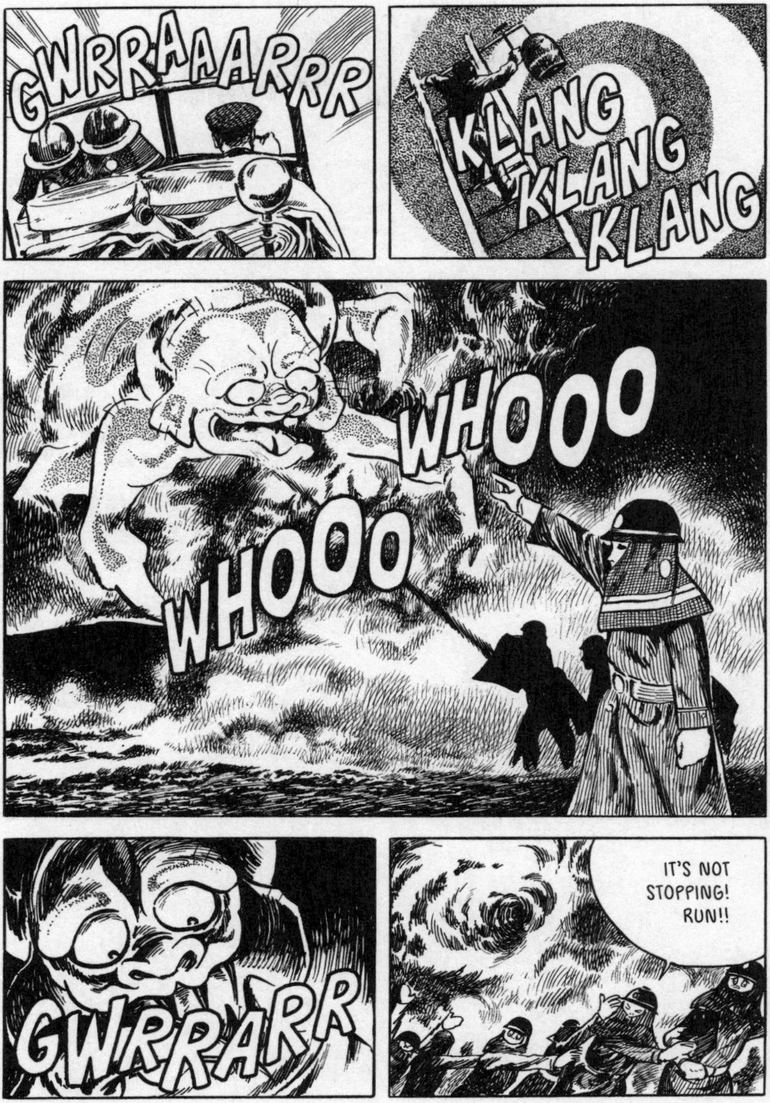
KLANG
KLANG
KLANG
GWRRAAARRRR
WHOOO
WHOOO
IT'S NOT STOPPING! RUN!!
GWRRARR

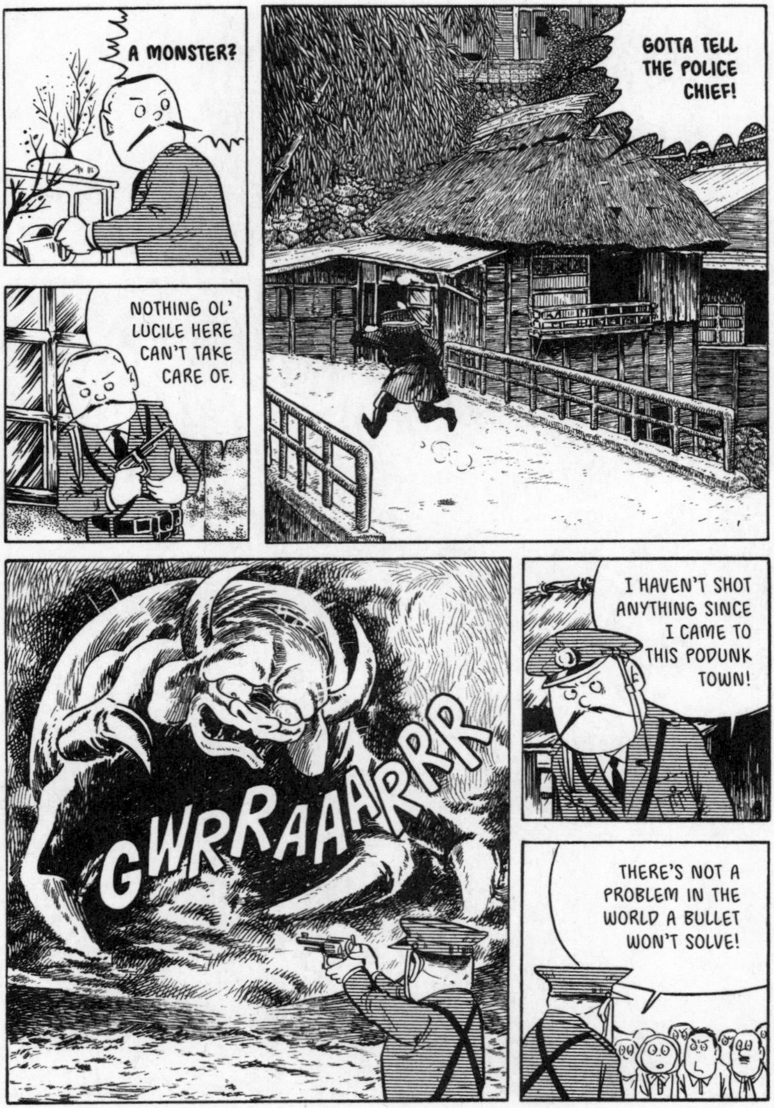
GOTTA TELL THE POLICE CHIEF!
A MONSTER?
NOTHING OL' LUCILE HERE CAN'T TAKE CARE OF.
I HAVEN'T SHOT ANYTHING SINCE I CAME TO THIS PODUNK TOWN!
THERE'S NOT A PROBLEM IN THE WORLD A BULLET WON'T SOLVE!
GWRRAAARRR

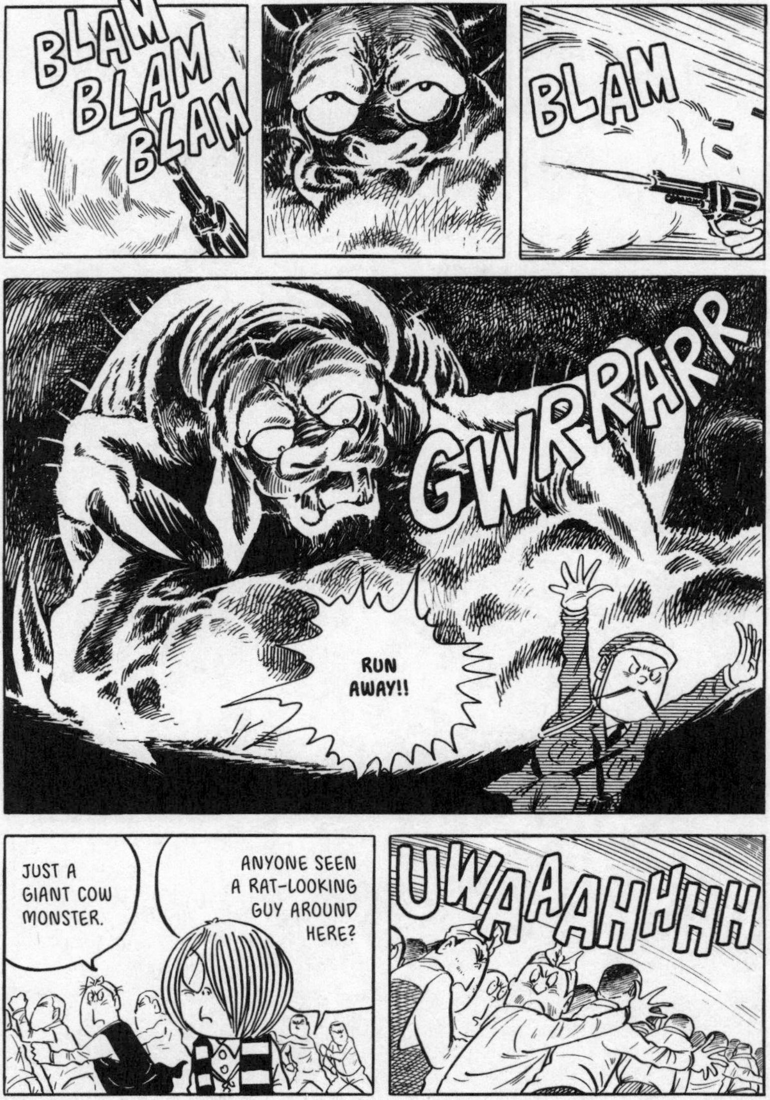
BLAM
BLAM BLAM BLAM
GWRRARR
RUN AWAY!!
UWAAAHHHH
ANYONE SEEN A RAT-LOOKING GUY AROUND HERE?
JUST A GIANT COW MONSTER.

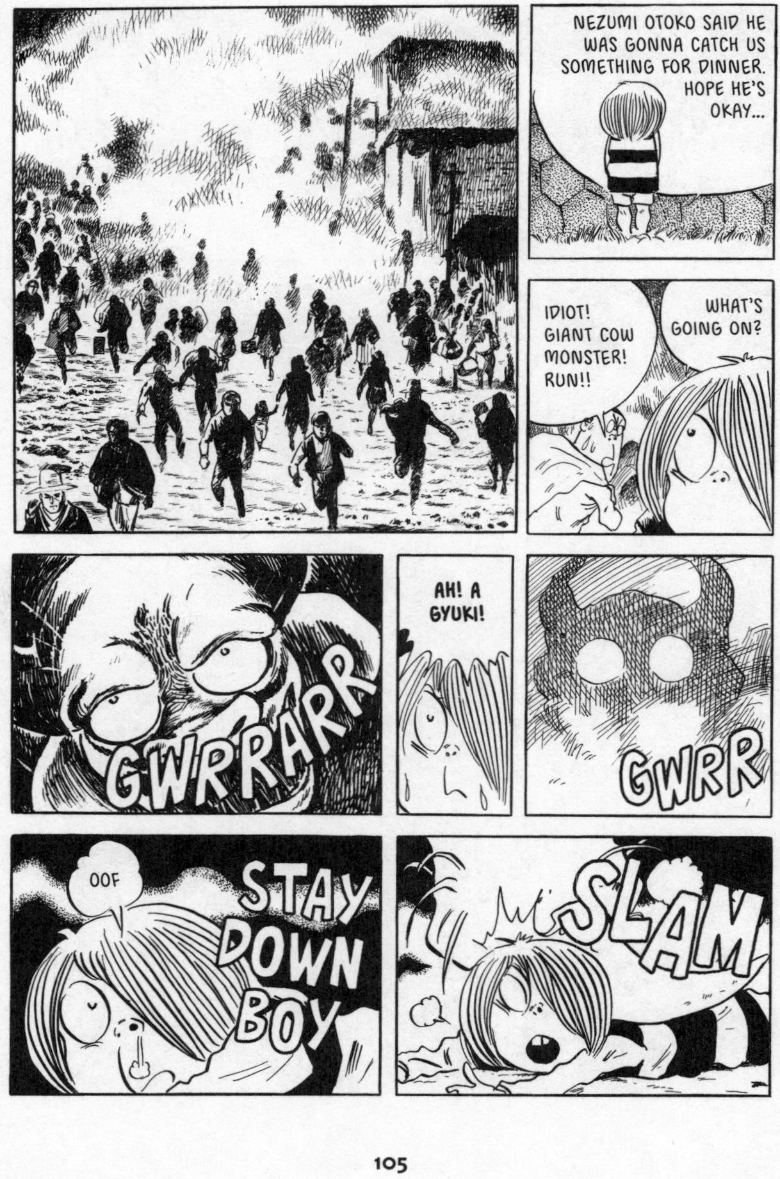
NEZUMI OTOKO SAID HE WAS GONNA CATCH US SOMETHING FOR DINNER. HOPE HE'S OKAY...
WHAT'S GOING ON?
IDIOT! GIANT COW MONSTER! RUN!!
GWRR
AH! A GYUKI!
GWRRARR
SLAM
STAY DOWN BOY
OOF

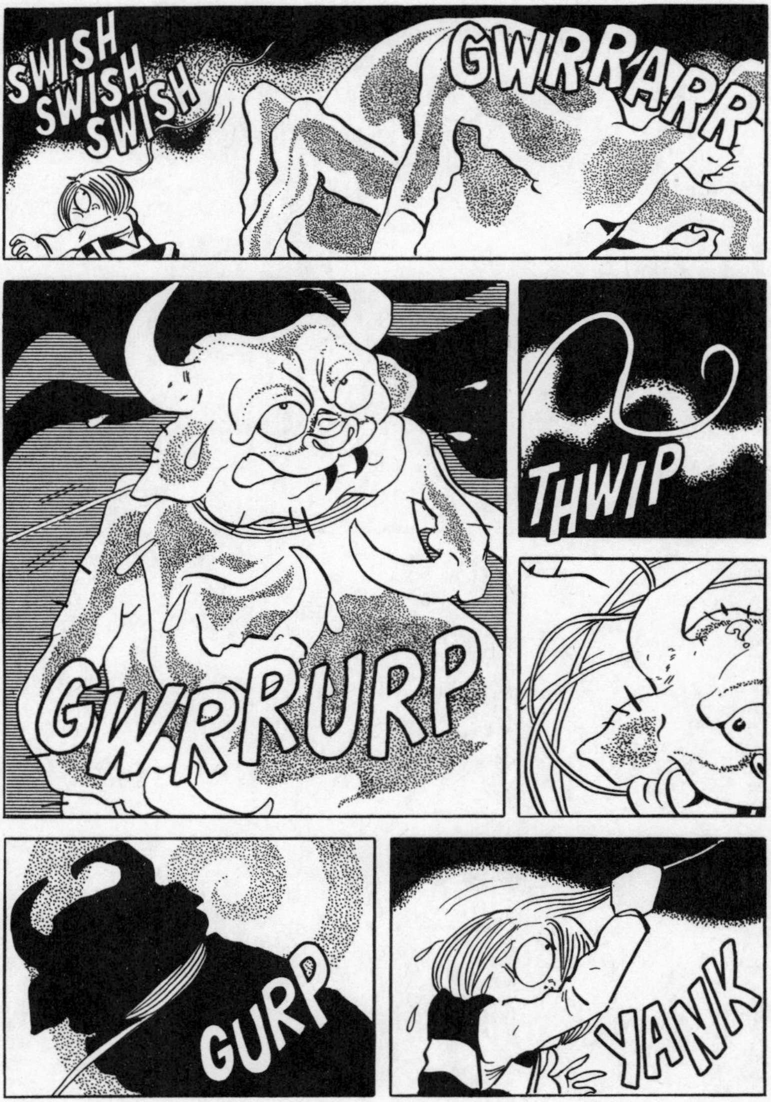
GWRRARR
SWISH SWISH SWISH
THWIP
GWRRURP
YANK
GURP

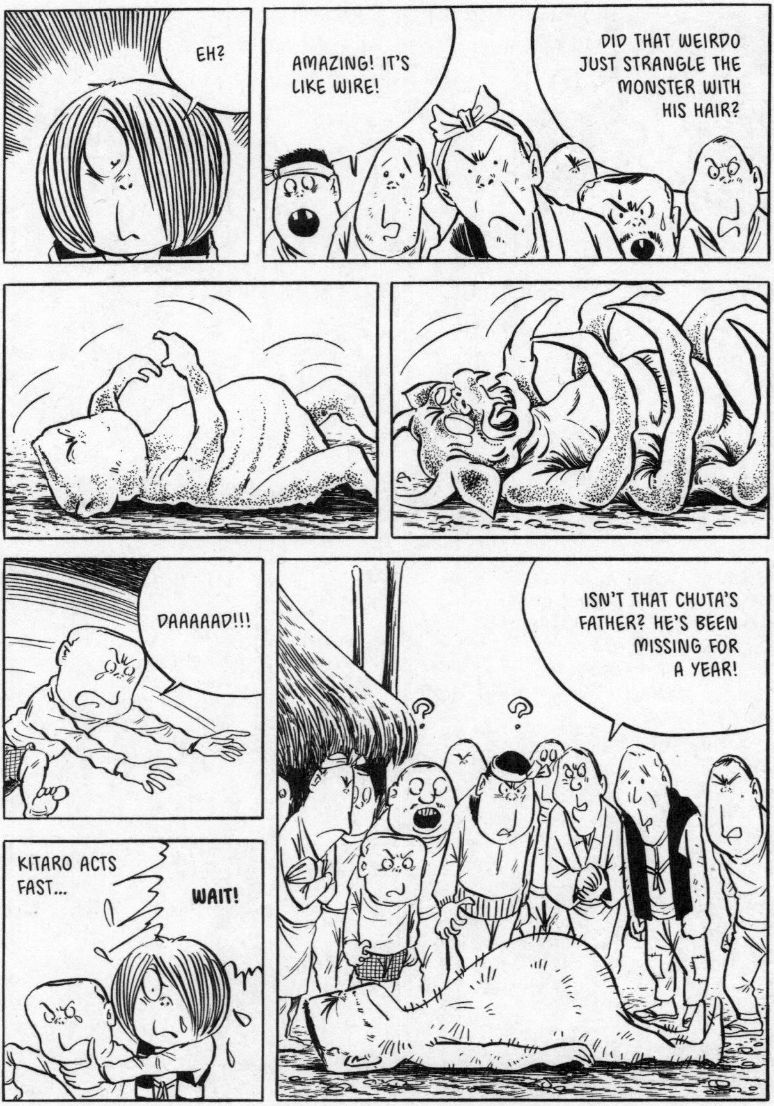
DID THAT WEIRDO JUST STRANGLE THE MONSTER WITH HIS HAIR?
AMAZING! IT'S LIKE WIRE!
EH?
ISN'T THAT CHUTA'S FATHER? HE'S BEEN MISSING FOR A YEAR!
DAAAAAD!!!
KITARO ACTS FAST...
WAIT!

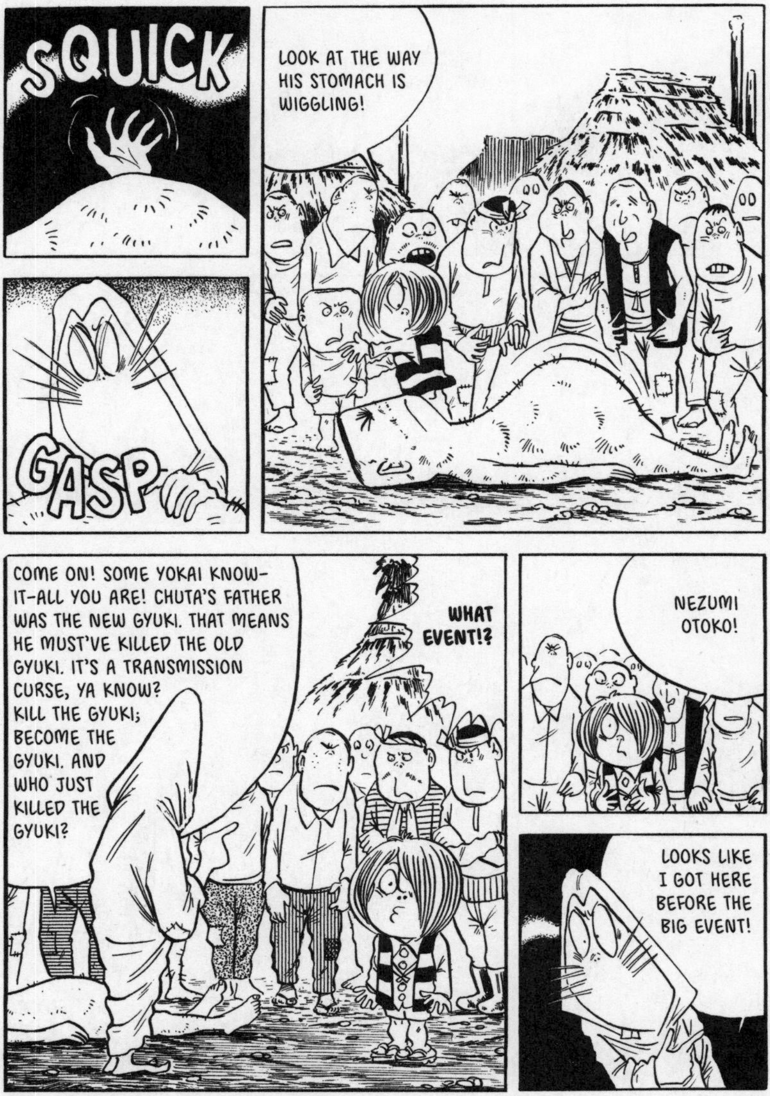

LOOK AT THE WAY HIS STOMACH IS WIGGLING!
SQUICK
GASP
NEZUMI OTOKO!
LOOKS LIKE I GOT HERE BEFORE THE BIG EVENT!
WHAT EVENT!?
COME ON! SOME YOKAI KNOW-IT-ALL YOU ARE! CHUTA'S FATHER WAS THE NEW GYUKI. THAT MEANS HE MUST'VE KILLED THE OLD GYUKI. IT'S A TRANSMISSION CURSE, YA KNOW? KILL THE GYUKI; BECOME THE GYUKI. AND WHO JUST KILLED THE GYUKI?

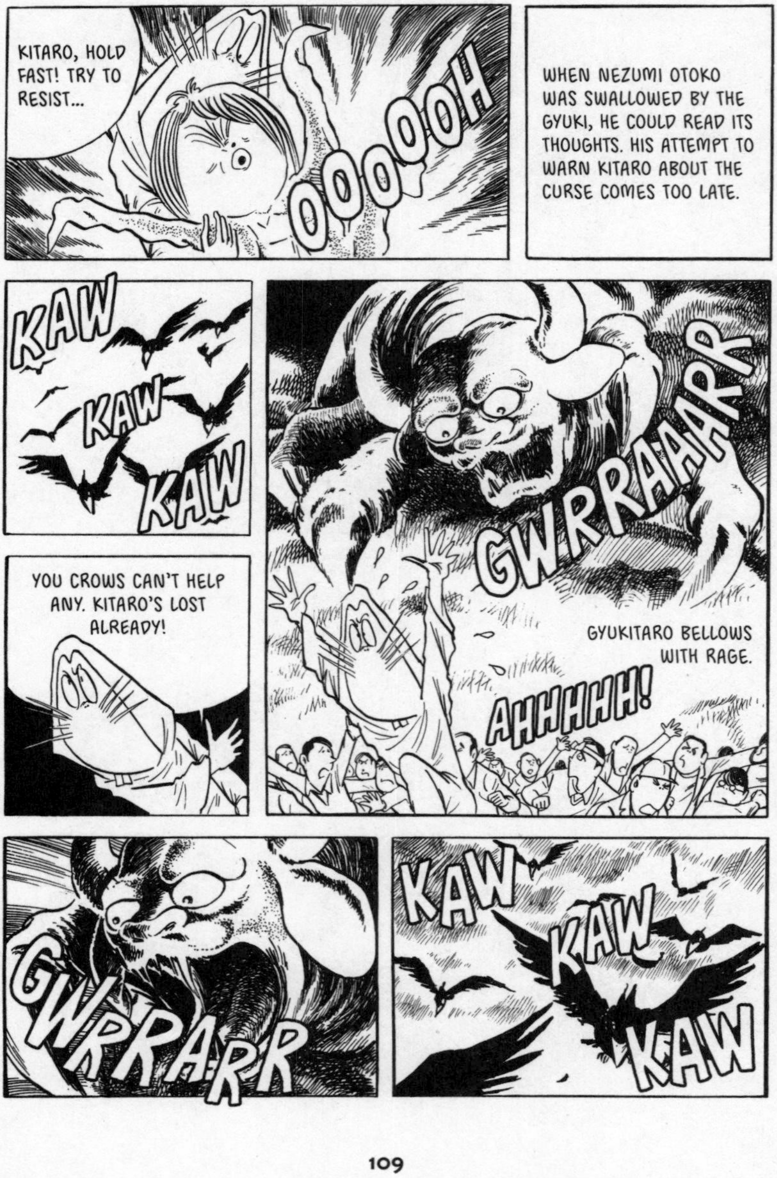
WHEN NEZUMI OTOKO WAS SWALLOWED BY THE GYUKI, HE COULD READ ITS THOUGHTS. HIS ATTEMPT TO WARN KITARO ABOUT THE CURSE COMES TOO LATE.
KITARO, HOLD FAST! TRY TO RESIST...
OOOOOH
GWRRAAARR
GYUKITARO BELLOWS WITH RAGE.
AHHHHH!
KAW
KAW
KAW
YOU CROWS CAN'T HELP ANY. KITARO'S LOST ALREADY!
KAW
KAW
KAW
GWRRARR

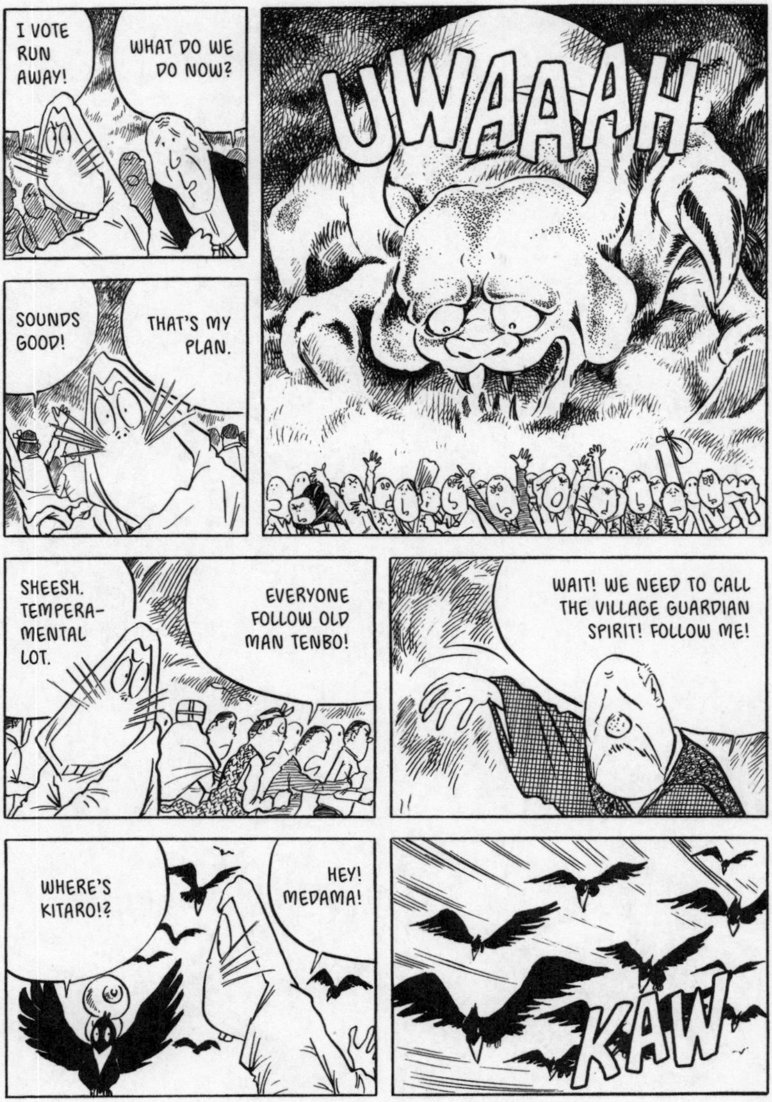
UWAAAH
WHAT DO WE DO NOW?
I VOTE RUN AWAY!
THAT'S MY PLAN.
SOUNDS GOOD!
WAIT! WE NEED TO CALL THE VILLAGE GUARDIAN SPIRIT! FOLLOW ME!
EVERYONE FOLLOW OLD MAN TENBO!
SHEESH. TEMPERA-MENTAL LOT.
KAW
HEY! MEDAMA!
WHERE'S KITARO!?

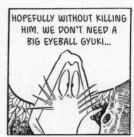

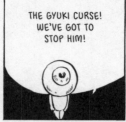

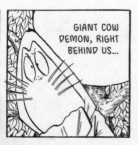

GIANT COW DEMON, RIGHT BEHIND US...
THE GYUKI CURSE! WE'VE GOT TO STOP HIM!
HOPEFULLY WITHOUT KILLING HIM. WE DON'T NEED A BIG EYEBALL GYUKI...
ONLY THE GODS CAN HELP US NOW. WE MUST GATHER AT THE SHRINE AND SUMMON THE GUARDIAN SPIRIT.
NON-SENSE!
BUT THE LEGEND OF THE GUARDIAN HAS BEEN PASSED DOWN FOR GENERATIONS.
MILLENNIA AGO, THE GUARDIAN ROSE TO SAVE THE VILLAGE. WE CAN CALL IT AGAIN...
WE MUST GATHER TO PRAY.
OKAY, BUT IT WILL TAKE ALL OUR COMBINED POWER.
ONLY OUR COLLECTIVE ENERGY CAN CALL HIM.

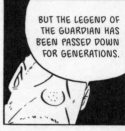

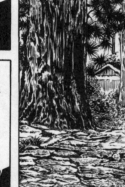

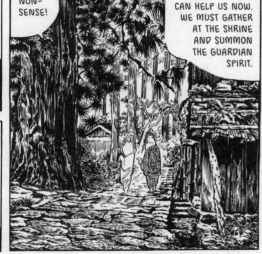

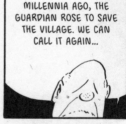

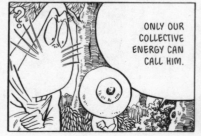

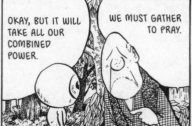

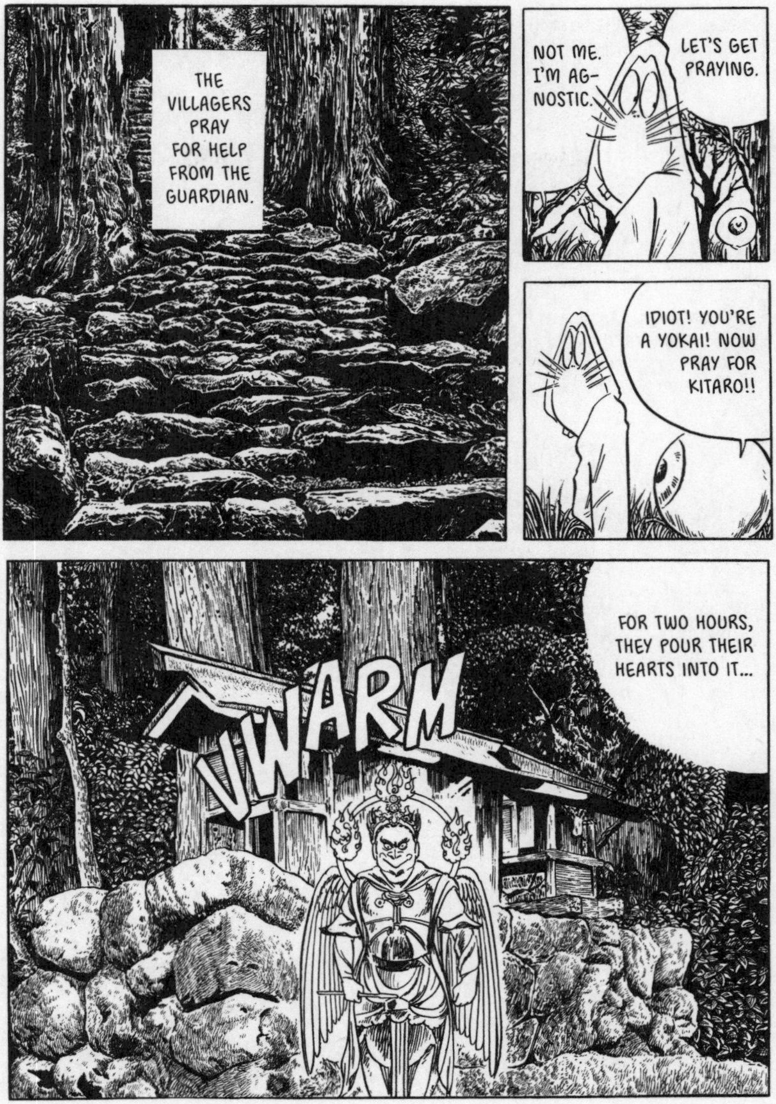
LET'S GET PRAYING.
NOT ME. I'M AG- NOSTIC.
IDIOT! YOU'RE A YOKAI! NOW PRAY FOR KITARO!!
THE VILLAGERS PRAY FOR HELP FROM THE GUARDIAN.
FOR TWO HOURS, THEY POUR THEIR HEARTS INTO IT...
VWARM

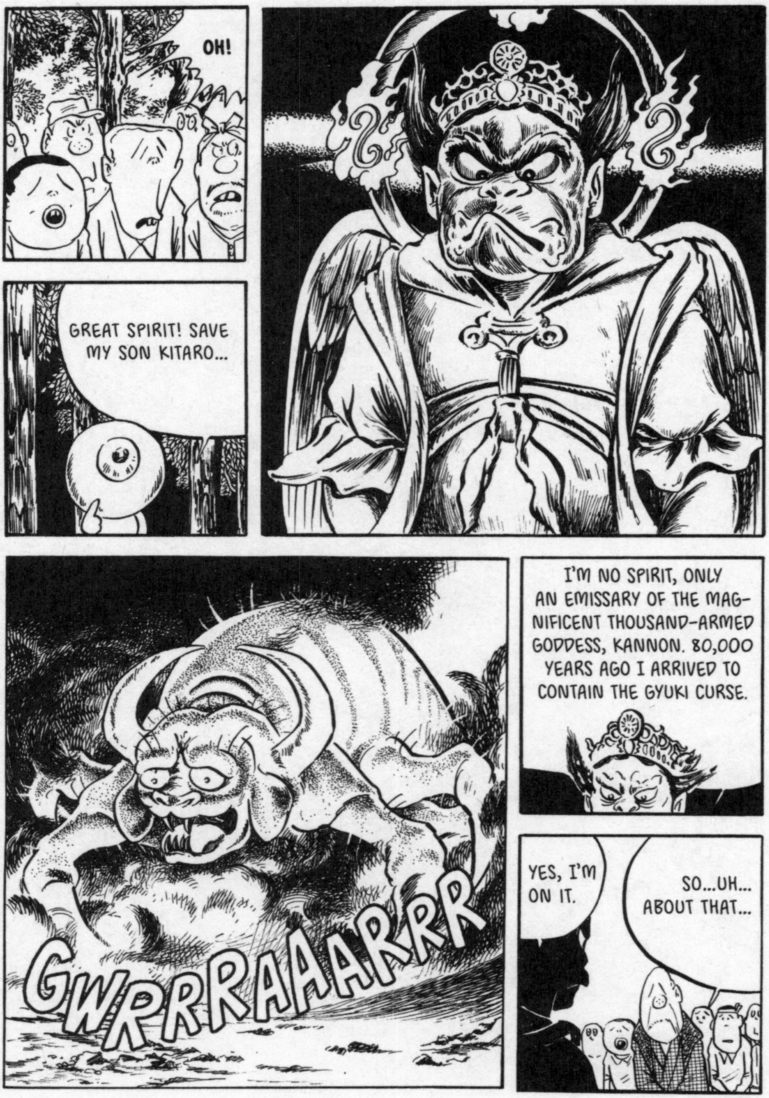
OH!
GREAT SPIRIT! SAVE MY SON KITARO...
I'M NO SPIRIT, ONLY AN EMISSARY OF THE MAG-NIFICENT THOUSAND-ARMED GODDESS, KANNON. 80,000 YEARS AGO I ARRIVED TO CONTAIN THE GYUKI CURSE.
SO...UH... ABOUT THAT...
YES, I'M ON IT.
GWRRRAAARRR

FWHOOOOO

DON'T FORGET THAT'S MY SON IN THERE.

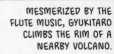

MESMERIZED BY THE FLUTE MUSIC, GYUKITARO CLIMBS THE RIM OF A NEARBY VOLCANO.

FWHEEE

GWRRARR

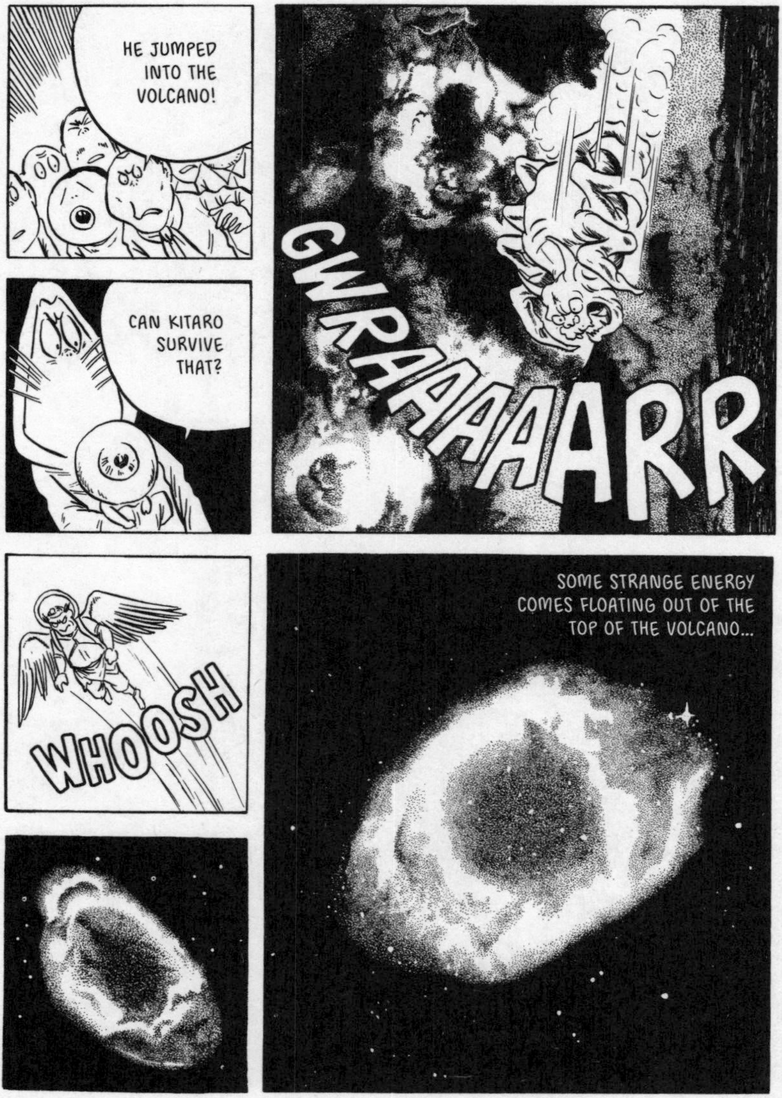
GWRAAAAAARR
HE JUMPED INTO THE VOLCANO!
CAN KITARO SURVIVE THAT?
SOME STRANGE ENERGY COMES FLOATING OUT OF THE TOP OF THE VOLCANO...
WHOOSH

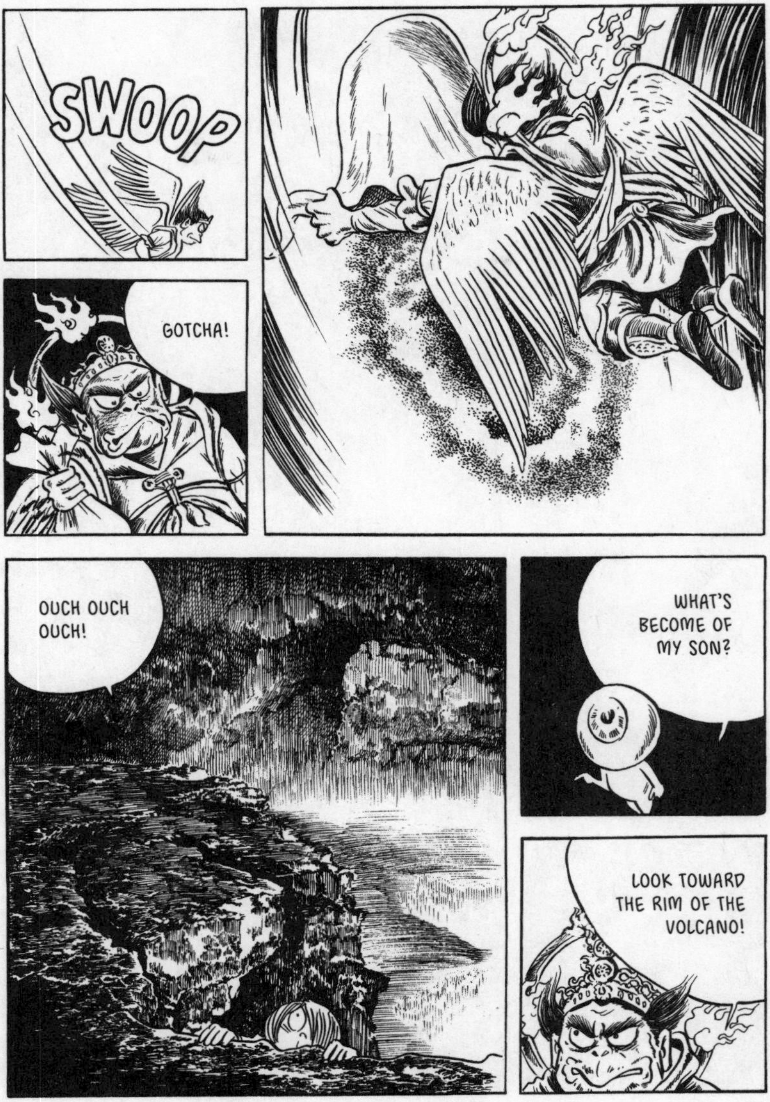
SWOOP
GOTCHA!
WHAT'S BECOME OF MY SON?
LOOK TOWARD THE RIM OF THE VOLCANO!
OUCH OUCH OUCH!

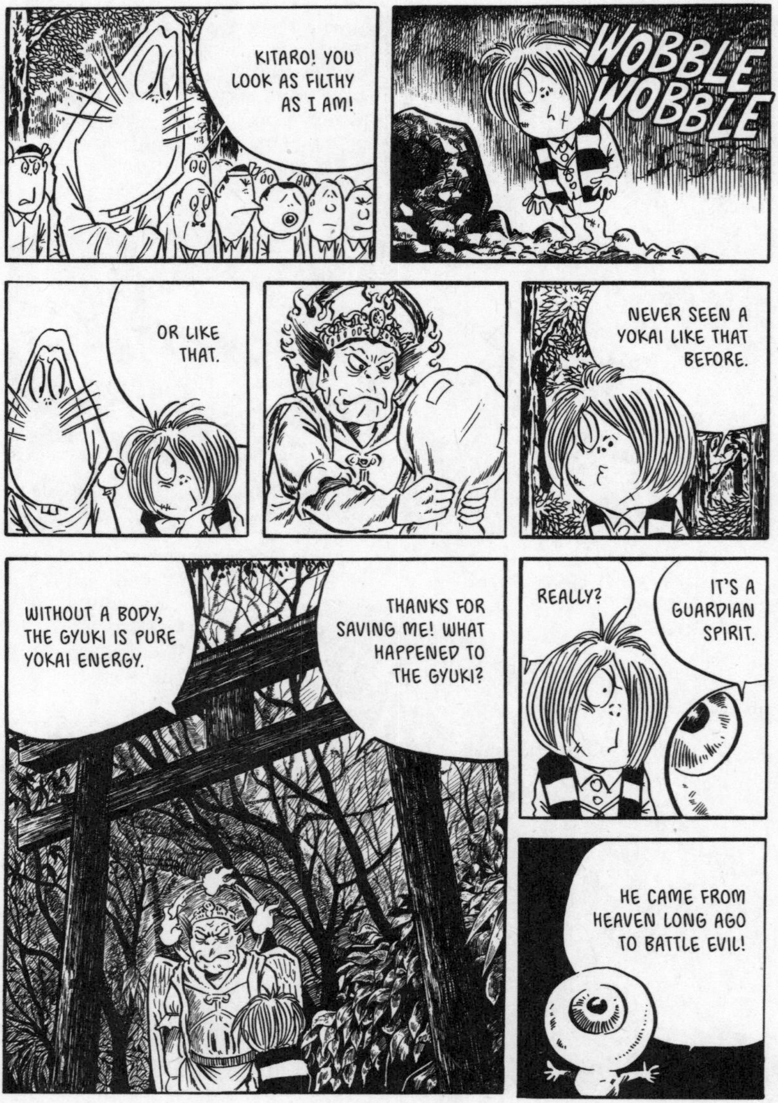
WOBBLE WOBBLE
KITARO! YOU LOOK AS FILTHY AS I AM!
NEVER SEEN A YOKAI LIKE THAT BEFORE.
OR LIKE THAT.
IT'S A GUARDIAN SPIRIT.
REALLY?
HE CAME FROM HEAVEN LONG AGO TO BATTLE EVIL!
THANKS FOR SAVING ME! WHAT HAPPENED TO THE GYUKI?
WITHOUT A BODY, THE GYUKI IS PURE YOKAI ENERGY.

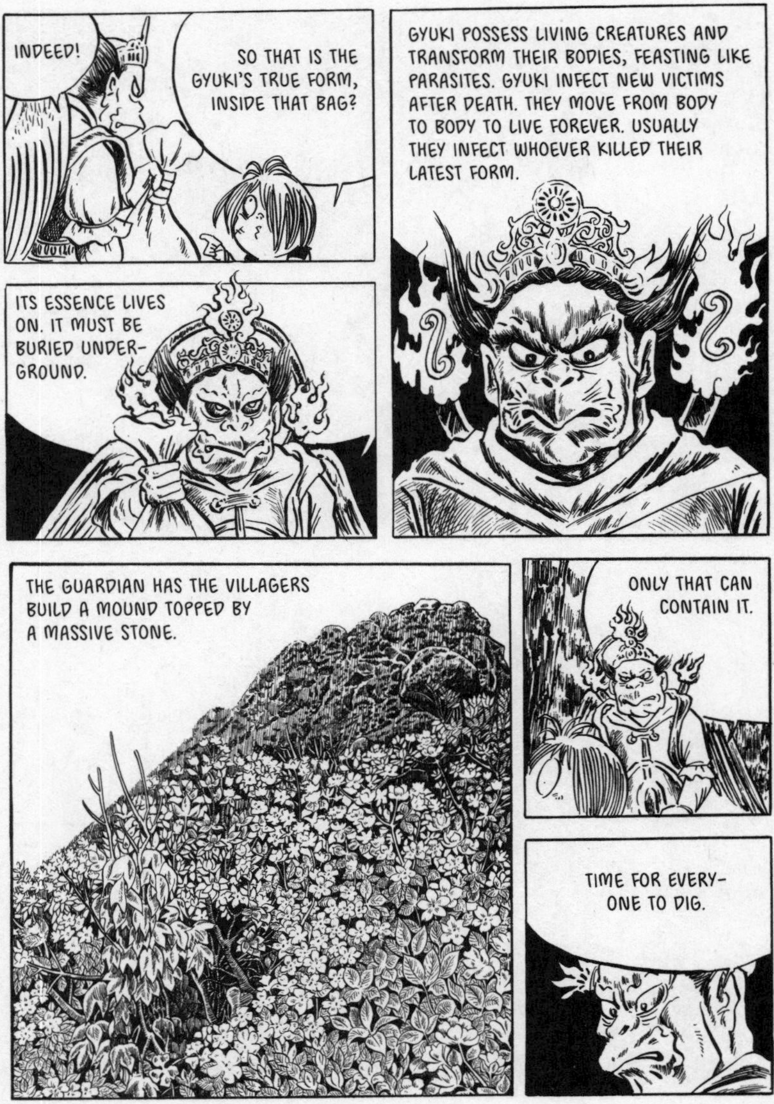
GYUKI POSSESS LIVING CREATURES AND TRANSFORM THEIR BODIES, FEASTING LIKE PARASITES. GYUKI INFECT NEW VICTIMS AFTER DEATH. THEY MOVE FROM BODY TO BODY TO LIVE FOREVER. USUALLY THEY INFECT WHOEVER KILLED THEIR LATEST FORM.
SO THAT IS THE GYUKI'S TRUE FORM, INSIDE THAT BAG?
INDEED!
ITS ESSENCE LIVES ON. IT MUST BE BURIED UNDER-GROUND.
ONLY THAT CAN CONTAIN IT.
TIME FOR EVERY-ONE TO DIG.
THE GUARDIAN HAS THE VILLAGERS BUILD A MOUND TOPPED BY A MASSIVE STONE.

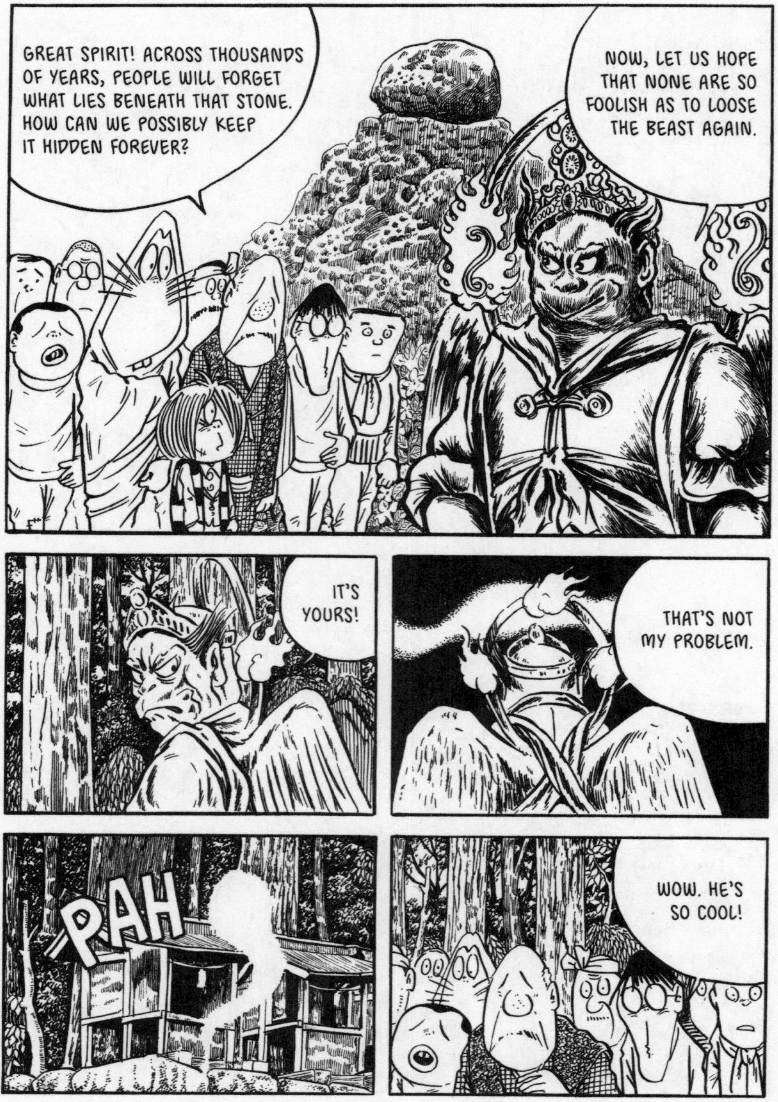
NOW, LET US HOPE THAT NONE ARE SO FOOLISH AS TO LOOSE THE BEAST AGAIN.
GREAT SPIRIT! ACROSS THOUSANDS OF YEARS, PEOPLE WILL FORGET WHAT LIES BENEATH THAT STONE. HOW CAN WE POSSIBLY KEEP IT HIDDEN FOREVER?
THAT'S NOT MY PROBLEM.
IT'S YOURS!
WOW. HE'S SO COOL!
PAH

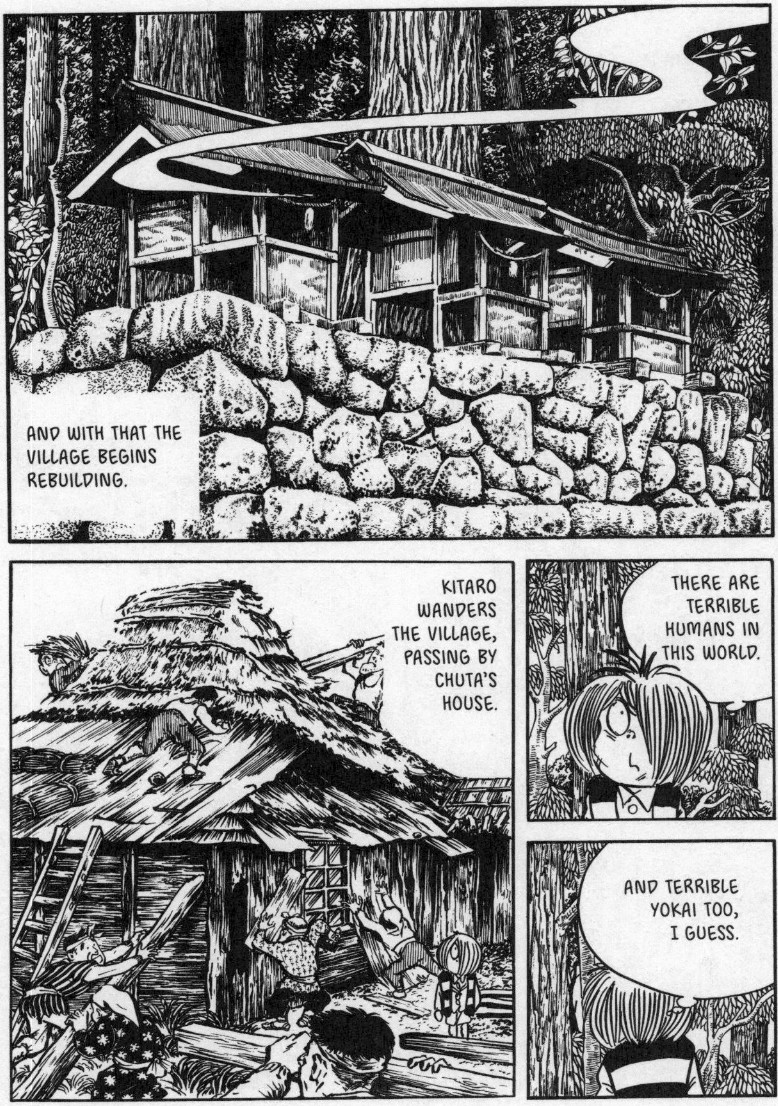
AND WITH THAT THE VILLAGE BEGINS REBUILDING.
THERE ARE TERRIBLE HUMANS IN THIS WORLD.
AND TERRIBLE YOKAI TOO, I GUESS.
KITARO WANDERS THE VILLAGE, PASSING BY CHUTA'S HOUSE.

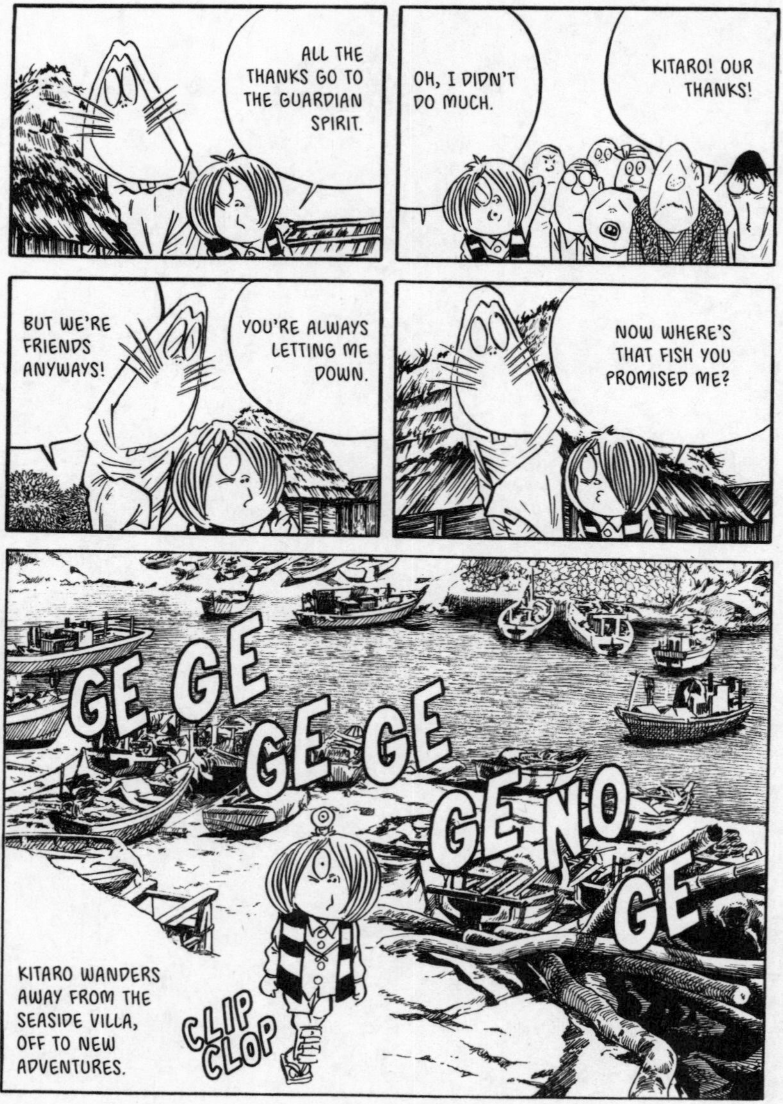
KITARO! OUR THANKS!
OH, I DIDN'T DO MUCH.
ALL THE THANKS GO TO THE GUARDIAN SPIRIT.
NOW WHERE'S THAT FISH YOU PROMISED ME?
YOU'RE ALWAYS LETTING ME DOWN.
BUT WE'RE FRIENDS ANYWAYS!
GE GE GE GE GE NO GE
CLIP CLOP
KITARO WANDERS AWAY FROM THE SEASIDE VILLA, OFF TO NEW ADVENTURES.

YOKAI OF THE MOUNTAIN PASS

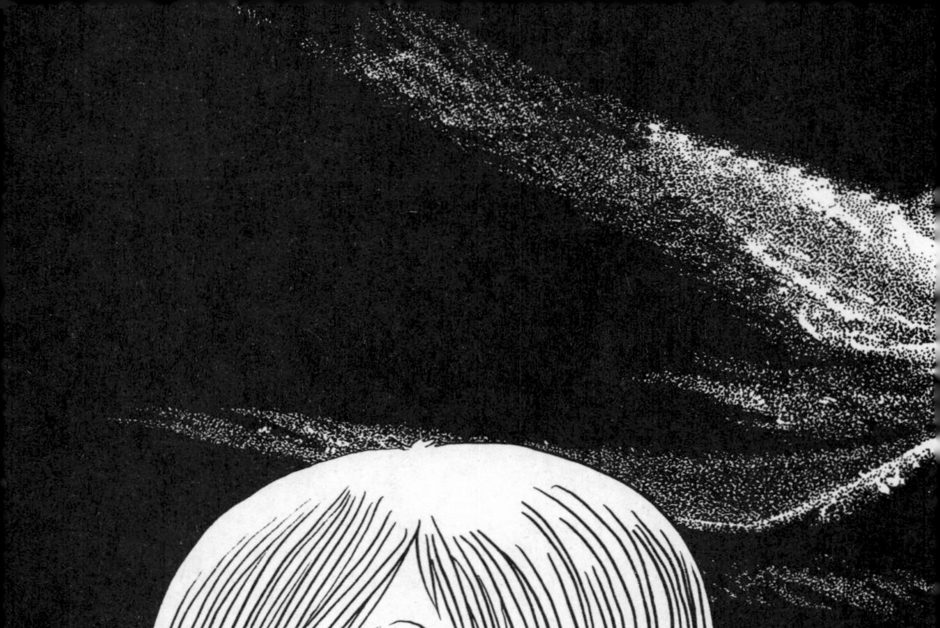

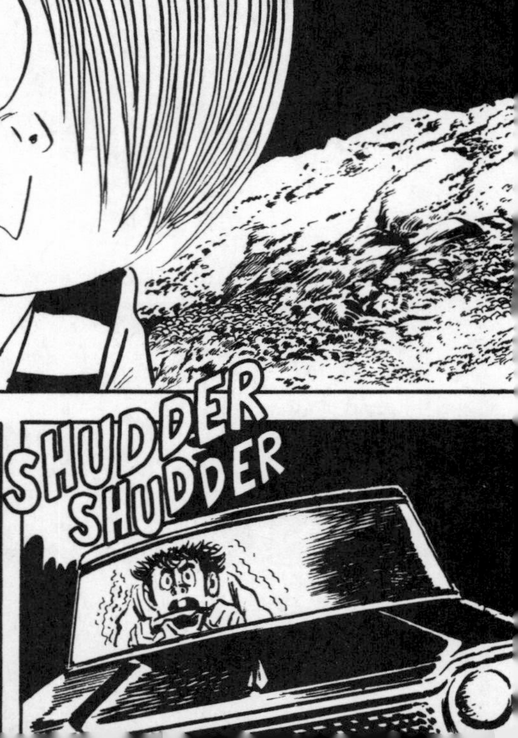
SHUDDER
SHUDDER

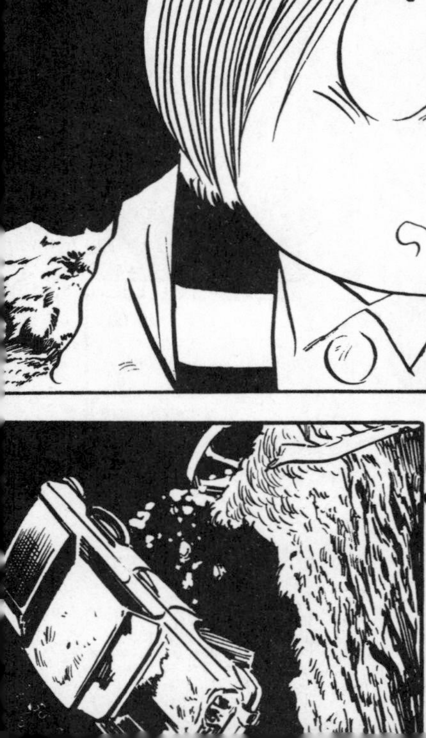

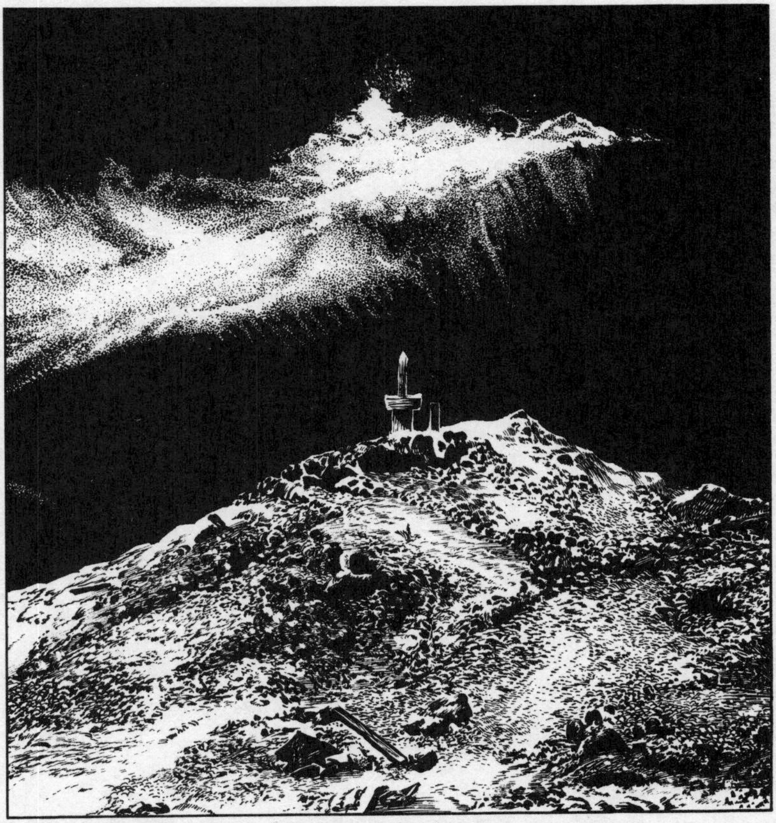

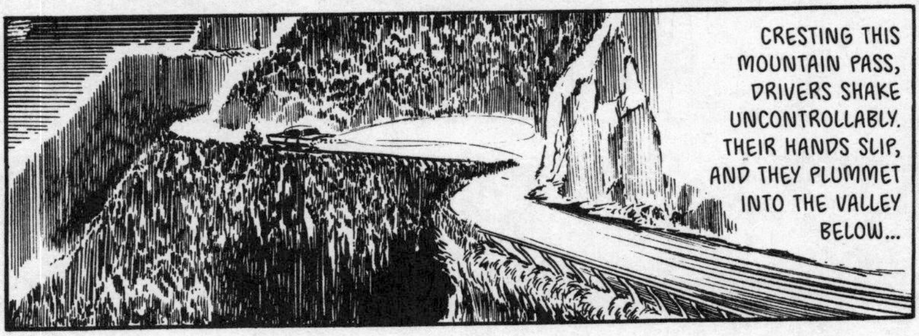
CRESTING THIS MOUNTAIN PASS, DRIVERS SHAKE UNCONTROLLABLY. THEIR HANDS SLIP, AND THEY PLUMMET INTO THE VALLEY BELOW...

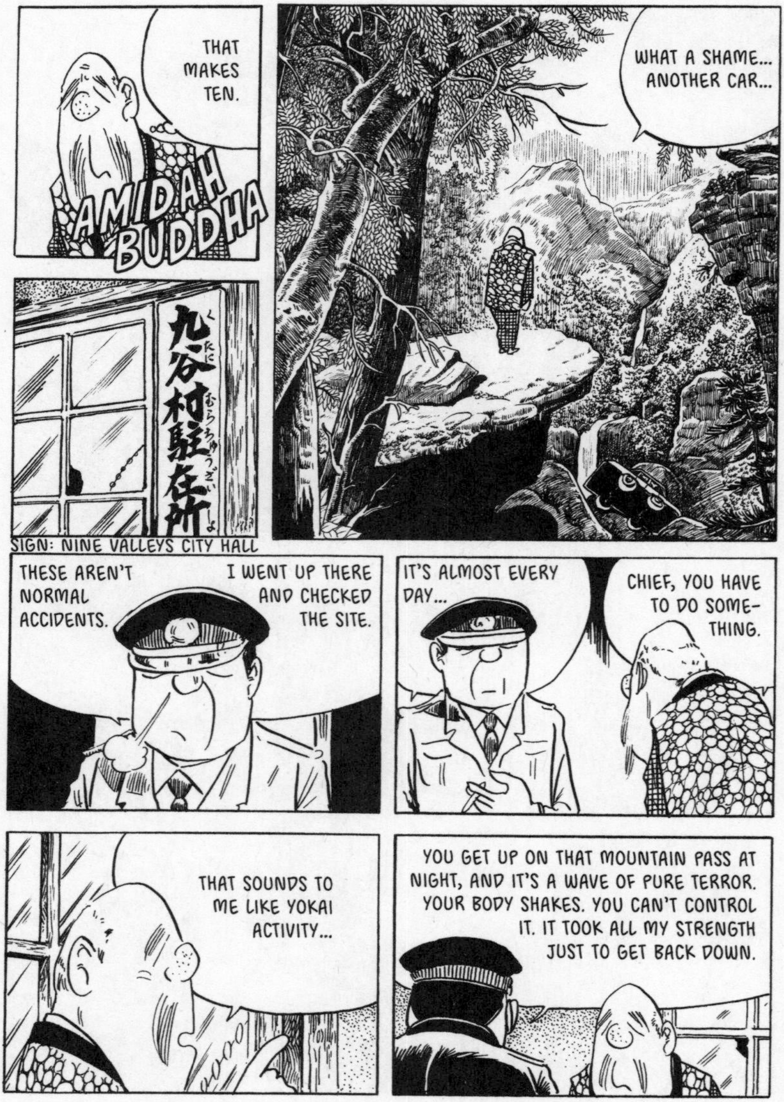
WHAT A SHAME... ANOTHER CAR...
THAT MAKES TEN.
AMIDAH BUDDHA
九谷村駐在所
SIGN: NINE VALLEYS CITY HALL
CHIEF, YOU HAVE TO DO SOME-THING.
IT'S ALMOST EVERY DAY...
I WENT UP THERE AND CHECKED THE SITE.
THESE AREN'T NORMAL ACCIDENTS.
YOU GET UP ON THAT MOUNTAIN PASS AT NIGHT, AND IT'S A WAVE OF PURE TERROR. YOUR BODY SHAKES. YOU CAN'T CONTROL IT. IT TOOK ALL MY STRENGTH JUST TO GET BACK DOWN.
THAT SOUNDS TO ME LIKE YOKAI ACTIVITY...

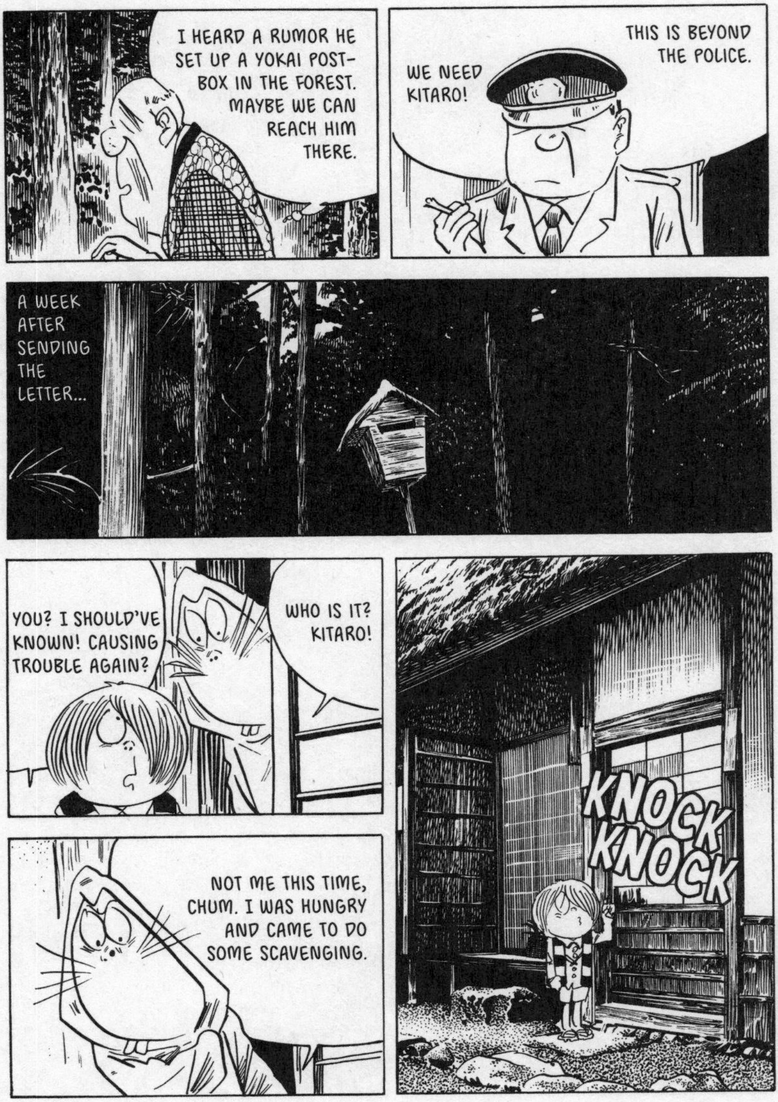
THIS IS BEYOND THE POLICE.
WE NEED KITARO!
I HEARD A RUMOR HE SET UP A YOKAI POST-BOX IN THE FOREST. MAYBE WE CAN REACH HIM THERE.
A WEEK AFTER SENDING THE LETTER...
KNOCK KNOCK
WHO IS IT? KITARO!
YOU? I SHOULD'VE KNOWN! CAUSING TROUBLE AGAIN?
NOT ME THIS TIME, CHUM. I WAS HUNGRY AND CAME TO DO SOME SCAVENGING.

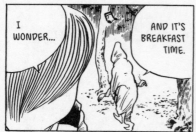

FOR REAL?
ABSOLUTELY! THERE'S GOOD EATS IN THIS FOREST!
AND IT'S BREAKFAST TIME.
I WONDER...
ARE YOU KITARO?
THAT'S ME. YOU KNOW THAT GUY THAT WAS JUST HERE...?
THAT VAGABOND? I FELT SORRY FOR HIM AND LET HIM STAY. HEH HEH HEH
COME ON IN.
I THINK I KNOW WHAT'S GOING ON.
DID YOU BURN ANYTHING LATELY? ANY OLD PICTURES OR KNICK KNACKS?
WELL...
I SUPPOSE WE DID. IT'S AN OLD HOUSE WITH LOTS OF JUNK. I WAS CLEANING OUT THE SHED AND FOUND A HUGE PAINTING, ALL FALLING APART.

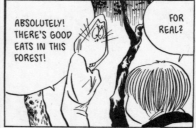

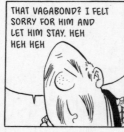

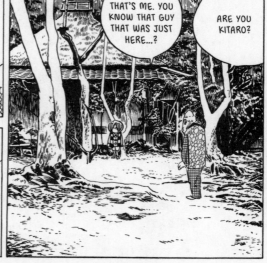

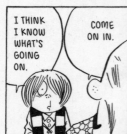

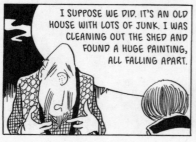

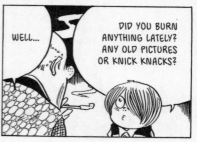

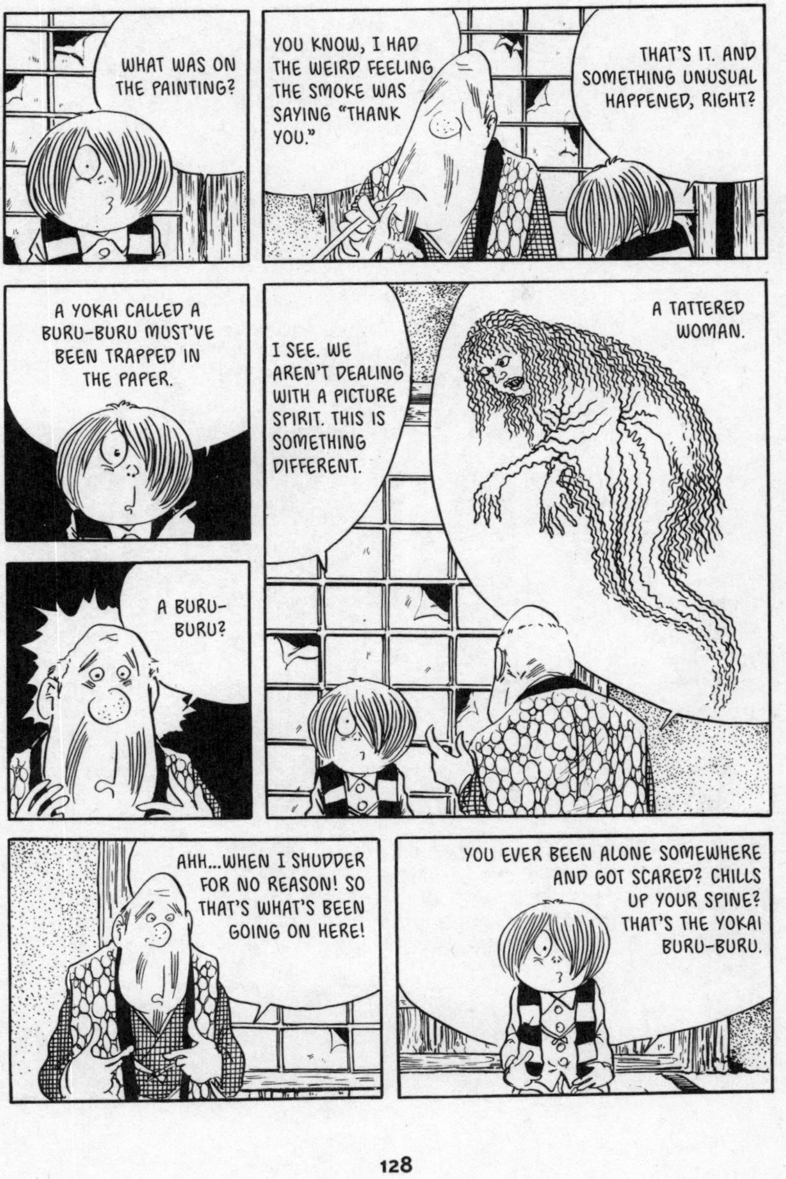
THAT'S IT. AND SOMETHING UNUSUAL HAPPENED, RIGHT?
YOU KNOW, I HAD THE WEIRD FEELING THE SMOKE WAS SAYING "THANK YOU."
WHAT WAS ON THE PAINTING?
A TATTERED WOMAN.
I SEE. WE AREN'T DEALING WITH A PICTURE SPIRIT. THIS IS SOMETHING DIFFERENT.
A YOKAI CALLED A BURU-BURU MUST'VE BEEN TRAPPED IN THE PAPER.
A BURU-BURU?
YOU EVER BEEN ALONE SOMEWHERE AND GOT SCARED? CHILLS UP YOUR SPINE? THAT'S THE YOKAI BURU-BURU.
AHH...WHEN I SHUDDER FOR NO REASON! SO THAT'S WHAT'S BEEN GOING ON HERE!

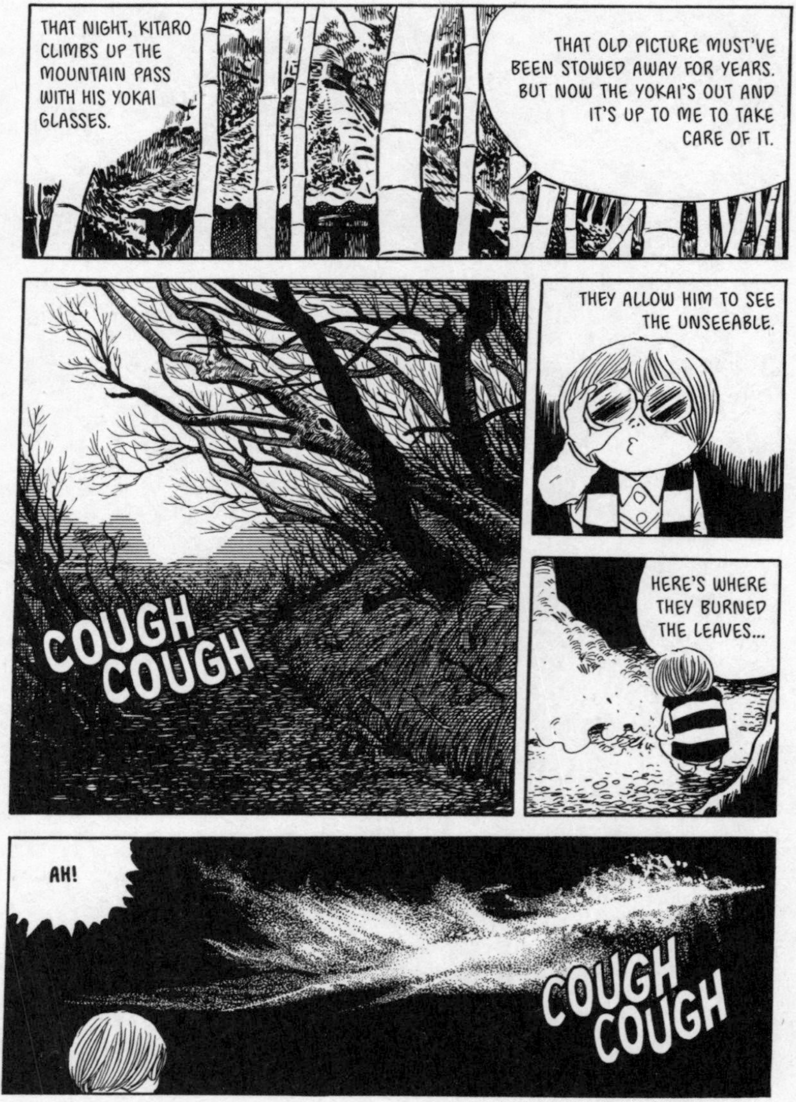
THAT OLD PICTURE MUST'VE BEEN STOWED AWAY FOR YEARS. BUT NOW THE YOKAI'S OUT AND IT'S UP TO ME TO TAKE CARE OF IT.
THAT NIGHT, KITARO CLIMBS UP THE MOUNTAIN PASS WITH HIS YOKAI GLASSES.
THEY ALLOW HIM TO SEE THE UNSEEABLE.
HERE'S WHERE THEY BURNED THE LEAVES...
COUGH COUGH
AH!
COUGH COUGH

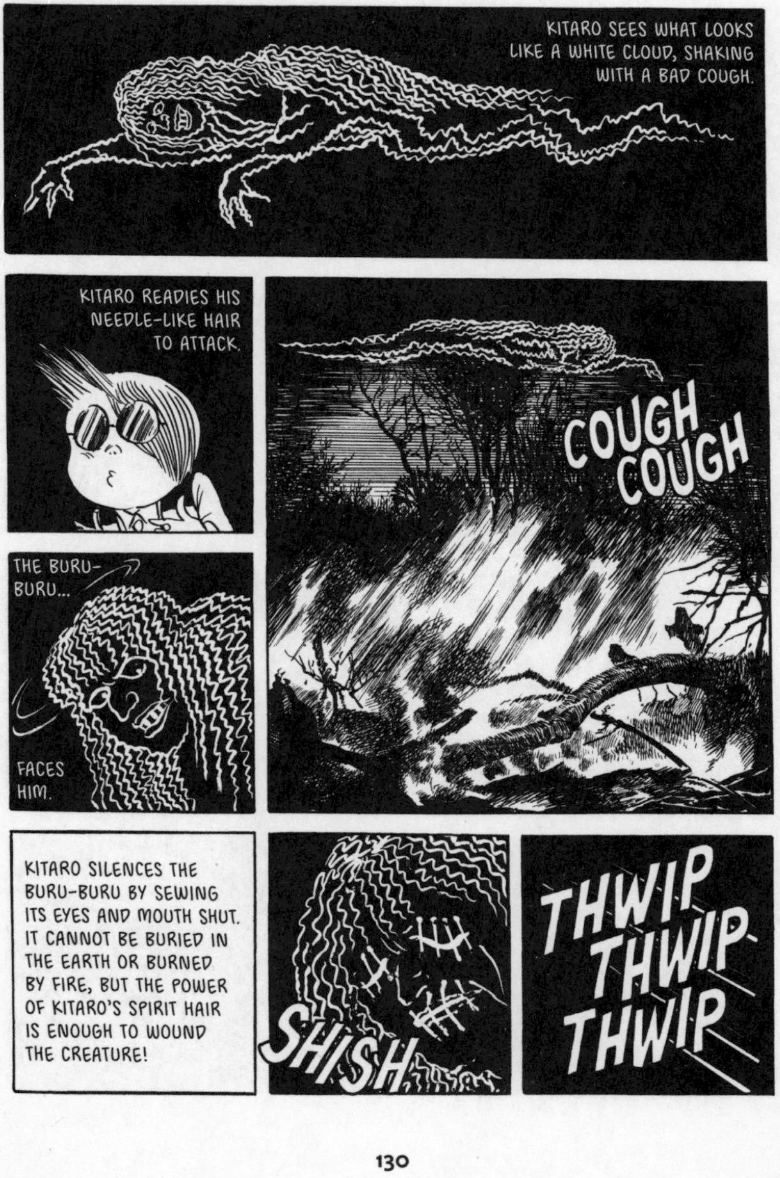
KITARO SEES WHAT LOOKS LIKE A WHITE CLOUD, SHAKING WITH A BAD COUGH.
COUGH COUGH
KITARO READIES HIS NEEDLE-LIKE HAIR TO ATTACK.
THE BURU-BURU...
FACES HIM.
THWIP THWIP-THWIP
SHISH
KITARO SILENCES THE BURU-BURU BY SEWING ITS EYES AND MOUTH SHUT. IT CANNOT BE BURIED IN THE EARTH OR BURNED BY FIRE, BUT THE POWER OF KITARO'S SPIRIT HAIR IS ENOUGH TO WOUND THE CREATURE!

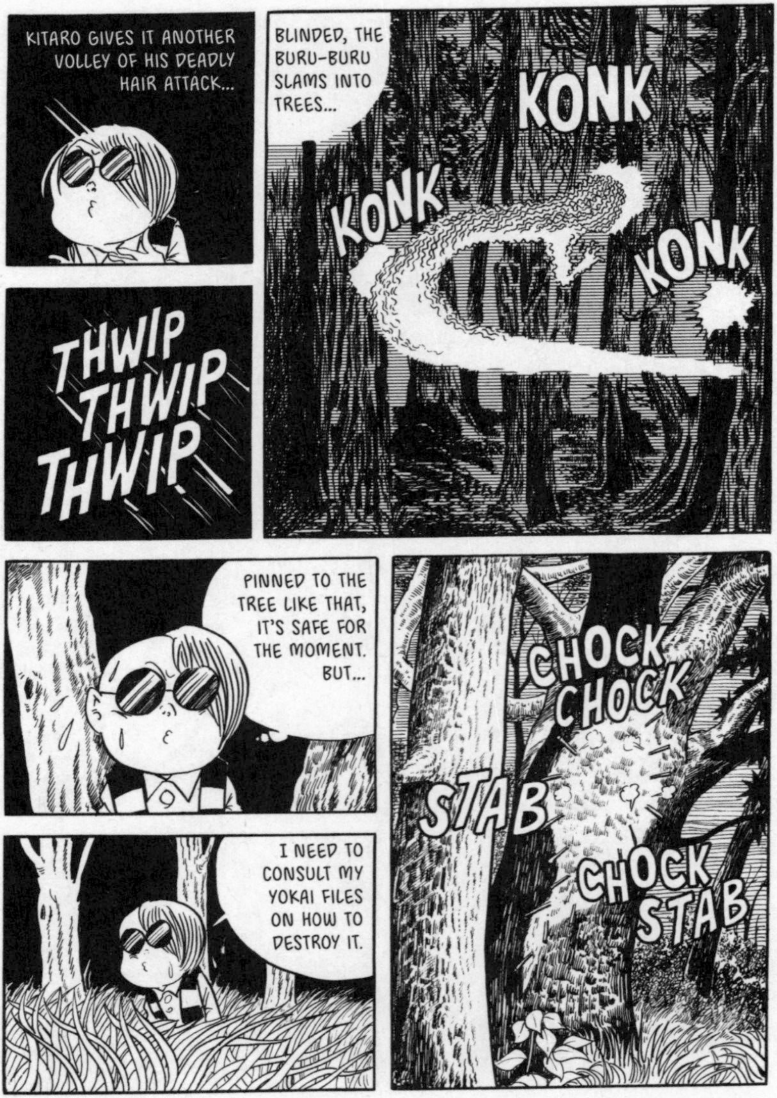
BLINDED, THE BURU-BURU SLAMS INTO TREES...
KONK
KONK
KONK
KITARO GIVES IT ANOTHER VOLLEY OF HIS DEADLY HAIR ATTACK...
THWIP THWIP THWIP
CHOCK CHOCK
STAB
CHOCK STAB
PINNED TO THE TREE LIKE THAT, IT'S SAFE FOR THE MOMENT. BUT...
I NEED TO CONSULT MY YOKAI FILES ON HOW TO DESTROY IT.

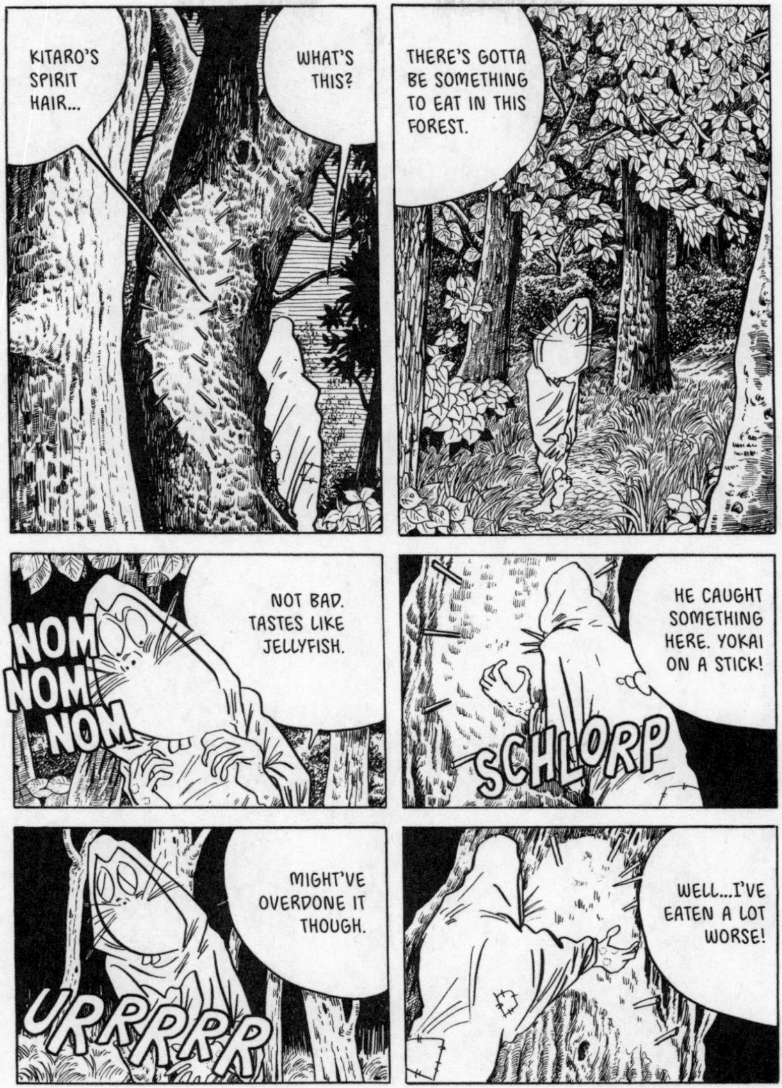
THERE'S GOTTA BE SOMETHING TO EAT IN THIS FOREST.
WHAT'S THIS?
KITARO'S SPIRIT HAIR...
HE CAUGHT SOMETHING HERE. YOKAI ON A STICK!
SCHLORP
NOT BAD. TASTES LIKE JELLYFISH.
NOM NOM NOM
WELL...I'VE EATEN A LOT WORSE!
MIGHT'VE OVERDONE IT THOUGH.
URRRRRR

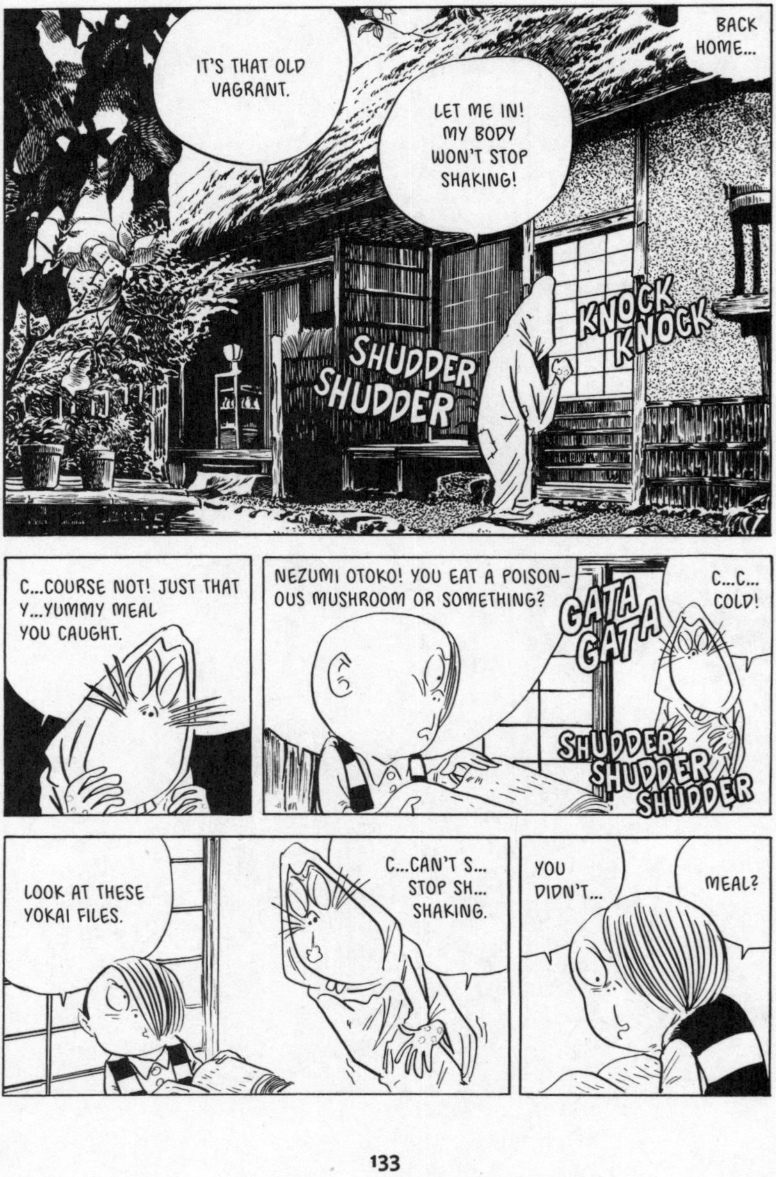
BACK HOME...
KNOCK KNOCK
LET ME IN! MY BODY WON'T STOP SHAKING!
SHUDDER SHUDDER
IT'S THAT OLD VAGRANT.
C...C... COLD!
GATA GATA
NEZUMI OTOKO! YOU EAT A POISON-OUS MUSHROOM OR SOMETHING?
SHUDDER SHUDDER SHUDDER
C...COURSE NOT! JUST THAT Y...YUMMY MEAL YOU CAUGHT.
MEAL?
YOU DIDN'T...
C...CAN'T S... STOP SH... SHAKING.
LOOK AT THESE YOKAI FILES.

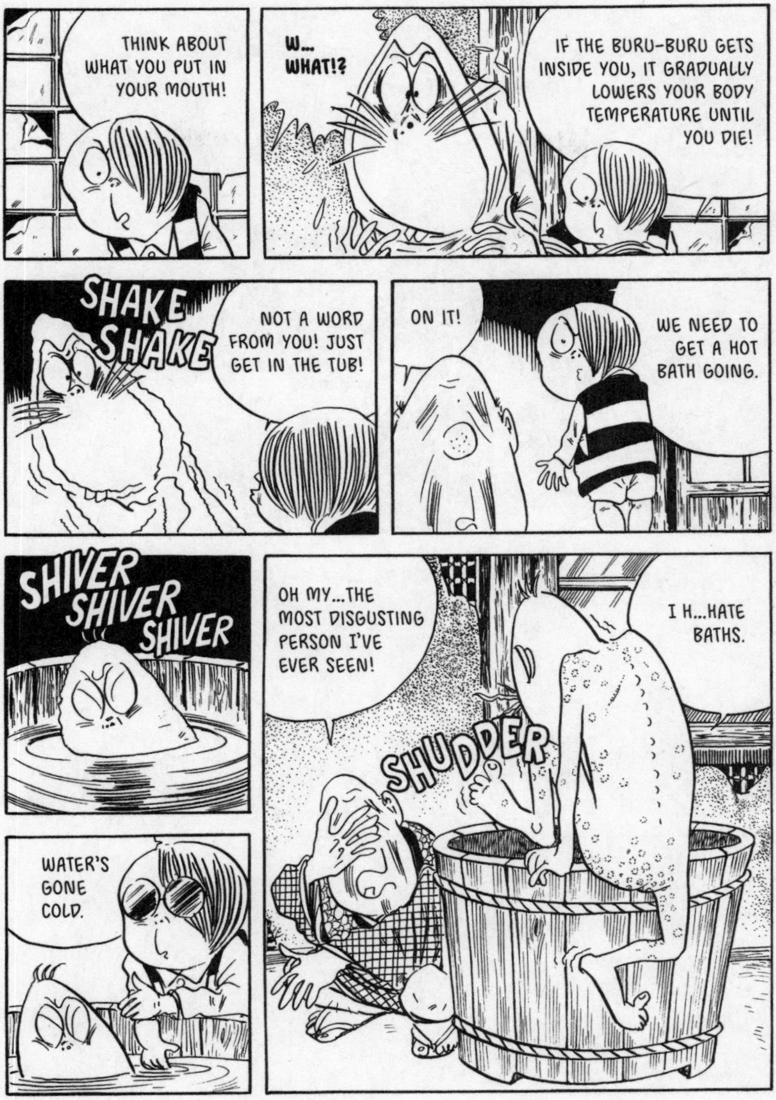
IF THE BURU-BURU GETS INSIDE YOU, IT GRADUALLY LOWERS YOUR BODY TEMPERATURE UNTIL YOU DIE!
W... WHAT!?
THINK ABOUT WHAT YOU PUT IN YOUR MOUTH!
WE NEED TO GET A HOT BATH GOING.
ON IT!
NOT A WORD FROM YOU! JUST GET IN THE TUB!
SHAKE SHAKE
I H...HATE BATHS.
OH MY...THE MOST DISGUSTING PERSON I'VE EVER SEEN!
SHUDDER
SHIVER SHIVER SHIVER
WATER'S GONE COLD.

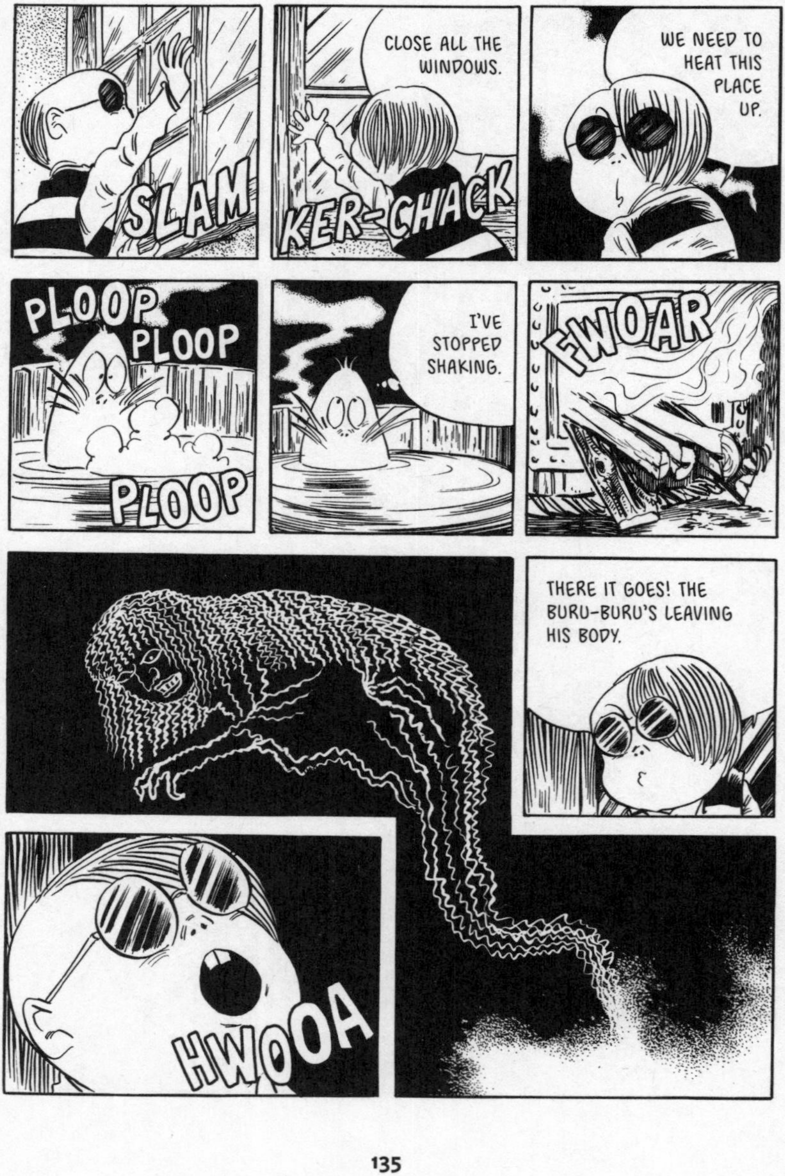
WE NEED TO HEAT THIS PLACE UP.
CLOSE ALL THE WINDOWS.
KER-CHACK
SLAM
FWOAR
I'VE STOPPED SHAKING.
PLOOP
PLOOP
PLOOP
THERE IT GOES! THE BURU-BURU'S LEAVING HIS BODY.
HWOOA

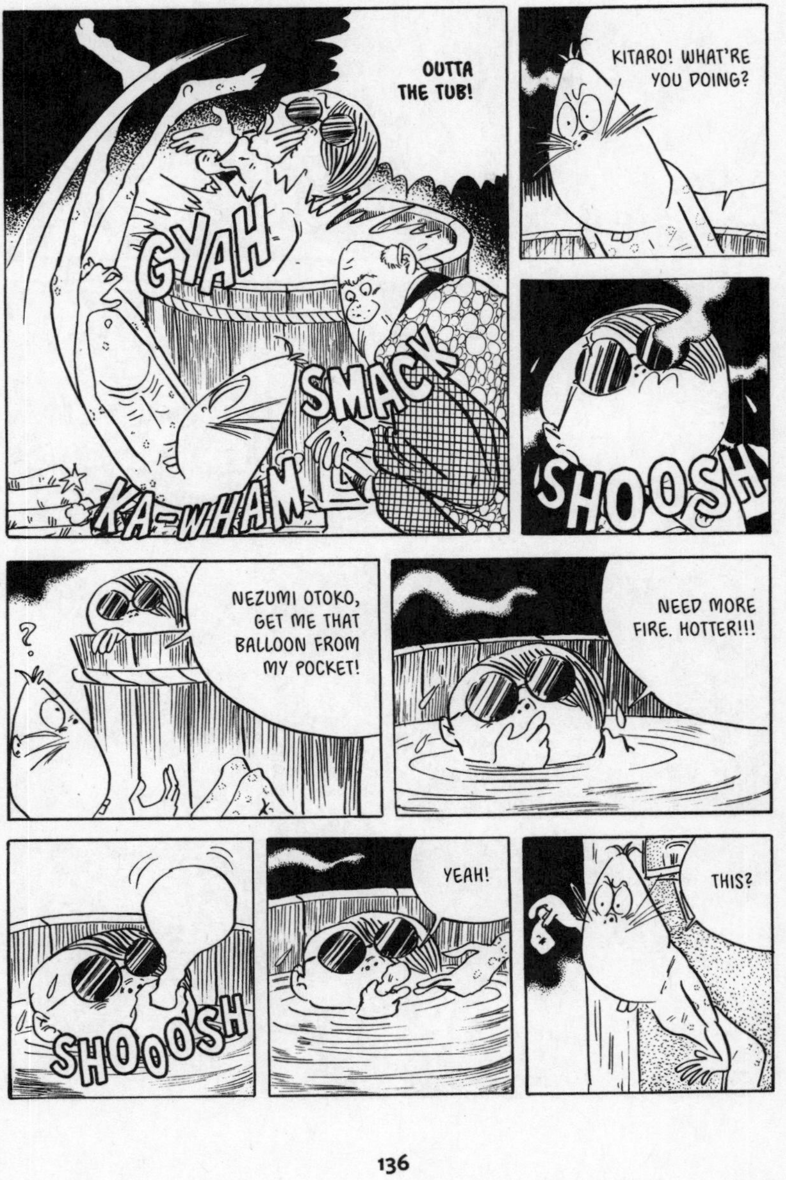
KITARO! WHAT'RE YOU DOING?
SHOOSH
OUTTA THE TUB!
GYAH
SMACK
KA-WHAM
NEED MORE FIRE. HOTTER!!!
NEZUMI OTOKO, GET ME THAT BALLOON FROM MY POCKET!
?
THIS?
YEAH!
SHOOOSH

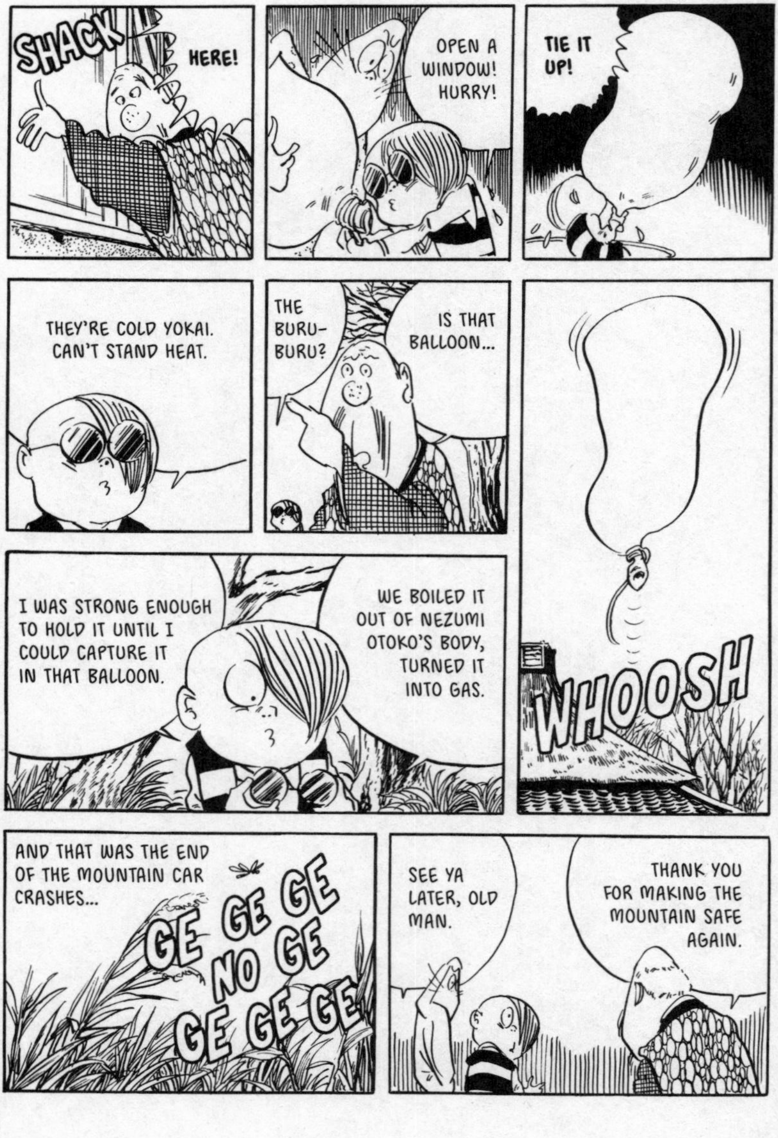
TIE IT UP!
OPEN A WINDOW! HURRY!
SHACK
HERE!
WHOOSH
IS THAT BALLOON...
THE BURU-BURU?
THEY'RE COLD YOKAI. CAN'T STAND HEAT.
WE BOILED IT OUT OF NEZUMI OTOKO'S BODY, TURNED IT INTO GAS.
I WAS STRONG ENOUGH TO HOLD IT UNTIL I COULD CAPTURE IT IN THAT BALLOON.
THANK YOU FOR MAKING THE MOUNTAIN SAFE AGAIN.
SEE YA LATER, OLD MAN.
AND THAT WAS THE END OF THE MOUNTAIN CAR CRASHES...
GE GE GE NO GE GE GE GE

MAKURA GAESHI

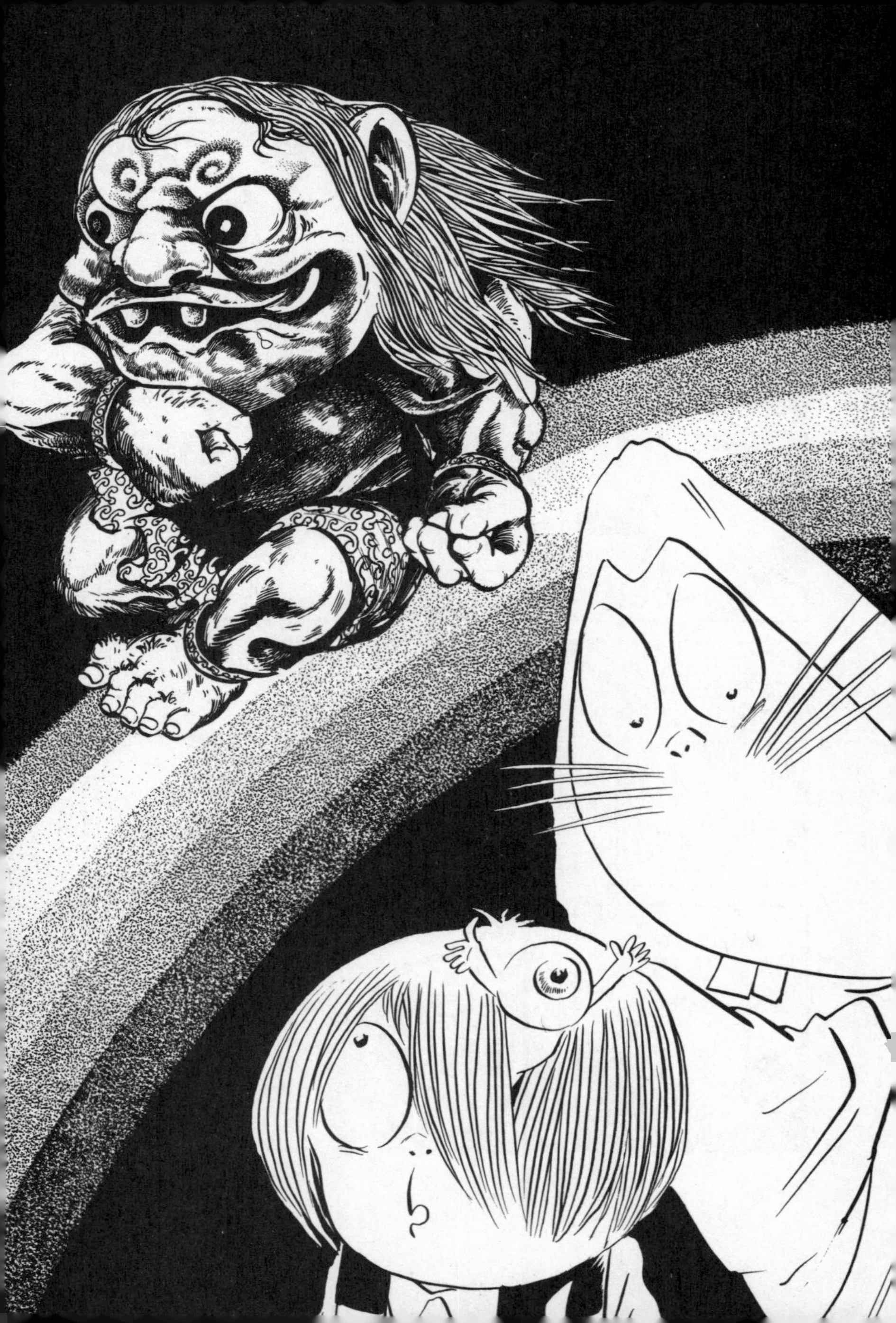

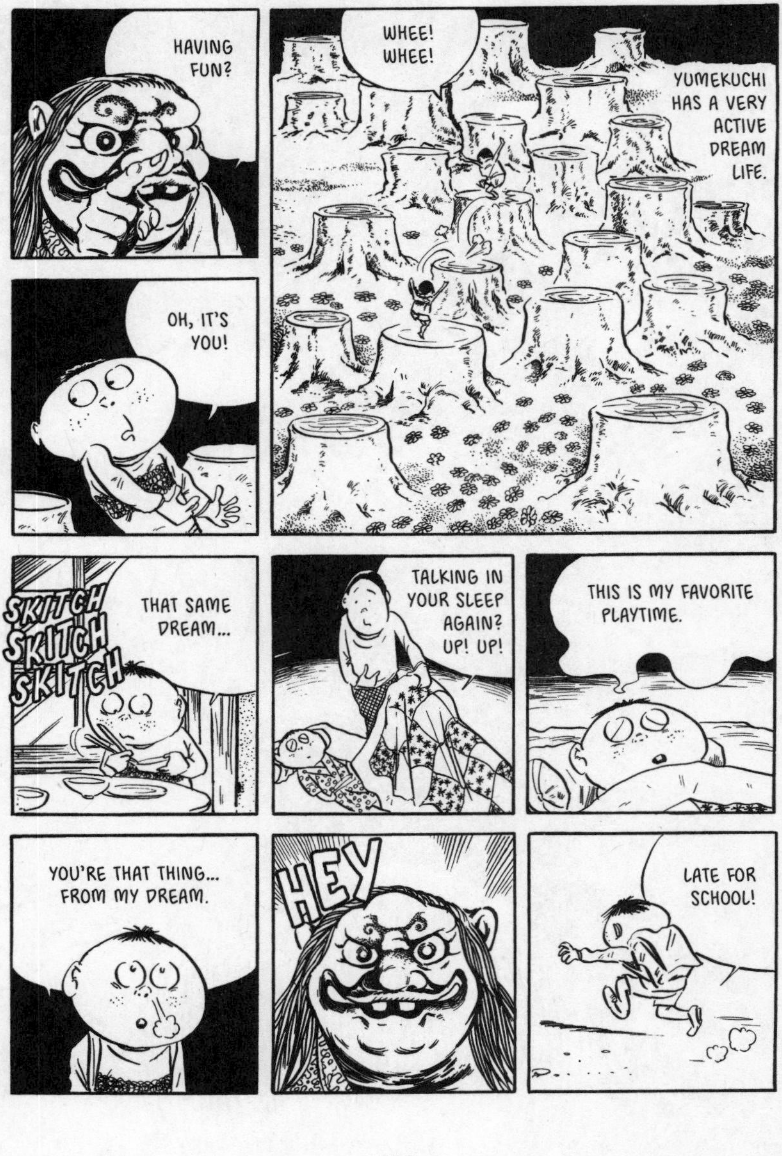
YUMEKUCHI HAS A VERY ACTIVE DREAM LIFE.
WHEE! WHEE!
HAVING FUN?
OH, IT'S YOU!
THIS IS MY FAVORITE PLAYTIME.
TALKING IN YOUR SLEEP AGAIN? UP! UP!
THAT SAME DREAM...
SKITCH SKITCH SKITCH
LATE FOR SCHOOL!
HEY
YOU'RE THAT THING... FROM MY DREAM.

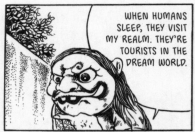

I'M MAKURA GAESHI, RESIDENT OF THE LAND OF DREAMS.
LAND OF DREAMS?
WHEN HUMANS SLEEP, THEY VISIT MY REALM. THEY'RE TOURISTS IN THE DREAM WORLD.
UNDERSTAND?
NOT REALLY. BUT I GOTTA GET TO CLASS.
I'LL BE WAITING HERE FOR YOU.
YUMEKUCHI DIDN'T COME HOME THAT NIGHT.
IT'S BEEN THREE DAYS.
THE POLICE HAVEN'T FOUND A CLUE. I'M WORRIED...
I WAS DOING MY OWN RESEARCH, AND I READ SOMETHING ABOUT A YOKAI CALLED A MAKURA GAESHI.
A YOKAI?
FROM THE DREAMLANDS.
YUMEKUCHI ALWAYS HAD THE STRANGEST DREAMS.

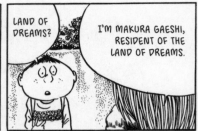

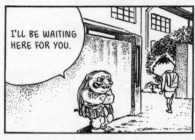

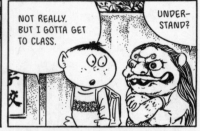

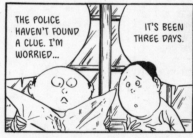

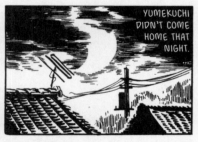

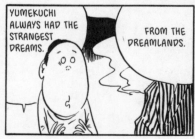

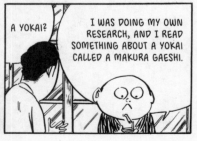

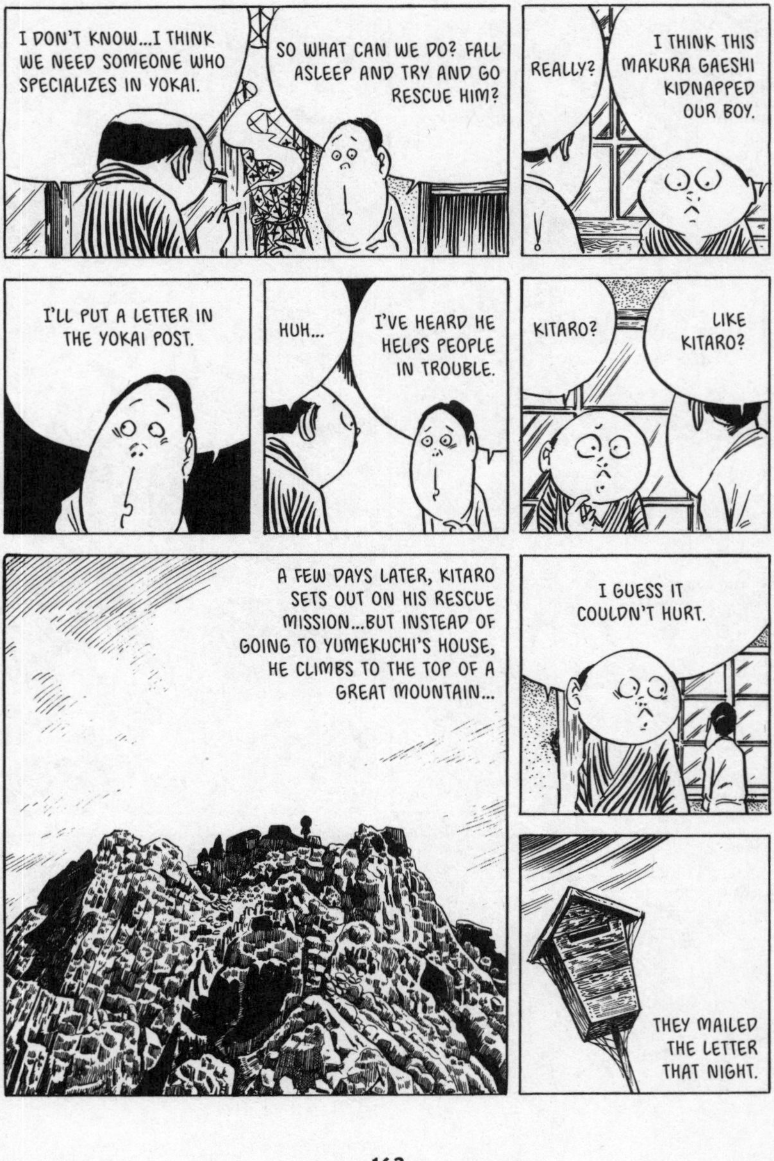
I THINK THIS MAKURA GAESHI KIDNAPPED OUR BOY.
REALLY?
!
SO WHAT CAN WE DO? FALL ASLEEP AND TRY AND GO RESCUE HIM?
I DON'T KNOW...I THINK WE NEED SOMEONE WHO SPECIALIZES IN YOKAI.
LIKE KITARO?
KITARO?
I'VE HEARD HE HELPS PEOPLE IN TROUBLE.
HUH...
I'LL PUT A LETTER IN THE YOKAI POST.
I GUESS IT COULDN'T HURT.
THEY MAILED THE LETTER THAT NIGHT.
A FEW DAYS LATER, KITARO SETS OUT ON HIS RESCUE MISSION...BUT INSTEAD OF GOING TO YUMEKUCHI'S HOUSE, HE CLIMBS TO THE TOP OF A GREAT MOUNTAIN...

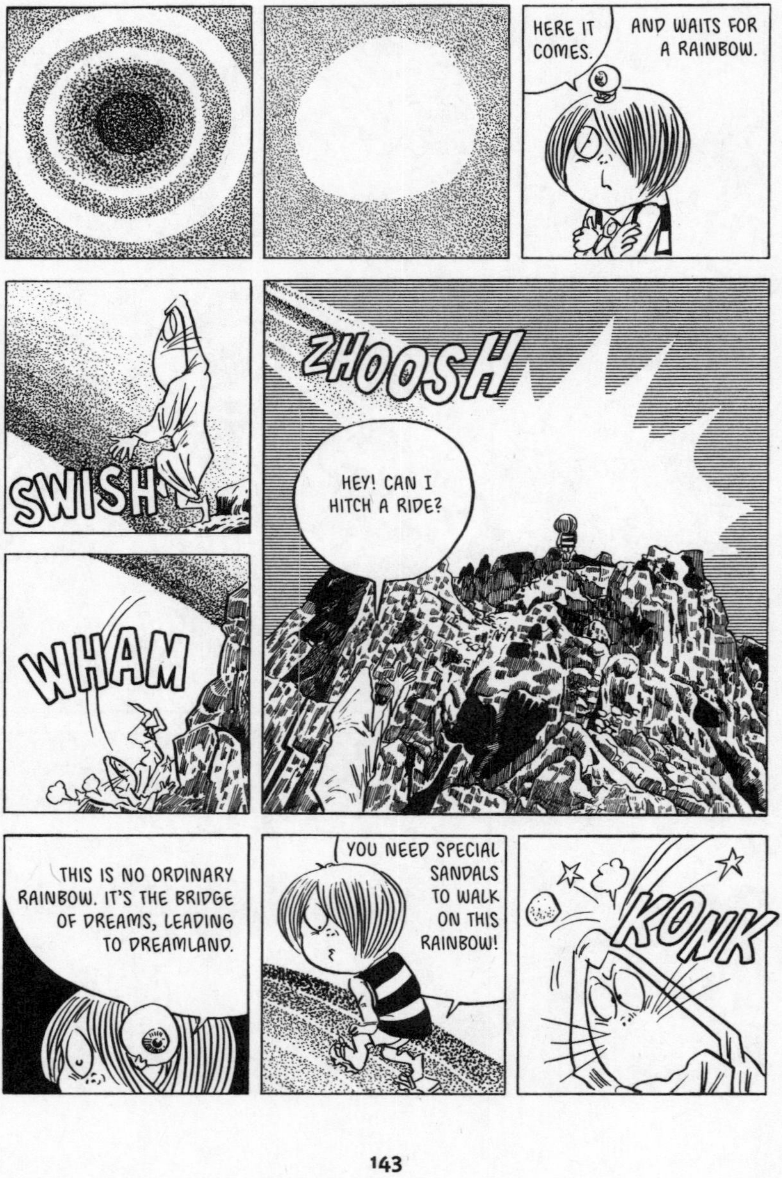

AND WAITS FOR A RAINBOW.
HERE IT COMES.
ZHOOSH
HEY! CAN I HITCH A RIDE?
SWISH
WHAM
KONK
YOU NEED SPECIAL SANDALS TO WALK ON THIS RAINBOW!
THIS IS NO ORDINARY RAINBOW. IT'S THE BRIDGE OF DREAMS, LEADING TO DREAMLAND.

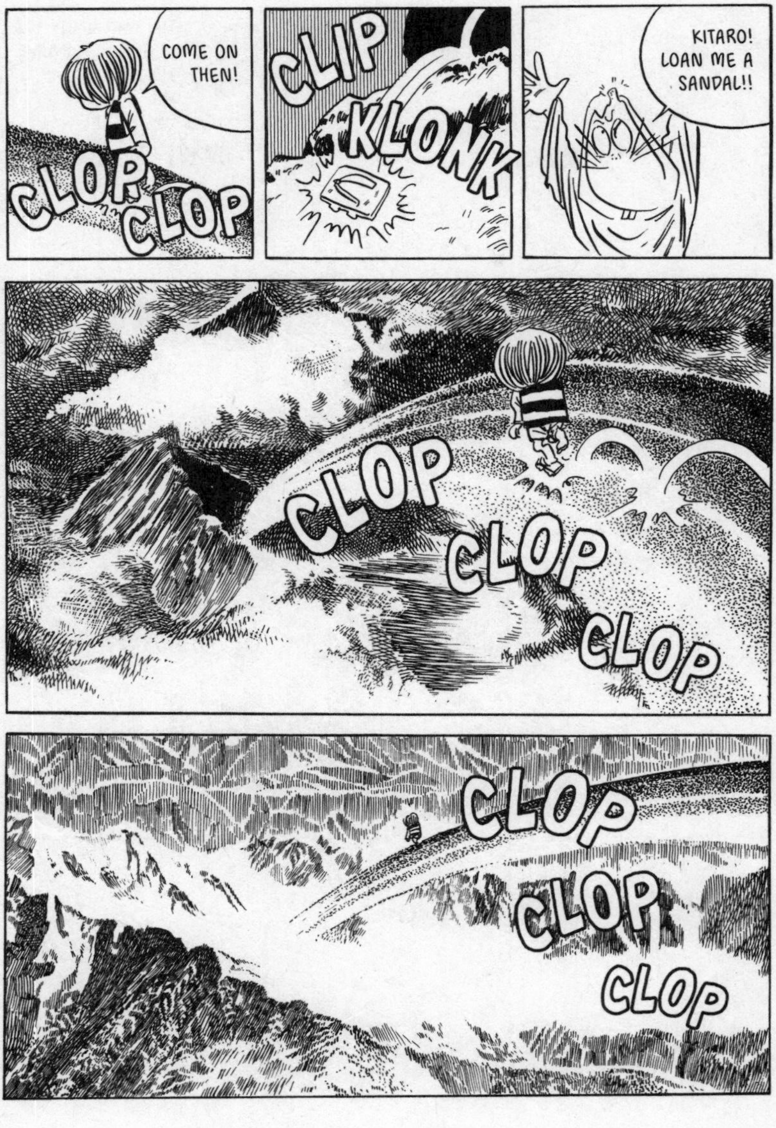
KITARO! LOAN ME A SANDAL!!
CLIP
KLONK
COME ON THEN!
CLOP
CLOP
CLOP
CLOP
CLOP
CLOP
CLOP
CLOP

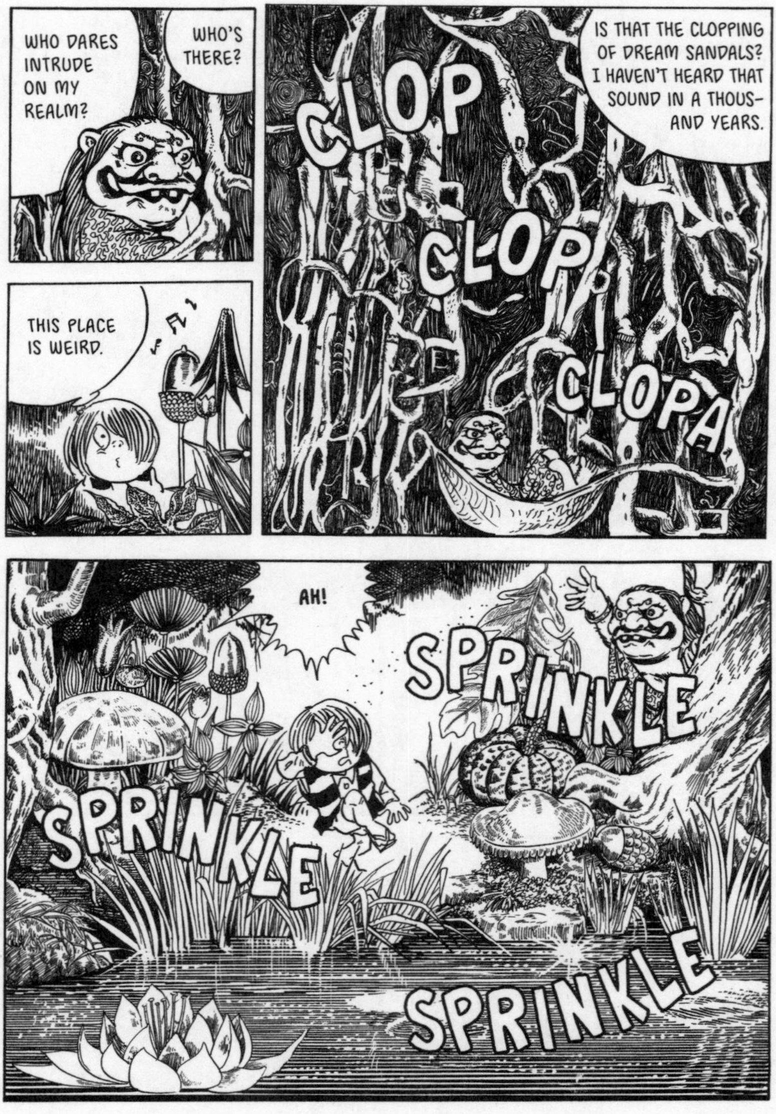
IS THAT THE CLOPPING OF DREAM SANDALS? I HAVEN'T HEARD THAT SOUND IN A THOUSAND YEARS.
CLOP
CLOP
CLOPA
WHO'S THERE?
WHO DARES INTRUDE ON MY REALM?
THIS PLACE IS WEIRD.
AH!
SPRINKLE
SPRINKLE
SPRINKLE

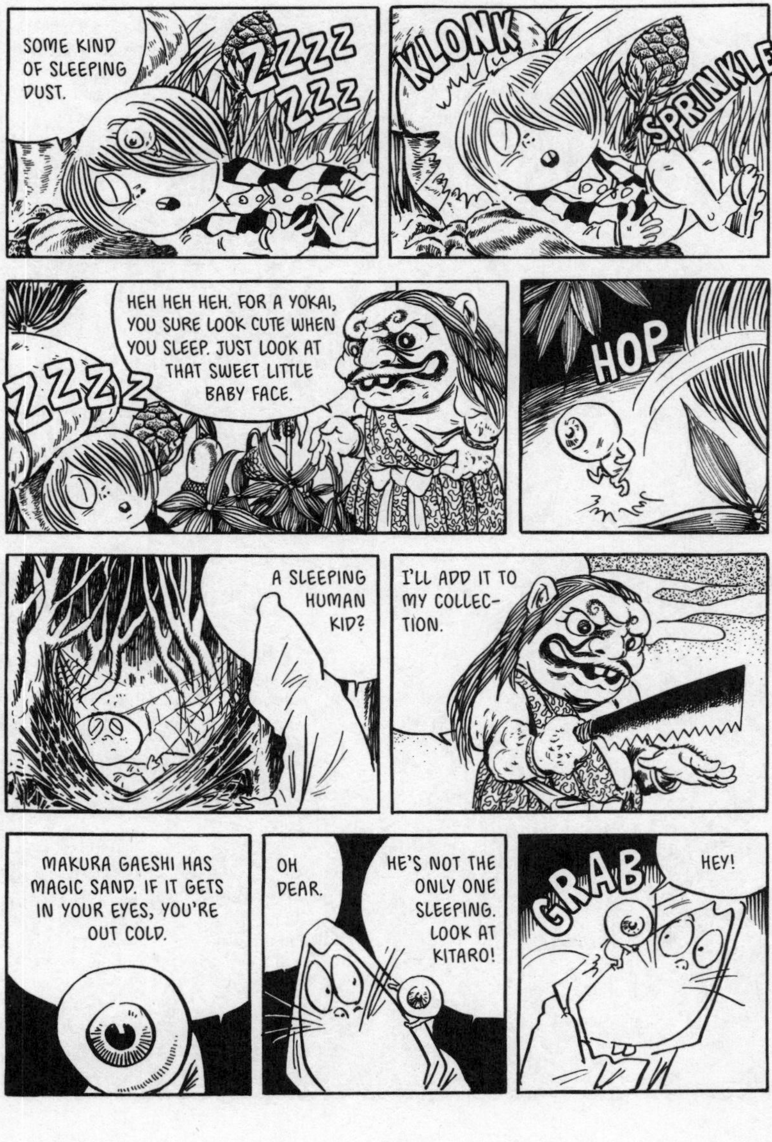
KLONK
SPRINKLE
SOME KIND OF SLEEPING DUST.
ZZZZ ZZZ
HOP
HEH HEH HEH. FOR A YOKAI, YOU SURE LOOK CUTE WHEN YOU SLEEP. JUST LOOK AT THAT SWEET LITTLE BABY FACE.
ZZZZ
I'LL ADD IT TO MY COLLECTION.
A SLEEPING HUMAN KID?
GRAB
HEY!
HE'S NOT THE ONLY ONE SLEEPING. LOOK AT KITARO!
OH DEAR.
MAKURA GAESHI HAS MAGIC SAND. IF IT GETS IN YOUR EYES, YOU'RE OUT COLD.

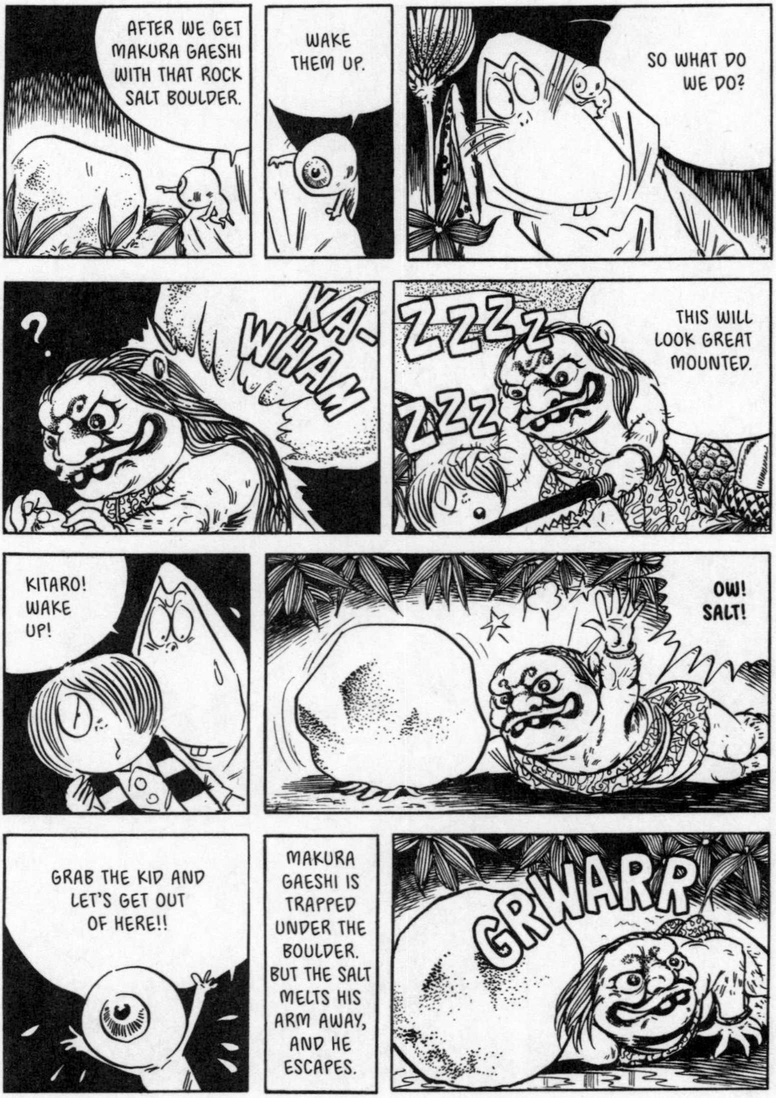
SO WHAT DO WE DO?
WAKE THEM UP.
AFTER WE GET MAKURA GAESHI WITH THAT ROCK SALT BOULDER.
THIS WILL LOOK GREAT MOUNTED.
ZZZZZ
ZZZ
KA-WHAM
?
OW! SALT!
KITARO! WAKE UP!
GRWARR
MAKURA GAESHI IS TRAPPED UNDER THE BOULDER. BUT THE SALT MELTS HIS ARM AWAY, AND HE ESCAPES.
GRAB THE KID AND LET'S GET OUT OF HERE!!

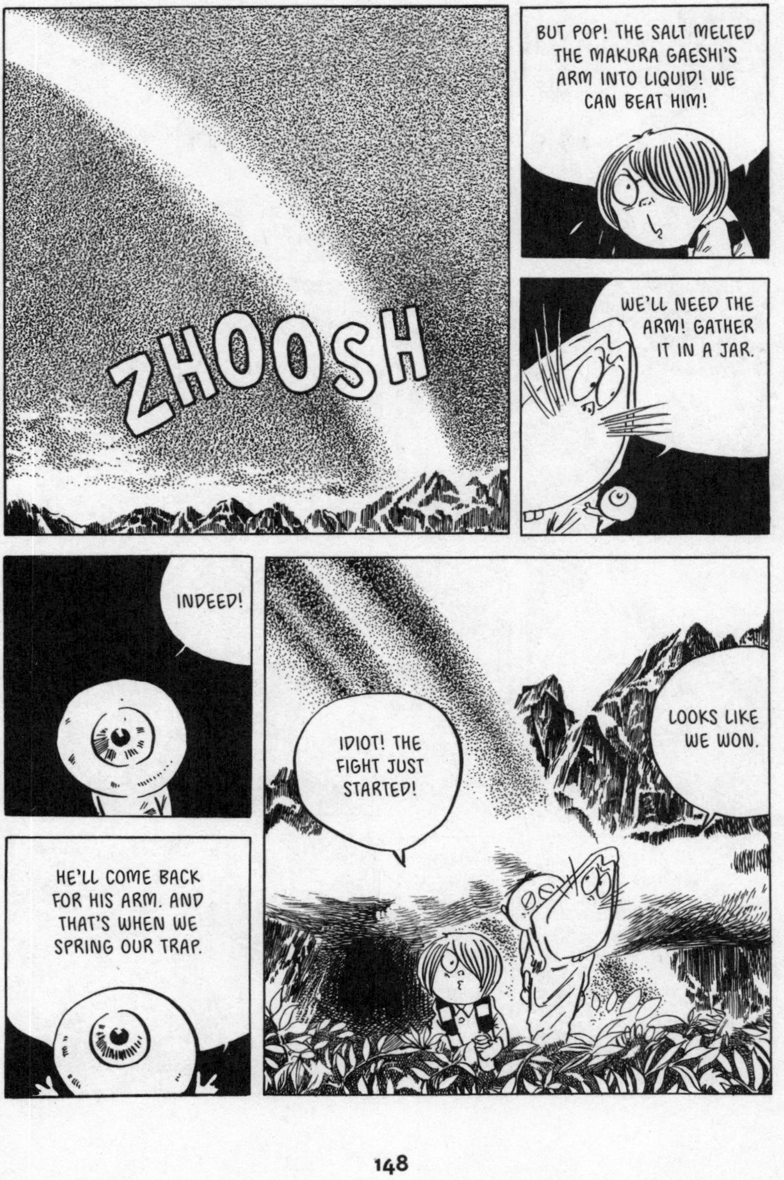
BUT POP! THE SALT MELTED THE MAKURA GAESHI'S ARM INTO LIQUID! WE CAN BEAT HIM!
WE'LL NEED THE ARM! GATHER IT IN A JAR.
ZHOOSH
LOOKS LIKE WE WON.
IDIOT! THE FIGHT JUST STARTED!
INDEED!
HE'LL COME BACK FOR HIS ARM. AND THAT'S WHEN WE SPRING OUR TRAP.

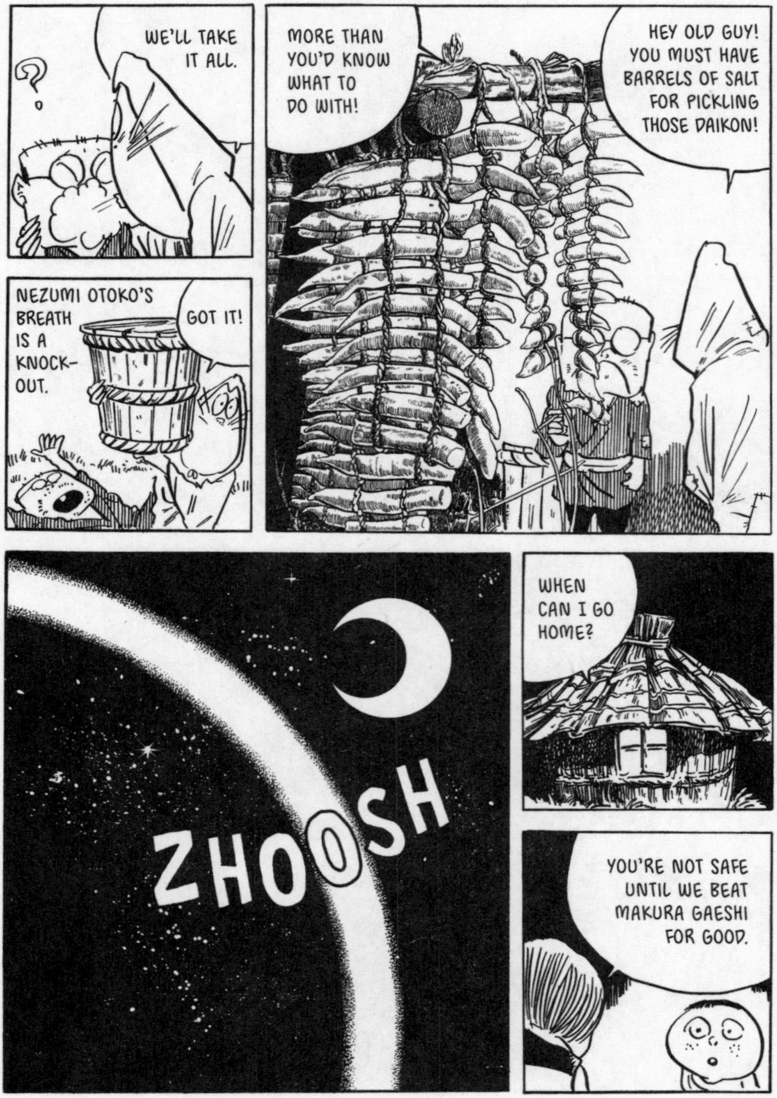
HEY OLD GUY! YOU MUST HAVE BARRELS OF SALT FOR PICKLING THOSE DAIKON!
MORE THAN YOU'D KNOW WHAT TO DO WITH!
WE'LL TAKE IT ALL.
GOT IT!
NEZUMI OTOKO'S BREATH IS A KNOCK-OUT.
WHEN CAN I GO HOME?
YOU'RE NOT SAFE UNTIL WE BEAT MAKURA GAESHI FOR GOOD.
ZHOOSH

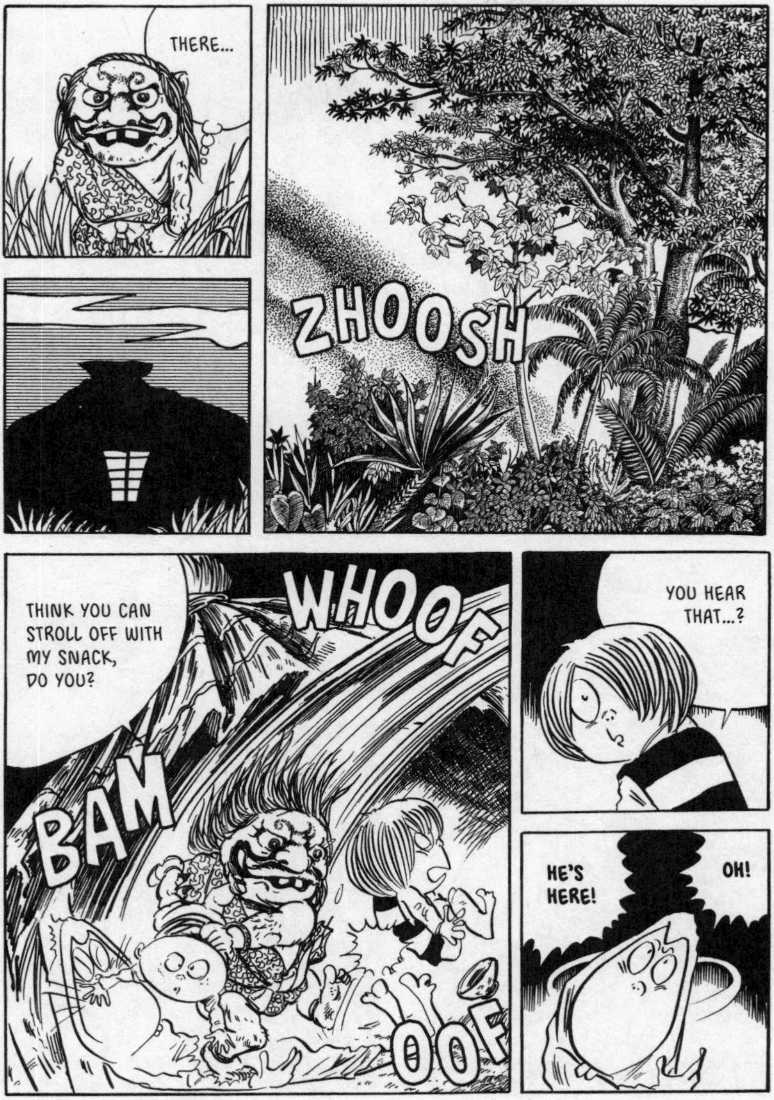
ZHOOSH
THERE...
YOU HEAR THAT...?
OH!
HE'S HERE!
WHOOF
THINK YOU CAN STROLL OFF WITH MY SNACK, DO YOU?
BAM
OOF

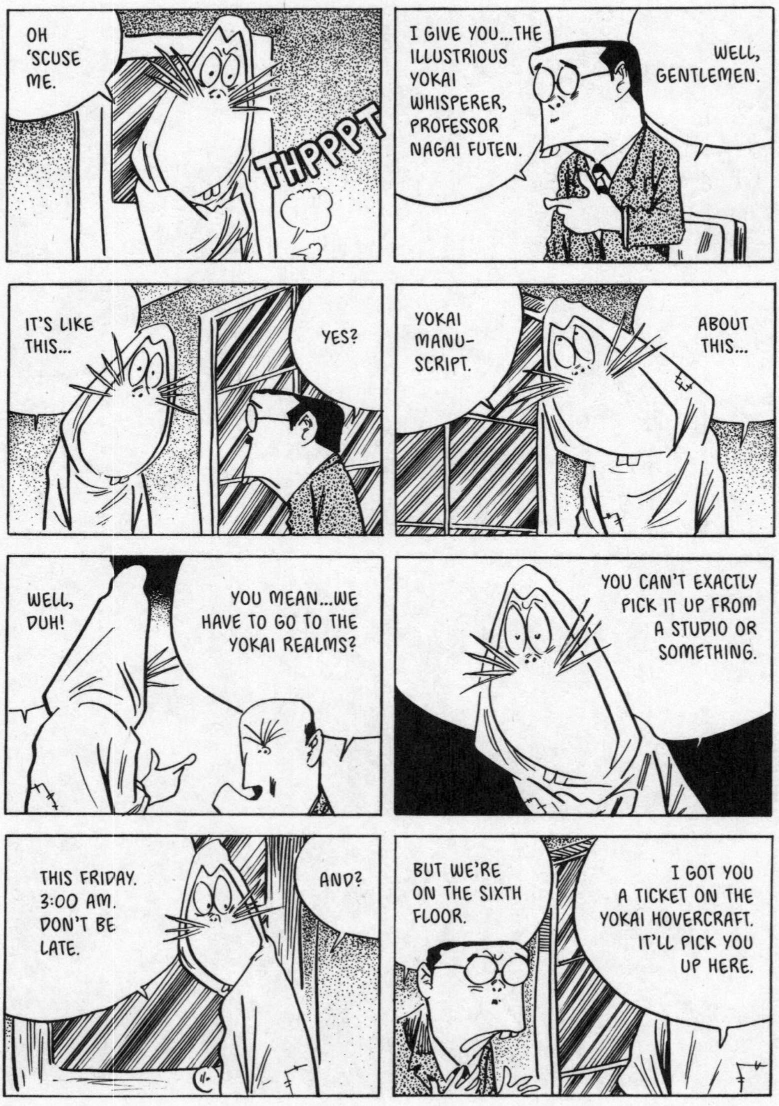
WELL, GENTLEMEN.
I GIVE YOU...THE ILLUSTRIOUS YOKAI WHISPERER, PROFESSOR NAGAI FUTEN.
OH 'SCUSE ME.
THPPPT
ABOUT THIS...
YOKAI MANU-SCRIPT.
YES?
IT'S LIKE THIS...
YOU CAN'T EXACTLY PICK IT UP FROM A STUDIO OR SOMETHING.
YOU MEAN...WE HAVE TO GO TO THE YOKAI REALMS?
WELL, DUH!
I GOT YOU A TICKET ON THE YOKAI HOVERCRAFT. IT'LL PICK YOU UP HERE.
BUT WE'RE ON THE SIXTH FLOOR.
AND?
THIS FRIDAY. 3:00 AM. DON'T BE LATE.

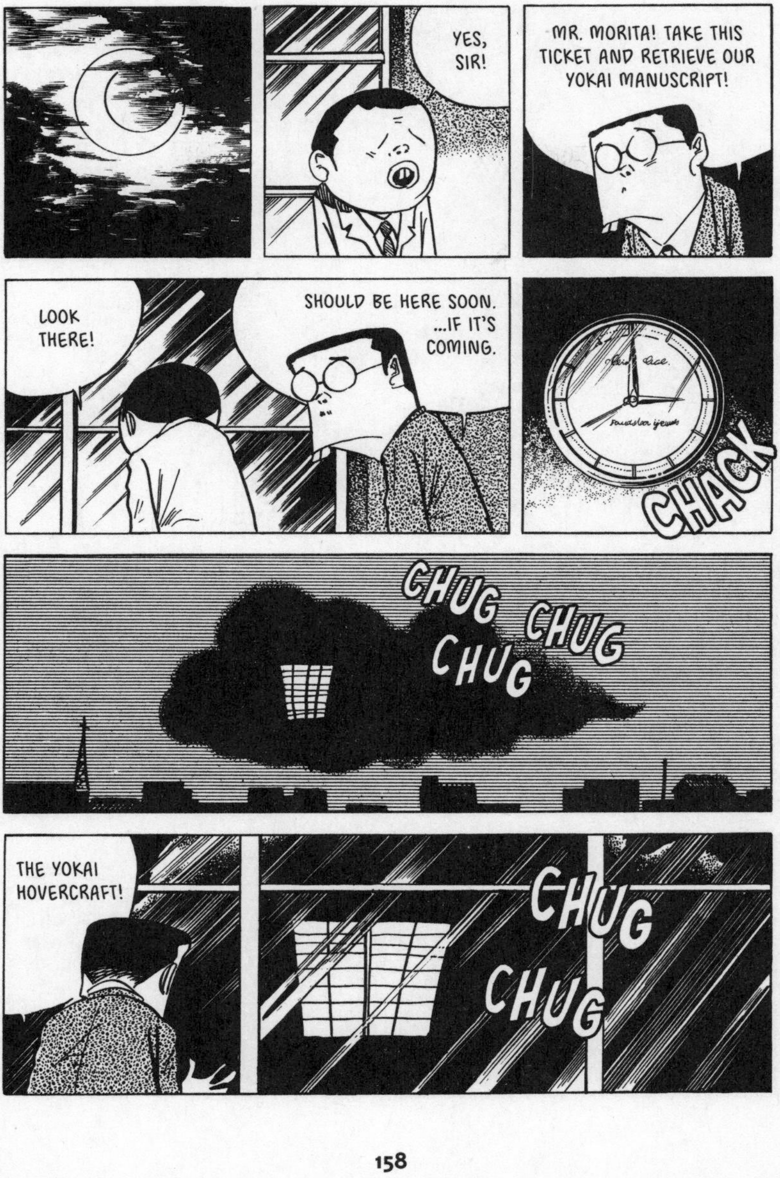
MR. MORITA! TAKE THIS TICKET AND RETRIEVE OUR YOKAI MANUSCRIPT!
YES, SIR!
CHACK
SHOULD BE HERE SOON. ...IF IT'S COMING.
LOOK THERE!
CHUG CHUG
CHUG
CHUG
CHUG
THE YOKAI HOVERCRAFT!

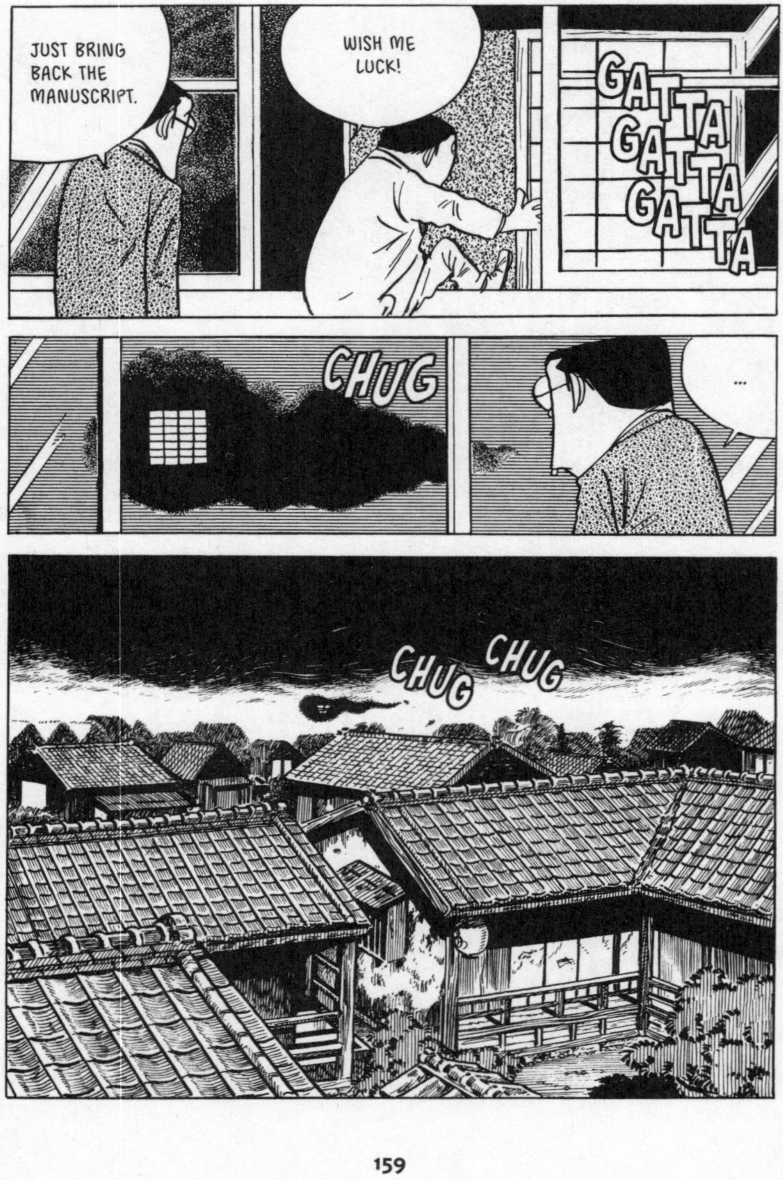
GATTA GATTA GATTA GATTA
WISH ME LUCK!
JUST BRING BACK THE MANUSCRIPT.
...
CHUG
CHUG CHUG

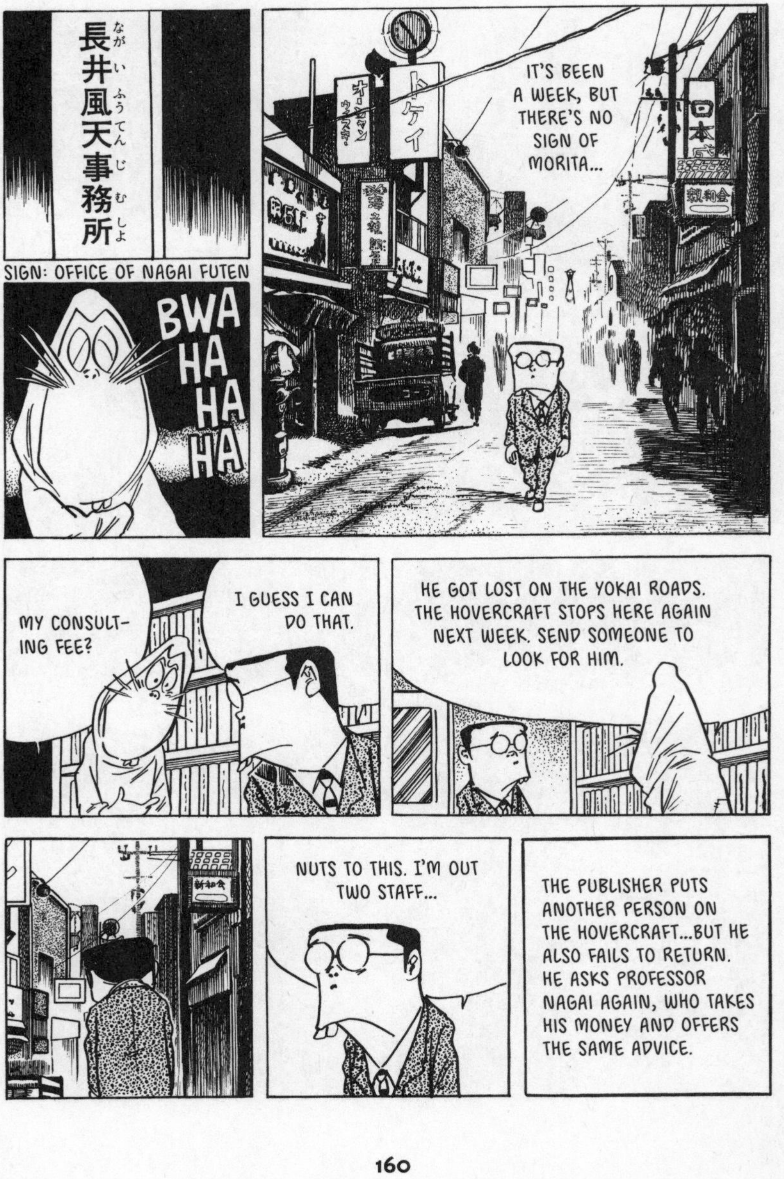

IT'S BEEN A WEEK, BUT THERE'S NO SIGN OF MORITA...
トケイ
日本
長井風天事務所
SIGN: OFFICE OF NAGAI FUTEN
BWA HA HA HA HA
HE GOT LOST ON THE YOKAI ROADS. THE HOVERCRAFT STOPS HERE AGAIN NEXT WEEK. SEND SOMEONE TO LOOK FOR HIM.
I GUESS I CAN DO THAT.
MY CONSULTING FEE?
THE PUBLISHER PUTS ANOTHER PERSON ON THE HOVERCRAFT...BUT HE ALSO FAILS TO RETURN. HE ASKS PROFESSOR NAGAI AGAIN, WHO TAKES HIS MONEY AND OFFERS THE SAME ADVICE.
NUTS TO THIS. I'M OUT TWO STAFF...

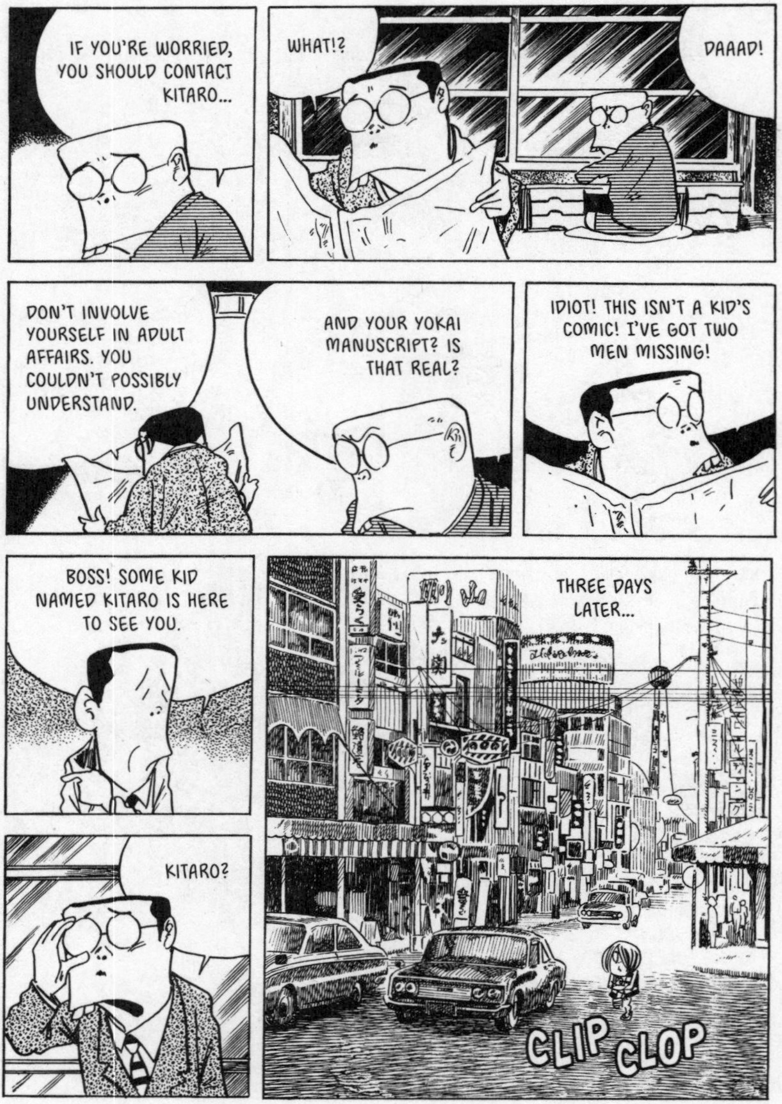
DAAAD!
WHAT!?
IF YOU'RE WORRIED, YOU SHOULD CONTACT KITARO...
IDIOT! THIS ISN'T A KID'S COMIC! I'VE GOT TWO MEN MISSING!
AND YOUR YOKAI MANUSCRIPT? IS THAT REAL?
DON'T INVOLVE YOURSELF IN ADULT AFFAIRS. YOU COULDN'T POSSIBLY UNDERSTAND.
THREE DAYS LATER...
CLIP CLOP
BOSS! SOME KID NAMED KITARO IS HERE TO SEE YOU.
KITARO?

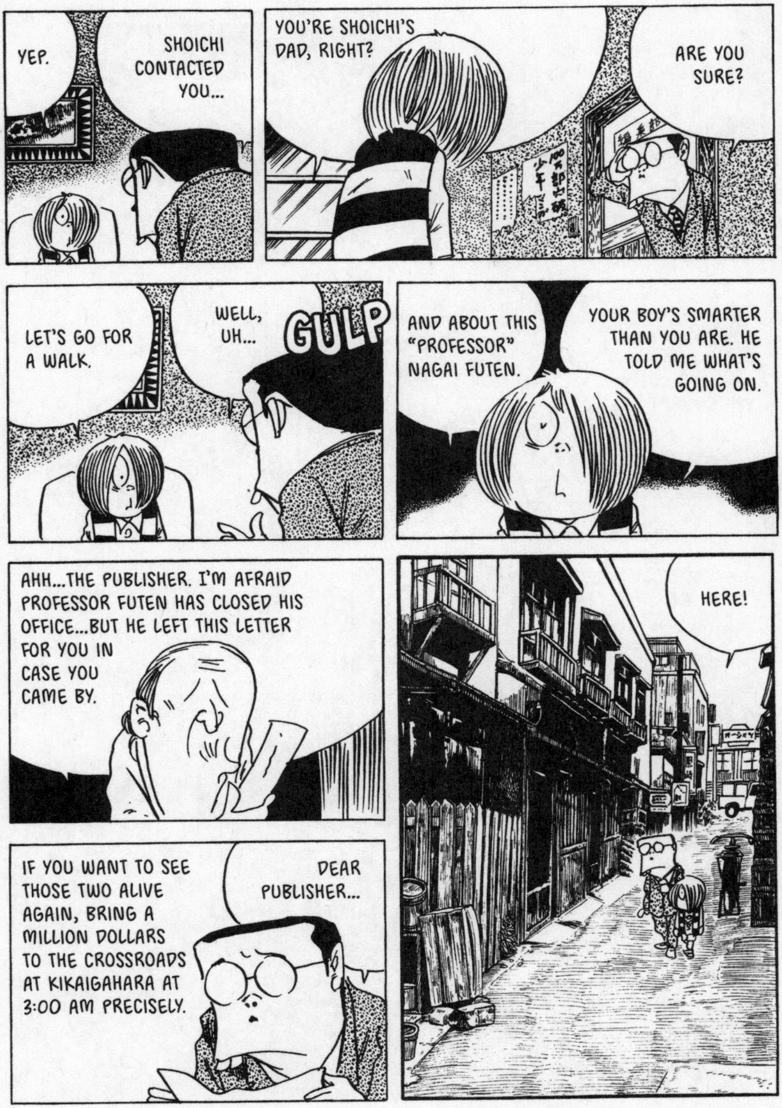
ARE YOU SURE?
YOU'RE SHOICHI'S DAD, RIGHT?
SHOICHI CONTACTED YOU...
YEP.
YOUR BOY'S SMARTER THAN YOU ARE. HE TOLD ME WHAT'S GOING ON.
AND ABOUT THIS "PROFESSOR" NAGAI FUTEN.
GULP
WELL, UH...
LET'S GO FOR A WALK.
HERE!
AHH...THE PUBLISHER. I'M AFRAID PROFESSOR FUTEN HAS CLOSED HIS OFFICE...BUT HE LEFT THIS LETTER FOR YOU IN CASE YOU CAME BY.
DEAR PUBLISHER...
IF YOU WANT TO SEE THOSE TWO ALIVE AGAIN, BRING A MILLION DOLLARS TO THE CROSSROADS AT KIKAIGAHARA AT 3:00 AM PRECISELY.

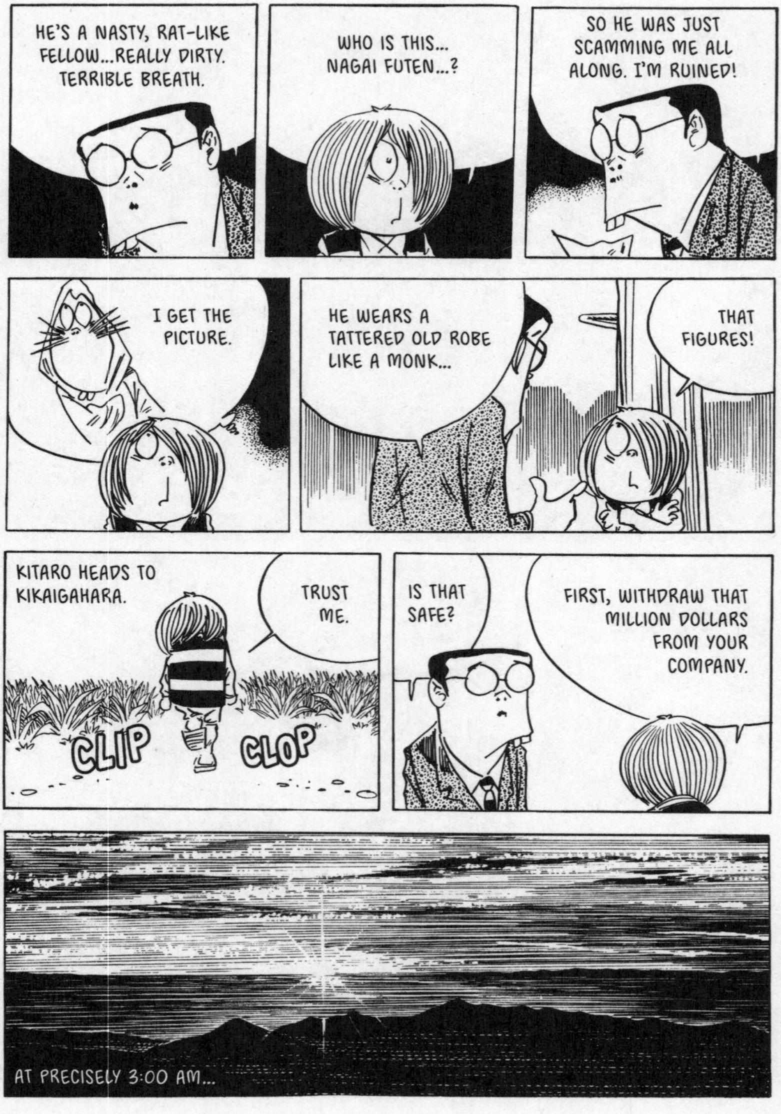
SO HE WAS JUST SCAMMING ME ALL ALONG. I'M RUINED!
WHO IS THIS... NAGAI FUTEN...?
HE'S A NASTY, RAT-LIKE FELLOW...REALLY DIRTY. TERRIBLE BREATH.
THAT FIGURES!
HE WEARS A TATTERED OLD ROBE LIKE A MONK...
I GET THE PICTURE.
FIRST, WITHDRAW THAT MILLION DOLLARS FROM YOUR COMPANY.
IS THAT SAFE?
TRUST ME.
KITARO HEADS TO KIKAIGAHARA.
CLIP
CLOP
AT PRECISELY 3:00 AM...

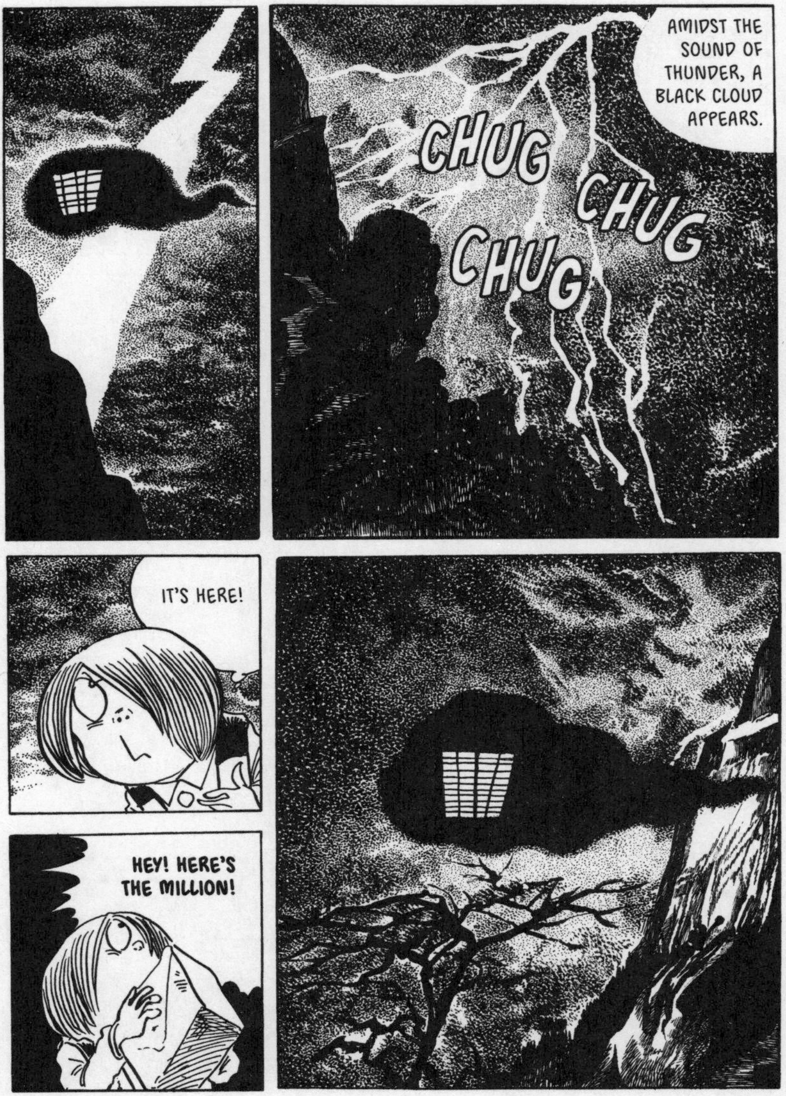
AMIDST THE SOUND OF THUNDER, A BLACK CLOUD APPEARS.
CHUG CHUG CHUG
IT'S HERE!
HEY! HERE'S THE MILLION!

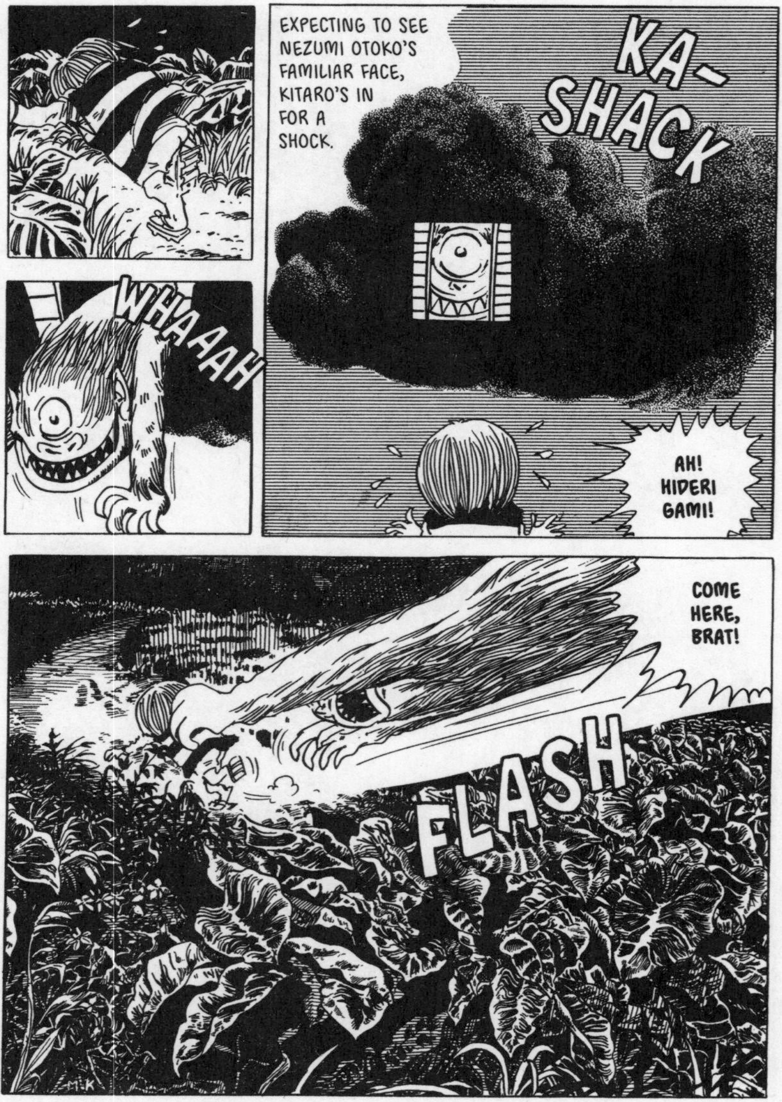
EXPECTING TO SEE NEZUMI OTOKO'S FAMILIAR FACE, KITARO'S IN FOR A SHOCK.
KA-SHACK
AH! HIDERI GAMI!
WHAAAAH
COME HERE, BRAT!
FLASH

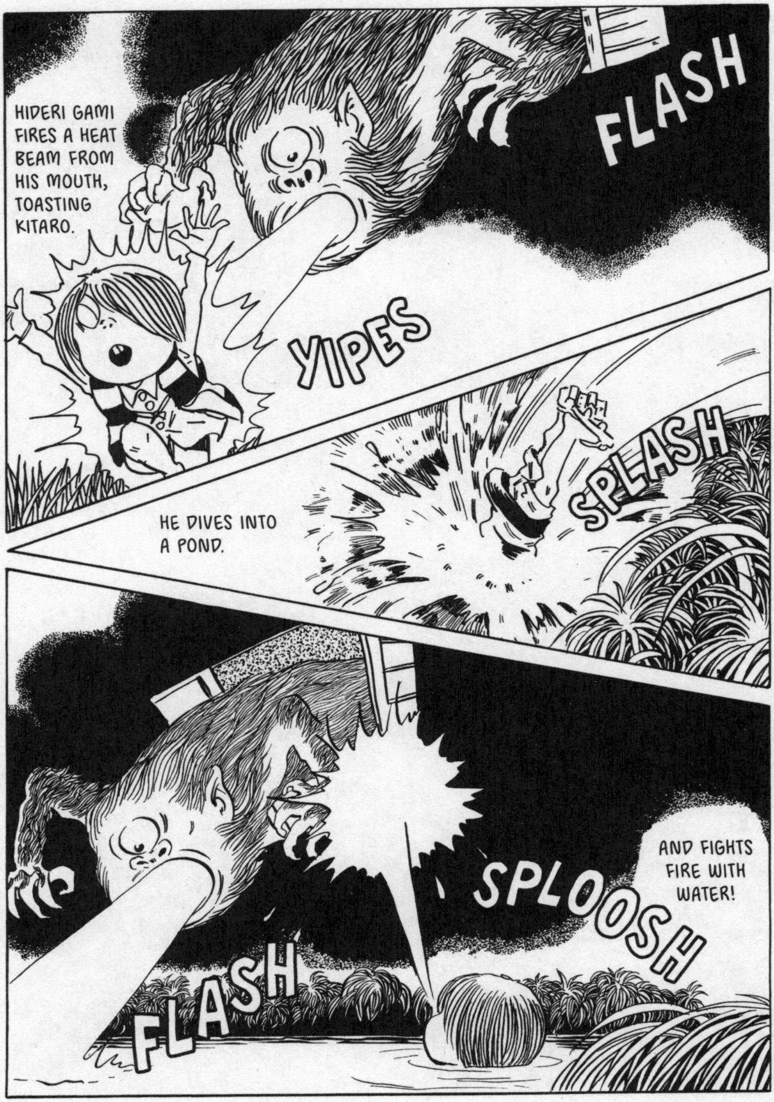
FLASH
HIDERI GAMI FIRES A HEAT BEAM FROM HIS MOUTH, TOASTING KITARO.
YIPES
SPLASH
HE DIVES INTO A POND.
AND FIGHTS FIRE WITH WATER!
SPLOOSH
FLASH

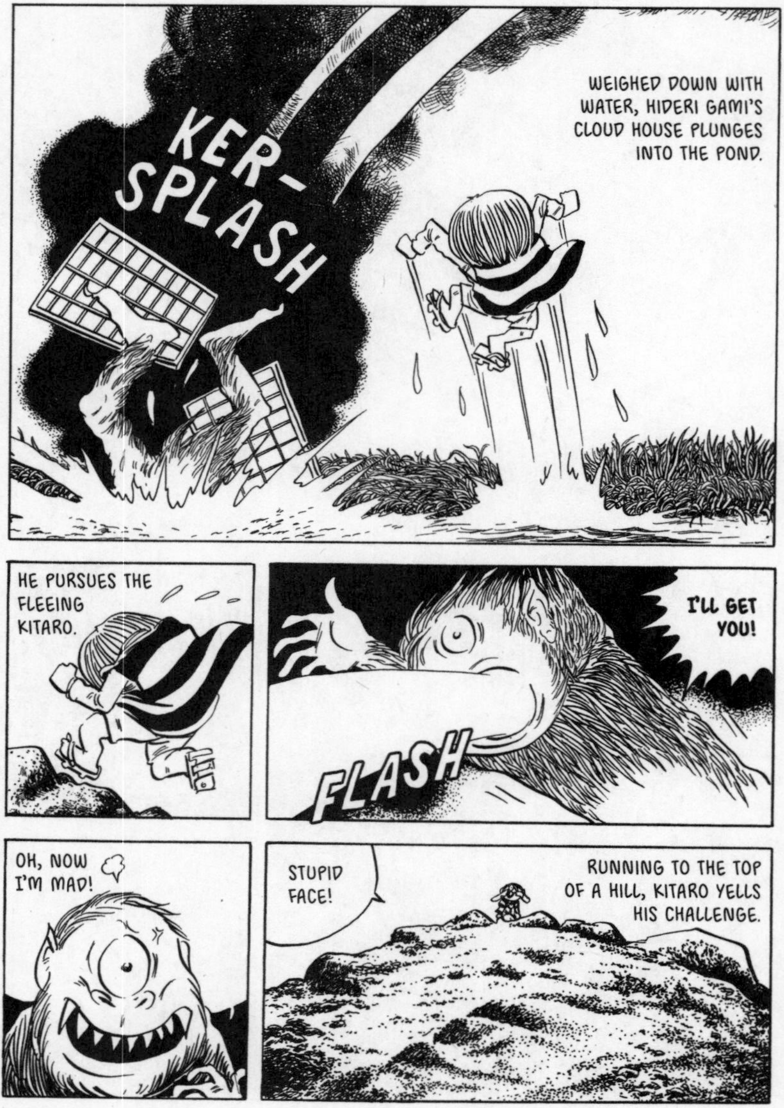

WEIGHED DOWN WITH WATER, HIDERI GAMI'S CLOUD HOUSE PLUNGES INTO THE POND.
KER-SPLASH
I'LL GET YOU!
FLASH
HE PURSUES THE FLEEING KITARO.
RUNNING TO THE TOP OF A HILL, KITARO YELLS HIS CHALLENGE.
STUPID FACE!
OH, NOW I'M MAD!

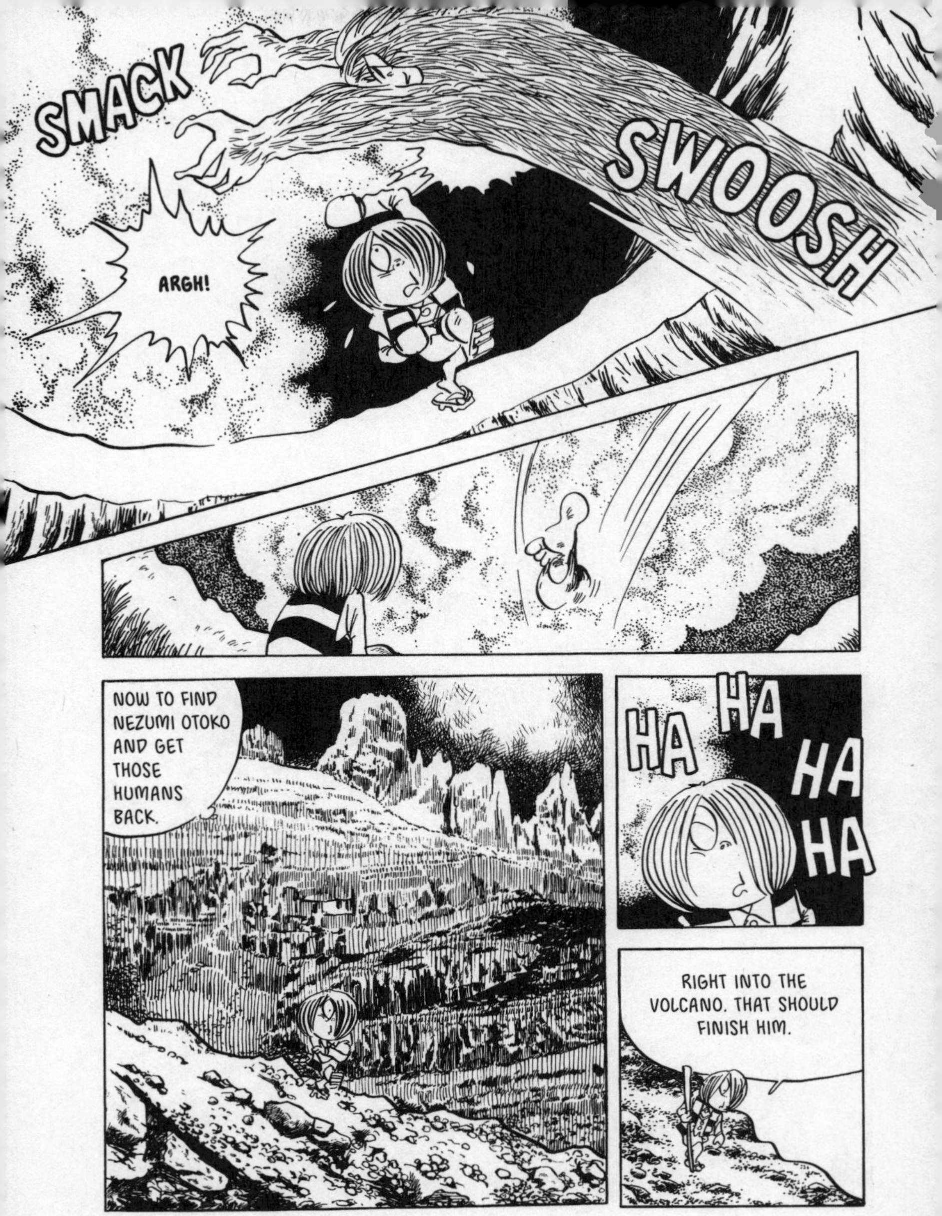
SWOOSH
SMACK
ARGH!
HA HA HA HA
RIGHT INTO THE VOLCANO. THAT SHOULD FINISH HIM.
NOW TO FIND NEZUMI OTOKO AND GET THOSE HUMANS BACK.

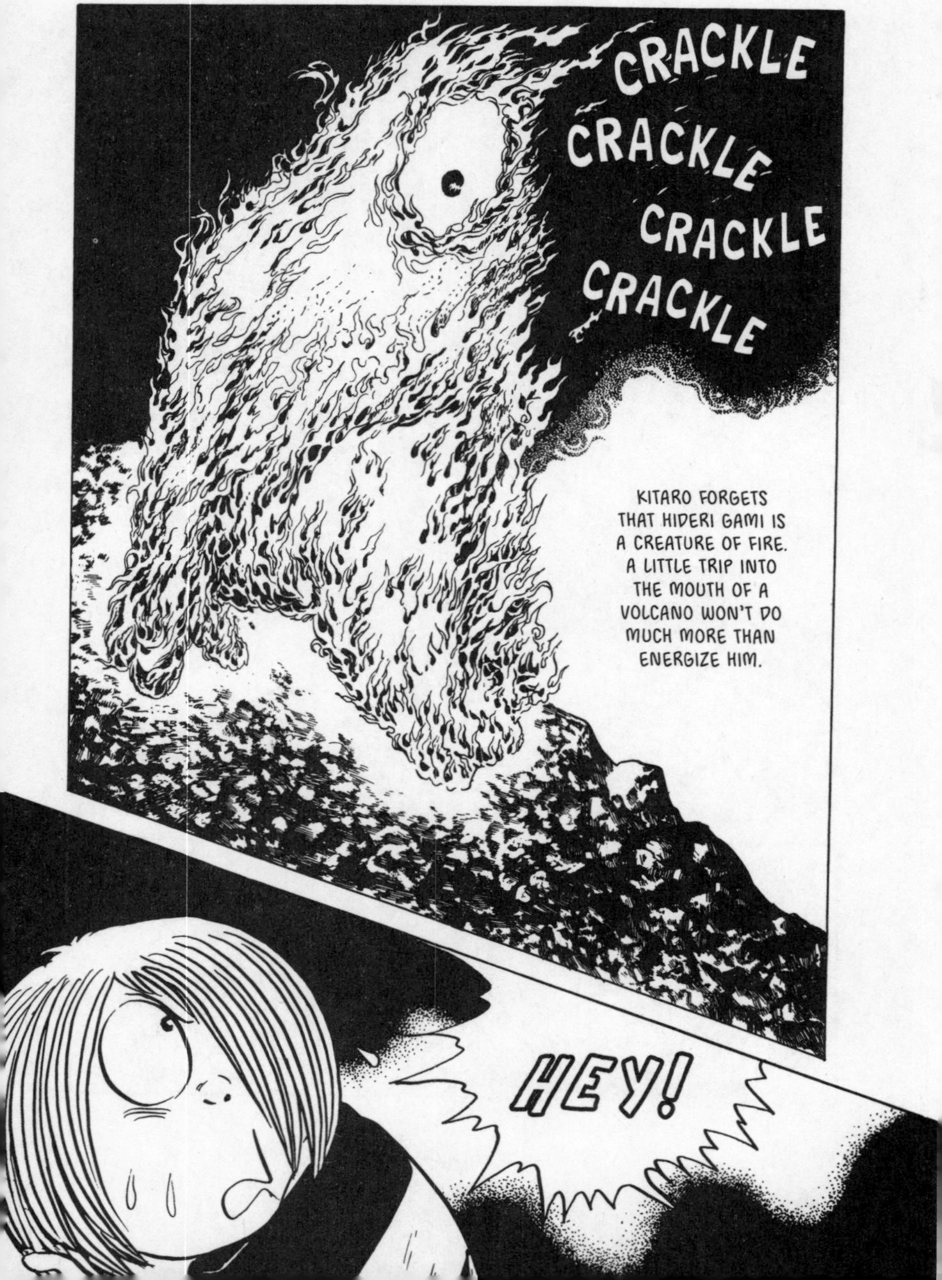
CRACKLE CRACKLE CRACKLE CRACKLE
KITARO FORGETS THAT HIDERI GAMI IS A CREATURE OF FIRE. A LITTLE TRIP INTO THE MOUTH OF A VOLCANO WON'T DO MUCH MORE THAN ENERGIZE HIM.
HEY!

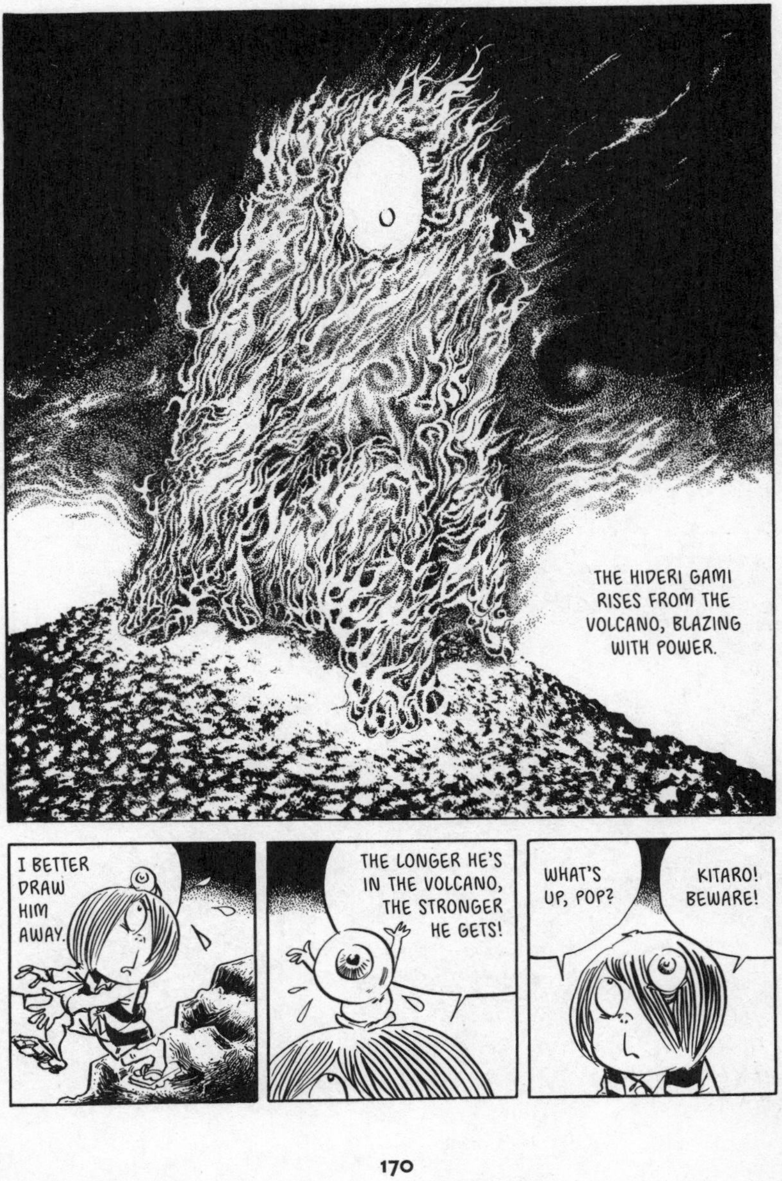
THE HIDERI GAMI RISES FROM THE VOLCANO, BLAZING WITH POWER.
KITARO! BEWARE!
WHAT'S UP, POP?
THE LONGER HE'S IN THE VOLCANO, THE STRONGER HE GETS!
I BETTER DRAW HIM AWAY.

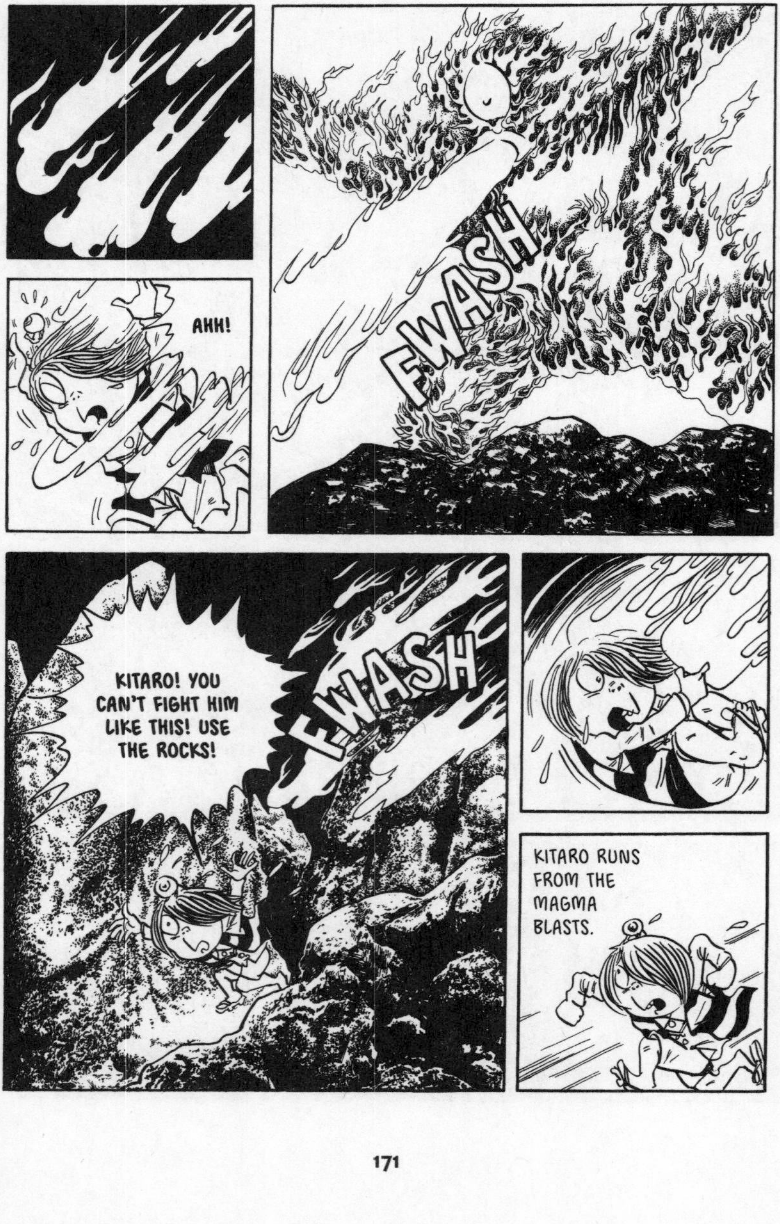
FWASH
AHH!
KITARO RUNS FROM THE MAGMA BLASTS.
FWASH
KITARO! YOU CAN'T FIGHT HIM LIKE THIS! USE THE ROCKS!

HEAVE!
WHAM
SCHLORP SCHLORP
HE ABSORBED THE ROCK AND JUST GOT BIGGER!
OUCH!
FWASH

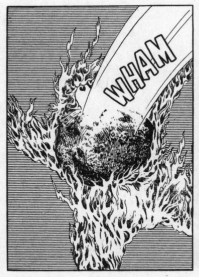

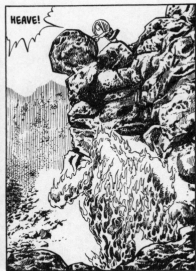

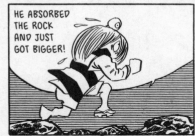

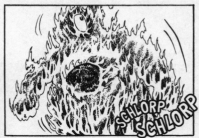

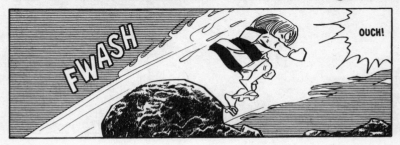

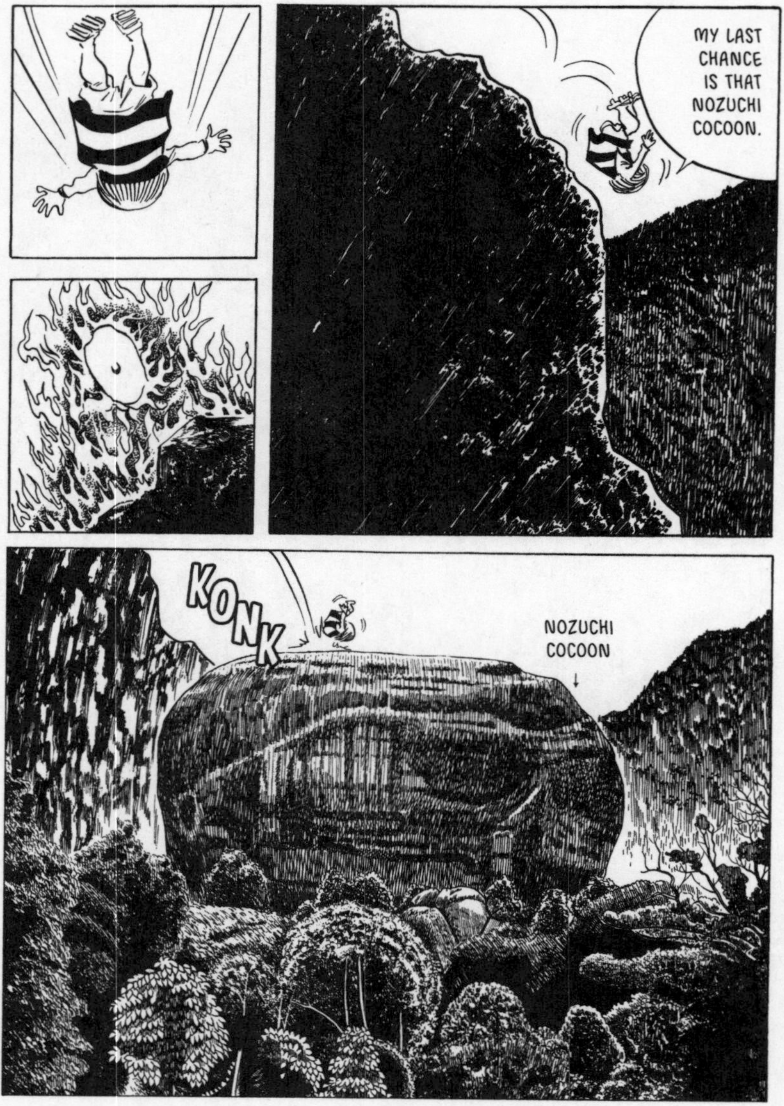
MY LAST CHANCE IS THAT NOZUCHI COCOON.
KONK
NOZUCHI COCOON

BOUNCE
RUMBLE
RUMBLE

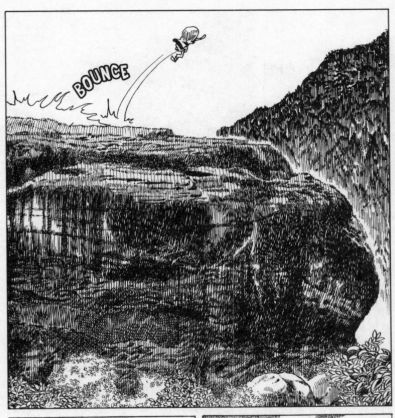

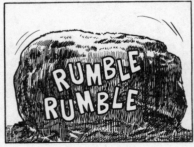

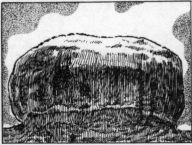

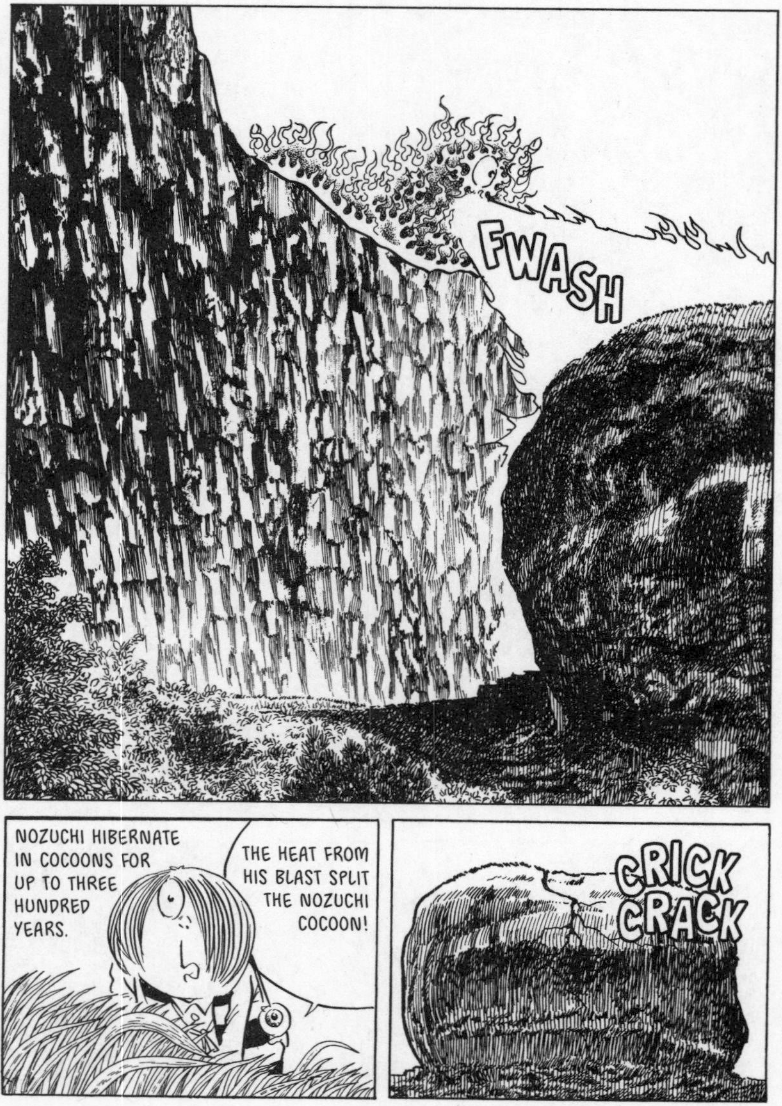
FWASH
CRICK CRACK
THE HEAT FROM HIS BLAST SPLIT THE NOZUCHI COCOON!
NOZUCHI HIBERNATE IN COCOONS FOR UP TO THREE HUNDRED YEARS.

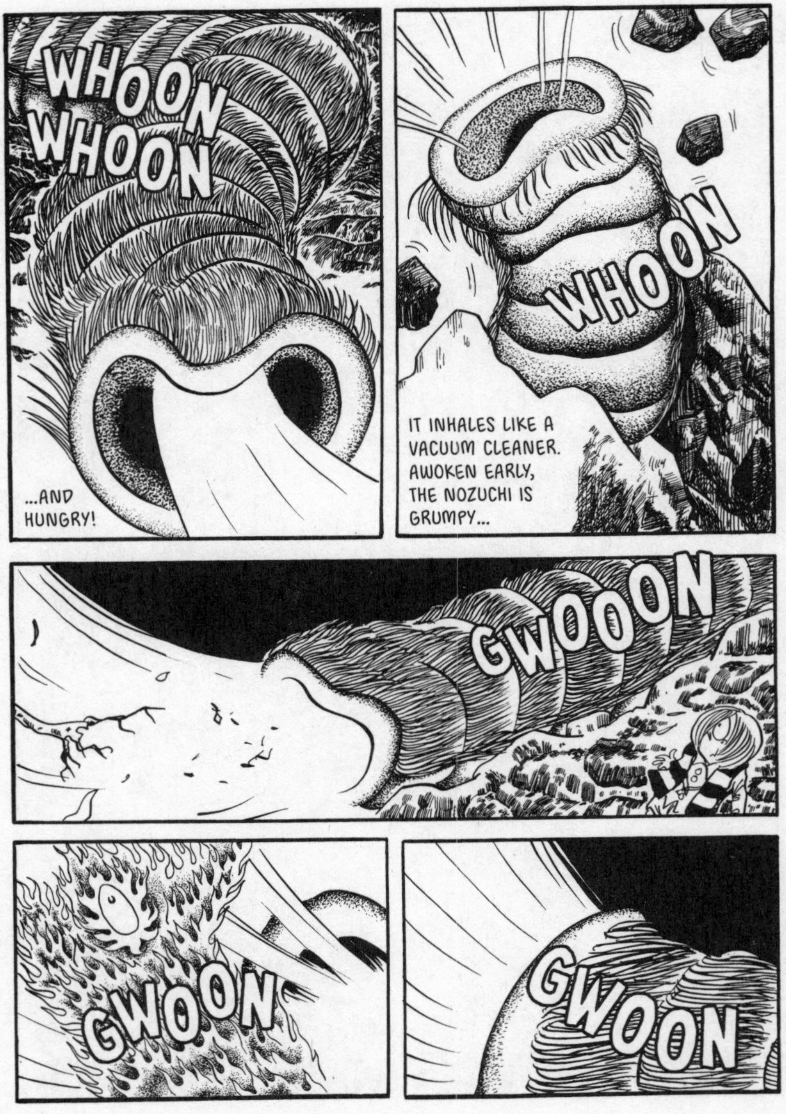
WHOON
IT INHALES LIKE A VACUUM CLEANER. AWOKEN EARLY, THE NOZUCHI IS GRUMPY...
WHOON WHOON
...AND HUNGRY!
GWOOOON
GWOON
GWOON

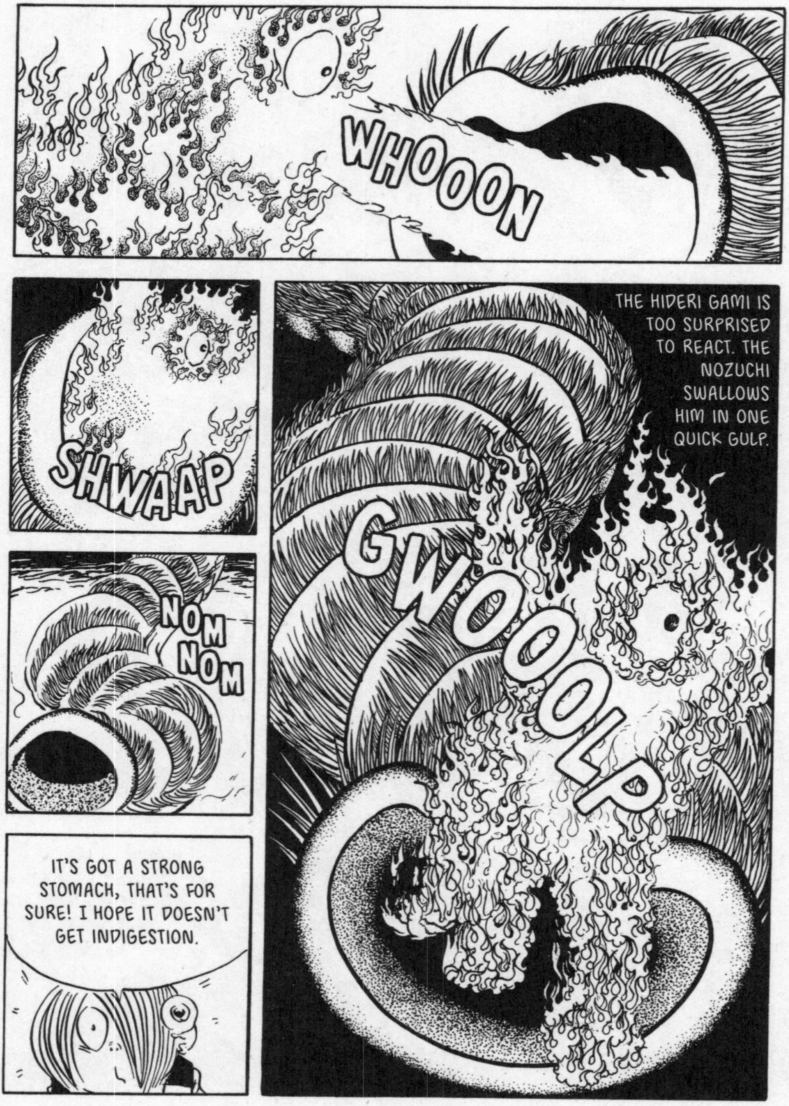
WHOOON
THE HIDERI GAMI IS TOO SURPRISED TO REACT. THE NOZUCHI SWALLOWS HIM IN ONE QUICK GULP.
GWOOOOLP
SHWAAP
NOM NOM
IT'S GOT A STRONG STOMACH, THAT'S FOR SURE! I HOPE IT DOESN'T GET INDIGESTION.

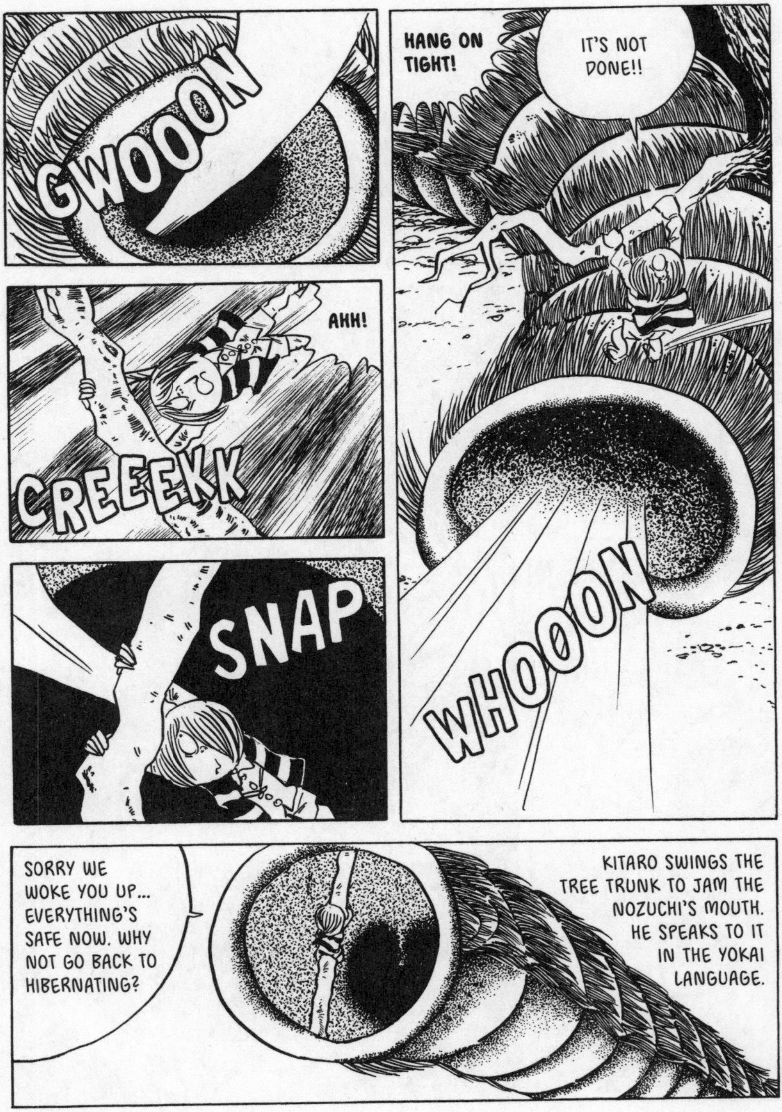

IT'S NOT DONE!!
HANG ON TIGHT!
WHOOON
GWOOON
AHH!
CREEEKK
SNAP
KITARO SWINGS THE TREE TRUNK TO JAM THE NOZUCHI'S MOUTH. HE SPEAKS TO IT IN THE YOKAI LANGUAGE.
SORRY WE WOKE YOU UP... EVERYTHING'S SAFE NOW. WHY NOT GO BACK TO HIBERNATING?

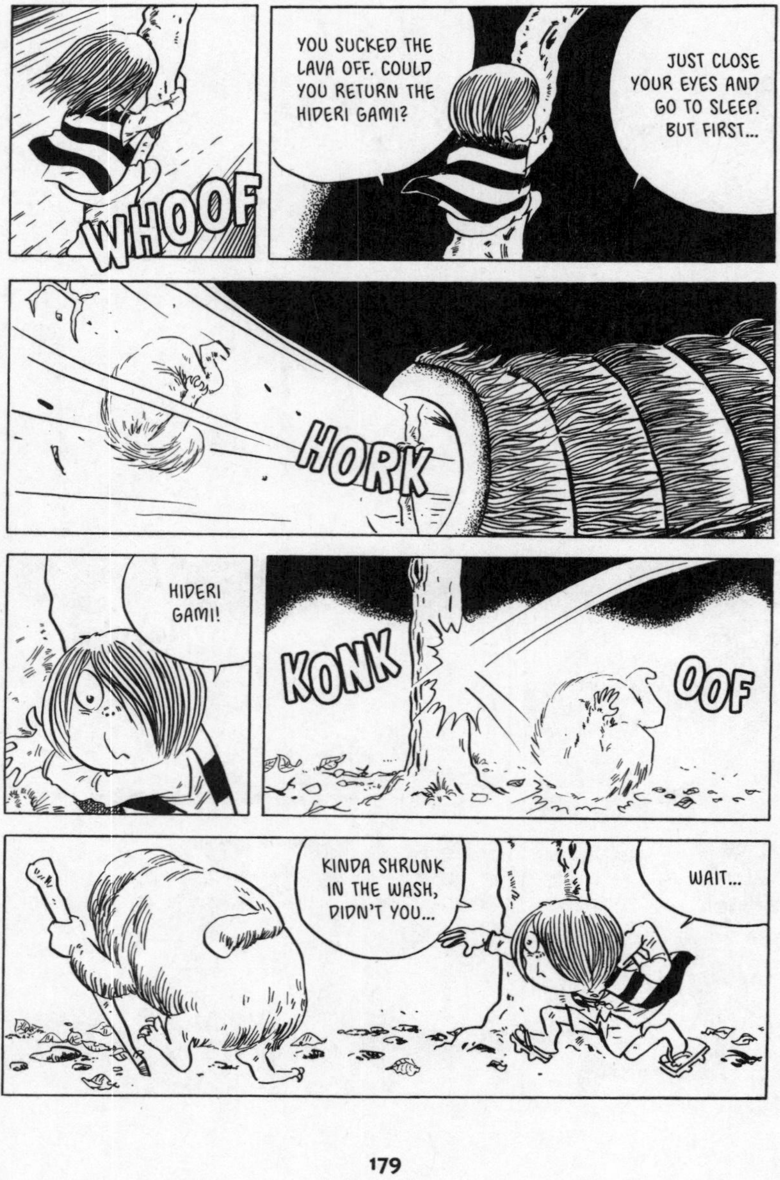
JUST CLOSE YOUR EYES AND GO TO SLEEP. BUT FIRST...
YOU SUCKED THE LAVA OFF. COULD YOU RETURN THE HIDERI GAMI?
WHOOF
HORK
OOF
KONK
HIDERI GAMI!
WAIT...
KINDA SHRUNK IN THE WASH, DIDN'T YOU...

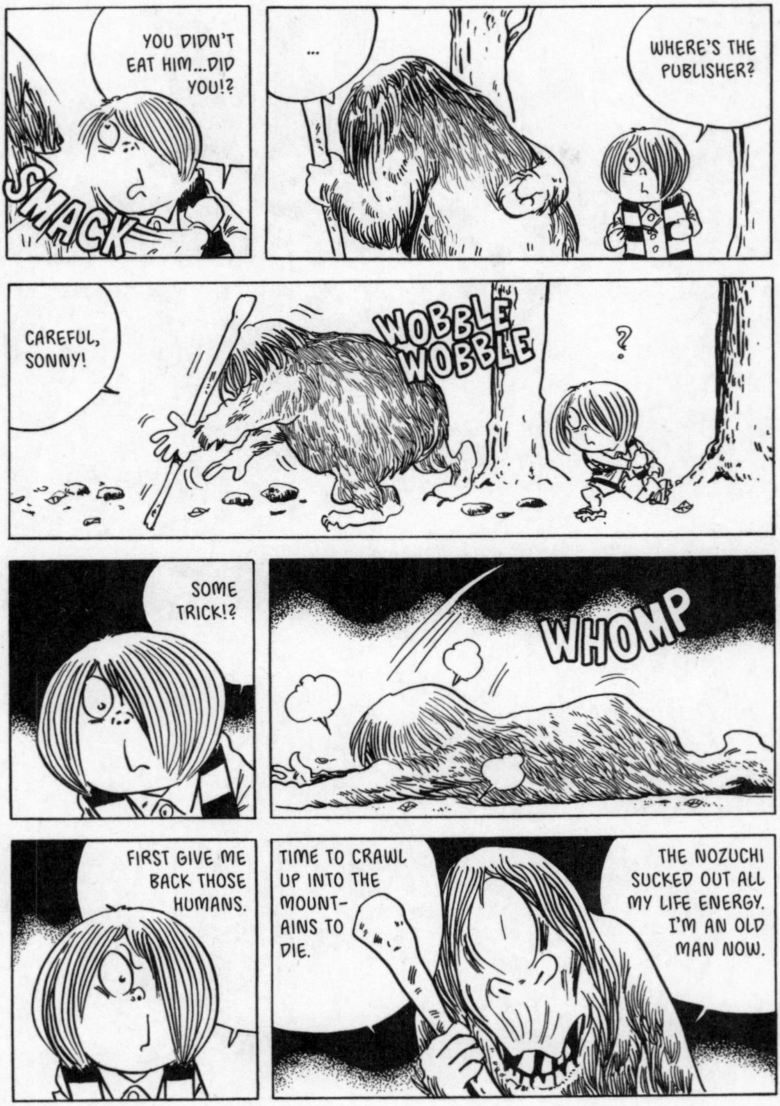
WHERE'S THE PUBLISHER?
...
YOU DIDN'T EAT HIM...DID YOU!?
SMACK
?
WOBBLE WOBBLE
CAREFUL, SONNY!
WHOMP
SOME TRICK!?
THE NOZUCHI SUCKED OUT ALL MY LIFE ENERGY. I'M AN OLD MAN NOW.
TIME TO CRAWL UP INTO THE MOUNTAINS TO DIE.
FIRST GIVE ME BACK THOSE HUMANS.

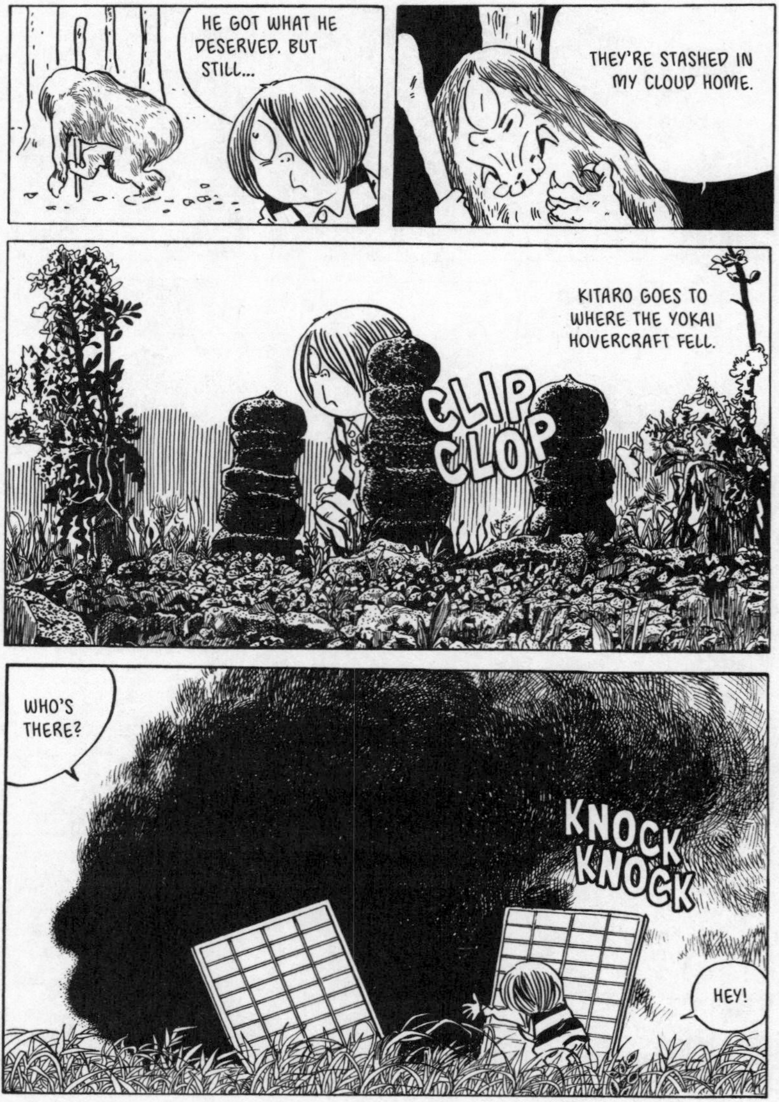
THEY'RE STASHED IN MY CLOUD HOME.
HE GOT WHAT HE DESERVED. BUT STILL...
KITARO GOES TO WHERE THE YOKAI HOVERCRAFT FELL.
CLIP CLOP
KNOCK KNOCK
HEY!
WHO'S THERE?

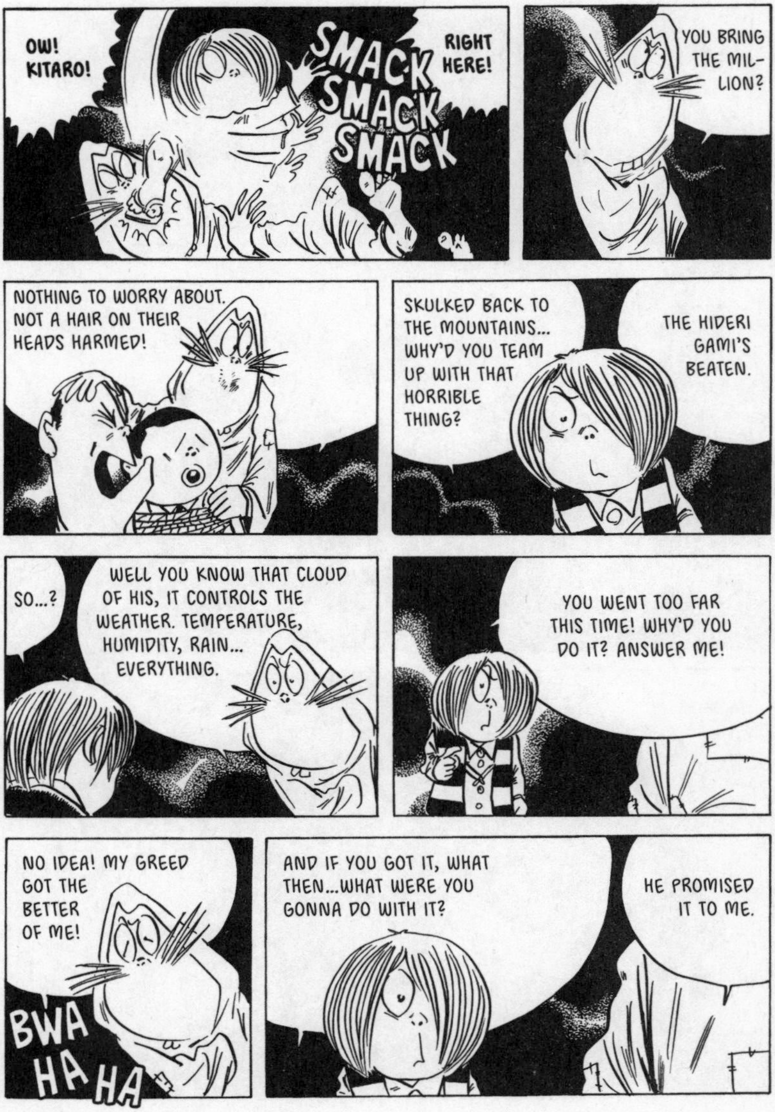
YOU BRING THE MIL-LION?
RIGHT HERE!
SMACK SMACK SMACK
OW! KITARO!
THE HIDERI GAMI'S BEATEN.
SKULKED BACK TO THE MOUNTAINS... WHY'D YOU TEAM UP WITH THAT HORRIBLE THING?
NOTHING TO WORRY ABOUT. NOT A HAIR ON THEIR HEADS HARMED!
YOU WENT TOO FAR THIS TIME! WHY'D YOU DO IT? ANSWER ME!
WELL YOU KNOW THAT CLOUD OF HIS, IT CONTROLS THE WEATHER. TEMPERATURE, HUMIDITY, RAIN... EVERYTHING.
SO...?
HE PROMISED IT TO ME.
AND IF YOU GOT IT, WHAT THEN...WHAT WERE YOU GONNA DO WITH IT?
NO IDEA! MY GREED GOT THE BETTER OF ME!
BWA HA HA

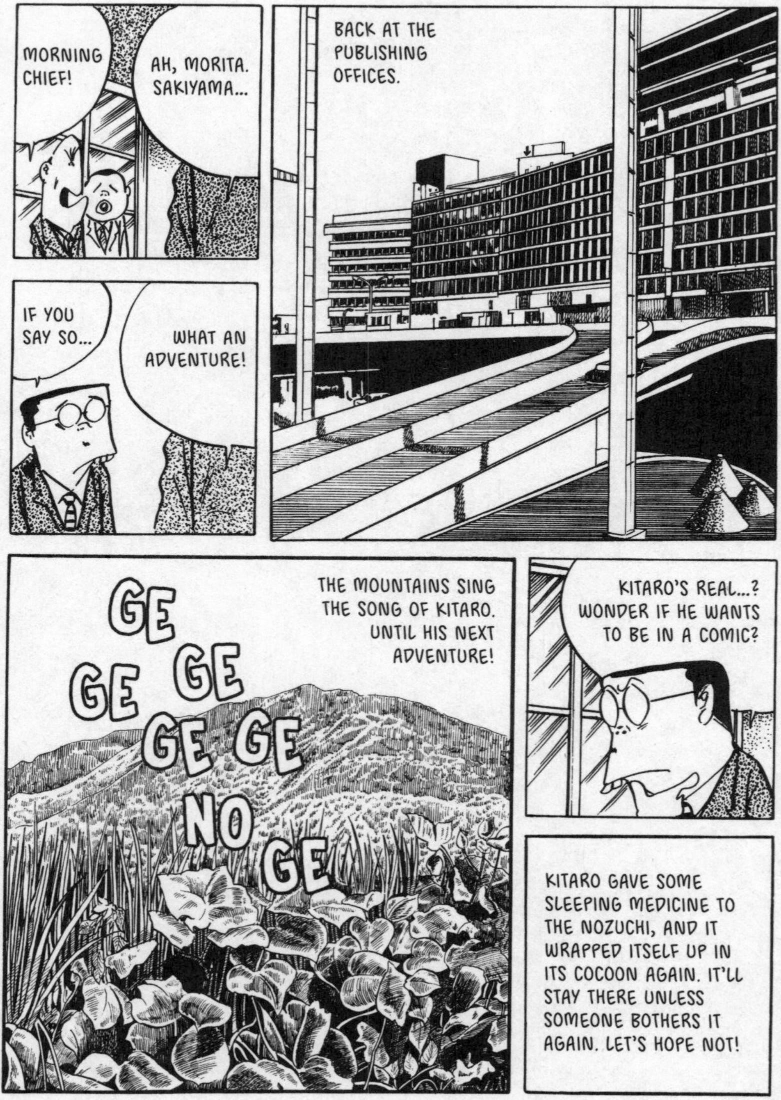
BACK AT THE PUBLISHING OFFICES.
AH, MORITA. SAKIYAMA...
MORNING CHIEF!
WHAT AN ADVENTURE!
IF YOU SAY SO...
KITARO'S REAL...? WONDER IF HE WANTS TO BE IN A COMIC?
KITARO GAVE SOME SLEEPING MEDICINE TO THE NOZUCHI, AND IT WRAPPED ITSELF UP IN ITS COCOON AGAIN. IT'LL STAY THERE UNLESS SOMEONE BOTHERS IT AGAIN. LET'S HOPE NOT!
THE MOUNTAINS SING THE SONG OF KITARO. UNTIL HIS NEXT ADVENTURE!
GE GE GE GE GE GE NO GE

YOKAI FILES

BY ZACK DAVISSON

WHAT ARE YOKAI?

You'll meet many different kinds of yokai in the pages of *Kitaro*, but it's not easy to describe exactly what that means. The word is difficult to translate, meaning something like "mysterious phenomenon." Yokai as a term encompasses monsters, spirits of rivers and mountains, deities, demons, goblins, apparitions, shape-changers, magic, ghosts, animals, and all manner of mysterious occurrences. There are good yokai and bad yokai, and some that are in between.

Some yokai are very old, with histories longer than civilization. Some are young, and have only appeared in the past couple of years. Some were once human beings who fell under a curse or otherwise changed, while some—like Kitaro and his father Medama Oyaji—were born yokai and have always been yokai.

Many are from Japan, but others are from China, Korea, India, or countries like Romania, the UK, Canada, the USA—or even outer space. Yokai can be legendary figures from folklore or urban legends, or characters from books or movies. They can come from anywhere. They can look like anything. Yokai can be giant monsters, unnatural plants, winds, or earthquakes. They can be visible or invisible.

Perhaps the best definition is to say that anything that can not readily be understood or explained, anything mysterious and unconfirmed, can be yokai.

HITODAMA are strange whorls of light and supernatural power that sometimes appear when yokai are near. They fly around like little fireflies, but rarely interact.

Are they souls (as the direct translation—human soul—might indicate) or small spirits attracted to bigger yokai? Or just an aftereffect like sparks from a fire? Nobody knows for sure.

NOPPERABO are one of the most famous yokai from Japanese folklore. They have a face as smooth as an egg, and delight in frightening humans late at night.

Nopperabo have traveled far from their native land of Japan, and recently sightings have been reported in Hawaii.

GYUKI, also called the *ushi oni*, are massive sea monsters with crab or spider-like bodies and giant bull heads.

They appear as far back as fourteenth century Japan, where they were the terror of coastal villages. There is one shrine in Japan that displays a pair of gyuki horns said to have been taken from the real thing.

KAMI are guardian spirits that protect the people and the country. According to Japan's native Shinto religion, the land is filled with them.

There are many shrines across the country, both large and small. Each of the shrines is the home to a kami, and each kami has its own particular legend, power, and appearance.

BURU-BURU is the cause of the mysterious chills and shudders you get when no one is around—rarely seen but often felt.

They are said to be born from acts of cowardice, like from warriors running away from a battle. They brush up against humans, sharing the same fear that created them.

MAKURA GAESHI are ancient monsters from the seventh century. Most stories tell of mischievous spirits who prank sleeping humans by yanking pillows from under people's heads and sticking them under their feet. Some other stories tell of a nastier creature who haunts the dreamlands and hunts people.

HIDERI GAMI are originally from China, and are found in some of the oldest Chinese legends. Stories tell of the legendary Yellow Emperor of China summoning the goddess Batsu to earth to fight for him. She won the battle, but used so much of her sun power she was unable to return to heaven. Angry, she fled to the mountains and gave birth to a race of terrible beings that burn with fire and evaporate water.

NOZUCHI are powerful snake-like creatures covered in fur like a caterpillar, and one of the earliest known yokai in Japan. They have no eyes or ears—just a sucking mouth. They eat everything that they can fit inside.

Nozuchi move by rolling down hills, then crawling their way back to the top like an inch worm.

YOKAI KNOWLEDGE CHALLENGE

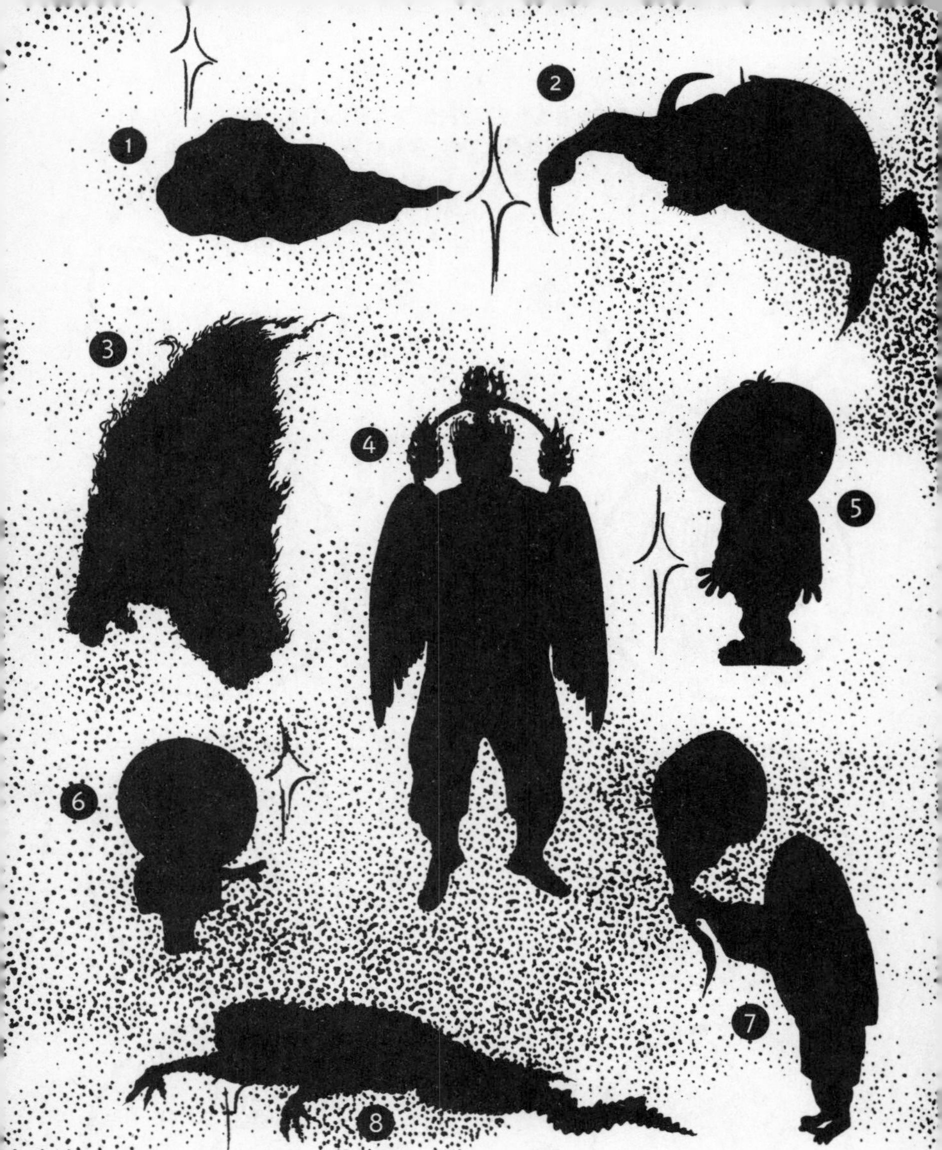
1
2
3
4
5
6
7
8

A TRUE YOKAI EXPERT CAN NAME THE YOKAI, EVEN FROM ITS SHADOW

Answers: 1-Hitodama; 2-Gyuki; 3-Hideri Gami; 4-Kami; 5-Kitaro; 6-Medama Oyaji; 7-Nopperabo (bonus points if you spotted that he's holding Nezumi Otoko's face!); 8-Buru-Buru.

THESE YOKAI HAVE LOST THEIR THINGS, BUT WHAT BELONGS TO WHOM?

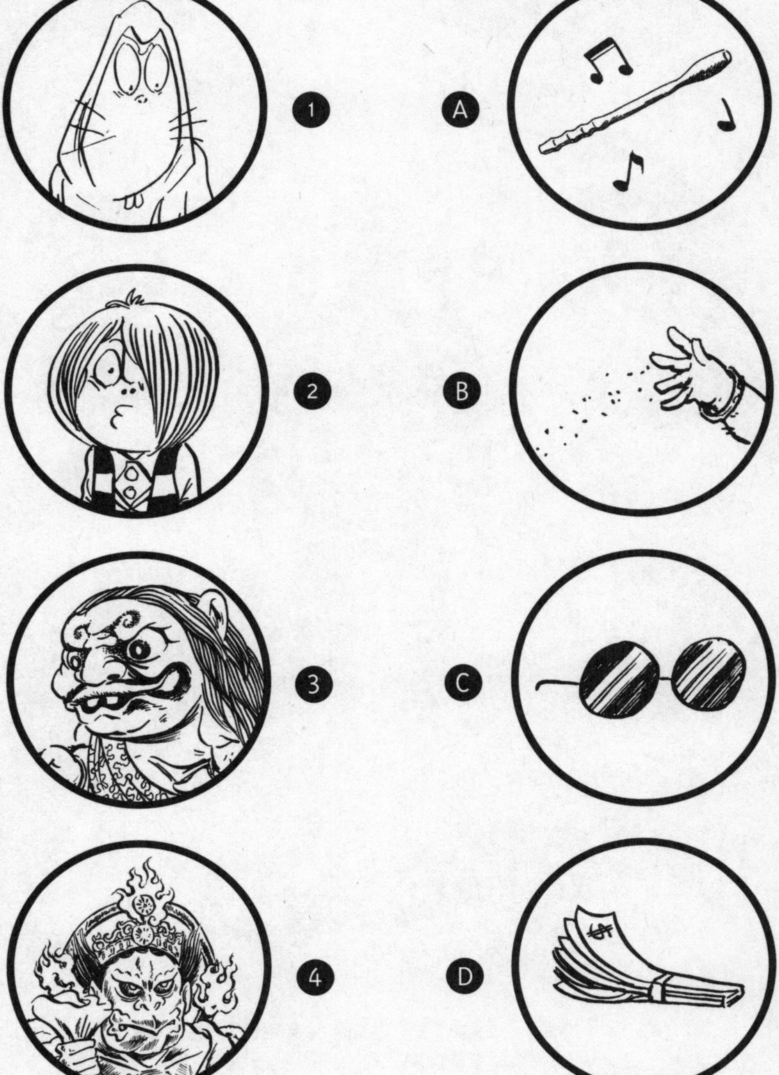
1
A
2
B
3
C
4
D

Answers: 1-D (Nezumi Otoko-Money); 2-C (Kitaro-Yokai Glasses); 3-B (Makura Gaeshi-Magic Sand); 4-A (Kami-Enchanted Flute).

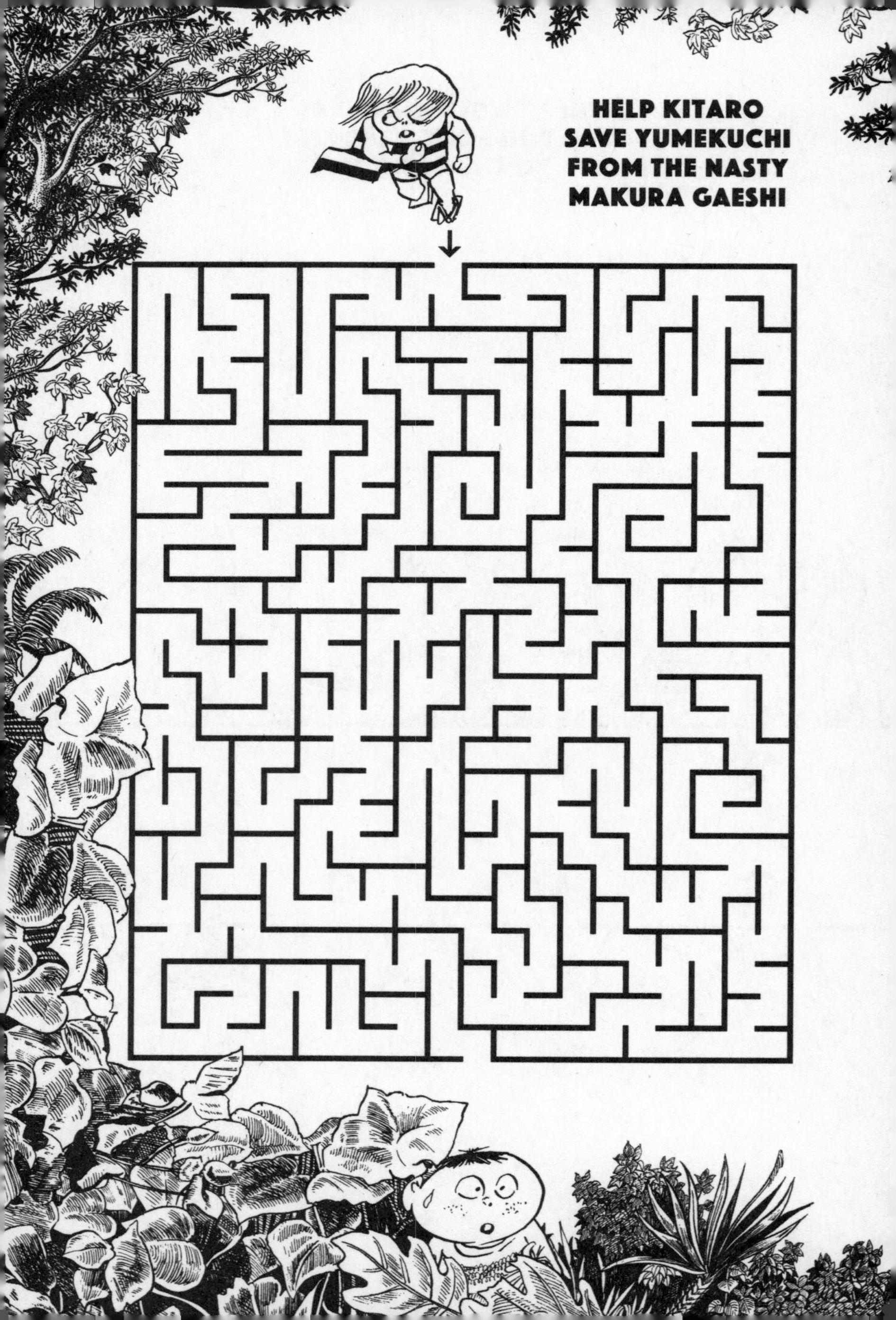
HELP KITARO
SAVE YUMEKUCHI
FROM THE NASTY
MAKURA GAESHI

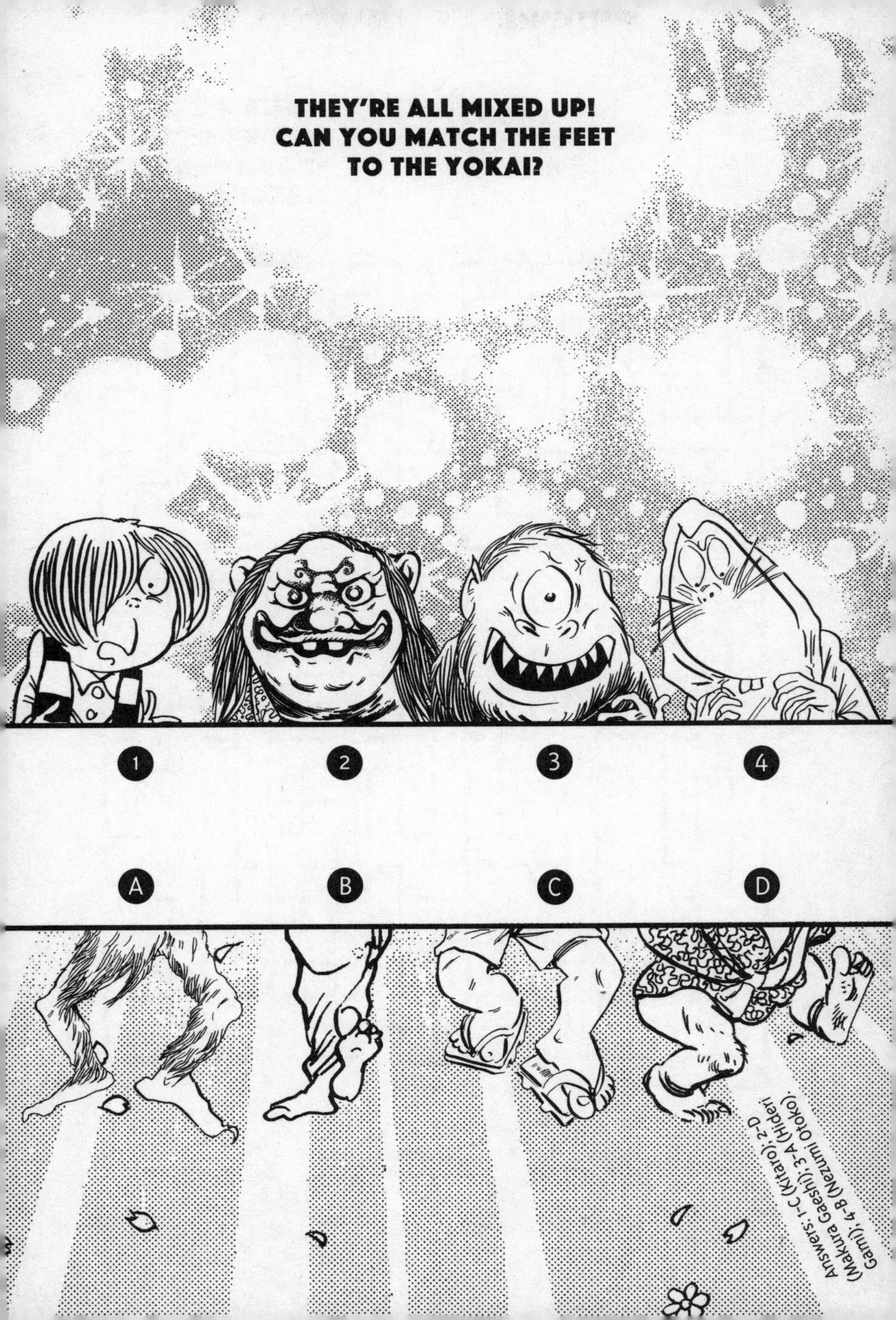
THEY'RE ALL MIXED UP!
CAN YOU MATCH THE FEET
TO THE YOKAI?
1
2
3
4
A
B
C
D
Answers: 1-C (Kitaro); 2-D (Makura Gaeshi); 3-A (Hideri Gami); 4-B (Nezumi Otoko).

HELP MEDAMA OYAJI BECOME WHOLE AGAIN BY DRAWING HIS MISSING HALF

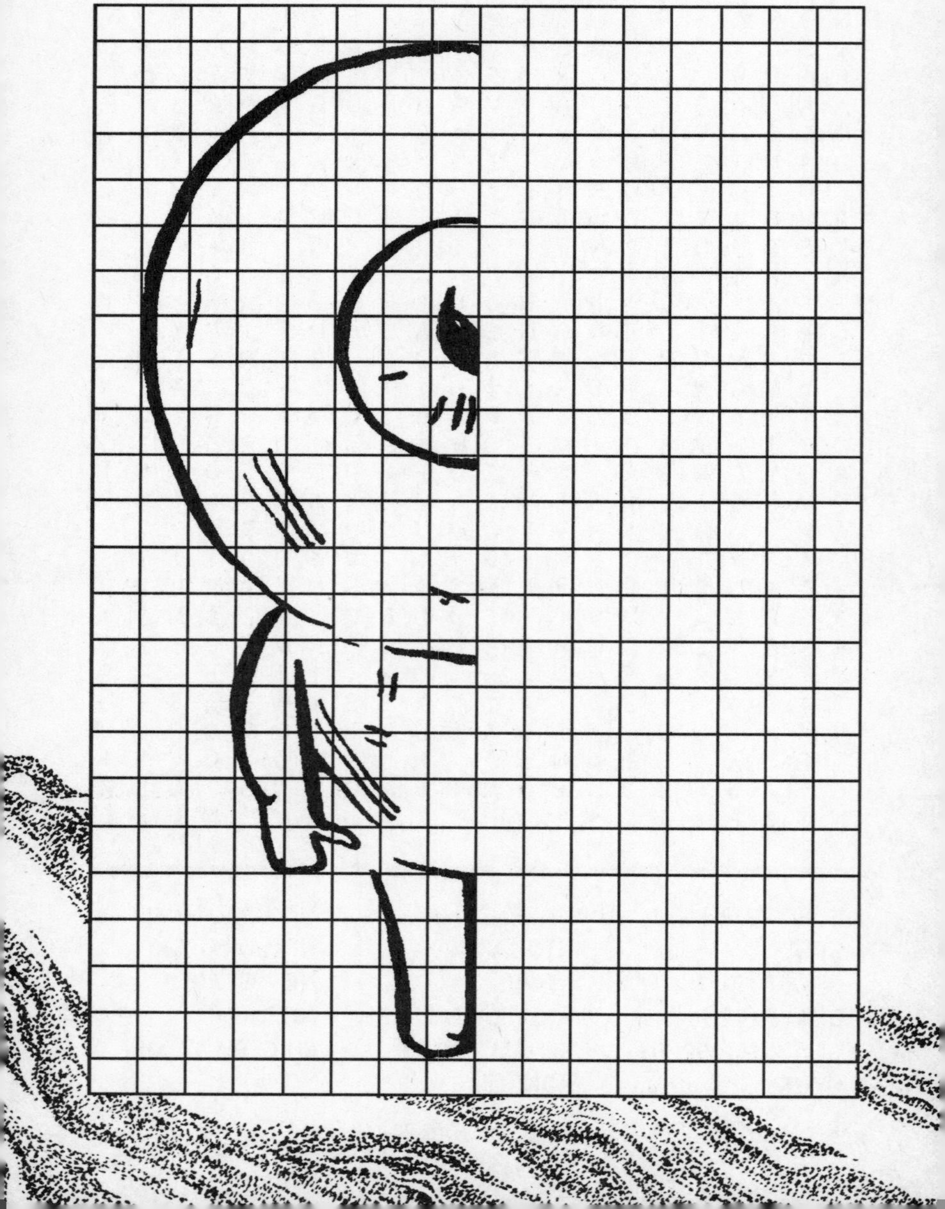

YOKAI WORD SEARCH: FIND ALL EIGHTEEN TO EARN YOUR YOKAI DETECTIVE BADGE!

```
N O K L S T Q U E S P E A I F G L C M B N Y
J G O R T S P O G R A V E Y A R D A O I A O
L A P O Q I O G R Y S T I K L U V Y T D M R
A R D N O Z U C H I V W A D O C A I R H A P
D T I G E H O K P O T A B L I S K H A D K S
Q S H I G E R U M I Z U K I K A G K C T U L
H O I U T H U B B E T U O C H M E A Y O R A
P U D T S I D W A K L A T R O U P J A K A R
K E E F O R P N O P P E R A B O D E F O G G
A S R T E S A P J W H N A P Z L O L Q W A T
I F I S A B A L A U D Q L D K F P A Z Y E Y
G P G E T D H O D G G H A U B U T I P Z S P
E M A M Y M I O E T H E O R U D E N S E H R
Z V M O N S T E R S T H I T R S Y O K A I A
S T I A N H O K S F O S B E U M A R G I G W
O I T H M E D I M T O M N R B E U P H D E O
R O Y O K P A S N Y E O E C U D H E O T N I
Q M N S A U M A L M I S Z O R A N G S I O S
W P I G T T A N E K O M U S U M E Z T P Z S
M A P Y I M O P N S E Y M F V A O R T I T E
E G E U R I F U Y K N S I W H O E P R X R P
B S Q K A E O P L I E D O N Q Y T D I N S I
R K T I S P D Q T E H T M O A M E B S X O O
N T Y C R N F P U A R E O B L J I G E T A S
T A Q A M I Z B L R I S K S B I W H A S Z U
V X P L D O S A L O A L O M R H M K O P G R
Y G U A R D I A N S P I R I T L O D Q V E I
C F A G C R Q U E A N F E M W I N S T O K D
X O Z P L A K S J D H F T A B Q M W N D S G
```

BURU-BURU	HIDERI GAMI	NEKO MUSUME
GETA	HITODAMA	NEZUMI OTOKO
GHOST TRIBE	KITARO	NOPPERABO
GRAVEYARD	MAKURA GAESHI	NOZUCHI
GUARDIAN SPIRIT	MEDAMA OYAJI	SHIGERU MIZUKI
GYUKI	MONSTER	YOKAI

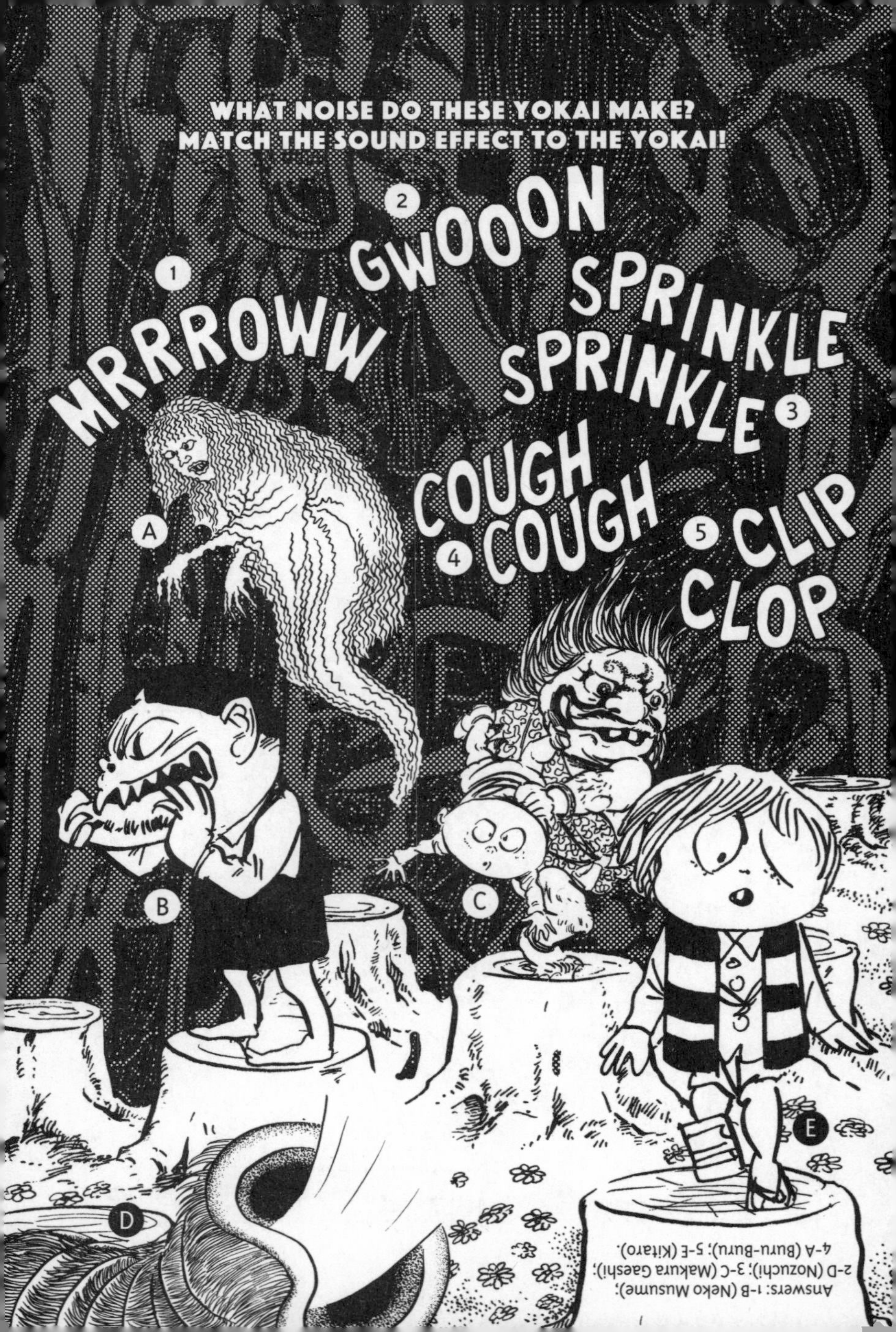

WHAT NOISE DO THESE YOKAI MAKE?
MATCH THE SOUND EFFECT TO THE YOKAI!
1 MRRROWW
2 GWOOON
SPRINKLE SPRINKLE 3
COUGH COUGH 4
5 CLIP CLOP
A
B
C
D
E
Answers: 1-B (Neko Musume); 2-D (Nozuchi); 3-C (Makura Gaeshi); 4-A (Buru-Buru); 5-E (Kitaro).

CAN YOU SPOT THE DIFFERENCE?
THERE ARE TWENTY IN TOTAL!

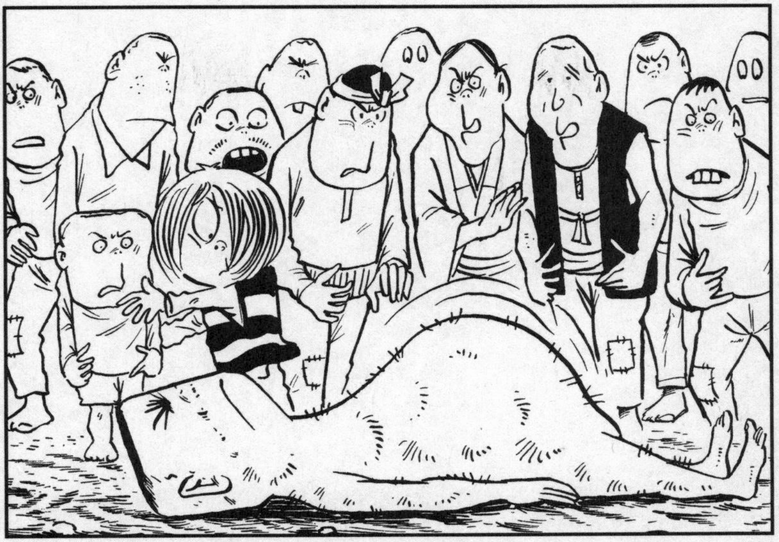

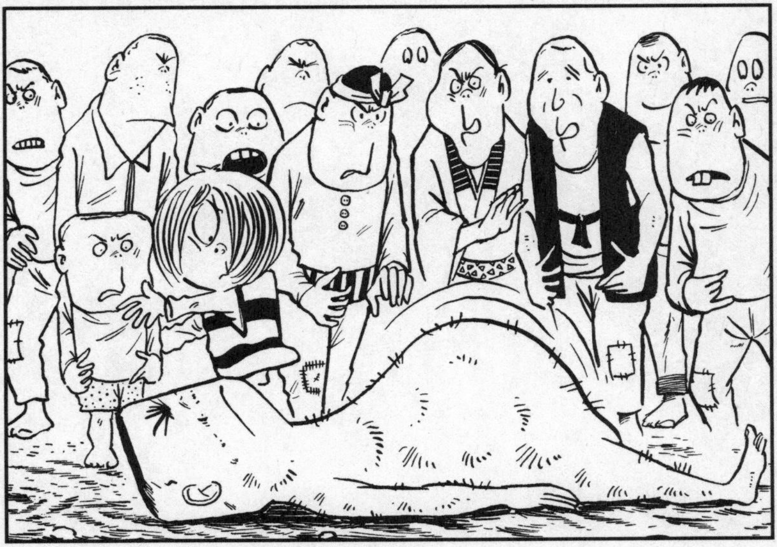

Font design: Kevin Huizenga. Drawn & Quarterly gratefully acknowledges Presspop Inc. and Maki Hakui for their invaluable assistance with the publication of this book.

drawnandquarterly.com. First paperback edition: May 2016. Printed in Canada.
10 9 8 7 6 5 4 3 2 1

Library and Archives Canada Cataloguing in Publication: Mizuki, Shigeru, 1922–2015. [Kitaro. Selections. English] *The Birth of Kitaro.* (*Shigeru Mizuki's Kitaro*) ISBN 978-1-77046-228-1 (paperback) 1. Graphic novels. I. Title. II. Title: *Kitaro.* Selections. English. III. Series: Mizuki, Shigeru, 1922–2015. *Kitaro.*
PN6790.J33M5913 2016 741.5'952 C2015-904933-4

Published in the USA by Drawn & Quarterly,
a client publisher of Farrar, Straus and Giroux;
Orders: 888.330.8477

Published in Canada by Drawn & Quarterly,
a client publisher of Raincoast Books;
Orders: 800.663.5714

Published in the United Kingdom by
Drawn & Quarterly, a client publisher
of Publishers Group UK;
Orders: info@pguk.co.uk

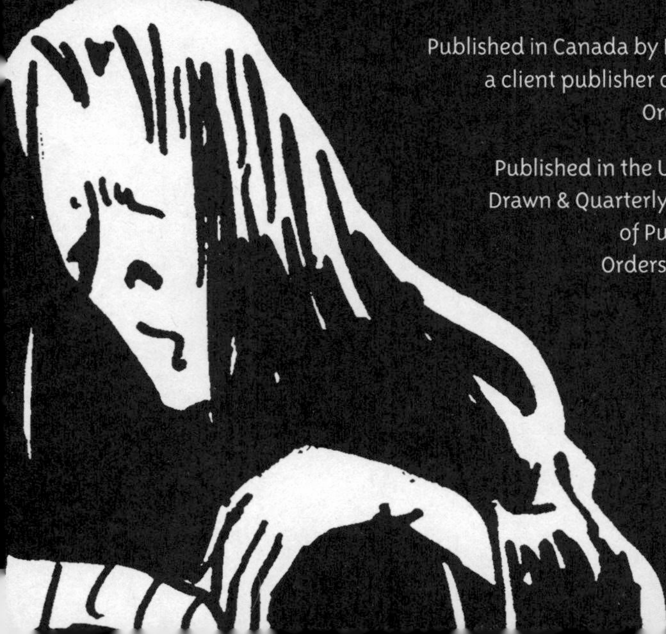

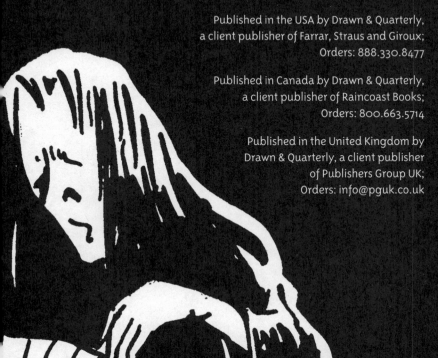

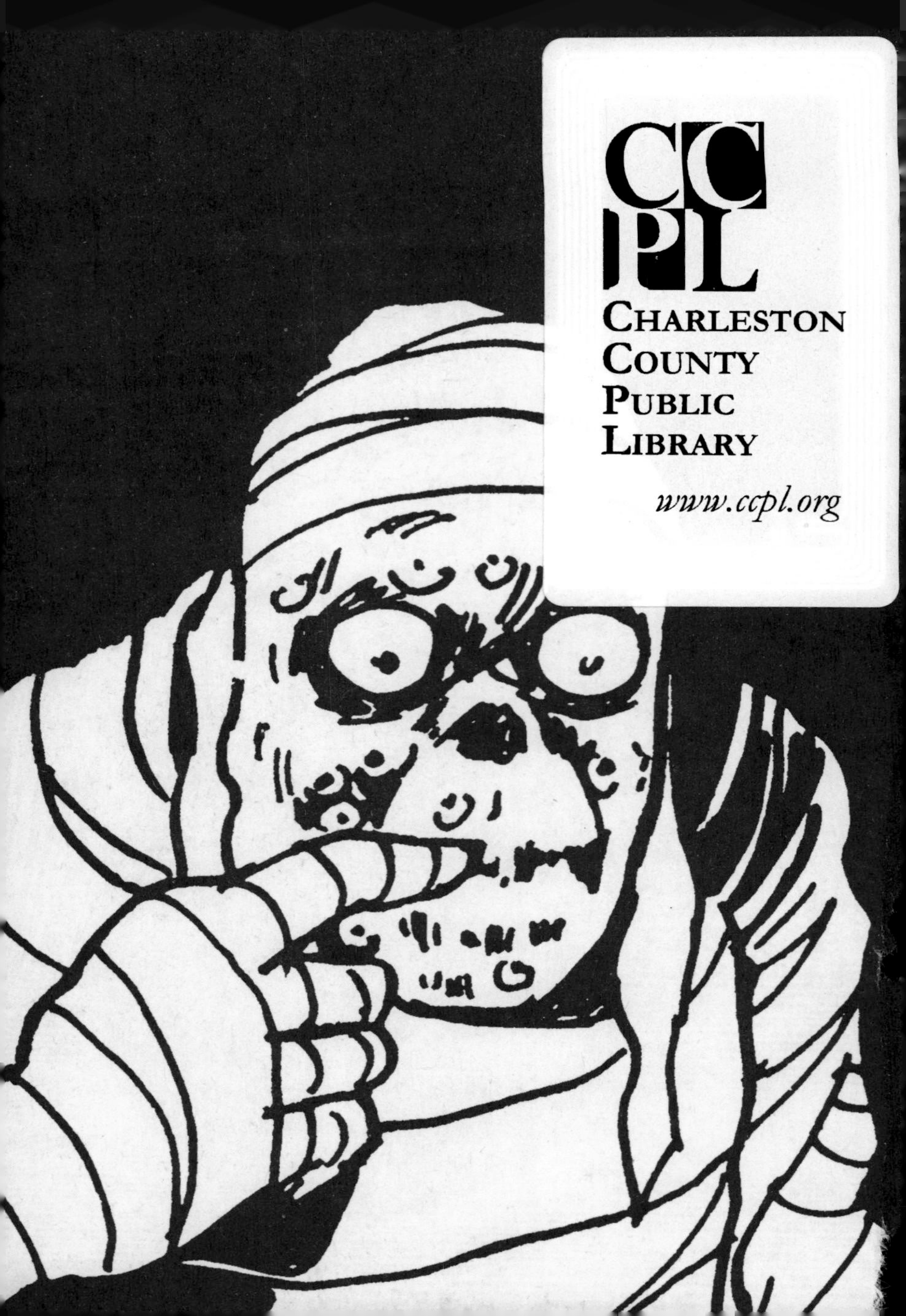

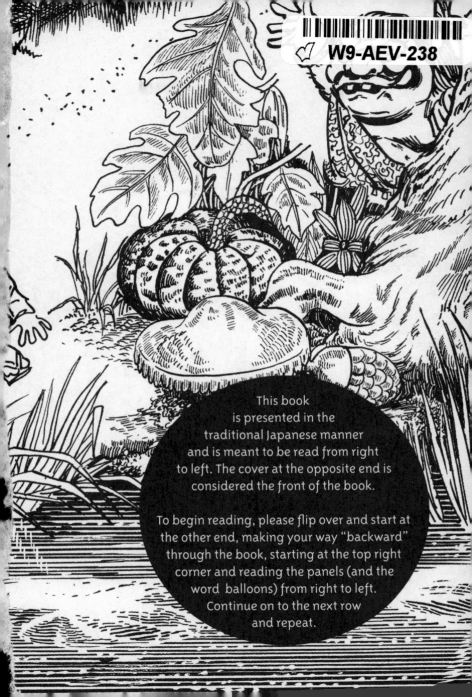

W9-AEV-238

This book
is presented in the
traditional Japanese manner
and is meant to be read from right
to left. The cover at the opposite end is
considered the front of the book.

To begin reading, please flip over and start at
the other end, making your way "backward"
through the book, starting at the top right
corner and reading the panels (and the
word balloons) from right to left.
Continue on to the next row
and repeat.